VISIONS

A COLONY SIX NOVEL

BOOKS BY TEYLA BRANTON

Colony Six
Insight
Sketches
Visions
Travels

Unbounded Series
The Change
The Cure
The Escape
The Reckoning
The Takeover

Unbounded Novellas
Ava's Revenge
Mortal Brother
Lethal Engagement
Set Ablaze

Imprints
First Touch
Touch of Rain
On the Hunt
Upstaged
Under Fire
Blinded

UNDER THE NAME RACHEL BRANTON

Lily's House
House Without Lies
Tell Me No Lies
Your Eyes Don't Lie
Hearts Never Lie
Broken Lies
No Secrets and Lies
Cowboys Can't Lie

Finding Home
All that I Love
Take Me Home

Other Books
How Far

VISIONS

COLONY SIX BOOK 2

TEYLA BRANTON

WHITE
STAR
PRESS

This is a work of fiction, and the views expressed herein are the sole responsibility of the author. Likewise, certain characters, places, and incidents are the product of the author's imagination, and any resemblance to actual persons, living or dead, or actual events or locales, is entirely coincidental.

Visions (Colony Six Book 2)

Published by White Star Press
P.O. Box 353
American Fork, Utah 84003

Printed in the United States of America
ISBN: 978-1-948982-00-9
Year of first printing: 2018

For my husband. The best is yet to come!

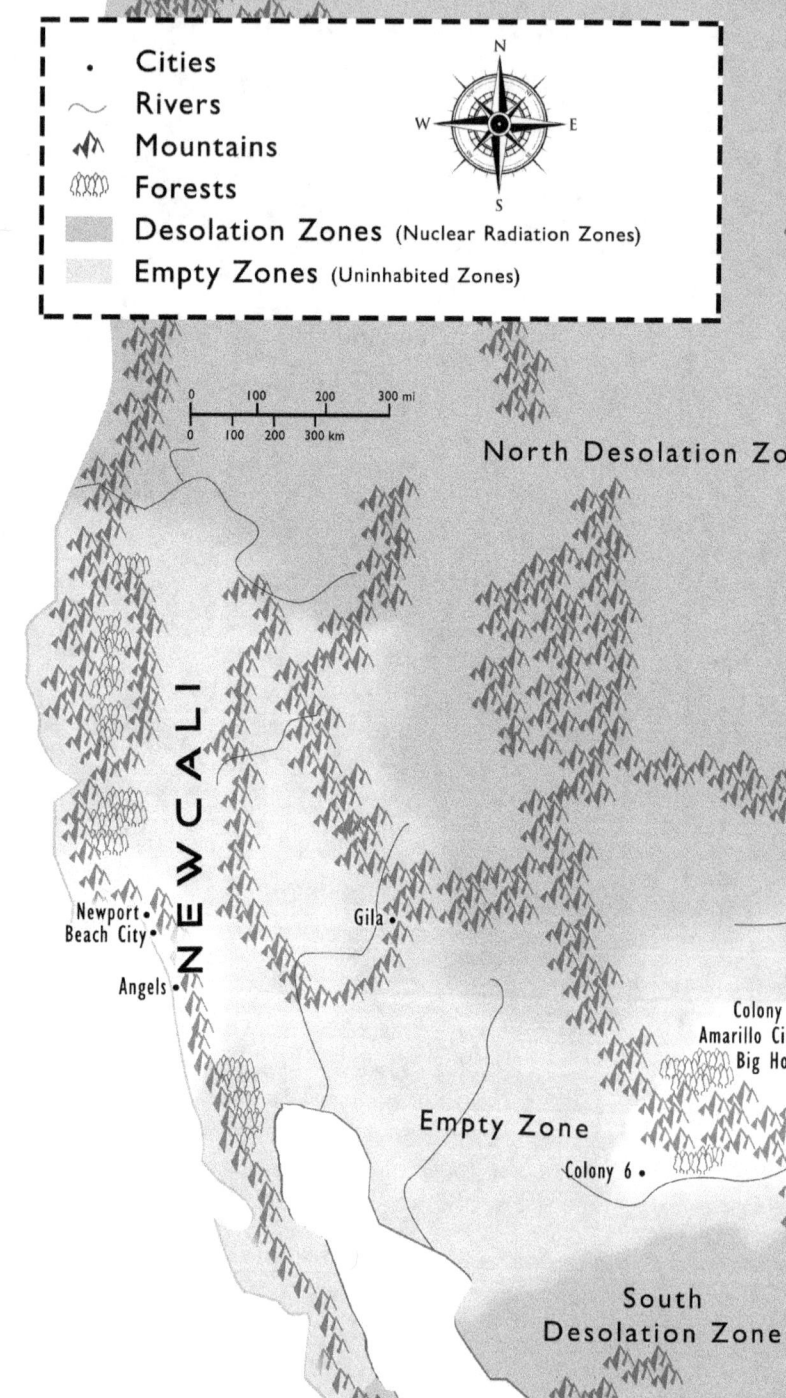

- Cities
~ Rivers
Mountains
Forests
Desolation Zones (Nuclear Radiation Zones)
Empty Zones (Uninhabited Zones)

N
W E
S

0   100   200   300 mi
0   100 200 300 km

North Desolation Zor

NEWCALI

Newport •
Beach City •

Gila •

Angels •

Colony
Amarillo City
Big Hor

Empty Zone

Colony 6 •

South
Desolation Zone

WELCOME TO THE CORE: COMMONWEALTH OBJECTIVE FOR REFORM AND EFFICIENCY

CHAPTER 1

Location: Amarillo City, Dallastar
Year: 2278, 80 years after Breakdown

The man's larger than life face on the holo screen was ordinary, typical of most of the two million CORE residents, whose features had blended together over hundreds of years. Brown eyes, medium brown skin, narrow face, and average weight. Brown hair long enough to cover most of his ears but short enough to be professional. Only the position of his eyes was notable, rolled upward as if searching the ceiling for answers.

"This is Dr. Sam Kentley," said Vic Brogan, captain of the Amarillo City Enforcer Division, commonly known as the AED. "He is your next assignment." His heavy-lidded eyes scanned those gathered in the Underground conference room where they met instead of at division where their conversation might be monitored. His body was all chest and arms like that of a boxer.

Enforcer Jaxon Tennant was still uncomfortable being part

of the underground. He'd trained for so many years to serve and protect the CORE he'd once believed in—and now knew to be a lie. How deep the lie, he didn't yet know, but like Captain Brogan and the others, he was determined to find out.

And not only because someone had murdered his mother.

"You are to travel to Santoni," Brogan continued, "and accompany the doctor back here."

"I'm assuming he's like us?" Across the table, Reese Parker, Jaxon's partner in the Violent Crimes Unit and also the division's sketch artist, looked up from her drawing pad, her pencil poised in the air.

"Like us" meant people from Colony 6 who had developed unusual abilities after generations of imprisonment and experimentation by the people who had pretended to save them—and who now wanted them dead.

Jaxon and Reese had grown up in the colony with most of the others in the room: Eagle Jensen, Dani Balak, and the twins, Lyssa and Lyra Sloan. As children they had fought to survive in the harsh environment and had been among the miraculous few who had been released from its confines. They had been a crew as children at Colony 6, and now on the outside, each had been found and hired by Captain Brogan to work at AED. Reuniting them as a team was an action meant both to protect and to use them.

Jaxon could never let himself forget that last part. They were here willingly, but if they chose not to be, they would conveniently disappear. They as individuals didn't matter in the long run—not when many thousands of lives weighed in the balance. They mattered only by how they could help free the citizens of the CORE.

"Yes," Brogan said. "He's like the six of you. If my intelligence is correct, Dr. Kentley is a healer unlike the CORE has ever seen. He has a near perfect record with his patients that can't be explained even by any pre-Breakdown medicines he might have rediscovered. None of his patients die while in his care, even those with severe radiation damage caused by exposure in the desolation zones."

"Unless he somehow has access to an alias, he's not anyone we knew," Jaxon said.

Brogan shook his head. "He's not from your same district in Colony 6, but he did grow up in the colony. Kentley brings our total to twenty people we've identified all together. Of all those allowed to leave the colony, we're nearly certain they're the only ones left alive. At least those still living in the CORE Territories."

"That's more than I hoped for," Reese said. She hadn't gone back to drawing, and her face looked haunted. Jaxon understood why. His mother wasn't the only victim. At least fifteen hundred children had leveled out of Colony 6 schools and left the colony over the ten years of limited integration with society, and Brogan had found only these twenty besides the six of them. That was a miniscule number when compared with the ten thousand children who grew up, remained in Welfare Colony 6, and were now registered as dead or completely missing from the population database.

"There may be more living under assumed identities, but these twenty who are still out in the open need to be our priority. Like Sam Kentley." Brogan waved two fingers in the air and the holo image of Kentley was replaced by the front of a short building. "This is where he works in Santoni. We are still tracing a home address. I'm not sure how much time we have left or why Special Forces hasn't detained him yet, but we've picked up increased enforcer activity in the area, which indicates impending action."

"No!" Dani Balak slapped her hand on the table, speaking for the first time at the meeting. "We don't have time for this.

What about Tauri?" Controlled anger threatened behind the measured words. Her unusual black skin masked any telltale emotion and her wiry blond hair jutted from her head at all angles as it normally did, but her splayed hand on the table trembled. Dani wasn't beautiful by any standard, but her features were well-formed, and the way she carried herself, exuding strength and confidence, made her a person who demanded attention.

Unlike the rest of the crew, Dani hadn't left Colony 6 to live in Estlantic or Dallastar, the two main territories of the CORE. Instead, she'd become a fringer, those who lived outside the CORE's influence and protection. Common belief taught that fringers were radiation-crazed killers, but like so many things, Jaxon had learned it wasn't true. While working with fringers in a territory they had named Newcali, Dani had saved people targeted for extermination by Special Forces, and her entire life's goal was to free all the colonies. She'd only recently agreed to take an undercover job at the division as Brogan's assistant in exchange for a promise, a promise Brogan hadn't yet fulfilled.

"You said you'd help me rescue my brother," she added, her words sharp and staccato. "That's the only reason I'm here."

Brogan let her words hang in the air for a moment without responding. *Did he hear the threat?* Jaxon wondered.

"I know this isn't what you hoped for," Brogan said finally, "but Sam Kentley is in immediate danger of being killed or taken by Special Forces. We can't stand by and allow that to happen. We need a healer in the underground, especially if what you tell us—and what others have confirmed—is true about those having abilities going insane. You are all at risk until we figure out why that's happening. The last thing we want is to be putting down our own people. Special Forces has done quite enough of that."

"Just so you remember that *my* priority and the only reason

I'm here is to free my brother." Dani's hand was no longer trembling. Had Jaxon imagined it?

Brogan's eyes narrowed. "I am very aware of your priorities. But you also agreed to help us in our joint mission to save the colonies, starting with the gifted who were permitted to leave. We're well into preparations to free Tauri, but a general location isn't good enough. We need more intel, and I won't risk the team—or you—going in early. You are all too valuable. The minute I think we can be successful, we'll go for him. Until then, we'll save as many others as we can. We'll need all of them if we are to beat the Elite." He held Dani's stare, the tension in the room thick enough that no one dared speak.

Finally, Dani gave a curt nod and lowered her gaze. Jaxon knew her well enough—from growing up together in Colony 6 and these past six weeks after the crew's reunion—to understand that she wasn't beaten. Dani was never beaten. She'd push them to Breakdown and back to get her brother out of Estlantic and the hands of Special Forces. If they didn't do it soon, they'd all better watch their backs. He rubbed the side of his temples to ease the building pressure there.

"And if Sam Kentley won't come with us?" Reese asked. She was drawing again, but with her right hand now instead of her left.

Brogan's heavy stare transferred in her direction. "Then you don't give him a choice."

"Of course," Reese said.

Jaxon felt her scrutiny, and when he met her gaze, a thousand words stared back at him from her green eyes. She knew every bit as much as he did that they skirted the law now, and there was no going back, not if they didn't want to end up dead. They probably would anyway. Watching her like this and wanting so much more for them both was an ache that never went away.

"We'll need to communicate," Brogan continued. "Off Teev feed, of course. Any communication there will be monitored. We'll have to use the hardware Dani provided from her people."

Jaxon wanted to protest his wording. He and Reese and the others were supposed to be Dani's people, her crew, but Brogan was right that the fringers came first with Dani now. And her brother.

The CORE controlled access to the Teev and monitored all its feeds continuously, but the fringers had created their own separate version of the Teev, called the T-link, which also contained back doors into the CORE Teev system. Their mobile unit was nearly indistinguishable from the CORE's iTeev, except the companion earbud was unconnected to the T-link itself by any wire. Dani had intended her contribution to aid in the rescuing of her brother, but the tech would also be useful to extract Kentley.

Brogan glanced at Eagle Jensen. "That means you're sitting this one out unless you've been able to refit your alternate pair of glasses with the fringer tech."

Eagle looked up from a piece of tech he was examining, his face as impassive as the dark glasses covering his eyes. Without them he was blind, or nearly so. "Needs more tweaks to be perfect, but it'll work well enough for this." He unfolded his tall frame and arose, taking the device in his hands to the tech-filled table that sat against the far wall of the conference room. "We leave in the morning?"

"Tonight." Brogan killed the holo screen with a downward sweep of a hand. "Santoni is over five hundred and fifty kilometers away, so the sky train will have you there in about three hours. Santoni's not much of a town, though, and you'll be noticed if you aren't careful. That means I want you to take civilian clothing and go incognito. By the time you arrive, Hammer will have sent Jaxon and Reese an encrypted file with everything you'll need, including the location of where you'll be staying. He suggests you leave on the seven o'clock train."

Eagle began packing items from the table into his bag.

"What about Lyra and me?" Lyssa asked. She glanced at her sister as she spoke.

Twin births were not permitted, at least outside the colonies, and the likeness in their thin faces was unsettling for most people. The women's familial features had blended over generations in the CORE melting pot, leaving only a tilt to their eyes and their ebony hair to firmly mark their Asian heritage.

"If this will involve our ability, we'll have to go," Lyssa added.

Brogan considered a moment. "How far is your projecting range?"

"Not five hundred and fifty kilometers," Lyra answered.

"Then I think the others can handle this one alone."

Lyssa looked disappointed. "Just when I finally learn to hit something when I shoot." She patted the gun on her hip. Working in dispatch, neither she nor Lyra wore enforcer blues, but she still worked for a division, and enforcement was the only CORE profession that allowed weapon privileges.

"This should not involve shooting." A slight smile tugged on one corner of Brogan's mouth. "We hope. But they'll need some tools." He opened a metal box and withdrew a short stack of thin cards. "With the Teev codes Dani has provided from the fringers, we've managed to hack into the CORE citizen database and omit the fact that any of you came from Colony 6, though it won't stand up to more than a cursory search, especially if, as we assume, they have a real database that lists everyone, including those they've made disappear altogether. Someone was responsible for sending that pus bag Bensell Summers after you six weeks ago, and that someone knows he failed. So you will need to use these identities during this operation." He pushed the box to Jaxon.

Jaxon removed a short bundle with his name written on the band holding the cards together. The false IDs looked like cash credits, but when activated, the IDs would override their implanted CivIDs and broadcast another identity. Placing the pad of a finger on the back would activate or deactivate them.

"You each have three to begin with," Brogan went on. "Make sure you take the stack meant for you and read the information we've programmed into them. Jaxon, I have included an alternate identity for Dr. Kentley with your cards. We've also included real cash credits for each of you, in case you need to make a purchase we don't want the CORE to track."

Jaxon passed the box to Dani, who took hers without comment. She'd had her CivID removed years ago by the fringers, of course, and the fake ID she used now was on a similar card that Brogan had also provided. She wasn't in the population database. For all the CORE knew, the real Dani Balak had never existed. Unless she was on some secret database.

"What about the cameras?" Jaxon asked.

Brogan chuckled. "I believe Dani can help us there."

She removed a small package from the pocket of her gray blouse, setting it on the table. From this she extracted a circular patch of indeterminate color and held it up so they could see. "My friends in Newcali have created these. We call them skin tags." She peeled something from the back of hers and slapped it slightly off-centered onto her throat. Within a few seconds, Jaxon couldn't see where she'd put it.

"They will immediately take on your skin color," Dani continued, "and once activated will distort your face on any electronic recording. Activate with one long press of your finger. Use a two-fingered long press to both distort your appearance and to mask any of your CivIDs, including your implanted one. Turn it off with three short taps with one finger. You will experience a tingle on your skin as it changes. Drones won't pick up the emissions because its function is to depress all emissions. Only detailed prison scanners might pick up their presence, at least ours do. Each tag will last up to two months and is nearly imperceptible to the naked eye."

"Nice," Eagle murmured. Jaxon was equally impressed, and he put his on immediately.

"Well, let's get to it." Brogan stood, signaling the end of the meeting.

Jaxon glanced at his iTeev secured to the sleeve of his enforcer uniform. The time on it read after five already. They needed to hurry.

Eagle shouldered his bag. "We should grab a little more firepower at division. Just in case." As the weapons expert, he had access to everything, including weapons Jaxon didn't want to know about. Eagle didn't much like guns, but he loved explosions.

"Good idea," Brogan said. "But first, I need a private word with Detective Tennant."

Jaxon hung back as the others left the room, where he knew they'd wait for him out in the old subway tunnels. He closed the space between him and the captain.

"I know I said that we omitted the Colony 6 origin reference in everyone's file, but Hammer had a problem with yours," Brogan said as the door shut. "Bottom line is he hasn't been able to do it, even with the codes from the fringers. There seems to be an extra layer of protocol attached to your file."

An eerie sense of unease teased at Jaxon's consciousness. That was often the sense he had before one of his premonitions, but when no vision came, he asked, "Any idea what it means?"

"I can't say, except that you're still a target for Special Forces. As long as you're from Colony 6, they'll suspect you have an ability. I can protect you here in Amarillo City, but you need to watch yourself in Santoni."

"You think it has something to do with Bensell Summers?" Summers was the man Jaxon suspected of murdering his mother, but in the end when Jaxon had killed him, he wasn't quite sure.

"It crossed my mind. But if it was that important to someone in the CORE Elite, it might also mean that they don't want you dead. Yet."

Small comfort, especially if there was any substance to the odd hints Summers had made about Jaxon's parentage. All his life Jaxon had wanted to know who his father was, but not if it meant being the son of a lying whore wrangler. Even if the whore had been his mother. He didn't blame her. She'd survived in the colony anyway she could, and that was more than many had done.

"I'll be careful," he said.

"Good." Brogan picked up a skin-like substance lying in a mass on the table and pulled it over his head. In the few seconds it took for him to settle the mask, he changed from the well-respected AED captain to El Cerebro, feared leader of the underground in Amarillo City. The thin, faintly reddish mask concealed his identity with success, but the smoothness of the fake skin made him resemble a Nuface addict. The evenness of his guise was marred only by the C-shaped tattoo on his fake cheek, easily recognizable, even by CORE residents who didn't deal with the black market. Fake brown hair followed the mask, covering his normal black. The whole ensemble was topped by a black knit cap, pulled low over Brogan's brow, that flattened the hair against his neck. The transformation was eerie. Only El Cerebro's top people knew his real identity, and he had to keep it that way if they had any chance of changing what was happening in the CORE.

"Keep me in the loop," Brogan said to Jaxon as they walked to the door together. "And keep an eye on Dani. We still need her."

So the captain—or was it the El Cerebro part of him?—had picked up on Dani's threat. Somehow Jaxon needed to hold it together for all their sakes.

Outside the door, two of El Cerebro's soldiers stood guard with assault rifles at the ready. The conference room was deep in the heart of an ancient, pre-Breakdown underground train system and also close to the undergrounders' main lair. Every time Jaxon had been below, at least two guards were standing watch.

The rest of Jaxon's crew waited with the guards, but they weren't alone. Nova, El Cerebro's niece, also stood outside, her eyes eager. "I volunteer to help, whatever it is you're doing." The child looked dirty as usual, her dark curls matted down her back, and she was so thin she looked younger than fourteen. Jaxon knew both the dirt and the innocence were fake. This was a child who'd once used pre-Breakdown tech to break into Reese's apartment and who tripped through the streets after curfew like she owned them.

"Not this time, Nova," El Cerebro said, his voice altered by a nearly invisible box on his throat.

"But it's been over a month since we did anything, except that one bitty raid on that electronics warehouse."

El Cerebro snorted. "The sales from that bitty raid are going to keep us in food down here for a year."

Nova was about to say more, but a look from her uncle froze the protest on her lips. Giving Jaxon an evil stare as if her exclusion were all his doing, she started down the dark tunnel, her heavy pack swaying and appearing close to toppling her over.

Jaxon shrugged toward Reese, and she hid a smile as they left El Cerebro with his guards and followed the others in the opposite direction from the one Nova had taken. "Looks like she's no longer pining after you," Reese said.

Jaxon snorted. "That's a good thing. I was beginning to worry she'd lock me in some abandoned room down here until I gave into her demands. Whatever those might be."

Reese laughed and engaged the projection light on her iTeev. "Sounds about her style."

The maze of tunnels was tricky, and they'd both gotten lost in them before, but Eagle could retrace his steps now even without his glasses, so they were in no danger of misdirection with him around. Jaxon could feel his suit's heat volume kicking up to account for the colder temperature in the tunnels.

They walked for a few minutes, and then Reese said, "This doctor, how far do you think his ability goes?"

"Grow back limbs? Raise the dead? Who knows?" He laughed as she snorted. For that moment, the conversation between them was easy, like in the old days, but it wasn't always that way now.

"Anyway, Brogan's right that we need him."

"You're having more symptoms?" he asked her.

She hesitated. "Alex gave me a neural suppressant and it did make the sketches come less frequently, but it's a little like seeing through a cloud, so I stopped taking them."

"Why didn't you tell me?"

"Because it wasn't necessary." She sounded angry, but he knew it wasn't directed toward him. "I just want to be able to control this thing like the others can."

On that he agreed. The rest of the crew could control their abilities far better than he or Reese, even the twins who sometimes "traveled" unintentionally in their sleep. Reese had no choice but to sketch images she saw from people's minds, including those she didn't want to see, and he had equally little control over the frequency or subject of his premonitions.

"It'll come." He hadn't told her everything either, and he didn't plan on it. Besides, the premonition he'd had of them together was so far off that he was beginning to wonder if it had stemmed more from his desire than from an actual vision.

The darkness in the tunnels seemed heavy and ominous. It was dangerous business, living this secret life. If they were discovered down here, working with El Cerebro, the punishment would be psychological reconditioning at the least and more likely surgical enhancement and permanent banishment to one of the welfare colonies.

Ahead, the twins were talking with Eagle, their lights moving as they walked, but Dani fell back with them. "We can use more healers in Newcali," she said.

Why was she so one-sighted? "You can't have him," Jaxon told her. "They need him here."

More than one undergrounder had died from a disease they were ineligible to obtain help for as long as they weren't valid citizens of the CORE. Others died from infection after digging out their implanted CivIDs or while giving birth to a non-authorized baby.

"I know." Dani didn't sound convinced. "Let's just get this done. I need to get to my brother."

The moment "brother" came from her lips, the pressure that had been building in Jaxon's head exploded in a flash of blinding light.

A man in enforcer blues stands over Dani, who is sprawled on the ground, an assault rifle aimed at her heart. "You can't dodge this many bullets," he says with a smirk. To his comrades, he adds, "She's from Colony 6, guys. No doubt about it. Cuff her and toss her into the shuttle. The Controller is going to enjoy this extra little gift."

Jaxon jerked from the vision, finding himself on the rocky ground and everyone staring at him, their lights shining in his direction. His arm went up to cover his eyes. If Reese thought her ability was out of control, his was impossible. Lately, even the mildest premonition caused that pressure at his temples and sent him scrambling to the ground. The more he tried to resist, the worse it became, but when he didn't fight them, he'd sometimes lose hours where he remembered nothing but the premonition. Only the hunches, gut feelings really, didn't cause a physical reaction, and those came less often now as the full-blown visions had taken over.

"Lights," Reese said, lowering her beam to the ground in front of him. The others did the same.

"Was it the doctor?" Lyssa asked. "Do we get him?"

Jaxon shook his head and gazed at Dani, finding her staring back at him, her black face blending in with the darkness around her, making the whites of her eyes that much more prominent. "You're going to be captured by Special Forces. They're going to take you to the controller."

"No," Reese said, her voice hard as she offered him a hand up. "We're going to make sure that doesn't happen."

But they all knew his visions came true. Always.

CHAPTER 2

R eese didn't require touch to receive a sketch, though proximity was important. Usually any strong image within one and a half meters would end up flashing through her mind, and eventually she'd have to draw it. This time she waited to draw the man from Jaxon's vision until they were out of the subway and seated in their shuttle.

Black and red stripes running down the silver sides of their shuttle marked it as an enforcer vehicle, but its larger engine was what really separated it from the public shuttles used by most of the two million residents of the CORE. Private cars on the road were far more rare, unnecessary with the free sky trains and shuttle system. Only the very rich had the time or inclination for them.

If it hadn't been important, if it had been a sketch of a clerk at a store or a child playing in the park, she would have pushed it off as long as possible with the hope that eventually one day she wouldn't have to draw the insignificant sketches at all, the ones that didn't relate to her cases. So far, she still had to draw them all, and each evoked the same amount of pressure in her mind.

A man formed under her hand, tall and lean, dressed in enforcer blues with the special patch that identified him as coming from the Headquarters Enforcer Division, or HED, so Jaxon was right about him being Special Forces. Dani appeared in the image next, lying at the man's feet on a floor made of stone, one hand out as if to block a blow. Reese wished she could see more of the scene, as she normally could when sketching someone's actual memory, but this was better than nothing.

Their shuttle made a perfect turn, gliding in and out among other automated shuttles to roll into the ramp leading down into the police shuttle bay. As she climbed from the vehicle, Reese passed the drawing to Dani, who studied it a long time before relinquishing it to Jaxon. Dani was already wearing the long, dark brown wig she used to cover her hair at division, her natural white making her stand out too much even in her relatively private occupation as Brogan's assistant.

"I'll ask Hammer to see if he can ID the man," Jaxon said, "and if there's a current location on him. There doesn't seem to be anything in the picture we can use to identify the location, so it might not happen in Santoni. We need to be as prepared as possible."

Dani nodded. "I'll meet you guys at the sky train. I have something to take care of first." She stalked off across the shuttle bay without waiting for a reply.

When she was out of earshot, Reese said, "We can't let this happen. She's given up a lot to help us."

"We won't," Eagle said. "I'll bring along a few extra toys." He had a smile on his face, and Reese was certain those extra toys would mean explosions.

"Remember, no civilian casualties," Reese said. "And we need the doctor alive."

Eagle laughed. "Have I ever let you down?"

Reese thought a moment. Though Eagle was technically an enforcer and had been through the training, he wasn't as skilled as she and Jaxon in combat, but growing up in the Coop, or chicken coop as they often called Colony 6, had toughened him in ways the average enforcer could never understand. More than anything, even as a child, he'd been dependable.

She set a hand on his arm. "Bring anything you want."

Lyssa was frowning. "We should be there too."

"No." Jaxon shook his head. "You two keep on the feeds from HED. We've got to figure out exactly where they're holding Dani's brother and what it takes to pull him out without getting caught. The sooner we get him, the sooner we can deal with the rest."

And not worry about trusting Dani. Though he didn't say the words, Reese knew he had to be thinking them. She was.

"We're recording everything we can on the TAD-Alert without setting off any alarms," Lyssa said. "I'm just not sure it'll be enough. It was meant for tracking and prioritizing emergency calls, not spying."

Reese had her doubts about that. The Teev Aided Dispatch Alert System, or the TAD-Alert, was a super Teev that tracked and recorded callers, prioritized emergencies, and recommended which enforcers should respond. Each enforcer division was equipped with one and could link instantly to most home or work Teevs in the entire city and beyond to have immediate eyes on the scene.

Using the TAD's recording capabilities, Lyssa and Lyra had come up with a set of supposedly innocent requests and had been sending them to the feeds at the Headquarters Division.

Altogether, the requests might have been flagged by someone in the Controller's office, but alone, they were either responded to or ignored. That was how they'd learned Dani's brother was at HED. But they didn't know much more than that about him. They were focusing now on the number of employees and daily schedules to see if anything was out of the ordinary.

"We're bound to find something soon," Reese said. "Hammer and the fringers are working on it too."

The twins separated then, Lyssa going to dispatch and Lyra heading to pick up Lyssa's daughter, Tamsin, from the sitter. The official records said Lyra was the mother, and her lie had prevented her sister from being punished for the unauthorized birth—and possibly saved Tamsin's life.

"Let's meet back here in an hour," Jaxon said to Eagle and Reese. "Unless anyone needs to go home for something."

"No, I'm good." Reese looked at Eagle, who nodded.

Reese went first to outfitting to pick up a clean set of enforcer blues and a battle helmet from the dispensing machine. The name "blues" was misleading because the bulletproof uniforms were completely black, including the shiny strips running up the sides of the pants and jacket. If there ever had been a reason for the name, no enforcer Reese had ever met understood it, and the tradition carried on, despite several attempts by the younger enforcers to change it.

Next, she chose a set of cool-weather civilian clothing, a protective undervest, and two extra sets of underclothing. Usually she preferred her own clothes for the rare times she wasn't in her uniform, but today standard issue would have to do. That also meant a pair of boots that didn't look like they belonged with her enforcer uniform.

From her private dressing cubicle, she retrieved her extra weapons, packing them in her weapons bag with her clothing. They'd need their enforcer CivIDs to take weapons onto the train, so it would be better for them to travel in their blues and change once they were closer to their location.

After packing, she hurried to her tiny office. The walls came alive with holo feeds, three depicting beaches from Haven in Estlantic, and the fourth a depiction of the transfer station from Colony 6. She kept it there so she'd never forget.

Setting her bag on the floor, she removed her iTeev from the sleeve of her uniform, unfolding the earpieces and putting it on like a pair of glasses. The plastic molded and settled against her skin. "Call Theena Parker," she said.

Her aunt—her great-aunt really, but they usually dropped that unnecessary detail—answered moments later, appearing in front of her in holographic form. She wore a flowing pink dress, and her ebony hair was down today, framing her face that was tight with Nuface therapy. She was seventy-five, but like most people her age, she appeared decades younger. The CORE might prohibit changing hair color or facial structure without submission of a Change of Appearance intention and resulting photographs for the annually updated database, but looking younger through Nuface therapy was encouraged.

"Hi, Aunt Theena."

"Reese, good to see you. Though you're looking a little tired."

Theena always said this, so Reese took it in stride. "Am I? Can't imagine why."

Her aunt rolled her eyes. "Too much overtime. I know how much you work. I'll be glad to get you home tomorrow night for the weekend. You can bring that doctor fellow you're dating if you want."

"About that," Reese began. "I know I promised to clean out all the stuff I've left at your house, but I've been assigned to go out of town tonight for work. It's possible I won't be back at all this weekend. I may not be able to call, either."

"Is it dangerous?" Theena sounded more interested than concerned.

Theena's tone didn't fool her. The old woman had raised Reese from age ten and was her only living relative. She'd be more than worried inside her calm façade.

"I don't think so, but I've a team backing me up."

"Jaxon?"

"Yes."

Theena's voice warmed. "Then you're in good hands, and so is he."

Reese hadn't told her about the others from Colony 6 also showing up, or the thousands of deaths. Theena was outspoken enough that she might get herself in trouble, and Reese wanted to protect her. Her aunt wasn't CORE Elite, but Theena's grandfather had been the Big Horn city manager, which was a lower level Elite position, and her aunt was well-known and respected in Big Horn. She still knew people in high places.

"I'll call you when I'm back in town. But don't worry, okay? I might be a few days."

"Well, I suppose I can always reach your captain if I don't hear from you."

Reese stifled a sigh. Theena had saved her in more ways than one, and she loved the older woman more than life, but she absolutely didn't need her calling the captain. "Please don't call. I'll be fine. It's just normal work."

"I can tell when you're lying." Theena put her hands on her hips. "You think I don't know you're hiding something?"

"It's classified, that's all. Sorry. You know I would tell you if I could."

"Hmmm." Theena's eyes narrowed. "I've heard some rumors . . ."

Reese's heart began to thunder. If Theena had become

connected with anyone who was openly discontented with the restrictions in the CORE, she would be in danger. But that would be far better than if she suspected the truth about thirty thousand imprisoned workers in the colonies, or that Special Forces had murdered over ten thousand residents of Colony 6 after the experimentation had created abilities that made them go insane.

"We'll talk when I get back," Reese said quickly. The Teeve feed was always monitored. Had she told her aunt that? She'd have to warn her again. "I have to go."

"I'll expect you next weekend then. And you can bring that handsome doctor. He can help you gather your things."

Reese stifled a flare of annoyance. She went to her aunt's precisely because the house was isolated, because dealing with only one person who might send her a mental sketch was a relief after holding it together during the work week. She'd filled an entire sketchbook last week alone, and while Brogan had reassured her that she would have as much of the rare paper as she needed, it was beginning to be ridiculous.

Her aunt picked up on her silence, and her next words came lightly. "Unless you don't want him seeing what's in the attic, that is."

She meant the bag of things Reese had brought with her from Colony 6 when she'd escaped after Jaxon's mother had been murdered and her father had run away scared. Nothing in the bag was important—maybe old clothes she hadn't looked at in twenty years or more. Whatever a poor child had owned or thought important. The only thing of real value were the drawing pads that held a visual record of her life in the colony, and those were already packed in a box at her aunt's.

"We'll see," Reese said. "Love you. I'll call as soon as I can."

She pulled off her iTeev, severing the connection, and breathed a sigh of relief. She was about to leave the room when a short ping from the door let her know someone was outside her office.

"Enter," Reese called. The door opened with a muted *whir.* "Alex," she said with a smile. Despite not wanting to take him to Theena's, it was still good to see him before she left.

Alex Andres stepped inside, his brown eyes somber. "I heard about the mission. Just my luck. I was hoping to spend time with you this weekend." He had a lopsided grin, due in part to the three-centimeter scar below the right side of his mouth, and a face that dimpled when he laughed.

"Sorry. You know I don't have a choice."

"I know." He glanced at the holo showing the transfer station, his nose wrinkling. "What in Breakdown is that?"

"Just a place I know." A place whose significance she'd never be able to make him understand. People who hadn't grown up in the Coop could never relate. He might be able to understand that it reminded her of what they were fighting for, but it wasn't only that. The transfer station, or rather the colony it represented, told her every day what all parts of the CORE were becoming—a thinly masked prison.

The station also reminded her of her crew. Of Jaxon, Eagle, Dani, and the twins. Of bonds forged by loyalty and love. She would still willingly die for any of them. She couldn't say the same about Alex. Yet.

Reese brought her hands up in a sweep and her Teev holo appeared over her desk. She typed out a few commands and replaced the transfer station with yet another beach landscape. Only a temporary switch. The next time she entered the room, the transfer station would be there waiting for her.

"That's more like it." Alex closed the space between them, his hand running through his light brown hair. "Wish I were going with you. You might need a doctor."

"We won't."

A frown tugged at the corners of his mouth. "It's just as well. While you were out, Chief Kirkpatrick made an announcement over the Teev. Apparently, it's no longer optional to carry a CivID card in Dallastar instead of an implant, and everyone who doesn't have it already will need to comply within the next three months. I received a personal message from the chief stating that I'll be responsible for making sure anyone we bring into division is fitted with an implant."

Kirkpatrick was the man over all of Dallastar, and all the division captains in Dallastar answered to him, including Captain Brogan, while Kirkpatrick answered only to the Controller himself at HED. Reese had never met Kirkpatrick, but she knew his power here was checked only by the captains under him and Brogan's alter ego, El Cerebro.

"We always knew that would happen," she said.

Estlantic, the other major territory in the CORE, had required implants for at least five years, and all residents in the six welfare colonies were given them at birth. Certain professions, like enforcers, had always been required to have them. But requiring them now for all of Dallastar meant more deaths because some would inevitably refuse. The people in Dallastar weren't as docile as those in Estlantic. Whether that was because of the distance from the CORE government, or their proximity to the fringers, she couldn't say.

"You think Captain Brogan heard about the announcement?" she asked. That Brogan had tasked them to rescue a doctor with abilities just as the chief announced the required implants seemed rather too coincidental.

Alex shook his head. "He's been vocal against it. I doubt the chief would have given him the heads up." He put his hands on her upper arms, gently rubbing. "I'm going to miss you." His head lowered, his eyes watching hers as he closed the gap between them.

She knew from experience that he was a good kisser, but she also knew that he was frustrated at the slow pace of their relationship. She had little choice in the matter. Because while she didn't need to touch someone to receive a sketch, the closer they were, the more likely she'd catch a glimpse of an image. It had been growing bad before she was sent to Dallastar, but she'd been able to control it a lot better since then. But her control had vanished when she'd started dating Alex. Thus the neural suppressant he'd given her.

His mouth touched hers, eager and seeking. She sagged against him, enjoying the feel of his body and the passion that ran through her veins, blotting out her worry about Theena and about helping El Cerebro save people. Those who needed protection comprised an ever-growing list—scientists who learned too much, people who spoke out, couples who grew tired of waiting their turn to have a baby.

Alex closed his arm around her, pulling her tighter. "How soon do you have to go?" he murmured against her lips.

She wished he'd stop talking and focus on what they were doing. Speaking always created an additional risk for sketches. "I'm meeting Jaxon and Eagle in a few minutes."

His chuckle was hoarse. "Plenty of time for this." He kissed her more deeply, but it was too late. A flash came to her, a clear image from Alex's mind. Of Jaxon, dressed in his uniform, standing in front of her, glaring, his fists clenched. Jaxon's eyes always burned a brighter blue when he was fighting passionately for something. She recognized Alex's medical office in the background. She had no idea how recent this image was, but it couldn't be that old. Jaxon's dark hair was shorter than it was now, but not by much.

She pushed Alex away. "Seriously? Do you really have to be thinking of Jaxon while you're kissing me?"

"Sorry." He shrugged. "You said his name."

"It's not the first time you've thought of him."

"He hates that we're dating."

"Because you put a tracker in me."

"I explained all that."

She swept her hand downward, killing the holo that still hovered over her desk. "You should have told me first." In the Coop, he'd have been kicked out of their crew for less. It was only the fact that Alex knew about her gift, his persistence, and their joint work in the underground that had gotten them this far into a relationship. She cared about him, but if she didn't learn to control her ability, she was going to have to end this relationship before it drove them both mad.

"I guess that means you're not taking the neural suppressant?" His voice was more sorrowful than accusing.

"I can't while I'm working. I need to be focused."

He nodded. "Of course. Maybe I can find something else."

"Maybe you should just stop thinking of Jaxon while we kiss."

"I will if you stop bringing him up."

Did she do that? This time it had been his fault, but she couldn't say that was always the case. The truth was, Jaxon was a part of her in a way Alex could never be. And while she was crazy attracted to Jaxon, she loved having him back in her life and couldn't risk their friendship with a fleeting romance. That made her choice to date Alex clear.

She bent to heft her bag. "I'd better go."

He walked with her to the shuttle bay, a slight awkwardness between them. "How's the language-learning coming along?" she asked, referring to the medical books passed down in his family that had belonged to his second great-grandmother, who had been a physician in a place called Denmark, wherever that was.

"Not well. So much of our data was lost during Breakdown.

Languages and medical knowledge are some of the worst hit. It's too bad there is no one out there left to share knowledge with."

She lowered her voice, glancing at the camera in the hallway. "We don't know that for sure. The CORE controls all communication. Who really knows what's left in the world?"

He sighed and took a step forward. "I think we would have heard from them by now."

"If they made it through Breakdown, they're probably just like us, trying to survive." Maybe they were also committing atrocities that were every bit as bad as those carried out by the CORE.

They paused at the shuttle bay doors, where Jaxon and Eagle were already waiting. "Hey guys," Alex said, dipping his head in greeting.

Eagle nodded, casting his usual friendly grin, but Jaxon ignored him and pushed open the door. Maybe it was the sketch she'd have to draw, but she saw Jaxon now as he'd been in Alex's mind, tall and strong, his hair darker than most, the intense blue of his eyes, and his tanned face sporting a couple days' beard growth that contrasted with today's freshly shaved face.

The men had been friends once, but ever since Alex had been a part of forcing them to work for El Cerebro, there had been tension between them, even if in the end they all knew it was the only responsible thing they could do. That Jaxon didn't seem to harbor the same resentment toward Evan Hammer, the Crime Scene Investigation team leader, who had played a similar role in tricking them to work for the underground, was strange to Reese.

"Take care," Alex said as she started to follow Jaxon.

Reese knew he was hoping for more than a casual wave-of-the-hand goodbye, but that was all he'd get with the others around. She didn't know enough about relationships to know how long that might last, but at some point, they'd need to address it. She was glad he wasn't going along on this trip.

The police shuttle dropped them at the sky train, one of the few intact remnants of a pre-Breakdown world. The solar-powered trains rose above all but the tallest of buildings, having replaced the overland and subway trains of decades past. They extended the length of the CORE, and many unused lines still existed in the uninhabited empty zones and in the radiation-filled Desolation Zones. After decades of disuse, CORE engineers had restored power to the sky trains and it now ran between cities and even to the welfare colonies as a free service to all citizens with valid CivIDs.

They passed a monitor at the station, which scanned their embedded CivID chips and allowed them to pass through the gates. With their enforcer status encoded into the CivIDs, they were permitted to bring weapons on board, which was no small thing since doing so had saved Reese's life in the past.

"Do you see Dani?" she asked, looking through the fifty-odd people gathered below the stairs leading up to the station itself.

"No, but something's going on here." Jaxon's hand hovered near his weapon. "Too many people are standing around for this time of day. Especially on a Thursday night. They should have gone home hours ago. No one's even going up to the train."

Thanks to the secret slavery inside the colonies, most CORE residents worked less than thirty hours a week, enforcement being one of the few exceptions. It was part of why enforcers were so well paid and given so many perks, but it also meant they'd have to deal with whatever was going on here before catching their train.

Reese hopped up on a bench and looked around for a body on the cobblestones or someone fighting—something to explain the gathering. The people looked average, dressed mostly in casual business wear. Dark hair and features for the most part, which was to be expected, but in the middle of the crowd, also standing on a bench, she spied a thin, wild-haired, bearded man wearing black pants and a tight green sweater. He held up a sign scratched on a piece of wood that he'd likely salvaged from an empty zone. It read in large bold letters: SAY NO TO IMPLANTS!

"The implants aren't just CivIDs," he was shouting. "They have all the information you've ever put into a Teev or given the government. It makes you traceable every second. You can't just put down your card and go into another room or go to the store and buy a smoke without them noticing. It'll be able to test your blood, monitor your heartrate, even know when you make love to your wife."

"Oh, go home," someone shouted. "You're crazy."

"It's already against the law to go around without the card!" a woman yelled.

"That's right," the thin man hollered back. "They already track us every minute. But the implant is worse. Do you know that one percent of you will die from the operation? Do you know the radiation it exposes you to over the course of your life is like walking into the North Desolation Zone? How many of us will die of cancer? Imagine that. A disease our ancestors had cured before Breakdown. Now our government is more interested in Nuface therapy than in curing diseases."

"That's not true!" someone shouted. "He's crazy."

This was met by a shove from others in the crowd.

"I've had Nuface," an older woman called. "It's great."

"Only because they gave you permission!" the wild man called back. "And how many years did you work to afford it?"

No response from the woman except a scowl.

"He's right about the emissions." This from a man in a suit.

"I work for the hospital, and it's true. But it's over an entire lifetime. It won't hurt anyone."

"Unless they're young or sick!" The thin man shouted. "Mothers, do you want your babies to die before you do? They already made you wait years just to get a child, and now they'll kill them. We have to stick together!"

"He's right!" a woman cried. "I've been denied a birth order four times already. Each time took me three months to apply with a six-month wait in between."

"Did you hear that?" The thin man waved his arms wildly. "She could have had four babies by then! Do you really think the CORE Elite have these implants? Do you think they pay what we do for Nuface therapy? Do you really think they have to wait to have a child?"

"No!" several people shouted. The mood was growing uglier by the second. Another dozen people had joined the crowd, with only a few hurrying away, casting frightened glances at the cameras that watched the square.

"And they have entire databases of pre-Breakdown information they don't share!" The thin man pointed his finger at members of the group. "That means you and you and you might die because those slut-munching pus bags care more about their smooth skin than keeping you alive. They glut themselves on our work, and tax us too much to support those lazy cotton-heads in the colonies. Don't let them continue! You need to stand up and be counted."

Murmurs of assent clearly showed which way the crowd was leaning. A chill shuddered through Reese that had little to do with the light breeze in the square.

Jaxon put on his iTeev, and his hand motions told her he was bringing up the holo feed from the cameras. Reese jumped down from the bench, removed her iTeev from her uniform sleeve, and slid it over her eyes, connecting it to

Jaxon's iTeev feed. Immediately small boxes with numbers popped up around the edges of her vision, each one with a narrow line leading to a person in the crowd.

"Just as I thought," Jaxon murmured. "Our preacher man isn't carrying a CivID." He frowned. "But it looks like he's not the only one."

"I count four more," Reese said.

"Those are the ones we need to worry about." Jaxon pulled out his temper laser, a mood-altering device that would calm all but the few that were immune. "Time to break this up."

Reese and Eagle followed his lead. "I don't know," Eagle muttered. "I'm counting seventy-eight people now. This could get bad."

Reese had to agree. And the closer they'd get, the more sketches she'd see from their minds, which meant she wouldn't be working at one hundred percent.

"We mostly have to worry about the five without the CivIDs," Jaxon said. "Eagle, you go for the guy on the left, I'll get the two in the middle. Reese, the one on the right and the preacher man are all yours. Keep your iTeevs on and put in your ear pieces so we can communicate."

Reese chuckled. "Only two for me? Put that way, it seems easy."

Jaxon shot her an amused glance. "Just try not to kill anyone else before you get to them. I signaled Lyssa to send backup. They'll need to track down and implant all these people."

"Poor suckers," Eagle muttered.

"You have an implant too," Reese reminded him. "It's not so bad."

Eagle simply stepped forward, a smile on his face, which made Reese wonder. Later she'd ask more. For now, she turned her temper laser on high and drew her stunner with her right hand. Her left was her dominant, but she could shoot equally well with the right, thanks to her time in the colonies. In practice, she always carried the deadlier weapon in her right hand.

"Look, there they are!" The thin man cried. "Enforcers. They'll take us all. Friends, save me!"

The crowd turned, a few separating themselves from the rest and sprinting away, a useless gesture because their CivIDs had already been recorded. One way or the other, they'd be found.

Reese hurried forward, pushing her way through the crowd. They only had a few minutes before their train arrived, and she wasn't going to miss it. Sketches came to her from the minds of those she passed. Images that she'd have to draw: an enforcer leading away a young man, an older woman weeping, a man pushing a mop as he stared hopelessly out a window. Then another sobbing woman, this time young, so very young.

Reese wanted to yell at them to shut up. To leave her alone. Her mind threatened to explode. She shoved a man from her path, wanting to hurry to her targets. Wanting to . . .

A sudden lethargy fell over her. Her steps slowed. What was she doing? Oh, that's right. The thin preacher and the guy on the right, the man who was pointing something at her now. Something that might be some kind of gun. Wasn't that interesting? She stared into the face of the man. His expression wasn't pleasant, but she found she didn't care.

"Go!" The man yelled at her. "You have better things to do."

He was right. She was hungry. When was the last time she'd eaten? There was a great little restaurant nearby with a handsome waiter she liked to flirt with just to tease Alex. If she left now, she might make it there and back to the train on time. Or not. Did it matter? First, she needed to sketch the images in her mind. After that, she'd eat.

She turned and walked back the way she'd come.

CHAPTER 3

"Break it up!" Jaxon shouted, sweeping the temper laser over the people nearest him. "Your CivIDs have been recorded. You need to go home or stand to the side. Go on now! You will all be contacted and interviewed about what went on here today. As of now, this is an enforcer matter."

That was enough to send more people scurrying away, but the crowd was still dense as he approached the preacher man's position. Reese should have been close to him by now. Where was she? One young man threw a punch at Jaxon, but he blocked it and shot his temper laser at him.

"Go home," Jaxon told him.

The man's shoulders slumped. "Hey, whatever," he said, and ambled away.

Jaxon swiveled, craning his neck to see how Reese and Eagle were doing, and was stunned to see that both of them had turned from their targets and were heading to the edge of the crowd.

"Hey!" he shouted. "Reese! What are you doing?"

Since they were still connected through their iTeevs, her voice came to him clearly, but sounded odd and detached. "Just going to draw a few sketches. Too many images in my mind. Then I'll grab a bite to eat. Would you like me to bring you something?"

Jaxon stared. What was up with her? She sounded drugged, distant. He scanned the crowd for danger. There, the four men without CivIDs were carrying laser-like devices in their hands, all of which were double the size of his temper laser.

"Reese, Eagle, they have some kind of temper lasers," Jaxon said, "and you guys have been affected. You should nearly be out of range, and the effect will fade, but I'm going to need your help sooner rather than later, so fight it and get back in here." The effects of a temper laser lasted an average of fifteen minutes, but this version seemed powerful.

All enforcers had to go through temper laser training, so Reese and Eagle should have developed at least some resistance. They had also been frequent receivers of temper blasts back in the Coop as children, which should lessen their recovery time. Of the crew, only Jaxon had been born with immunity, along with less than one percent of the CORE's two million people.

Jaxon watched Reese turn to him, her eyes shuttered by her iTeev. "Come on!" he yelled, knowing his voice would ring through her comlink. "Get back here and finish your job. Now! That's an order!"

Without waiting to see if she or Eagle responded, Jaxon grabbed the bystander in front of him and threw him out of the way. One of the men with the temper lasers laughed at him and turned his weapon in Jaxon's direction.

Jaxon dived toward him, simultaneously exchanging his own temper laser for a stunner. This guy didn't deserve the soft treatment. He fired and a little dart shot out, hitting the man in the neck. The thug shuddered with shock and went down.

Two of the remaining three rushed Jaxon, exchanging their useless temper lasers for their fists. Jaxon got one with the close-contact feature of his stunner before it was wrested from his hand. At least they couldn't use it on him without a team code or the correct fingerprints. From the corner of his eye, he saw the fourth guy grabbing the preacher and pulling him off the bench he'd been standing on. They'd get away unless Reese and Eagle could shake off the effects of the laser.

A fist slammed into Jaxon's head, reminding him he had more immediate concerns. He scrambled to regain his balance and punched at the big man attacking him, who barely seemed to notice Jaxon's blow. The man lunged wildly toward Jaxon, his leap exposing his stomach. So not a professional. Jaxon put all his strength into an upper cut, one that should have stopped the man instantly. Instead, he simply coughed and threw another meaty fist at Jaxon's face.

Jaxon dodged. *He's hyped up on juke.* This close it was easy to see the glassy, bloodshot eyes. He wouldn't feel anything Jaxon did to him for thirty minutes or more, and with the guy's longer reach, it'd be a challenge to get him down quickly with only his fists. Jaxon faked a punch to his face and reached for his gun. The man grunted and sprang at him again, punching Jaxon's hand away from his weapon. Jaxon lashed out with his foot, crashing it into the guy's stomach. The man gasped for breath but kept moving forward.

There, an opening. Jaxon twisted, ducking close to the man and punching into his chin, snapping his head backward. He followed with a hammer punch and another kick. The man fell.

"Stop!" Reese shouted.

Jaxon turned to see one of the other men he'd taken out behind him, his temper laser raised to smash into Jaxon's head. The man shuddered and crumpled as Reese got him with her stunner.

"Thanks," he said.

She nodded with an expression he knew too well. She was blaming herself. Her gaze went beyond him where Dani was fighting both the fourth man and the preacher. Dani moved with so much speed that for a moment Jaxon was mesmerized. Her gift was utilizing oxygen in such a way that she was faster and stronger than any man or woman had a right to be. She could run all day without tiring, stay underwater for hours, and she healed faster. Everything that humans needed oxygen for, she had improved upon. Within seconds, she had disarmed the men and had her assault rifle aimed at their stomachs. She turned and gave Jaxon a gloating smile, the locks on her long brown wig slightly askew.

Jaxon wiped the blood from the side of his face and helped Reese cuff the fallen men. Eagle appeared in time to help with the third before picking up one of the oversized temper lasers. "This is new," he said. "I don't usually react so badly to a temper laser."

"Here comes our backup," Reese announced.

Dani dragged her prisoners over to them, their hands cuffed. "Sit," she said, pointing at the ground. In her hands was the temper laser that had belonged to the fourth man.

"You're immune to the temper?" Jaxon asked her, his voice low. She hadn't been as a child.

She cracked a sardonic grin. "No, I just moved fast. He didn't get a chance to use it on me."

"These belong to fringers?" Eagle indicated the laser he was carrying. In the CORE, only enforcers and doctors who conducted psychological reconditioning had access to temper lasers, so it was a logical question. "Too strong and it could cause brain damage."

Dani frowned and indicated their iTeevs, reminding them that as long as they were connected to the feed, they were in danger of being overheard. Jaxon, Reese, and Eagle shut down their units and moved a short distance away from the prisoners.

"Without doing more research," Dani continued, "all I can tell you is that they resemble weapons we have in Newcali. Like ours, they aren't activated by fingerprints, and we've improved on many weapons that were still available after Breakdown. We don't stifle creativity or research. But these men are not ours. I've already sent their images to our database, and they aren't Newcalians."

"Undergrounders, then?" Reese asked.

Jaxon had been wondering the same thing, but El Cerebro didn't usually go for public disturbances unless it was to cover up another secret operation, and the only operation he was aware of right now was saving Dr. Kentley. Then again, he didn't know everything about the underground leader.

"Well, if they're with the Underground," he said, "we'll leave them to Brogan."

"And if not?" Reese cocked her head at him.

He sighed, but it was Dani who answered, "Then we've got another player on the scene. Saca, for all we know they were sent by Special Forces to weed out sympathizers."

"Paranoid much?" Eagle gave her a placid smile. "They could be just what they seem—disgruntled citizens. They probably want more pay, were rejected for a business license, or had their birth order denied."

Jaxon stared at their captives. Despite the increasing chill as night approached, the thin man had laid down on the cobblestones, his hands under the back of his neck as if he hadn't a care in the world. He didn't look like Special Forces or Elite, but whether or not he was an actual disgruntled citizen, Jaxon couldn't tell. "Or she might not be paranoid enough," he said.

"They could be from one of the fringe groups living in the empty zones," Reese suggested.

Dani nodded. "Though most of the groups near here are connected with Newcali, there are several groups that aren't. Some of them are vicious. They periodically attack our people."

"Maybe Hammer and Brogan can figure it out before we get back." Jaxon could already hear the humming of the tracks above them. "Train's coming. We've got to pass these guys off quickly."

Eagle stuffed the oversized temper into his already bulging weapon's bag, seemingly uncaring about appropriating evidence. "If you send them your feed of the event, we can file our reports on the train."

Jaxon motioned for an approaching enforcer to take care of the prisoners, then tapped into the AED general enforcer channel and explained the situation to the backup team as he and his crew ran up the metal stairs to the station platform. The train slid into place before them, wind whipping at his face even at its drastically reduced speed.

Inside they chose the table cars, with three seats abreast on either side of the table. Jaxon threw his bag into the overhead compartment and slid in next to Reese. She was closer to him than the window, and their legs touched, but she didn't move away. Delicious heat flooded his body.

"Sorry about what happened back there," she said to him. "I knew what I was supposed to do. I just cared more about other things. I've always been able to reorient quickly, but this time it took forever to shake."

"These tempers seem stronger than ours," Jaxon reminded her. Her scowl showed she didn't care to accept the excuse. She slapped a drawing pad on the table and began sketching.

Eagle removed the oversized temper laser and set it on the table before stowing his heavy bag. "Double check your iTeevs," he said. "Let's make sure they're off before we talk about anything important."

Jaxon had already removed his iTeev from his face, but he checked the unit on his sleeve anyway as the others stored their equipment. Only Eagle kept his special glasses on so he could see, disabling his connection to the feed.

"You know," Eagle said, settling next to Dani. "That guy was right, the one Jaxon called the preacher. The CORE does tax everyone fifty percent."

"Yeah, and they're only pretending to send that money to the colonies." Dani's voice was acid. "Tell me, where is that money really going? Because no matter how you look at it, the only ones enjoying life in the CORE besides the Elite are enforcers like you. And that's because they're getting paid enough to look the other way."

Jaxon couldn't protest. None of them could. Even a few months ago, he'd been blind to what was going on, but after learning about the slavery in the colonies and nearly being killed by Special Forces, he'd begun noticing the furtive looks in the faces around him. How they flinched from him whenever he approached. Life outside the colonies for him had been so much better than inside that he'd swallowed the rhetoric completely. He hadn't noticed the quiet suffering of people who were too frightened to speak out. Now everywhere he looked, he saw the fear.

"Right," said Eagle, "but people don't know the colonies aren't being supported."

"Or do they?" Reese countered, not looking up from her sketches. "The underground exists, scientists have been contacting the fringers for years for help in getting out of the CORE Territories. Maybe people know more than we give them credit for."

"Whatever they believe," Dani said, "slavery doesn't just happen. Someone trapped people in the colonies on purpose, someone experimented on us there. Someone's pulling the strings. It's a matter of finding out who."

"It has to be some of the Elite," Reese said, her gaze crossing Jaxon's.

He nodded. "They're the only ones not afraid. The question is, what are we going to do when we find them?"

"We kill them," Dani answered. "Exactly the way they killed over ten thousand of our people."

Jaxon wanted to protest that they had no idea how far up the corruption went. Because if it went all the way to the top, they'd more likely end up in padded cages or have their ashes trampled in the dust than succeed in killing anyone.

No one else had an answer for Dani either.

"Anyone hungry?" Jaxon's stomach had been sending urgent messages since before leaving the division. Everyone nodded.

"I'll help." Reese set down her pencil and followed him into the aisle.

In silence, they made their way to the back of the train car where the readymeal dispenser stood. Jaxon turned on his iTeev, linked to the enforcer credit in his account, and sent it to the machine. Reese began pushing buttons. The machine whirred as it sent the cartons of food through the microwave before popping out of the slot. Jaxon chose a variety of drinks to wash the sometimes tasteless food down.

As they waited for the meals to cook, Reese stared at the passing landscape, her eyes distant. Her hands twitched.

"Are you all right?" he asked softly.

She didn't meet his gaze. "Just a bit on edge. I need to sketch more."

"How bad is it?"

She waited so long to reply that he almost thought she wouldn't speak at all. "Bad." She sighed and added, "I told you that I haven't been taking the neural suppressant Alex gave me because it makes me feel fuzzy. But what I didn't say was that I can barely touch anyone without it."

Which was how the suppressant had come into play at all, he suspected, especially since she was dating Alex. It was probably wrong of Jaxon to be glad things weren't working well between them.

"On a brighter note," she added. "I can now wait up to ten hours before I'm forced to get the sketches on paper. And I don't have to make them as detailed."

"That's good." He'd seen her go from calm and controlled to a quivering mass of need in less than an hour in the past when she'd seen too many sketches. Her ability made her the perfect enforcer sketch artist, but it was slowly driving her crazy. He started to put a comforting arm around her, then hesitated.

She leaned into him. "I can feel sketches from you," she said. "And the others in the crew, but not all the time. You are a relief to be around compared with other people. At least most of the time. Except when you have premonitions near me."

Which he tried not to do, if he had any warning at all. He always put as much distance as possible between him and Reese, in case the vision was of them together. As long as she was dating Alex, he couldn't let her glimpse that intimacy. Among other reasons, it seemed too desperate on his part. Embarrassing that he could want it—want her—so much.

"Why would it be different for us?" he asked.

She shrugged, giving him a flat grin. "Maybe it's because I already filled an entire sketchbook with images from your mind."

Or maybe it was because they spent almost every day together and she'd built up an immunity to him. Whatever the reason, Jaxon was willing to accept her explanation at face value.

"Looks like our food is ready." He piled the readymeals on a disposable tray. "Grab the drink skins, would you?" She swept up the skins and preceded him up the aisle.

Back at the table where the others waited, they doled out the readymeals. Dani wrinkled her nose but said nothing as she dug into hers. Eagle ate as he chatted about the cool features on the new temper laser. Reese began drawing again.

There was a picture of him, Jaxon saw, more detailed than the rest. Who had sent her a mental image of him? He was willing to bet it wasn't anyone from the crowd at the train station. Should he ask?

She caught his gaze and turned the page. *Later then,* he thought.

The train slowed abruptly as it raced into another station. The doors clanged open and a few people entered. They took one look at the uniforms Jaxon, Reese, and Eagle were wearing and moved to the next car. Had that always happened?

"Better make our reports now," Jaxon said. "We don't want to send them anywhere close to Santoni."

They spent the next hour filing their reports, and then took turns changing into civilian clothes in the train restroom before each activated one of the fake CivID cards Brogan had given them. Their enforcer IDs had been useful to get their weapons onto the train, but now their uniforms and IDs would only bring attention to themselves. Back in Amarillo City, Evan Hammer would be busy planting false information into the camera feed that would make anyone monitoring the train, or who later reviewed the recordings, think the team had left at another station.

Hammer also sent Jaxon an encrypted file over his T-link with the details about their trip. Aside from the lodging reservations, Hammer had hacked into the doctor's daily schedule and made an appointment for Reese in the morning under one of her fake CivIDs to talk to the doctor about back pain. She was to get him alone and explain that she was also from Colony 6 and get him to accompany her back to Amarillo City willingly. If not, the rest would step in and take him by force.

"Apparently, our only option is to approach him at work," Jaxon said. "Looks like his listed address is his receptionist and her husband's apartment, but he doesn't actually live there. Since he doesn't keep regular hours on Saturday or Sunday, tomorrow is our only shot."

Dani scowled. "Sounds like he's got something to hide."

Of course the doctor was hiding something—his ability at the very least—or Special Forces wouldn't be after him. Reese going in alone did seem to be the least threatening option. Unless Jaxon's visions kicked in and said otherwise, she was also the logical choice to fill him in about the danger he faced. A simple sketch glimpsed from his mind would prove her ability and her Colony 6 origins.

Jaxon regarded the others. "Unless anyone has an objection to the basic plan, let's go over what Reese should say. We'll also need to discuss what to do if he rejects her invitation and how we'll deal with Special Forces if they show up, which given Brogan's intel seems likely."

"I was thinking we might need a distraction if Special Forces looks like they'll make a move while we're at the doctor's office." Eagle held up a device. "Something like this planted at the sky train station would be the best, I think. It can ignite a fire close to the control booth that will sound the alarms. The stations are always unmanned, so there's no chance of it being put out too quickly, and the sirens should bring Special Forces to investigate. With a few carefully placed clues that hint at finding the vandals, we could probably entice them over to a river that runs by the town and buy ourselves a little more time to pick up the good doctor."

"I like it," Jaxon said.

"If he doesn't come willingly," Reese said, "we could use a temper laser. He's probably not immune."

They talked over additional possibilities until people gradually filled up the train car and privacy became an issue. By then they were only rehashing old ideas. The train nearly emptied again as they reached the last large city before hitting Santoni. Only a knot of people at the far end of the car and Jaxon's crew remained.

Jaxon went over the plan again in his mind to see if they'd overlooked anything, but his thoughts were interrupted by a commotion at the end of the car.

"Stop!" a man yelled. "Thief, thief! I've been robbed!" He jumped from his seat and began running after a small figure with a blue hat pulled low over its head.

Instinctively, Jaxon jumped to his feet, his hand going to a hidden weapon. The small figure bore down on him, followed closely by the man. He reached out and grabbed the figure. The hat fell off, revealing the dark curly hair and narrow face of a street urchin Jaxon recognized only too well. Nova, Brogan's niece.

Jaxon sprang forward and caught the man's fist as he launched it toward Nova's face. "I don't think you want to do that," Jaxon said. "You could go to jail."

"She's the one who stole from me," the big man said.

"Did not!" Nova shouted, anger radiating from her like heat from a cup of brew. "Prove it."

"Give it back," Jaxon said to her. "Or I'll make sure you answer to Captain Brogan."

The girl's face darkened. She pulled an iTeev from under her ratty sweater and shoved it at the man. "It's old anyway. Stinkin' pus licker."

The man's face flushed, and he looked ready to pounce on

Nova, but Jaxon pulled her away. "I'll see that she's turned in to the authorities," he said. "I have connections."

The man paled and backed away. "Fine. Thank you." He was back in his seat before Jaxon hauled Nova to where the others waited.

"Seriously, Nova?" Reese said as Jaxon thrust the girl into the seat. "What are you doing here?"

Nova's chin jutted out. "Just going for a ride. Sky train's free, ain't it?"

"Lovely. Just lovely," Dani muttered. "Now we have to babysit."

The speakers on the train came to life. "Next stop is Santoni," came a pleasant voice. "If this is your stop, please gather your possessions and prepare to leave."

"I can help," Nova said. "I lived in Santoni for two years before my father died. I know every part of it. That's why I came when I figured out where you were heading."

"And how did you find that out?" Jaxon demanded.

Nova shrugged, leaning over slightly as the train came to a stop. "I'm El Cerebro's niece. I know everything."

"Uh, you might want to be a little careful who you announce that to," Eagle said, his eyes pinned to the window. "I think our friends out there might be more than a little interested in that kind of information."

Jaxon followed his gaze to see a group of enforcers, who were exiting a train on the opposite side of the platform, the train that had come from the direction of Estlantic. Each of the four wore a Special Forces patch on their sleeves.

Nova gasped and ducked instinctively, while Jaxon gave Brogan silent thanks for their civilian clothes and their new CivIDs. If they'd come in as enforcers, no doubt they would have alerted these soldiers to their presence, which might be a problem if there were complications with the mission.

"This might move up our agenda," Jaxon said. "We may have to act tonight."

"Except we have no idea where he lives," Eagle reminded him. "His receptionist may have no idea either. Unless Special Forces has figured it out, they're as stuck as we are until morning."

"I'll follow them," Dani said. "I'll contact you through the T-links and let you know what I find out."

"I'll go with you." Jaxon shouldered his bag.

Dani gave him a withering stare. "If I go alone, I won't be seen."

She had a point. With her gift, she could move much faster and more subtly without him. She could climb buildings or run around to other streets without breaking a sweat. Telling her he didn't quite trust her wasn't going to win him any points with her or anyone else in the crew.

"Okay, but I want you reporting in every fifteen minutes."

In a smooth motion, Dani grabbed her bag and sprinted from the train.

Jaxon turned to see Reese staring out the window. "What is it?" he asked.

"Are you sure that's a good idea, letting her go? I don't think any of them were in my sketch of her, but there might be more Special Forces waiting wherever they're going."

Jaxon reeled. He hadn't thought to look for the man in his vision, the one who would capture Dani in the future, and now it was already too late. The Special Forces and Dani were gone. With only a sudden pressure as warning, the world disappeared as another vision descended on him, stealing his breath and moving him to an entirely different place and time. Not to the vision of Dani and the enforcer as he expected, but something much worse.

Children sprawl over the floor, their skin eaten away with blistering sores. Their mouths open in soft moans, their breaths coming so faintly, he can't be sure how many still lived. Their makeshift beds look inadequate and uncomfortable. One tiny figure is covered completely by a ragged brown blanket. Too late for that one. A loud, agonized wail fills the room, its concrete wall pitted with structural damage . . . and imbued with human suffering.

"Come on." Eagle tugged at him, pulling him to the door and off the train.

Jaxon stumbled blindly along with Eagle, his vision clearing only as he felt the train speed from the station. Eagle handed him his bag. Reese propelled Nova forward, gazing at him in horror. No chance she hadn't received a sketch of that. He pitied her, knowing it would be bright and vibrant in her mind until she transferred it to paper.

I'm sorry, Reese, he thought

She ran to the nearest trash receptacle and began vomiting into it. He glanced around the platform, but it was empty. No one was interested in leaving the train at Santoni, except for them and Special Forces.

"What is it?" Nova asked, looking around her anxiously. Her hand went to the small knife he knew she carried at her waist.

He shook his head, unwilling to share with this child, no matter how jaded she was, no matter how her father had died of radiation poisoning.

"She needs to go back," Reese said, staring at Nova. Her hand clenched at her sides, a sure sign she was fighting a sketch. The one from his mind plus however many she had glimpsed from strangers on the train.

Nova's face showed betrayal at Reese's comment. "I thought you would understand. They killed my father just like they did yours. This is my fight too."

"We'll deal with her later," Jaxon said. "Let's get to the C-lodge where Hammer made us reservations."

"We're staying at a C-lodge?" Nova perked up. "I've never been to one before. No one I've ever known has, except maybe my uncle."

Jaxon had stayed at only a few himself, normally while on vacation when he'd lived in Estlantic. All C-lodges, or Commonwealth lodges as they were formally called, were owned by the CORE, and the fees for renting a room included the usual boxed readymeals. A few of the larger places he'd stayed at in New York also had an adjoining restaurant where he'd bought a fresh meal at almost the same price as a room for the night. No, he didn't guess that the average resident would spend much time in a C-lodge, much less an undergrounder like Nova, even if she had a valid Civ-ID in her bag of tricks.

They hurried through the streets, not bothering to call a shuttle because the C-lodge in Santoni was close to the station. Inside, the gray-haired woman at the desk pointed her iTeev at Jaxon and appeared satisfied with whatever appeared on her screen.

"A two-bedroom suite," she said. "The charges will come automatically from your account." She flashed them an insincere smile. "Thank you for visiting C-lodge Santoni." Without waiting for a reply, she turned back to the large Teev holo screen behind her where a couple was kissing with exaggerated passion.

Before entering the room, Jaxon checked Nova's CivID to make sure it was a valid one. One never knew where the child was concerned. Anyone entering a room at a lodge was scanned and recorded, and the last thing they needed was Nova bringing down the local enforcers upon them.

"Welcome Reba, John, Ernest, and Nora," the room chimed as they entered. Nova rolled her eyes at the fake names, which

Brogan had presumably chosen by the sole fact that they began with the same letter as their real names.

Jaxon turned off the automatic greeting, signaling Eagle to check to see if any recording devices were on in the room. After pulling equipment from his bag and fiddling with it, Eagle shook his head.

"We're clear. But no doubt the surveillance hardware is in place, so I'll leave up a monitor, just in case." Eagle set a device on the table. "I brought a 3D printer, so I'll make monitors to put in the other rooms as well."

Eagle busied himself unpacking his equipment. With the new interface Brogan had provided from pre-Breakdown tech foraged from the desolation zones, Eagle could connect his mental 3D renditions directly to the 3D printer. Jaxon had little idea how any of the pre-Breakdown tech worked, except that it used brainwaves and attached to the surgical implants Eagle already used for his regular glasses. But the combination of his ability and the printer meant the team was now limited only by the schematics he could create, the materials they could carry or get hold of, and the size of the printer.

"I don't volunteer to tell Brogan about her," Reese said to Jaxon, casting a glance at Nova, who was already choosing a readymeal from the dispensing machine in the small alcove of a kitchen. "I voted for her to go home."

"No one has to tattle," Nova retorted. "I promise, I'll just stay here out of the way." She sank onto a couch and waved her hand to turn on the life-sized Teev holo.

Jaxon shut it down with a reverse motion. "Not now. I have to call Dani." Like Reese, he also worried about telling Captain Brogan that Nova was with them, and at the same time he felt a strange reluctance to send the child home. Whether because she might get in trouble on her own, or because she might be useful, he wasn't sure.

A tap at the door made them all jump. Jaxon pulled his gun and Reese did the same. He motioned her behind the door, as he turned on the door's viewscreen to see who was outside. He half expected Special Forces.

"Stand down," he said to Reese. "It's Dani." He opened the door. "I thought you were following the enforcers."

"I did. You'll be happy to know they are just downstairs. They checked in a few minutes before you did, so I was already here. I followed you up." Dani doffed her bag and set it by the door. "They met two others. I wasn't able to hear much, but I did set a pressure pad outside their door. It'll send me a warning if they leave. Catching up with them won't be a problem."

"You have a pressure pad that works?" Nova asked. "Cool. We found a couple in the empty zones but never could get them to work."

"There's a reason we're helping the CORE scientists escape." Dani sat down on the couch and began to unlace her boots. "It's one more thing we have that the CORE doesn't. They don't care about a lot of tech these days."

"Why should they?" Eagle looked up from the counter he'd strewn with enough banned equipment to get them all sent back to Colony 6. "They have surveillance everywhere and that's really all they need to remain in control. That and enforcers."

Dani gave him a grin. "Well they don't have cameras in the corridors of this C-lodge. Apparently as of a few minutes ago, spider webs have seriously obscured some key angles. We'll be able to get in and out without being examined too closely. Should take a day or two for them to figure it out."

"By which time we will have left town." Eagle bumped his closed fist to hers. "Nice."

"Let's get some sleep then," Jaxon said. "We have to beat them there in the morning."

"First I should set up the distraction we discussed on the train." Eagle picked up his bag that still looked half full. "With the arrival of the additional Special Forces, we'd probably better set off the blast tomorrow morning as soon as they leave their room. I'll need help gathering and setting the false vandal trail. I'm thinking leaves and mud from the river as a path leading them away. We'll have to use the skin tags Dani provided so the cameras don't catch us."

Dani jumped to her feet. "I'll help. I want to do some recon anyway. I need to stretch my legs."

If Dani said she needed to stretch her legs, her fidgeting would drive them all crazy within a few minutes, so Jaxon was glad she'd volunteered and that Eagle would be around to keep an eye on her. "We don't know what Special Forces' time-table is," Jaxon reminded them, "which means the distraction may still be only a backup. They might be planning on more surveillance or a direct offer, not to kidnap him."

"Oh, you mean like they did to us?" Reese's smile held no mirth. "I seem to recall too well the knife they used during our first so-called invitation, and then the guns on our second meeting."

"Which is why Eagle's plan is a good one. Nothing is for certain." Jaxon waved Eagle and Dani to the door. "Go on and get it done. Reese and I will go over her approach to the doctor tomorrow."

Hopefully, Kentley would come without protest—and before Special Forces showed up.

"We don't need to go over it again," Reese said as the door shut behind their friends. "Unless you have anything to add from our discussion on the train."

"Maybe we can agree on a few signal words. In case you need to send us a message over the T-link while you're talking with him."

"Good idea." Reese glanced at Nova, who was eating and watching them with intense eyes. "Let's talk in the bedroom."

"Can I watch the feed then?" Nova asked plaintively.

"Yes," Jaxon told her. "Don't turn it up too loud."

Reese scooped up her bag and headed for one of the two bedrooms. Jaxon hefted his own bag and followed her. The room wasn't a luxury suite by any means, but it held two large beds. She sank onto one of them and began drawing rapidly on her ever-present pad without any hesitation. She knew where each line should go, almost apparently without looking.

Jaxon knew what she was drawing before it came to life under her hand. The sick children in his vision, looking even more lost and forlorn in her pencil sketch. Though he'd seen them in color, her vibrant image leapt from the page, burning his eyes with its offense. His premonition might not come true for months or even a year, which so far had been his longest vision, but it would still come to pass.

"It could have been us," she said. "The Coop was close to the radiation zone. I used to think that's why my father and the other adults were so angry all the time."

He knew what she meant. Radiation poisoning could excuse a world of hurt in a child's heart.

He sat next to her and took her hand. When it was just the two of them like this, the old days didn't seem so old. She was still his best friend, and it didn't matter that his adult self was also in love with her.

"If we find the children—when we find them—we have to help." Her hand tightened on his. "No matter what."

"Of course."

Their world had gone crazy. The CORE was rotten, corrupt, and someone had to figure out who was behind the rot and fix it. Brogan had chosen them.

CHAPTER 4

Lyssa Sloan sat back in her seat and stared at the holo display of the TAD-Alert. There was only one active call at the moment, about vandalism near the Freedom Fountain, and her co-worker Zevolun was handling it, though the Teev program had already identified which enforcers they should send out.

Nothing like the gathering at the sky train station that had required a dozen enforcers with weapons. The participants had been subdued quickly, thanks to Jaxon and the others, but the reports submitted by the crew were unusual, especially in regard to the powerful temper lasers. The man Jaxon called the preacher was in lockup now, denying any wrongdoing and insisting that it wasn't his problem people had stopped to listen to him. He claimed he hadn't planned a gathering or broken any laws.

Except he *had* broken laws. Even if he hadn't planned the gathering or invited people, talking out about CORE policies was punishable by reconditioning or medical enhancement. Dozens of troublemakers Lyssa knew or had heard about had been sent to a colony after enhancement, where they were supposedly supported by the CORE in a safe environment. But Lyssa knew confinement meant working sixty hours a week until they died or weren't useful anymore. If they didn't have family in the colony at that point, they would conveniently disappear.

It made Lyssa's life seem easy by comparison. She worked the required thirty hours a week, grouping them all into three days so she could be with her daughter, Tamsin, the other four days. On the days Lyssa worked, Lyra dropped Tamsin off at a sitter's, who would take her to school, and Tamsin was later picked up by the sitter until Lyra arrived to get her after work.

For those three days at work, Lyssa was herself. On the other four, the days she spent with Tamsin, she pretended to be Lyra, who was Tamsin's officially recognized mother. Pretending to be Lyra at home also meant pretending to be married to Kansas, Lyra's husband.

Lyra and Kansas, stepping in when they did to marry early and claiming Lyssa's illegal child as their own had saved Lyssa's life, both figuratively and literally. Yet even that wouldn't have worked if Kansas hadn't been able to use his pull in the CORE transportation office to get a birth order, a feat he'd not been able to repeat in the decade since Tamsin's birth.

Which left them all in a strange sort of limbo, tied by the child they each adored, but whose existence imprisoned them all in different ways. Kansas loved his wife, Lyssa had no doubt of that, but Lyra's once-strong emotions for her husband were frozen in cravings for her own child, one she was denied because of Tamsin's existence.

By practice, each of the two million CORE residents was allowed the right to replace him or herself, which meant couples should be able to win two birth orders, and single people one, but more and more people like Lyra and Kansas had been rejected for a second child. Some were even denied one. With a required six month-wait after each rejection before applying again, the three-month application process became even longer and more tedious.

Lyssa's guilt ran deep. Which was why six weeks ago, when Lyra and Kansas's application had been rejected yet again, Lyssa had applied for a birth order herself. While single mothers weren't ideal birth candidates, they weren't prohibited from submitting an application, and it meant their family had that much more of a chance for a baby. With Brogan's help and fake CivIDs, it would be possible for Lyssa to trade lives with Lyra in the real world long enough for Lyra to become pregnant and give birth. Lyssa hadn't told her sister about her application yet, not after the devastation of her last rejection, and as birth order announcements were made every three months, Lyssa still had weeks to wait before learning her status.

The CORE Elite said birth orders were being rejected because people were living longer and expanding was impossible at this time. But Lyssa was one of the few who knew the whole truth, the ugly truth, that the CORE was largely sustained by the number of people imprisoned in the colonies. If more births were allowed, they would need more buildings, more food, more enforcers, which to the Elite meant another welfare colony. But where would they put it? And who would volunteer to populate it? Times were nowhere as desperate as in the days after Breakdown when the Elite had convinced those in the dregs of society to build the colonies, where each had tiny houses and jobs and twenty-meter walls to keep them "safe." Birth rules were the most protected CORE law, and unless residents wanted to brave the desolation zones and risk punishment, they had no choice but to submit.

Checking to make sure the displays were still quiet, Lyssa sat back in her chair and closed her eyes. She wanted a glimpse of her baby. The room dissolved around her as part of her consciousness traveled from her body, searching for her sister. There she was. In Tamsin's room, where the child was already climbing into bed. She resembled Lyssa and Lyra, her long ebony hair engulfing her thin body. She looked younger than her ten years, though sometimes Lyssa thought she seemed far older.

"Is Mommy going to be back before I go to sleep?" Tamsin was asking Lyra.

Lyra glanced over to where Lyssa was now standing, a shadow of her real self but clearly visible to Lyra. In the early days it had taken effort to make themselves seen and heard by the other twin, but now it came easily. They theorized eventually it might be possible to connect with people besides each other, but it hadn't happened yet.

"I think you'll be asleep before she gets here," Lyra said to Tamsin. "She traded a shift with someone today because she had a meeting earlier."

Tamsin heaved a sigh. "I miss her when she's gone."

"Well, the good news is that because she's working late tonight, she gets to go in late tomorrow, so she'll be able to take you to school. Maybe even stay there for a bit with you."

Tamsin grinned. "Good, then I'll be able to show her my new holo designs. I've been working on them really hard."

"I'm sure she'll love them." Lyra climbed into the narrow bed and put her arms around Tamsin, much the way Lyssa did when she put the child to bed. Yes, Lyssa had to push back a surge of resentment that she wasn't the one in the room, but mostly she felt grateful that her sister loved Tamsin as much as she did.

"I love you, Aunt Lyssa," Tamsin said.

The name on her daughter's lips sounded wrong, no matter how many times Lyssa had heard it in the past decade. A part of her longed to tell her daughter that she was really Lyssa, and that it was her aunt who was actually married to Kansas. But the pretense was the only way to make sure Tamsin—and their whole family—remained safe.

"I love you too, baby girl," Lyra said.

Tamsin sighed and snuggled up to her, her eyes drifting to where Lyssa stood at the foot of the bed, as if she too could see her. But she couldn't. Both Lyra and Lyssa tested her often. Even if Tamsin did have their ability, she might need the drugs the CORE had tested on Colony 6 to activate it. Lyssa was both relieved and saddened that Tamsin might never know how to "travel."

"Thank you," Lyssa whispered into the silence, words only her sister would be able to hear.

Lyra nodded and buried her face in Tamsin's neck. Lyssa hoped it gave her comfort. *My fault, my fault,* she thought. Now such a mistake as Tamsin was impossible, but a decade ago, sometimes birth control implants failed or lapsed, or weren't renewed in time.

The door opened, and Kansas came inside, his guitar in hand. Lyssa's incorporeal gaze fixed on him. He was a dark, bronze man with short hair that curled tightly against his scalp, and the way Lyssa felt about him made all other men pale in comparison. She hoped her sister's husband never discovered that bit of truth about her.

"Want a song, sweetie?" he asked, rubbing his finger over the strings.

Tamsin opened her eyes. "Yes, Daddy. Please."

Lyra stayed as her husband played the song, her eyes closed and a half smile on her lips. The way she lay, Lyssa could see the tiny mole on the right side of her neck under her ear. It was the only physical difference between them.

When Lyssa was home getting Tamsin to bed, she always

left the room when Kansas came in to say goodnight, partly because she knew her presence made him uncomfortable but mostly because it hurt to have him so close. If Lyssa had let them raise Tamsin alone as Kansas had requested, would Lyra now still want a child? To feel her own baby growing and kicking inside her? To have something of her husband's? Or would Tamsin be enough?

They would never know.

Lyssa walked closer to the bed, reaching out a hand to place on her daughter's cheek. Tamsin didn't look her way. Lyra's eyes opened, though, and she dipped her chin slightly in farewell.

Lyssa had sent enforcers out on a dozen more calls and was rechecking the TAD-Alert's holo displays when Gemma, another co-worker, sailed through the door.

"Sorry, I'm late," she said in a voice that was entirely too husky for her voluptuously feminine appearance. Her brown hair was on the lighter side, but her eyes were as dark as Lyssa's own.

"You kidding? You did me a huge favor by coming in for me and splitting your shift." Lyssa arose and arched her back to apply a little stretch.

"How'd the appointment go?"

"Oh, fine. It should go away on its own." Lyssa had forgotten the made-up excuse of a doctor's appointment for a growth on her toe. She couldn't exactly tell Gemma the truth, and having Brogan excuse her without apparent reason was too suspicious to continue regularly. Sometimes if she couldn't get away and it wasn't busy in dispatch, Lyssa could attend the meeting by traveling to her sister or vice-versa.

Gemma's eyes strayed to the screen. "So how's it been. Quiet?"

"Getting calls pretty regularly, except for the past half hour, which was why I told Zevolun to take a break, but he should be back soon. The only real problem we had was around seven."

"Oh?" Gemma's round face turned eager. She sat down and rolled her chair close. "Tell me."

"A man was speaking out about the CORE at the train station. A group gathered to listen. When enforcers arrived, the man's friends pulled temper lasers."

"Probably some punk bucket trying to get back at an Elite." Lyssa shrugged. "Maybe."

"Well, thanks for staying so late. I finally got to see my boy." Gemma's face looked bleak for a moment, and Lyssa stifled her pity. Her son was one of the rare invalids born in the CORE. With genetic testing done before birth orders were issued, rigorous doctor care, and forced termination for detected flaws, it was rare to see anyone with a congenital disease. The three-year-old now lived in a special hospital in another town, so she didn't get to see him often.

"How is he?" Lyssa forced herself to ask, already knowing that it probably wasn't good.

Gemma glanced toward the holo displays, her mouth pursing. "Fine, fine. They take good care of him."

There was more, something she wasn't saying, but Lyssa understood her trepidation. The TAD-Alert heard everything, and while Gemma would never be allowed to have another child because of her son's defect, she had her husband and aging mother to worry about.

"That's good." Lyssa said. "Everything looks calm, so maybe I can leave before Zevolun comes back."

Gemma laughed as a soft bell went off. "Go ahead. It's not like the TAD can't handle this practically alone anyway." She put on her headset and looked at the holo that was already spitting out images of an angry woman shaking a knife at her husband.

"This is TAD-Alert," Gemma answered the call, "What's the nature of your emergency?" They always said that, but she tapped at a holo control, which would send the enforcers the system had already recommended to respond. With a few more hand motions, she commanded the TAD to monitor their heartrates and scan the room for other people, drugs, or possible weapons.

With a sigh, Lyssa unhooked her jacket from the back of her chair and turned from the scene. Domestic disputes usually weren't reported to the division, but there had been more and more of them lately. Those and vandalism. Brogan wouldn't be able to put off reconditioning on this one. Or worse.

In the hallway, Lyssa checked to make sure it was empty before turning down the first corridor on the left, pausing at a door that led into a room on the other side of the TAD. This was where most of the super Teev's hardware resided, and Brogan had somehow connected backup holo emitters there that would allow her, and anyone else he admitted into the room, to use the TAD out of sight of prying eyes. He hadn't asked her to stay later to work on the problem of Dani's brother, but she'd seen the desperation in Dani's eyes at the meeting. If they didn't find a way to save him soon, she'd do something they might all regret. She placed her hand on the door, and a soft whir told her it accepted her print.

Evan Hammer looked up from the display as she entered. "Hey, Lyssa," he said casually.

She nodded at the big, ponytailed man. "Hammer." She waited a few seconds before adding, "Any word?" She knew Jaxon and Reese wouldn't be using the regular Teev channels to talk with them while they were in Santoni.

"They're okay." He sighed. "But Jaxon says Nova's there. I haven't relayed that information to Brogan yet." By the sound of his voice, he wasn't looking forward to it.

She wanted to ask more, but even though Hammer, who was by day the crime scene investigator supervisor, had verified the TAD wouldn't record them there, she didn't trust the Teev, not after having used it to peruse the hallways of HED. Did the Elite have any idea how powerful the machine was?

Probably.

"I'm here to do a little more research," she said. "I have an idea."

"Oh?"

She shook her head. "I'll let you know if anything comes of it." Brogan would probably tell him before she did.

He waved his holo display closed and stood from the only chair in the room. "Well, go ahead. I'm beat anyway. Have to be back in the morning too early." His presence engulfed her. Though he moved delicately despite his bulk, there was power in every motion, and it contrasted so much with her own small stature that he made her uncomfortable.

Maybe she was still having trouble trusting him. For all the nearly five months she'd known the enforcer, he'd been living a double life with Brogan in the underground. She'd sent him out on calls, looked things up for him when he needed, and calmed the victims he'd thought needed a woman's touch and she'd never suspected him. He was probably the best liar she knew.

Except for herself.

Had he been surprised to learn that she had a daughter? He'd been there when Lyra had told the others the truth, and so far he hadn't brought it up.

Hammer paused as he reached the door where she stood. His cheekbones were accentuated by how his hair was pulled back, and his brown eyes were deep and endless. "Lyssa," he said. "I hope all is well with your . . . at home."

She nodded. "It's good. Thanks." She wondered if he had anyone waiting for him. He wasn't married, she knew, but a man that powerful and good looking must have a lot of women friends.

"I thought maybe . . . maybe we could grab a glass of chotks sometime." He said it casually, but she was so surprised by the words that for a moment she couldn't speak. No, she wanted to say. Never. But what was her excuse? He was too big? She found him unattractive? That he scared her?

No, not scared. She'd faced down much worse than him back in the Coop.

"Yeah sure. It'd be fun. But just so you know . . . I'm sort of seeing someone."

He considered that a moment. "Ty Bissett in personnel?"

So he'd noticed, though she'd tried to be discreet. Or Jaxon had told him, which seemed more likely. The two were good friends.

"Yeah." Would he tell her how pointless it was dating a dead man? And maybe the fact that Ty was as good as dead was why she dated him. It meant she could never be serious about him, not in the way that Lyra and Kansas were.

"Well, that just takes the pressure off." His laugh didn't sound forced.

Did he mean that the pressure would be off because Ty wasn't competition since he didn't have a future? Or because she and Hammer wouldn't have to worry about romance mucking up their relationship.

"Well, have a good night," she said, slipping past him.

"Night."

She waited until the door was shut before changing the holo to reflect the inside of HED. The Headquarters Enforcer

Division's lobby and public areas were easily accessible, as were the corridors around the offices and common areas, but the simple commands she had at her disposal hadn't allowed for much snooping. She couldn't even get the blueprints of the entire building without alerting them that she was breaking protocol, and Brogan hadn't thought it wise to bring down more notice on them.

Today when the TAD-Alert had responded to the emergency at the sky station, she had clearly seen the warning on the screen that the preacher wasn't broadcasting a CivID, and a new idea had come into existence. She couldn't tell the machine to give her eyes in all the hallways at HED without authorization, but she could enact a code that was already in the system: to look for non-compliance with CivIDs. Not carrying an ID was an active threat, especially inside HED.

While she was at it, she'd also have the machine search for absence of the markers left by the immunizations and additives that were required by law and put into the readymeals everyone ate. Everyone except Fringers and a few of the older generation who still had access to small gardens in their yards would have the markers in their bodies. These violations the TAD would see as a threat because it endangered the welfare of the CORE as a whole.

She sent Captain Brogan a message before she started working, which though encrypted, was vague enough that anyone intercepting it might think she was talking about monitoring their division and not HED. After a few hours of work on the request, she was ready to put it in. If Brogan agreed.

There was no message from him yet, though, so she'd have to call or leave it for morning. Yet even as she started to punch his icon, a message from Brogan appeared on her iTeev: *You are cleared to run the test.*

Well, at least she wouldn't have to talk to him personally, which was good in light of what Nova had done. If Hammer had already told him about his niece, he wouldn't be in a pleasant mood.

Lyssa typed in the command: *Possible fringer activity. Scan noncompliance in all areas. Report location and type of noncompliance.* She added the HED initial, which she hoped was close enough to their own AED to be misconstrued as an accident if the request was intercepted. But she didn't think she'd be caught. It was perfectly acceptable to have the TAD search for noncompliance as reported by the many Teev cameras throughout the CORE. What remained to be seen was if it might give them any insight as to where Dani's brother was being held and how to get him free.

She pushed enter. It was done now, for good or bad.

With a little sigh, she looked down at the folded square of her iTeev. "Call Ty Bissett," she said. "Audio only." She didn't want to explain this room.

He answered so quickly, he might have been waiting. "Hey, Lyssa."

"Hi. You have time for a drink?"

"Love to. You just finish your shift?"

"Yes."

"Meet you at the usual place?"

They'd found a bar that was far enough from the division that it didn't attract other enforcers, so they could be discreet about their relationship. Her requirement, not his, and though the secrecy bothered him, she couldn't explain that it was for his safety. Tonight the bar seemed like too much work. "No, I'll come to your apartment. I'll bring chotks."

"Nice." His voice was low and sexy, and she could picture his compact form and eager smile. His dark eyes framed by black hair that was surprisingly soft and fine. There was nothing about him that stood out, and she'd once thought him too quiet for her. But he kissed like a prince and made her forget, if just for a short time, about Kansas, and her situation with Lyra.

She could almost forget Jaxon had seen him die—and that maybe her dating Ty was the reason for the vision. Whatever the reason, the premonition couldn't be unseen now.

"Hurry," he said, a note of playfulness entering his voice.

"I have a shuttle waiting."

The shuttle was courtesy of Kansas, or she would have used up her monthly shuttle allotment already. Unlike the sky train, use wasn't unlimited, but as an employee of the transportation office, Kansas had a car and unlimited shuttle use for his family. After Lyra told him about people from Colony 6 going missing, he had insisted on sending a shuttle for both of them every day.

"Good," Ty said. "See you soon."

"Bye." Lyssa disconnected and glanced once more at the TAD's display. No result yet, but the command was working. She'd set up an alert to notify her if it was able to find anything.

She hurried down the hall to the front division doors, passing the janitor she knew only by his first name, Castiel. He was tapping gently on a Teev screen embedded into a boxy cleaning machine that was roughly sixty square centimeters wide and as tall as his waist. The cleaner moved over to nearly touch the wall with its gently-rounded edges, whirring as it sucked up dirt no one could see.

Castiel's face bobbed in her direction, his eyes unfocused, his mouth smiling. Distaste filled her. While the number of people sent to medical enhancement in Amarillo City was the lowest in the CORE Territories, the city did have its victims. Castiel had once been an enforcer here, long before her time, but still remembered by others. Now he walked with the cleaners.

Or supervised them, rather. It wasn't a necessary job, because the cleaning machines generally could work on their own, but Lyssa suspected Brogan felt a sense of obligation. Given what she knew about the rate of disappearance or banishment of those like Castiel who didn't have family, Brogan had probably saved his life.

But for what? Wouldn't his life be better sacrificed for a new child? She bet his mother wouldn't think so. Just as Gemma wouldn't wish her son dead.

"Hi, Castiel," she said.

His head bobbed and his smile widened. "Have a good day," he responded.

She hurried past him outside to the waiting shuttle.

CHAPTER 5

Before the sun rose Friday morning, Reese showered and dressed carefully, making sure her thin, protective vest and her Enforce brand nine mil weren't visible under the loose gray blouse and matching slacks that were part of her civilian disguise. Nothing remarkable or memorable.

Slipping her knife into the boot that didn't contain her back-up pistol, she returned to the room where she'd slept. Where Jaxon still slept in the second bed after having tossed the pillows to the floor. She'd worried he'd keep her awake all night with images from his dreams, but there had been nothing, and she suspected he'd been out on the couch most of the night.

She walked over to see if he was near waking, but he didn't move. The tiniest stream of light filtered through the blinds, throwing a slash across his face. He was curled in a fetal position, as he'd slept as a boy, as she'd also slept as a child. Was it an attempt to be small and unnoticed or simply a remnant of a time before birth when they hadn't known fear?

She stifled the sudden urge to touch him, to crawl in bed

with him and feel his arms around her. But if she did that, it would change everything, and she'd only just gotten him back. She couldn't risk what they had now. There was so much about him she didn't know, so much that had happened in the twenty years that separated them. Every day together seemed to erase more of those years, but there were still things they hadn't shared, things she'd probably only share with Jaxon.

Not with Alex? Not likely when she couldn't even spend the night at his place without seeing sketches from his dreams. She really needed to get a handle on her gift.

Jaxon's hand was on the mattress by his face, and before she could stop, she reached out to touch him. At the contact, she felt a slight tug in her brain and a sketch came from his mind—of an older woman with frightened eyes and a scared smile. Not his mother or anyone Reese knew, yet the woman stood on the step of a tiny colony house. Must be from the time after his mother was murdered and he'd been taken from Colony 6 and placed in a foster home.

Jaxon stirred, and she didn't want to be caught staring down at him, spying on his private thoughts, so she grabbed her gear and went to the main room. On the couch, she thumbed through the many drawings she'd finished last night until she got to a fresh page where she could draw the woman from Jaxon's dream. She must mean something to Jaxon if he'd been thinking, or dreaming, rather, about her so vividly.

The woman was too thin, as were most people in the colonies, and she had a kind face, but the eyes—the eyes told the story of a lifetime of fear. Not simply overwork, exhaustion, and discouragement, but constant mortal fear. Reese recognized the emotion. She'd experienced it while living with her drunken father, and she'd felt it every day for months before coming to Dallastar. Ever since the Kordell Corp, or the KC, had targeted her back in Estlantic. The KC was the largest business in Estlantic that wasn't owned by the CORE, and when she'd linked one of their executives with running juke and he was sent to medical enhancement, the company had nearly killed her when they caught up to her. The five months Reese had spent in a hospital because of their retaliation had been the darkest days she'd spent since Jaxon's mother had been murdered in the Coop. She still had nightmares of the attack.

Her pencil continued to glide across the page as if memories of the KC didn't matter. The house behind the woman was telling. The paint was new and the yard and flowers neatly tended. The woman loved growing things. At least she'd had that little bit.

Reese snapped the book shut as Eagle came from the second room. Even this early he wore his dark glasses, though they couldn't possibly be comfortable for sleep. She'd asked him once about the darkness indoors, and he'd explained that the glasses transmitted the world to his brain through his temples, and he was so close to blind that the lenses could have been rainbow colored for all it mattered to his natural eyes.

"Good, you're up," he said, running a hand through his hair. "I want to show you something." He shrugged off a large case slung over his shoulder with a strap.

"What is it?" she asked.

"It's a nyckelira case." He grinned and added, "With a few alterations. It's something I've been working on in the underground. I printed it on the large printer before we left."

Nyckeliras were sixteen-string, fiddle-like musical instruments with dozens of keys that intersected the strings. The instrument was held like a guitar, but the strings played with a short bow while fingers of the left hand pushed the keys. The instruments were all the rage among the youth of the CORE, bought at local furniture shops, though no one seemed to know exactly who was manufacturing them. It had become common to see people wearing the cases and gathering to play the instruments. Reese and Jaxon had recently broken up several groups at Freedom Fountain that had exceeded the twenty-citizen gathering limit.

"I chose a nyckelira because the case wasn't too wide or long to fit into my supply bag and because with some slight adjustments, it can hold an assault rifle and more." He set the case on the second couch and flipped it open. "See, it fits a rifle perfectly, even with an oversized magazine and two extra clips." He ran his fingers along the weapons. "But the real beauty is when you flip it over." He shut the case and turned it. "See this seam? Well, it looks stitched like they used to do pre-Breakdown, but it's fake. A certain series of taps in the right order will trigger a sensor I designed and . . ." He tapped quickly before pulling the case apart at the seam to reveal the temper laser he'd taken from the man at the sky train in Amarillo city and a tiny nine mil. "It's a tight squeeze, but since this temper is stronger than ours, I printed a new barrel with an alternate design to make it fit."

"Nice." Jaxon said from behind Reese, startling her a little. He was already dressed and his face was newly shaven. "I was wondering how we'd take our weapons through town without being too obvious. With Special Forces hanging around, we can't all take our bags."

Eagle shut the case and tossed it to him. "It's all yours, since you're the one who's waiting outside the doctor's building for Reese. Dani and I can stay off the main street until you give us a signal."

"Show me the code again," Jaxon said.

Reese left them with the case and went to the readymeal dispenser. She wasn't hungry, but she would eat to make sure she didn't lack energy later on.

"Where's Dani?" she asked.

"She sacked out in here last night," Eagle answered, "but you know she doesn't need more than a few hours of sleep. No idea where she is now. And before you ask, the kid's still sleeping in the room. With any luck she'll stay there."

Reese doubted it. Nova had already demonstrated that she didn't think twice about throwing herself into the path of trouble.

"That reminds me," Jaxon said. "I told Hammer about Nova, so hopefully he'll pass on the word to the captain. I haven't heard back from either of them."

"Coward," Reese shot, not hiding her grin.

Jaxon shrugged. "Guilty as charged where that kid is concerned. You know how the captain feels about her."

The men joined her in eating, finishing before she did. One last weapons check and they slipped from the room without waking Nova. Dawn was already giving way to the morning sun, and it was cool enough even this far south that Reese was glad for the long sleeves of her blouse.

"Keep your T-links open on our feed," Jaxon told them. "And let's activate the skin tags Dani gave us. Just one press, though. We don't want the cameras in the city recording our faces and connecting us to the doctor's disappearance, but we do want them to read our fake CivIDs."

Reese pressed the skin tag on her neck firmly, waiting for the minute electric tingle, and then adjusted the T-link over her eyes. The construction felt similar to her iTeev, except for the superior wireless earbud.

Without warning, Dani appeared on the sidewalk a meter away from them. Reese saw her come from the building's shadow, but the movement barely registered. It was almost as if she wasn't there one moment and magically appeared the next.

"Still nothing from our friends," she said, her gaze flicking toward the C-lodge. "They haven't left."

"Good." Jaxon smiled. "Let's do this then. The office will be opening in twenty minutes. The shuttle I ordered from the room Teev should be here already."

There it was, a small blue shuttle rolling down the street toward them. The door slid open as it approached, having scanned the fake CivID Jaxon's card projected. Reese climbed into the back with Eagle.

"Good morning," chimed the onboard Teev. "Time to destination is five minutes. Do you wish to make another stop after?"

"No," Jaxon said. "Please turn off audio."

"Turning off," came the pleasant voice.

Compared to Amarillo City, Santoni was tiny. Like all of the smaller cities, the buildings predated Breakdown, and some hadn't been properly repaired. There were no private cars in sight, only more public shuttles. At least the road seemed in good repair.

People began appearing on the sidewalks, nodding to each other with courteous smiles as they passed. Reese found herself exchanging nods right along with the strangers. *Friendly people,* she thought.

The doctor's office was at the west end of town, nestled between a shopping district and a group of apartment buildings. The shuttle stopped at a bakery some distance before the doctor's building, and Reese climbed out. Nodding farewell to the others, she sauntered down the street, pausing to look at a display in a window before moving on. She passed the doctor's office and circled around the apartments to see what was on the other side. Nothing but sparse woods, which was a rare find. Like most trees in the CORE, they were protected by law in an effort to restore the huge forests that had been destroyed during Breakdown. Only the forests near Colony 3 were used in manufacturing, carefully replanted and tended by the colonists. No, by the slaves.

From the corner of her eye, she caught a glimpse of Jaxon, who was doing his own reconnaissance, the nyckelira case over his shoulder. He'd know as well as she did that the woods might be a good place to hide in a pinch.

When she arrived once more in front of the doctor's office, she went inside, surprising a young receptionist who was removing her brown jacket. "Good morning," the woman said in sing-song, tossing the jacket over her chair. "May I help you?"

Reese pocketed her T-link and smiled at the real welcome in her voice. "Yes, I have an appointment at eight with Doctor Kentley."

"Of course." The woman picked up an iTeev, folded in a square, and held it up in her direction. "Let's check your CivID. Okay, it's Reba, isn't it?" As Reese nodded, she continued, "Your file says you're here for back pain? Sorry about that. But you're all checked in. Please have a seat." She indicated the flowery upholstered couches in the lobby. "I'll call you when the doctor is ready for you. We still have a few minutes before your appointment."

"Thank you." Reese started toward the couches, rubbing the small of her back for show.

"Oh, and just a reminder: if your CivID isn't implanted yet, you should schedule that appointment very soon. We'll be doing those at the hospital, so we have limited openings. And you don't want to miss the deadline." Her smile this time was strained. Reese wanted to ask if the receptionist's ID was already implanted and why it was necessary to do it at the hospital.

"I'm just here about the back pain," Reese said. "I'll take care of the rest with my regular doctor. Thank you."

The younger woman nodded, tucked her dark hair behind her ear, and waved her holo screen to life.

"Jaxon?" Reese whispered as she walked away. "How's it looking out there?"

"No sign of Special Forces."

Dani's voice cut in. "Actually, I just received a signal from the pressure pad. Our friends at the C-lodge are leaving. My guess is they're heading your way."

"How many left the room?" Jaxon asked.

"Hard to say, but I think at least five. Probably all six."

"Eagle," Jaxon said, "now might be a good time for your little fire. In case they are heading to pick up the good doctor. Even if they aren't planning to grab him, the distraction may lure them away from this area."

"Sending the signal now," Eagle responded. "The alarms will go off in less than sixty seconds."

Reese took a deep breath and sat on one of the flowered couches. The enforcers had come on the train, but their friends might have a black Special Forces shuttle. That meant less than five minutes away. "Be on the lookout for one of those black shuttles," she whispered.

"Nothing yet," Jaxon assured her. "But Reese, I've got eyes on two men entering the building. They . . . they're dressed like Newcali soldiers."

"What?" This from Dani, who seemed offended even by the idea.

"Same gray cement color," Jaxon said. "A little more worn maybe, but the same color."

A sliver of unease shot through Reese. Had Dani betrayed the doctor's whereabouts to her fringer friends? She'd made no secret that Newcali wanted—no, needed him.

"Cotton-headed, pus lickin' jukeheads," Dani swore. "I'm going to smash in their punk bucket faces." Which Reese could only assume meant she had told her friends, and they were taking matters into their own hands.

Reese could see the men now, hurrying to the desk where they consulted with the receptionist in low, urgent tones. Reese sprang to her feet and hurried over.

"Go on back," the woman said to the men, casting a nervous glance around them at Reese. "Be quick, though."

The shorter of the two men briefly met Reese's gaze as they hurried through the door the receptionist had indicated. Tension tightened his forehead under the shaggy hair, and his brown eyes were both hard and lost at the same time. Reese understood that he'd do anything to accomplish whatever he was here to do.

Well, so would she.

"How long before I can see the doctor?" Reese asked. "It's eight now."

The receptionist's pale face blanched further. "They'll only be a minute."

Something didn't ring true in her words, but unless Reese was willing to barge back there and shoot the fringers, she'd have to be patient. She turned away from the counter.

"Jaxon," she said softly, putting space between herself and the receptionist. "They went into a back room to see him. Someone better watch the rear in case there's another entrance."

"On it," came Dani's hard voice.

Could they trust her, or would she help the fringers escape with the doctor?

Jaxon must have had the same thought. "I'll head there too. That leaves you with the front, Eagle."

"The alarm has gone off at the train station," Eagle said. "I'm monitoring the general local enforcement feed via one of Dani's T-link back doors. Let you know in a minute if Special Forces diverts. If they don't, we won't have much time."

"They should divert," Jaxon said. "With a threat to the sky train."

Reese thought so too. Santoni wasn't a large city, and the enforcer division here was likely a subdivision, a smaller unit in place mostly to prevent possible fringer intrusion on their border.

"Uh, Reba?" The receptionist's voice penetrated Reese's thoughts.

"Yes?" Reese turned and strode over to the desk.

"Bad news, I'm afraid." The receptionist frowned, closing her desk's holo feed. "Doctor Kentley just let me know he has been called to deal with an emergency. We're going to have to reschedule."

Reese glanced toward the door where the fringers had disappeared. "I can't reschedule. I really need to see him now."

The young receptionist blinked, as if it was the first time anyone had contradicted her. "Well, I'm sorry. He has to leave. I could put you in with his nurse in an hour, if that helps." An image flashed from the receptionist's mind—of Kentley, his eyes wide and his face scared. Was that how he'd looked just now when he'd talked to the receptionist on the holo screen, or had the image come from another day? Reese had no way of knowing.

"Heads up, guys," Eagle's voice said in Reese's ear, pulling her out of the sketch. "Special Forces is apparently not responding to the fire diversion. I repeat, they are *not* responding. When local enforcement contacted them, Special Forces exact words were, 'If you let anything happen to the sky train, we'll have you shot and thrown into the South Desolation Zone.' Worse, I'm on the roof next door, and I can see a black shuttle coming down the street. We've only delayed them a little, if that. Looks like we'll—"

"Kentley's going out the back!" Jaxon interrupted.

Ignoring the receptionist, who was still trying to reschedule, Reese sprinted to the interior door and yanked it open.

"Wait! You can't go back there!" called the receptionist.

On the other side of the door was a hallway with various doors. Reese sprinted past them all, pausing when a woman in blue scrubs holding an iTeev nearly ran into her. Reese pulled her stunner and pointed it at the woman. "Where's the back door?" When the woman hesitated, Reese pushed the stunner close to her face and shouted, "Now!"

With a little gasp, the woman angled her arm and pointed down the hallway. "At the end, turn left. Please don't hurt me!"

Reese pushed past her and ran to the end of the hallway, skidding a little as she careened around the corner. She dived for the door and pushed it open, nearly falling over a pile of old furniture just outside the door.

"Hold it right there," Dani shouted. She had her gun out, pinning the doctor and the two fringers in place behind the building near the border to the woods.

Reese glimpsed Jaxon angling around to the side. Reese replaced her stunner with her Enforce nine mil and ran to help Dani.

"You aren't from Newcali," Dani said to the fringers. "Where'd you get those uniforms?"

"Whatever Newcali is," said the taller of the men with a snort. "We're fringers, though, if that's what you're asking."

"Please," the doctor said, holding up his hands. "I don't know who you are, but it's a matter of life and death that I go with these men."

"No, it's a matter of life and death that you come with us," Reese countered. "Your life and death. And theirs. We're here to help you, Dr. Kentley. El Cerebro sent us."

The shorter of the two fringers pulled his weapon, aiming it at Dr. Kentley's head. "You let us go, or I shoot him right now. He's no good to us if you take him."

Dani fired so fast the man didn't have time to react. His gun went flying. He cursed, shaking his hand. Reese reached for her temper laser. She didn't want to leave them confused for Special Forces to pick up, but she would if she had to.

"Special Forces is here," Eagle said in Reese's comlink. "Two heading inside and four around back in full gear. I think they expect him to run. Should I start firing?"

"It's your call," Jaxon said, "Dani, Reese, get Kentley into the woods."

Dani flicked a look at Reese. "I'll distract Special Forces. You take care of them." She turned, her body nearly blurring in Reese's sight as she sprinted away.

The taller man stepped behind Kentley, hunching behind him so that neither Special Forces or Reese had a clear shot. "I've got a gun at his back now," he sneered at Reese. "Let's see you try to hit that."

Anger burned in Reese's gut as the man stepped backwards into the woods, pulling Kentley with him. "Jaxon, I don't have the shot," she said.

"Neither do I," came the response. "Follow him."

A gunshot blasted through the quiet morning, whizzing past Reese. Special Forces had apparently spied Dr. Kentley. "What about Dani?" Reese asked.

"I'll stay behind with her. Go!"

Reese dived into the trees after the men, her heart thudding as a bullet ripped into the tree next to her. She glanced back to see Dani lunging at an enforcer, a patch of red blossoming on her right arm. Dani hit? The idea was inconceivable. Two enforcers were down but still moving, another was exchanging gun fire with Eagle on the top of the next building. Reese's last view was of Dani flipping an enforcer up in the air and slamming him into the side of the next building.

Reese ran. This uneven terrain wasn't familiar, but her daily enforcer workouts had prepared her for endurance, at the least, and she'd keep up. The men were just ahead, with Dr. Kentley running with them. If he'd been under pressure to go with fringers, it didn't seem like it now. Maybe he was more afraid of her than he was of the men. Branches whipped her face, growing thicker by the moment, until she couldn't see the men but only hear them ahead of her.

On any other day, she would have stopped to marvel at the beauty of the trees, the smell of the leaves, the feel of the bark. But now thoughts of her crew pushed all the wonder from her mind.

More shots rang out behind her, and Reese was tempted to turn back. Her team was under fire, and if this was the event Jaxon saw in his premonition . . . no, she couldn't think about that. Dani had said these fringers weren't from her group in Newcali, but Reese had no way of verifying that because Dani hadn't shared much intel about her group. They knew only that the Newcalians were located on the west coast. How many they numbered, their plans for the future, and most of their technology, Dani hadn't shared.

Abruptly, the forest began to change, as if taken by a sudden blight. The trees were set farther apart and their leaves were withered. Instead of earth and loam, the aroma was sulfuric and rotting. The rustling up ahead abruptly stopped. Reese pushed herself forward, her lungs burning. Dani should have been following the doctor. With her ability, she would have already caught up. Did that mean she'd meant for the fringers to get away?

Reese burst through the ravaged trees into a tiny clearing. She stared around her, seeing no signs of the men. She stilled her breath, listening. Nothing. They had disappeared.

CHAPTER 6

J axon let off a couple shots with his pistol at the Special Forces as he tried to free his rifle from the nyckelira case. Dressed in enforcer blues, helmets included, they were completely protected, but a few well-placed bullets could incapacitate them at least temporarily.

Dani had somehow lost her gun, probably when the bullet hit her arm, but she didn't need it. She moved so fast, Jaxon was afraid he'd accidentally hit her. The two Special Forces she'd already downed had learned the danger of getting hit by her fists. But the two from inside the doctor's office had joined their companions, and they spread out, using the edges of the buildings to hide behind and protect themselves. One enforcer had made it to the black shuttle and was driving it into the narrow alley between the buildings. Jaxon guessed they planned to take Dani alive, or they would have placed a bullet in her head by now.

"I can't hit any more from up here," Eagle said. "They know

where I'm at. I'll have to move. And with their armor, I need direct hits to do any good."

"Target their shuttle with everything you've got," Jaxon ordered, ducking behind a mound of dead trees near the edge of the woods. "Something big. Hurry!"

"Will do."

From Dani there was nothing over the T-link except the occasional grunt as she slammed her foot or fist into one of the Special Forces. She downed another, leaving only two standing, plus the one in the shuttle. Then a loud *crunch!* and all sounds from her stopped. Had her T-link fallen or been damaged?

Hunching over, Jaxon began working his way to the end of the pile. The next second, he stumbled, falling to the bare earth as a sudden disorientation overtook him.

Dani lies on the ground, staring into the barrel of an automatic rifle held by a man with a Special Forces patch on his enforcer uniform. A black shuttle moves up behind them, coming close to their position. A huge explosion rocks the alley. Dani and the enforcer disintegrate into pieces, taking half the doctor's building with them.

In horror, Jaxon gagged. Had it happened in real life or was this a premonition?

He strained to see, realizing his eyes were shut. He was still on his knees. *Vision, then,* he thought.

"Eagle," he grunted, "don't hit the shuttle. Whatever you do, don't hit it!"

No response. Was he too late? He couldn't tell, he was still blinded. The first vision hadn't shown any explosion, only Dani captured. Had Jaxon seen more of his earlier vision, or an alternate future? He couldn't tell.

Shouting broke through the premonition's hold. Now he could see the real Dani sprawled on the ground, a gloating enforcer laughing over her like in Jaxon's premonition. Why wasn't she moving? The assault rifle could spit out bullets fast, but the first bullet would be limited by the reaction of the enforcer holding it. Surely Dani could use her faster response time to rush him. Even if one or two bullets hit her, she was wearing protective gear under the civilian clothes and with her ability could push past the pain. Or was she hurt more than Jaxon knew?

Jaxon yanked his rifle from the nyckelira case and fired, drawing the enforcer's attention. *Run, Dani!* he thought.

Eagle appeared at ground level at the edge of the building next door. In his eagerness to free Dani, he was about to be overtaken by an enforcer coming at him from an angle. Jaxon shifted his aim and shot the enforcer in the chest, knocking him over. Eagle turned to retreat, but the man holding Dani at gunpoint shot him in the back.

Eagle crumpled. The man Jaxon had shot was back on his knees, laying down cover fire as his partner dragged Dani to her feet and shoved her into the waiting black shuttle. Jaxon half expected it to explode, but it didn't.

Which meant his vision hadn't come true. Had he changed the future or had the vision been from another time entirely?

The shuttle started moving forward, and the man laying cover fire dived inside with his two partners and Dani.

"Eagle, get out of there!" Jaxon shouted, firing at the shuttle. The bullets bounced off the armored surface. The shuttle rolled toward Eagle, turning partially sideways to protect one of their downed men as they jumped out to collect him. Eagle started crawling.

Jaxon stood, spraying the shuttle with bullets. The men leapt back inside and the vehicle moved forward. Abandoning the pile of dead trees altogether, Jaxon ran toward Eagle, the nyckelira case banging against his hip. He dragged Eagle to his feet. Shots came again from the shuttle, but in the next instant the bullets stopped as return fire came from the trees.

Reese, Jaxon thought, half carrying Eagle toward the woods. His friend groaned with each step, his face a mask of agony. The protective vests could only do so much. At least no blood showed through his green shirt, so as long as he hadn't punctured anything vital, he'd probably feel better once the shock wore off.

Reese appeared in front of them as they entered the trees. She let off another volley of bullets before looping one of Eagle's arms over her neck and urging them deeper into the woods. "They'll come after us," she said.

"Maybe not," huffed Eagle. "I'm pretty sure we killed two of them. They won't be anxious to face us alone. And they got Dani. They'll think they can make her talk."

"They'll still come," Jaxon said, pushing them forward. "They want to find the doctor. And the local enforcers won't be far behind." He glanced at Reese, who shook her head.

"The doctor and the fringers disappeared. Literally. One minute I was following them, and the next, they were gone."

"Tunnels?" Jaxon asked. He edged them around a fallen tree.

"Has to be. I didn't have much time to look around before you guys started yelling." She gave him a hard look. "I made the choice to turn back."

He wanted to protest, but she was right. "We can't go back to the C-lodge. They'll look there for strangers." Or Dani might break, but he wouldn't say that aloud.

"Nova," Reese breathed out the name, her pace faltering for a few steps. "We have to tell her."

"And we have to contact Brogan. He should know of a place we can hunker down." The Dallastar underground had connections everywhere, Brogan had reiterated so many times in briefings at the AED that Jaxon had stopped listening. That was before he'd known Brogan was El Cerebro.

Sirens filled the air, signaling that at least some of the local enforcers were abandoning the sky train fire and heading their way. "They're coming," Reese said.

Eagle moaned. "For once, I'd like Jaxon to be wrong about these things."

Reese chuckled. "Don't worry. He's wrong a lot. Just try and move a little faster, would you? We can swap Jaxon-is-wrong stories later to your heart's content."

Eagle choked out a laugh and pushed harder.

"Try not to break any branches," Jaxon said. "We'll be harder to follow." He tapped the side of his T-link, which was miraculously still over his eyes. "Call Nova," he told it. "Audio only." He paused and added, "Someone did route her into this network, didn't they?"

"Me," Eagle grunted. "Sort of. It uses a back door to link to her illegally manufactured iTeev rip-off."

Which sounded just right for an undergrounder.

After a long wait, Nova picked up, also on audio only. "What?" she barked. "I'm not doing anything I shouldn't, if that's why you're calling."

Which meant she was doing exactly what she shouldn't, Jaxon was sure. "Fringers got the doctor," he said, "and we had a run-in with Special Forces. They have Dani. You need to leave the C-lodge now. I don't know if they'll check there, or if our covers will hold up."

"What about you guys?"

"We need to find some place to hole up until we talk to El Cerebro."

"I know a place in town," she said. "When I lived here, my uncle told me I'd always be safe there. But it's been a few years."

Jaxon considered a moment. It was possible the safehouse had been moved, but his team's options were limited. Special Forces would have access to pre-Breakdown spy drones, and that made remaining in the woods dangerous. If the people currently occupying the safehouse weren't allies with the underground, they'd simply have to take over the place.

"Send us the address," he said. "And try to contact your uncle to verify the house." It'd be easier to have allies.

"Sending the location to the three of you now. You need to approach from the back to get in. But can't *you* call my uncle?" A whine had entered Nova's voice.

"No. We're a little busy at the moment trying to stay alive. You broke his rules, and you'll have to deal with him eventually, so it might as well be now. We need the help."

The words had the desired effect. "Yes, sir," she said. "I'll send you a new address, if he has one. I'll meet you there."

"Stay safe."

She was silent for an instant. "I will. You too."

Jaxon tapped the side of his T-link to end the call.

Reese met his gaze around the back of Eagle's neck. "We're going someplace Nova recommends? Really?"

"The tracking drones will be out. We won't even notice them until it's too late. Even if we turn off the T-links so they can't trace the electronic signals and mask our CivIDs, these woods aren't that big. They'll find us. We need to get inside."

"Provided we can reach the safehouse," Eagle put in. "I knew I shouldn't have left my new drone at the C-lodge. It could have at least warned us if one of their drones was close."

"Nothing we can do about it now." Jaxon's T-link was already showing him the address. They'd have to circle half the city on foot to get close, but they couldn't risk the cameras in town.

Reese shook her head, pulling them to a stop. "There's no way we'll make it." She removed Eagle's arm from her shoulder. "We need a shuttle. You keep on going south, until I let you know where to meet me. I'll run ahead and get a shuttle. One person alone will have a better chance of going unnoticed. But until we get there, we should mask our CivIDs completely with the skin tags. They'll have recorded the ones we were using at the doctor's anyway, and we'll need to switch out before we're seen in public again."

It was a good call. "Go," Jaxon agreed, reaching for his skin tag, pressing two fingers against it. The tingle under the patch was almost comforting.

Reese took off running, slipping through the trees, much as twenty years ago she'd darted through the close-set houses in Colony 6. She looked fierce and determined.

"Can't reach." Eagle was struggling to make his hand obey him.

"I'll get it." Jaxon felt Eagle's neck for his skin tag and pressed. "You feel it?"

Eagle nodded. The masking wouldn't prevent drones from detecting their heat signatures or tracking the T-link emissions, but at least their identities would remain hidden, perhaps giving them time to destroy the drones and get away.

Eagle coughed. "Feels like I fell off the roof of that building."

"You're lucky you had on a vest or we wouldn't be having this conversation."

"Believe it or not, I'm almost wishing we weren't."

Jaxon didn't answer but started forward, staggering under Eagle's weight without Reese's help.

"Sorry about Dani," Eagle panted. "I should have done something. I just didn't think she'd need help. You've seen how she is in practice. None of us can touch her."

Jaxon thought about his surprise at Dani not rushing the

enforcer and how she'd lost her gun. She'd been injured, but with her ability, she'd have to be hurt a lot more for her endurance to diminish.

He gave a bitter chuckle. "It was her plan all along."

"What?" Eagle's pained face twisted in his direction.

"To get captured. I bet she thinks they'll take her to her brother."

"No," Eagle said. But in the next breath, he added, "Yeah, that's her. And it explains why her T-link isn't working. She must have disabled it. We have to get to her before they make her talk, or Brogan and the entire underground is at risk."

Jaxon knew, but he held back a comment, pushing both himself and Eagle harder. Tree branches tugged at his clothes and smacked him in the face. The smell of earth and crushed leaves was drowned by the stench of his own sweat and fear. Every sound made him look behind them, fearing to see Special Forces or one of the tracking drones.

Eagle was stumbling more often now, and his face was closer to green than white. "Let's take a few minutes," Jaxon said, coming to a stop. He propped Eagle against a tree. "You want to sit?"

"No, I might not get back up." Eagle started coughing. He doubled over, clinging to the tree, spitting up blood. Cursing under his breath, Jaxon put his arm around Eagle's waist and was about to pull him onward when the world around him stuttered.

Jaxon sees smooth male hands touching the nyckelira case on a desk. The wood looks real, instead of the customary hard plastic molds, and is decorated with elaborate carvings.

The hands flip the case open, revealing an empty interior. Strong, rough fingers, different from the smooth ones of before, reach out and stroke the black velvet lining.

A sharp slap on the face brought Jaxon back to himself. He

opened his eyes to see that he was on the ground with Eagle on top of him. "Sorry," Eagle groaned. "I tried to pull you out of it, but I fell. Look, I think someone's coming."

"How long have I been out?"

"Five minutes maybe."

Three more minutes than he'd planned to stop, extra minutes they didn't have.

"What's going on?" Reese said in his ear.

"Nothing," Jaxon heaved himself to his feet and pulled Eagle up after him.

"Right." Reese paused disbelievingly before saying, "I have a shuttle. Sending my location to you now. Heading in your direction. When you see a tall purple building, look for me in the alley there. That's as far as I'll be able to come."

Jaxon could see the building now, though it looked more gray than purple. "Almost there," he said.

"Actually, that's a good two kilometers away," Eagle informed him. "That's ten minutes on a good day." He could mentally diagram it down to the centimeter, so Jaxon didn't protest.

"I'll leave the shuttle and meet you," Reese said.

Jaxon thought a moment. "Okay, but turn off your T-link now. Even if Dani disabled hers, Special Forces might figure out how to use it to pinpoint our location. Then they wouldn't need to wait for drones to pick up our heat signatures or T-link emissions."

Eagle, still clinging to Jaxon, said, "He's right. I'm sending a delete code to erase any information and shut down the connection to Nova. I also just sent Reese the coordinates where to meet us. Even without a link to the feed, the compass on her T-link will get her there."

"You just sent . . .?" Jaxon stopped talking, remembering that while Eagle's special glasses supported hand motion control, they didn't require them. A few flicks of his sightless eyes were every bit as effective. CORE iTeevs supported a few similar eye commands, but most people never used them.

"Reese, you hear that?" Jaxon asked.

"Yep. Doing it now."

Jaxon's lungs were burning from lack of air by the time he spied Reese ahead in the thinning trees. Without a word, she put his assault rifle back into the nyckelira case, grabbed Eagle's arm, and started pulling them both back the way she'd come.

"Hurry," she said. "They sent an alert to all public shuttles for everyone to be on the lookout for three people. We may have a problem, unless one of you knows how to prevent it reporting back."

Eagle coughed once, spitting up more blood. "Our IDs are masked, so as long as I can disable the weight sensor," Eagle said, "it won't be able to estimate how many we are."

"Actually, I'm not masked, or I couldn't use the shuttle," Reese told him. "I'm using a second CivID. But go ahead and do it anyway. Better to burn another ID than to have it realize I picked up two more people."

"They'll expect something like that," Jaxon said as they cleared the trees. "We won't have much time."

Reese smiled grimly. "We won't need it. Once we get to the shuttle it's only six minutes to the safehouse. I'll stop and let you two out there and go on a bit to throw them off. The shuttle won't be able to record any of our faces, so they'll have nothing."

They reached the shuttle, looking conspicuous in the alley near the purple building. She helped Eagle inside, who began pulling open panels. Seconds ticked into minutes. "There," he said finally. "It won't be able to report normal weight until it connects the sensor to the feed again."

"How are you preventing it from connecting?" Jaxon asked.

"I pulled out the wire."

Jaxon barked a laugh. "I guess that's as good a way as any. It'll report an error and go in for repairs. It might even make our trail harder to track."

Eagle made a face. "Well, I also pulled the speech and audio wires. I wasn't sure which was which."

"Finally some good news," Reese muttered. "I hate it talking to me."

"We don't want it recording anyway," Jaxon added.

Eagle scooted to the next seat and Jaxon climbed in the back, while Reese took Eagle's vacated seat. On the manual shuttle controls, she punched in an address near their destination, choosing the highest speed possible.

They'd been driving only two minutes on the main street when a large silver enforcer shuttle passed them at high speed. Like their own smaller shuttle, the windows were one-way glass and the inside hidden from view, but Jaxon could imagine a full squadron of enforcers with assault weapons inside. He gripped his gun long after they passed, half-expecting them to turn around and give chase.

Eagle was coughing again and spitting blood. "He might be bleeding internally," Reese said.

Jaxon nodded. "We have to hurry."

CHAPTER 7

Lyssa awoke as Ty stroke her cheek and leaned in to kiss her. She sighed with pleasure until she realized where she was. She jerked upright and scrambled for her iTeev.

"Don't worry," he said with a laugh. "It's still early. You don't have to be to work at five, remember?"

"I'm getting my niece off to school, though." Niece, not daughter. It came off her tongue easily enough, but the word tasted bitter. She breathed a sigh of relief when her folded iTeev screen showed there was still plenty of time to get home before Tamsin needed to be up for school, which started at nine. Lyssa hadn't meant to pass out here last night, but one glass of chotks had turned to another, and being with Ty was so uncomplicated compared to the rest of her life.

Except for the fact that he was going to die. There was that.

He sat next to her on the bed and nuzzled her cheek with his lips. He was fully dressed, ready to go in to division, and she had to leave soon herself, but she gave into the need to kiss him. His compact form fit hers perfectly, and she never felt afraid of him. He was warm and strong, and his freshly washed smell was tinted by some kind of cologne that reminded her of a teacher she'd had once in school. She'd had a serious crush on him too.

Grief crept up from somewhere inside her, and she clung to Ty more tightly than she should have. She stared at the wall and the beautiful painting he had of Freedom Fountain and the Plaza outside the CORE management building that housed the city manager and other government workers.

He pulled away slightly to look at her face. "What is it?"

Her eyes caressed each curve. His face was kind, and there was an underlying strength that made her wish she could confide in him. "Nothing," she said.

His mouth turned slightly downward. Not what he wanted to hear, apparently. "Look," he said. "I know you want to take this slowly, but I've been thinking that maybe in a month or so, you'd like to move in. If things are still going well, of course, as I hope they will be. You probably don't have a lot of space there with your sister and her family."

His words pierced her heart like radiation from a desolation zone. She could never leave Tamsin, and she could never explain why. Because doing so would risk Tamsin, and she couldn't trust her daughter's life to him. He had no relationship with her and would have no reason to develop a deep enough one to permit disclosure.

What was she thinking, getting involved with him? Or with anyone? There would be too many questions. Since the moment she'd decided to go against the laws of the CORE and keep Tamsin, she'd given up so many other choices.

And she'd do it again.

She pushed away from Ty, faking nonchalance, though he'd likely glimpsed her terror. "Maybe. Let's wait for a few more months and see." He'd probably be dead by then.

Lyssa had questioned Jaxon regarding the timeline of his visions, and while most of them came true within a few weeks, others hadn't happened for months. One vision of Reese coming to Amarillo City he'd had a year in advance. But whatever the length, time wouldn't stop. They were already nearing the two-month mark for the vision of Ty.

"Lyssa." Disappointment spilled from the single word, but she pretended not to notice, knowing he wouldn't push her.

She hopped out of his bed. "I'd better get going or Lyra will be late. If you wait a few minutes, I'll drop you at the station."

"It's okay," he said stepping toward the door. "I have a few errands to do on the way."

She blew him a kiss and hurried into his bathroom for a quick sonic cleansing that would make her presentable for Tamsin, even in her dirty clothes from yesterday.

The worry set in almost immediately. What sort of errands did Ty have? Would one of them be the reason someone would break his neck?

Cutting her cleansing by less than half, she ran from the room and gathered her clothes, pulling them on as she hopped to the door. This was the other part of seeing Ty. Worry that never ended. Worry that something she did or didn't do would cause Jaxon's vision to come true.

The blue shuttle was waiting for her, either having sat outside all night or returning this morning at the time she'd requested yesterday. She didn't know or care which. She could see Ty striding down the street. She wished the public shuttles allowed manual control like the police ones, but she was stuck having to tell the shuttle to move down the road slowly.

She expected Ty to head from his apartment to the sky train, which was only a ten-minute ride to the main station near their division. Instead, he crossed the street and headed the other way, hurrying slightly now. She told the car to follow as she had on numerous occasions when they met at the bar. More than once, she'd seen him give credits to a few street punks that somehow managed to continue avoiding enforcer sweeps. She'd begun to wonder if that was wise. Conceivably, they could be the reason for his impending demise, though Ty's connection with her was far more likely as a cause, at least while she remained a target for those who suspected her Colony 6 origins.

More shuttles were filling the streets now, as people began their day. While most used the sky train, some spent their shuttle allotment on errands or to reach destinations not along the sky train routes. Some worked for members of the CORE Elite or their relatives.

Lyssa checked the time and continued her surveillance. Though she carried a gun, she didn't have a lot of confidence that she'd be any help to Ty should someone dangerous come looking for him.

On he walked, turning down random roads until finally he stopped and swiveled around, folding his arms over his chest, and staring at her shuttle as it approached. He wouldn't be able to see inside it, or know it was her, but he might suspect. Especially if he'd noticed the shuttle awaiting her outside. Whatever he'd been planning, it looked like he wasn't going anywhere until the shuttle was gone.

"Go home," she told the shuttle wearily, not wanting to face him now. She wanted—no, needed—to see her daughter. Ty could get himself killed for all she cared.

The ache in her chest renewed, but she inclined the seat and ignored it.

"Destination home," the shuttle said cheerfully, as if happy to be fulfilling its purpose. "Time to destination is fifteen minutes."

When she arrived at the ninth-floor apartment she shared

with Lyra and Kansas, Lyra was alone in the kitchen. Her delicate face was almost lost in the mass of long black hair, the hair she could never cut unless Lyssa did too.

"Good, you're here," Lyra said. "I was about to get her up, but if I don't have to take her, we can let her sleep a few more minutes."

Lyssa heard the accusation in her twin's voice, even if it didn't exist. "Of course I'm here." *Like I am every day that I'm off work.*

Lyra nodded. "It'll be nice for you to have this extra time together. She missed you last night."

"I missed her too." It was like an ache similar to the grief she felt for Ty, only more intensified.

Lyra stepped toward her. "You really shouldn't see him," she whispered. "It'll be that much harder when it happens."

"I tried to stay away." What she wouldn't add was that at least she could have a part of Ty and that was more than she'd ever have with Kansas.

Lyra nodded. "I'm sorry." She hugged Lyssa, and for a moment they clung together as they had in the Coop when their father had died at the factory, and when they'd awoken in the night listening to their mother's hacking coughs. She'd lasted only until they'd leveled out of school and left the Coop, and only since Tamsin's birth did Lyssa understand how she'd held on even that long.

"Thank you for being here." Lyssa knew she said it too often, and it normally irritated Lyra, but today she only smiled.

"I told Kansas about Dani," she said. "Well, not her name or that she's working at division, but just that she was one of those we grew up with. I told him she normally lives in Newcali."

"And?" Lyssa's swallow sounded too loud in the room.

Lyra sighed and released Lyssa. "He reminded me that even

visiting the fringers would put us all at risk. Or further risk, rather." Because Kansas also understood that their Colony 6 connection somehow put them at risk, thus the extra shuttle service, but he didn't know how they'd almost been killed six weeks ago.

Lyra frowned and continued. "Still, I think I'll ask Dani to take me there, to see what it's like. To make sure it's not worse . . ."

Worse than here, she meant. Because there were no birth orders in Newcali, and if Lyra and Kansas moved there, Lyra could have her dream.

"We'll figure this out," Lyssa said.

"What if we can't?" Lyra stared at her, anxiety furrowing her brow. "What if this is just the way the world is always going to be? What if they're right that there isn't enough land to sustain more people? What if they're telling the truth?"

Anger grew inside Lyssa. "They lied about killing our friends. The colonies are also a lie. You heard what Reese told us about her visit to Colony 6. They're paying bonuses so women there will have more children. Instead of giving women like you babies, they're creating more workers to take the place of those they killed after they went crazy from the experiments. You know there's room for more settlements in the empty zones. And maybe we'll end up having to leave the CORE, but we need to see if we can fix it first. For Tamsin. For all the other kids. For your child when you have him."

Lyra's face hardened, as if the thought was too much. She swept her bag from the kitchen table. "I'm heading to work a little early so I can stop at that bakery Kansas likes."

"Good idea. I'll be there soon."

Lyssa watched her sister leave before checking on Tamsin. The child was fast asleep, lying on her side with her blanket off, her knees tucked and her arms spread out as if she were reaching for something. "I love you, baby," Lyssa whispered, stifling an urge to wake her with kisses.

Lyssa went to her own room next door for some clothes and then to the bathroom for a proper cleansing. By the time she returned to wake Tamsin, the girl was already stretching, her mouth open in a huge yawn.

"Mommy!" Tamsin said, reaching for her.

Lyssa went to the bed and sat, scooping her baby into her arms. She smelled of soap and a hint of peppermint. Her body felt warm and slightly humid. "Hi, sweetie."

"I missed you last night."

"I missed you more." Lyssa kissed her nose.

Tamsin giggled. "If I hurry to get ready, can we go to the river and see the ducks first?"

"Sure, we have time."

"Good."

Tamsin buried her face in Lyssa's chest and for that moment there were no aches. But later as she put in two readymeals for their breakfasts, Tamsin said, "I had a weird dream last night. You were sleeping in a bed, and there was a man with you." Her face crunched as she stared at Lyssa. "It wasn't Daddy."

"That is a weird dream." Lyssa opened the readymeal and placed it in front of her daughter. Steam wafted out, and an aroma that might resemble cooked eggs. The box said some kind of egg casserole, but it was debatable how much egg it actually contained. Readymeals were mostly synthesized food substitutes. "Did he look like someone you know? Maybe a teacher? Dreams do that sometimes. Mix up things in your real life."

"I never saw him before. He had short hair. It was black, and he wasn't wearing a shirt." She giggled. "He was smaller than Daddy, and his skin was lighter." She frowned as she took a bite of eggs. "At least I think so. The light was just coming through the curtains. It seemed so real, like I could reach out and touch you."

"Don't talk with your mouth full," Lyssa said automatically.

Tamsin swallowed. "I liked the painting, though."

"What painting?"

"On the wall where you were sleeping in my dream."

Lyssa's heartbeat went from normal to high speed in the space of two seconds. "What painting?"

"Freedom Fountain and the plaza. It looked just like it did when my class went to see it."

Lyssa sat down abruptly, her own readymeal left unopened. Tamsin had seen Ty's apartment, and what that meant for her, Lyssa couldn't begin to understand. That was how it had started for her and Lyra. First realistic dreams, and then it began happening while they were awake. The first time they'd understood it wasn't in their imaginations had been on the day Tamsin was born.

"Mom, what's wrong?" Tamsin was staring at her.

"I have weird dreams sometimes too," Lyssa said. She still traveled without meaning to when she was asleep, and so did Lyra, though they could control it in their waking hours. "Want to know what I do?" When Tamsin nodded, Lyssa continued. "I just think about my bed, tell myself to get back there, and then it goes away. Can you try that next time?"

Tamsin laughed. "That's silly. It's just a dream. It can't hurt me, and it was kind of fun."

Be calm, Lyssa told herself. If Tamsin had traveled, it had only been to find her. She shouldn't be able to visit anyone else except Lyra.

She sighed. As if she needed one more thing to worry about. Regardless, no one must know about Tamsin, except maybe

Lyra. Not even the rest of the crew. Not yet. Certainly she couldn't report this to Tamsin's doctor. She'd be in danger of being taken by Special Forces—or worse.

"Hurry and finish," she said. "We need to leave soon if you want to walk by the river."

Minutes later, they left the shuttle near the river, where Tamsin found little sticks to throw into the water. Lyssa kept her eyes rolling over the area, glad for the small bulge of her pistol. There was no telling how safe they really were, even with Brogan's tinkering of their personnel files.

As they approached the school, where the shuttle now waited for them, Lyssa's iTeev vibrated gently, flashing a message onto the screen from the TAD-Alert.

Non-compliance negative at HED, it read. *Two locations not scanned.*

Not scanned? Lyssa hoped this was the break they needed.

CHAPTER 8

After Jaxon's call, Nova retreated from the novelty store where she'd picked up a few knickknacks for the kids back in the underground. Some of the items she'd even bought with a cash card she had for emergencies. Most of them, however, she'd simply taken. The shop owner was stupid and inattentive, like so many CORE residents, and it was almost a sin not to take advantage of it. Nova figured the residents had to be that way or they wouldn't allow the CORE Elite to tell them what to eat, where to work, and how many children to have like obedient little drones.

Not me, Nova thought. She thrived in the underground, taking what they needed and fighting the CORE from within.

She was curious about Newcali, though. From what little she'd gotten from the fringer Dani Balak, it was a beautiful place. Dani didn't seem as if she'd ever let anyone push her around, so maybe it really was nice. Maybe people there didn't whisper in the dark and tense up whenever an enforcer walked by, or clippers as she called them. She'd felt that way too. Before knowing Jaxon and Reese.

Now Dani had been captured. Nova had seen her friends die, but this was different. Dani was one of the strange ones with abilities from Colony 6. She was both frightening and special.

Nova scanned the area carefully as she walked down the bright street. No one had asked her why she wasn't in school, which surprised her. Because even at the eighteen her current CivID broadcasted, she didn't look that old, and eighteen-year-olds outside the colonies were required to be working on a certificate of education, usually in an area of their choice, unless they hadn't passed the aptitude tests. Failing meant being sent instead to job training in another area of work that required less skill.

At first, she'd worried about the lack of interest in her seeming disobedience, but maybe Santoni wasn't as blinded by the CORE as she assumed. In Armarillo City, she had to keep to the shadows and make sure she was masking her CivID always, or people threatened to turn her in.

The sudden wail of a siren compelled her into a nearby building. Some kind of business where people dressed up in suits. The air inside was cool and fresh, contrasting with the heat descending on the city as the sun gained altitude in the sky. It was warmer here than in Armarillo City. She remembered that now, and she was pretty sure she could smell the ocean, even if she couldn't see it.

On the phone, Jaxon had told her to stay safe, which he probably said to everyone he worked with, but had she imagined the softness in his voice? Not that she was crushing on him anymore, of course. He was old, old, old. Thirty, at least.

She'd need to hire a shuttle to get close to the safehouse, but what if the others were caught? They'd probably be tracked to the C-lodge, so it was good she was accustomed to bringing all her belongings with her and didn't have to go back there. She frowned at the thought. The others had left bags of equipment at the C-lodge, though. Would they need them? Nova stopped, kicking the cement sidewalk with the front of her shoe. One thing for sure, if Special Forces saw the enforcer blues there, they'd realize the group wasn't what they seemed.

Saca, I'll have to go back, she thought.

Better now than later. She started walking as fast as she could, using her iTeev to call a shuttle to meet her. The closer she came to the C-lodge, the harder her heart pounded. She'd have to switch her CivID to the one she'd used earlier to enter the room, and then switch back. With whatever Dani had done to the cameras, that should be enough to get her away without being traced. But she might change to another ID after leaving just to make sure. Good thing her uncle made her carry at least three at all times.

She could see the C-lodge now, and nothing unusual appeared to be happening there. She went inside, activating a new CivID as she rounded the corner leading to the elevator. She bypassed that and used the stairs. One of the first rules of the underground was to never get caught in a small space.

Nova held her breath as the door opened for her on the second floor. This was the most dangerous part. If Special Forces had already traced the others' fake identities here, there might be a trap waiting to be sprung.

The suite was empty. She grabbed everything, checking all the rooms, and shoved the items into two bags. Heavy, but mostly because of Eagle's junk and Reese's assault rifle. They were both going to owe her big time. In the hallway, no one yelled at her to stop, and she switched IDs again as she entered the stairwell. So far so good.

She was drenched in sweat with effort as she finally exited the C-lodge. The shuttle was waiting outside, a shiny blue tetrahedron under the morning sun. With relief, she heaved the bags inside and threw herself in after.

"Please state your destination," said the onboard Teev.

"Just drive. I'll tell you in a minute." At least it didn't somehow detect that she had weapons like the sky train did. Or had it already sent an alarm to the local enforcers. *No,* she couldn't think that way.

"Driving." The shuttle started into motion.

It had gone only a half block when three enforcer shuttles pulled up at the C-lodge behind them, the black and red stripes prominent along the silver sides. Nova stared out the window of her shuttle, glad for the one-way glass.

You shouldn't have gone back. The voice in her head was her uncle's. Imaginary, but it shamed her none-the-less. This was one of those impulsive decisions she shouldn't have made, another example of why he didn't allow her to participate in any but the most basic operations. Her life wasn't worth the risk, her uncle would say. Instead of being smart, she'd put herself in danger once again. It wasn't only her uncle she continued to disappoint but also herself. Would she ever be able to tell the difference between a calculated gamble and an unacceptable risk?

She'd be lying if she didn't confess, at least to herself, that part of her actions had come from a desire to put off the necessary call to her uncle to check on the status of the safehouse.

"Enable privacy mode," she told the shuttle.

"Privacy mode enabled," it answered. "Audio recording is off."

Nova scavenged through the duffels until she came up with one of Eagle's detection devices. When she turned it on, it glowed red, which meant the shuttle was lying. Possibly it was a city-wide override because of what had happened. She'd have to text her uncle instead.

She pulled her iTeev from her eyes, folding it into a square that now showed the map of the city. "Take the next right turn and then a left," she said. "Then keep going until I say."

She cleared the map and began texting. *Dani's been captured. The crew needs a safehouse. Is it the same? Please don't yell at me.*

The message had to route through the layers of protection Brogan had enabled, but the return message came back more quickly than she'd dared hope. *Yes. But proceed with extreme caution.*

Well, that didn't go too badly, she thought. There would be consequences, though. When she got back. If she got back.

She was about to fold the iTeev when another message appeared on the screen: *Are you okay?*

Nova bit her lip as tears came to her eyes, tears she was glad no one was around to see. Her uncle was the meanest, strongest, most awful person she'd ever known, but he was also the smartest and the most caring, and she loved him more than she'd even loved her father, the father she still mourned. While her father had sacrificed his life to get her out of Colony 4, doing so meant he'd left her alone in the world. Brogan hadn't. His sentencing might be harsh and swift, but at the bottom of it all, he lived. For her. To keep her safe. Above or below in the underground.

I'm okay, she wrote. *And I'm sorry.*

Keep your knife ready.

There was nothing more, which was somehow worse than if he'd threatened her with some sort of discipline, but the warmth in her chest was still there.

I gotta be stronger, she thought. *I'll make him proud—and make them pay for my father's death.*

Her uncle had warned her about focusing on revenge, but

sometimes it was all that kept her down in the underground. Otherwise, she might be tempted to accept his invitation to live in the world above, to go to a CORE school and be a drone. His position would allow it, and she'd no longer have to fear being picked up and sent back to a colony.

But then she'd betray her father. She'd betray herself.

The apartment buildings around her turned into houses. Single-family dwellings weren't permitted in new construction these days, which made sense with so few birth orders being handed out, so these had to be pre-Breakdown. It meant she was closer to her destination.

She gave more directions to the shuttle, waiting with impatience until she'd passed the safehouse. "Stop at the next corner," she said. "I'm pretty sure my tutor lives there." *Not that you're recording,* she added silently.

The shuttle glided to a stop. Nova hauled the bags out, staggering under their weight. What was she going to do with this stuff? If she let on that she'd gone back for the equipment, she'd never be let out of the underground again, especially after her narrow escape. She'd have to figure out what to tell them later. Right now she had to make sure the safehouse was just that—safe.

She headed around the back of the house on the corner, moving slowly until the shuttle was out of sight. Then she cut across the yard, hoping no one was home and that they hadn't joined the surveillance craze and put up their own cameras that hooked into the Teev feed. Unlike the enforcers, she didn't have one of Dani's skin tags to mask her face in the recordings.

Once in the back yard of the safehouse, she eyed the rear entrance with interest. The door appeared boarded up and the porch sagged as if it were seconds from falling into pieces. Looked like the right place.

Keeping only her own pack, she stashed the bags behind a

shed, cutting a few branches from an overgrown bush to cover them. Then she slipped her knife up her sleeve, wishing she was wearing her ratty old sweater, which was much better for concealment than this stupid yellow blouse she was wearing as part of her "good-little-citizen" disguise. Pulling out her iTeev, she tapped in a code and pulled it over her eyes. At once, the back of the house shimmered and the dilapidated porch disappeared, replaced by a sturdy one. There were no boards on the door now.

Definitely the right place.

She headed up the stairs. Dropping her pack, she'd lifted a hand to knock when a pistol shoved into her ribs. "Who are you?" growled a masculine voice.

"I'm Nova." She raised her hands carefully so the knife wouldn't be obvious. What had her uncle said? *Proceed with extreme caution.* She should have remembered that part. "El Cerebro sent me."

The man behind her snorted. "Prove it. Anyone could say that."

She dared turn her head slightly, catching sight of dark hair and eyes. He was more boy than man, maybe only a few years older than herself. He held the gun in his right hand. Did he even have real bullets? Unless you were an enforcer, owning a gun in the CORE meant immediate medical enhancement, so he was either willing to risk becoming a vegetable or he was connected with the local fringers. Or both.

"Not someone who can do this." She stepped backward into him, spinning to her left and capturing his gun hand with her arm. Her knife slipped into her hand, and she held it against his throat. She hadn't knocked the gun from his hand, but if he tried to yank it from her arm, she could slice his esophagus without too much effort. Tiny drops of blood were already appearing under her blade.

"Come now, is that any way to treat our guest, Thaniel?" A thin, bearded man stepped into her view. He relieved the younger man from his gun, casually training it on Nova. "I believe that El Cerebro sent you, child. Please, be at ease. We won't hurt you."

Nova really didn't have a choice with that gun now pointing at her. She stepped back quickly, lowering the knife. Her knees were shaking, so she thought it best to sit on one of the chairs that happened to be on the back porch.

To her surprise, Thaniel was grinning. "That was cool. Where'd you learn to do that?" He came to sit beside her, swiping a hand across his forehead to push his black hair from his eyes.

She shrugged. Was he for real? "From my . . ." She'd been going to say, "my uncle's second in command," but it was probably best to keep her relationship with El Cerebro quiet. "Just from some friends," she said. "They'll be here shortly."

The bearded man regarded her with bottomless dark eyes. "We heard the sirens. What happened?"

"I'll let them tell you. I don't know the details." Nova felt suddenly weary. She wasn't too sure these people could be trusted—especially given her uncle's warning—but she'd let Jaxon and Reese deal with it.

The young man was staring at her. "I'm Thane," he said, offering his hand.

"Nova." Not really her name, but the only one she answered to. It had been her father's nickname for her. Thane's hand felt warm on hers. Nice. She pulled away.

"You look familiar," he said. "Are you from around here?"

"I used to live nearby." She hadn't remembered the city at all as she'd expected. Maybe because most of her memories were a nightmarish blur, like the years she'd spent in Colony 4. But now that Thane wasn't holding a gun to her back, he did look like someone she might have known—if she could only remember past the haze. "It was a long time ago. I didn't go to school."

He was still grinning. He had a pleasant face, one that made her want to keep looking. "Neither did I." He leaned over to whisper, pointing at his chest, "Illegal child."

That made him even more interesting. He was close now, and she could smell him. A bit of sweat mixed with something nutty. It wasn't unpleasant. Her heart beat a bit faster.

"Get brew for our guest, Thaniel. She looks tired."

Thane pulled away. "Yes, Father."

Father and son. Envy slid over Nova's heart. Did he have a mother too?

The bearded man took his son's place on the chair next to hers. "Maybe you should call your friends," he said.

Nova noticed the gun still in his hand. "Extreme caution," her uncle had told her. She hoped she wasn't bringing Jaxon and Reese into a trap.

"I don't have to," she said. "They'll be here as soon as they can."

Or at least she hoped.

CHAPTER 9

Reese hurried back to where she had left Jaxon and Eagle after asking the shuttle to pause momentarily. They were no longer there, which was a good sign. Cameras were likely picking her up now, but that couldn't be helped. She was still masking her face with the skin tag and now tapped it to also hide the CivID.

The safehouse was in a residential area that was different from the apartment housing they'd seen in Santoni thus far. These were single family dwellings, set close and small, but still something of a luxury for someone who'd spent her first ten years in a welfare colony.

She found the men resting against the side of the safehouse, out of sight of any visible camera. Seeing them was a bit of a shock, and she couldn't say which of them looked worse. Jaxon was almost as pale as Eagle, and his bright eyes were feverish.

"Should we activate new CivIDs?" Eagle asked.

"No. If these people are who we hope they are, they won't

care," Jaxon said. "If they aren't, the less they know about us the better."

"There is another option," Reese said, still not comfortable trusting Nova. "We could turn on our real CivIDs and go to the local division. We might be able to track Dani that way."

Jaxon shook his head. "We can't risk it. Even if we convinced them we just happened to be in the neighborhood, those enforcers saw our faces, and they may not be able to trace us electronically because of the skin tags, but they'll recognize us this soon after our confrontation. And Eagle's been hit. We can't exactly walk him in there and say we were attacked."

"You could leave me here." Eagle wiped blood from his mouth onto his shoulder.

"No," Reese and Jaxon said together.

"Dani made her choice," Jaxon added. "We stay with you."

"You really think she wanted to get caught?" Reese found it hard to believe Dani would decide that was the best way to free her brother.

"I know she did it on purpose," Jaxon insisted, "And we're not risking the rest of the crew until we find out more about where they're holding her."

No one had a response.

Reese peeked around the house. "Uh, we might have a problem," she said. "There doesn't seem to be a way in. Just a boarded door. Porch doesn't even look safe."

Jaxon started to speak but doubled over instead, grabbing at his head and then curling down and clawing at the ground as his knees buckled.

In a brilliant flash, Reese saw again the children she had drawn the night before. She sucked in a breath that seared her throat and made her want to vomit. The images from Jaxon's mind brought to life all the nightmares she'd ever experienced about radiation and the desolation zones. Colony 6 was near enough that everyone living there had worried about getting sick, about becoming one of the crazed.

By the CORE, Reese thought. *Those poor children.*

Reese tightened her fists to stop her shaking. Who were the children? And how were they connected with their future? Hopelessness spread through her. Jaxon's visions always came true. There was never a change, except when he saw two separate visions of the same event, and that had happened only once, one premonition right after the other. She wanted to blame him for showing her the horror—to blame anyone— but it wasn't his fault. He twisted his neck to look up at her sorrowfully, his face as haunted as she felt.

She extended a hand, but he shook his head and lifted himself up. She knew he was trying to spare her, but it was too late. She'd seen the sketch and would have to draw it. Again.

She looked away. "You good to move, Eagle?" she forced out.

"Sure. This is nothing that rest and heavy painkillers can't cure." He sounded breathless. "I wish I'd thought to take some from my blues."

She thumbed in her pocket for a tiny tube. "Took this from the emergency kit in the shuttle. It's not much, but maybe it'll help."

"Thanks. Can you open it? I don't think I . . ."

She broke off the lid and held the tube to his lips. By the time they finished, Jaxon's eyes had lost their intensity. He held a pistol in one hand and pulled the nyckelira case onto his shoulder with the other.

"Let's go then." She grabbed one of Eagle's arms and put it around her neck. On the other side, Jaxon did the same.

"Who's holding who up," Eagle rasped, but he fell silent at Jaxon's glare.

Reese wasn't exactly sure where they were going, until she detected the slightest shimmer over the back of the house. *Ah, a holo* she thought. "They could be watching us already," she whispered to Jaxon. "Better put away the gun."

His jaw clenched, but he nodded and slid the Enforce nine mil inside a hidden holster. But his hand hovered nearby. Reese shook out her own hand that was itching to draw the children—no, that demanded to draw them. The image still seemed to dance in front of her eyes.

Don't lose it now, she told herself.

They walked forward slowly, expecting . . . what, Reese didn't know. She put a foot onto the step and then the next, and suddenly the world around her changed. The boarded door vanished, and the porch was strong and solid under her feet. Two people sat on the porch. One was Nova, her eyes looking wide in her narrow face but otherwise undamaged. The other was a gaunt man with a black beard and dark eyes that held an unmistakable suspicion. In his hands he held a gun. which he didn't raise but angled so that it was almost on Nova.

"So, these are your friends," he said.

Nova bit her bottom lip, probably to stifle a crude retort. "I just told you they were as they walked up here. El Cerebro sent all of us."

The stranger inclined his head. "Then welcome. I won't ask names, but you can call me Silas."

"Thank you, Silas," Jaxon said. To Nova, he added with a touch of concern. "You okay?"

"I'm fine," the child insisted.

Reese tried to look at her more closely without taking her eyes completely from the man. In fact, Nova seemed completely changed from the undisciplined undergrounder Reese normally saw. Her hair was carefully combed and held back in a clip, her face clean, and she was wearing a tailored yellow blouse and gray pants. Reese had seen Nova looking "normal" once or twice before but only briefly. She hadn't expected it today.

"I'm fine." Nova glanced at a boy who came out the back door, a mug in hand.

Reese could smell some kind of brew. Not the expensive kind from the guardana leaves grown in Colony 2 that made her mouth water, but the bitter stuff from the stems that still had the same kick. He handed the mug to Nova, who nodded at him graciously instead of rolling her eyes.

"Look, our friend's hurt," Reese said. "Do you have a med kit?"

"No," Silas said. "Or not one with anything in it to help him. We've been stretched thin, and medical supplies are difficult to purchase. Go on inside," he told Reese and Jaxon, obviously wanting to keep them in his sights. To the boy, he added, "Hold the door, Thaniel."

Reese tugged at Eagle and got him moving again. The door led directly into a kitchen, which was larger than the nice one in Reese's apartment, but barren except for a large table, a sink, an ancient refrigerator, and a stack of unopened readymeals on a narrow counter next to the sink. The single cupboard held only a few dishes. The aroma of brew was stronger here.

"Let's get him on the table," she told Jaxon. "We need to see the damage."

Eagle groaned as they hefted him on the table, his leg dangling over the edge, where Reese unfastened the hooks in his shirt, removing it.

"Hey, that's a clipper vest!" the boy exclaimed. "Are you enforcers?"

Jaxon appeared ready to pull his gun, but Silas didn't seem concerned. "If he's hurt wearing that, I hate to see what hit him."

Reese released the magnetic seals on the vest's sides and eased it off, wincing at the damage. Eagle's back had become a mass of red and mottled skin that was rapidly turning green and black. Beads of blood had come to the surface and now smeared over his skin. Whatever he'd been shot with, it hadn't been only one bullet, but a spray, at the least. It was a wonder his vest had stood up to such force. He began coughing again, and blood stained his lips.

"We need to lay him down." Reese asked Silas. "Do you have anything to put under him?"

Silas motioned to Thaniel, who disappeared from the room and returned shortly with a blanket and two tattered rags. "The rags are for the blood he's coughing up," explained Silas.

Eagle appeared better lying down, even with his feet still poking over the edge, but Reese's eyes met Jaxon's. "We need a med kit."

Nova started for the door, and Silas stepped in front of her. "Where are you going?" he asked, his voice harsh and suspicious.

"I have their med kit," she said. "I left it outside."

"And why did you do that?"

Nova gave an exasperated sigh, sounding more like her old self. "Because I had no idea what I was walking into. El Cerebro wasn't quite sure about you."

Silas didn't react. "Go with her, Thaniel," he ordered.

The boy looked only too eager to go with Nova.

Silas retreated from the table, gun still in hand, though pointing toward the ground. "Why are you here?" he demanded. "What do you expect from us? What does El Cerebro expect?"

Reese tore her eyes away from Eagle, wishing Alex were with them. She might feel ambivalent about their relationship, but he'd know how to fix Eagle. "Just a place to hide until this passes over. And information."

"Hide from who?" If anything, Silas grew more wary.

Reese and Jaxon exchanged another glance before Jaxon said, "Special Forces."

"And what do they want?"

"A doctor," Jaxon said readily, "and we interfered, so now they're after us."

Not exactly all of the truth but close enough. Reese was content to let Jaxon's words stand. "One of our friends was taken," she added. "I know the whole city is on alert, but we'd like to find out where Special Forces is keeping her." They wouldn't relinquish Dani to Brogan's custody, but he might be able to stall their taking her to HED in New York. Maybe they'd come up with something.

"I can ask around," Silas said, "but she's probably in the division prison. You won't be able to break her out. Not without inside help." He let that hang, but neither Reese nor Jaxon took the bait. "About the doctor," Silas continued. "Was it Doctor Kentley?"

Reese arched a brow as a sketch of Kentley came to her from Silas's mind. "You know him?"

"Of him. Everyone does. He's revered in these parts. He's not above helping people who can't legally get medical care."

"I see." Jaxon studied the man, as if considering his words. "El Cerebro sent us to talk to him, but he left with two men in gray uniforms shortly before Special Forces came to detain him."

Silas's gaze became hooded. "How bad do these Special Forces want him?"

Reese considered his expression. There was something Silas wasn't telling them, but she didn't know the right questions to ask. "They won't stop unless he's dead. Or captured."

Long moments of silence passed before Silas spoke again. "Then you can't stay here. They'll search door-to-door. You have to leave as soon as possible."

"Where do you suggest we go?" Jaxon's words were tight and hurried, as if he expected Silas to call Special Forces and turn them in himself.

"There is a place in an empty zone west of here. They'll be watching everywhere else." Silas's voice held a challenge.

"Fine," Reese said after meeting Jaxon's eyes and seeing agreement there.

Silas jerked his head at Eagle. "Then get him ready to leave. I'll need to contact some people. I'll also ask about the Special Forces to see if anyone has heard of a prisoner, but I think your friend is long out of reach." Silas finally tucked his gun into the belt holding up his brown pants, and took out an iTeev, unfolding it to a larger screen. His thumb swiped over the surface.

"What about Dr. Kentley?" Jaxon asked. "Can your connections trace him?"

Silas shook his head. "If he knows Special Forces is after him, he'd be a fool to return. You won't find him in Santoni. Or anywhere nearby."

Reese stifled her frustration. He was right. The doctor, wherever he was, would stay hidden. "The men he left with, you think you might know them?"

Silas shrugged. "It's possible. Most of us do favors for each other, like I'm doing for you, but fringers are not all the same."

"So I'm learning. What about the gray uniforms?"

He shrugged. "Could be scavenged. Like your friend's protective vest." His tone invited confidence, which Reese ignored.

Nova had returned with two of the weapons bags they had left at the C-lodge. Admiration swept through Reese. "You thought to bring them?" she asked.

Nova hesitated. "Oh, right. I was at the C-lodge when Jaxon called. It made sense for me to grab them as I ran out the door." Her smile widened, and her eyes were perfectly innocent, which was exactly how Reese knew she was lying. But she'd deal with that later.

Every enforcer carried nominal medical supplies on their blues, three of which were in Reese's bag, but she'd also stashed a larger med kit inside, which meant she didn't have to bring out the uniforms and endure more scrutiny. Silas was already eyeing the bags hungrily. Reese looked at Jaxon and flicked her gaze at Silas, warning him to be on the lookout. He immediately stepped back from the table to keep a closer eye on the older man.

"I'm really fine now," Eagle protested. "Must have broken a rib or two. That's all."

Reese put her hand on him to keep him down. "Lie still. I'll give you a stronger painkiller." She held a blue pain hypo against his arm and pressed the button on the end. It wouldn't be too much, even with the medicine from the shuttle.

Seconds later, he breathed a sigh of relief. "Ah, much better."

She dabbed the blood from his skin, gently rubbed ointment over his back for the bruising, and sealed it all with a large patch of RealSkin, which was normally used for deeper wounds that had been repaired but would stop the blood from beading again. Lastly, she gave him an injection with standard issue, emergency-use only nanoparticles. They weren't the more effective pre-breakdown nanobots that Alex had access to, but they should help Eagle heal faster, as long as he wasn't too bad to begin with. There was a laser, too, in the bag, but that was for surface wounds that needed sealing and wouldn't be any better than the RealSkin here.

"Thanks," Eagle said, relaxing now that she wasn't hurting him. He closed his eyes.

Reese returned the med kit to her bag and set it on the floor near Jaxon, who was keeping an eye on everyone in the room. Nova and Thaniel had pulled two chairs to a corner of the barren kitchen and were chatting like old friends. Silas was tapping again on his iTeev.

"My son will take you to the empty zone," Silas said, looking up from his screen. "There you will all be able to rest in safety. However, you will need to agree to be blindfolded part of the way. You understand, I'm sure. Your young friend has the code, which tells me El Cerebro sent you, and he himself knows of the place we are sending you, but he may not know everything about you, and we are not under his command. We have our own to protect."

"I understand," Reese said.

"And our supplies?" Jaxon added. Reese knew he really meant their guns.

He shrugged. "You may take them with you, but understand if there is any problem, El Cerebro will not be able to count on us again—for anything."

Reese nodded. "The place you're taking us to is in no danger from us."

Silas didn't release her gaze. "I hope that is true. El Cerebro will still owe me a debt. Don't forget."

Reese didn't suppose any of them would. "Thank you. Any word on our friend or the doctor?"

Silas shook his head. "Nothing good. There were six Special Forces. One is dead. One is close to death. Ten minutes ago, three of the remaining four got on a sky train heading east. They had a female prisoner."

Reese's gut wrenched. So, Special Forces had acted quickly, apparently not willing to give them any chance to free Dani. Anger and relief boiled inside Reese. Anger because Dani was part of their crew, and relief because they might be tempted to risk anything for her and now they'd be forced to plan more carefully.

Jaxon blew out a frustrated breath. "The doctor?"

"I have no news for you there." Silas pulled his son away from Nova and stepped into another room, presumably to give the teen instructions.

Jaxon moved closer to Reese. "He's hiding something," he said quietly.

"He's probably hiding a lot of things." Reese glanced past him at Eagle, who appeared to be asleep on the table. He didn't look comfortable, though the meds had eased his pain. "But he's risking his life and his son's life. I don't see that we have a choice."

"They know about the doctor," Nova said, appearing next to them with a stealth Reese hadn't expected but should have.

"What do you mean?"

"Thane's an illegal child, and the doctor delivered him. He spent most of his years hiding in an empty zone." She frowned. "I think I might have known him or seen him before, but I just can't place where."

"You've been in the underground for what—two years?" Jaxon said. At Nova's nod, he continued, "A lot of time has passed. Kids change a lot."

"Just keep thinking." Reese moved closer to the table to see if Eagle's RealSkin was dry and holding. "It might come to you." The moment she'd seen Jaxon, she'd known him, even after twenty years apart. But they had spent their first decade together, neighbors and best friends in the Coop.

As if hearing her thoughts, Jaxon's eyes met hers, their intensity back. She didn't look away, but after a few seconds, he retreated, heading for the door, one finger kneading at his temple. "Going to get some air," he said. Reese and Nova watched him leave the kitchen. Out on the back porch, they heard the scrape of a chair.

"I'll be outside too." Nova started after him.

"Nova," Reese said, and the girl paused. "Thanks for getting the supplies. However you got them."

The girl shrugged uncomfortably. "Like I said, I was already there."

"No, you weren't. It was a brave and stupid thing you did."

One side of Nova's mouth quirked upward in a half smile. "Looks like we all did stupid stuff today." She took a few more steps and then paused to ask, "How are we going to get Dani back?"

Reese shook her head. "I don't know. Her T-link is completely dead, so she probably disabled it. We'll have to trace her the hard way."

"Her friends in Newcali might be able to help."

"Maybe. But we've turned off the T-links for now. Special Forces might be able to track us through her set if we use them."

"Great, one more thing to worry about." With a sigh, Nova disappeared through the door.

Reese shook Eagle awake and was relieved to see that he was able to sit up without pain. His color wasn't any better, but he hadn't rested long.

"We have to go," she said. "You think you can walk?"

"Yeah. I'm fine." He gave her a smile that almost held his usual humor. "I could use a cup of brew."

Reese reached for a red hypo in her pack. "A stim will give you a boost." She held it against his arm.

"Thanks."

He'd just put on his vest, hastily wiped down with a rag, and his shirt when Thane and Silas rushed into the room. "You have to go now," Silas ordered. "They've tracked a suspicious shuttle to this street."

Reese didn't ask how he knew.

"Follow my son. We have someone waiting. You'll go by

car some of the way, and then by tunnels." He waved at them, panic in his motions. "Hurry!"

Reese shouldered the two overloaded supply bags and ran to the door. Eagle followed almost as quickly, the stimulant she'd given him apparently kicking in. She hoped it wasn't masking his symptoms, though. She didn't like his color.

On the porch, Jaxon was already on his feet, and his hands reached for one of the bags. Wordlessly, they ran across the neighbor's yard, and into the yard of the house behind where a battered yellow car waited in the front. It was an old model, more round than sleek like the tetrahedron shuttles. It was too small to fit them all, but somehow Reese, Jaxon, and Eagle pushed into the back seat and Nova sat half on top of Thane in the passenger seat in the front. Reese noted that on the dashboard where an onboard Teev might have once been, there was now only a gaping hole.

The driver, a rotund, cleanshaven man with a shaved head, sped away. "The cameras have all failed here, but only for three more minutes until they reset," he said as they careened around a corner, knocking Reese painfully against the door.

More turns and then an abrupt stop. Houses reached in every direction except to their right, where a thick group of trees jutted from the earth, looking more like dangerous green spikes than the things of beauty Reese had noted earlier.

"Hurry!" the driver barked. "One minute!"

They tumbled from their cramped confines, bumping and hitting into each other, and followed Thane into the woods. Behind them, the yellow car sped away. Thane ran on a narrow path through the trees and brush at full speed, and it was hard to keep up with the heavy bags. Eagle was wheezing. But even when the road was no longer visible, Thane didn't stop.

Abruptly, he disappeared in front of them. There one minute and sinking and gone the next. Nova did the same.

Reese hurtled after them down a brush-covered slope. She could see the others now, descending in front of her. She dared a backward glance to make sure Eagle and Jaxon were keeping up. She could no longer see the woods except for the tops of some trees and the brush in this indentation.

Thane stopped and began clearing away a mound of branches, vines, and brush that hid an opening. Inside the dark hole was a set of crumbled stairs, also covered in leaves and twigs. This must be one of the tunnels Silas had talked about.

Once inside, Thane pulled back the covering over the opening and turned on a handheld light before leading them into the increasing darkness. Then he jumped down from a cement platform to where four metal lines dug into the ground, partially covered by dirt and debris.

"It's like El Cerebro's underground." Nova sounded almost happy.

Thane laughed easily. "Yeah. In fact, it was him who sent us the plans and helped us find it. These tunnels are so old, even the CORE has forgotten them. They've saved hundreds of lives. Come on. We don't want to miss our next contact."

He led them through the tunnel almost at a run, occasionally turning at intersections, first one way and then the next, as if his memory never faltered. But Reese began noticing symbols on some of the walls they passed, though she hadn't figured out which he was following.

Thane finally came to a stop, his chest heaving with effort, "I'm sorry, but this is where I need to blindfold you. We wouldn't be too bad off if this tunnel was discovered, but where we go next . . ." His voice held a plea, and though Reese had noticed the bulk of a gun at his waist under the back of his shirt, he had to know he wouldn't stand a chance against them. His only choice would be to refuse to lead them.

"We could make you show us," Nova said.

His chin jutted out, and his smile vanished. "I'd just lead you around until our contact left. I'm telling you that now because I don't think you're here to hurt us."

"Do it," Jaxon said.

Nova sighed and turned her back to the boy. Thane took a length of cloth from the bag he carried and tied it over her eyes, suddenly all gangly arms and extra thumbs. Reese hid a smile. Obviously, he liked the girl.

When they were all securely blindfolded, Thane gave them a rope to hold onto and was careful about rounding corners and deviating around debris. He could have no way of knowing that Eagle would be able to map the direction in his 3D brain simply by calculating the steps he took. It might help them later if they needed somewhere to hide out.

"This has to be how Kentley got away," Reese said in a low voice to Jaxon. "Through a tunnel like this one."

"That's my guess. They probably all intersect." Reese tried to peer under the blindfold, but the cloth was tight, and with Thane's light the only one in the tunnel, she couldn't make out anything. "You think it's wise to trust this kid? He could lead us into a trap."

"El Cerebro has a lot of pull with these people, regardless of what Silas said, or they wouldn't have helped us at all. They won't risk his retaliation. I think they're just trying to protect themselves. Besides, he's an illegal child, remember? He won't be going anywhere near enforcers."

Reese hoped he was right.

The walking wasn't difficult, and Reese felt they made good time considering the blindfolds. But they were unnaturally close, and sketches from the others' minds pressed in on her. More moments in time that she'd have to draw. From Nova she caught a glimpse of a boy from the Underground and her uncle in both his identities. From Eagle a snatch of the 3D mental map he was creating that would challenge her artistic skills, and from Thane a thought of Nova sitting next to him. Only Jaxon's mind didn't send her a sketch, for which she was grateful. She hoped he wouldn't have a premonition while they were in the tunnels, because she'd see an image of that for sure, and just thinking about the one she still needed to draw of the sick children made her chest ache.

After about thirty minutes, light began filtering in through the edges of her blindfold and their path angled steeply upward. Within seconds Reese could feel wind on her face, and it was all she could do not to rip off the blindfold and pull her gun.

"Are we out?" Nova demanded.

"Just a minute," Thane said. They tramped on, tripping over debris. *The woods or an empty zone,* Reese thought. She sniffed, but it didn't smell like the woods. The aroma was closer to dust, though the wind might carry the hint of a sea breeze.

She brought a finger up to tug at the blindfold, but Thane chose that moment to stop. "Okay, you can take them off," he said.

"I can't, you half-witted, punk bucket fringer!" Nova retorted. "You tied it too tight."

"I'll get it," came Thane's hurried voice. Then, "Hey, watch it with that knife!"

Reese had to cut her blindfold off too. She looked around with relief. In every direction lay mounds of rubble, the skeleton of some buildings reaching as high as twenty stories into the air. The occasional hardy weed stuck through the broken glass, shattered concrete, and twisted metal that covered the ground. Reese shivered. An empty zone, an area that marked the border between the inhabited CORE Territories and the desolation zones where the radiation was deadly.

"Now what?" Nova sounded angry. Her hair had come loose from its clip and the curls were everywhere, growing more ratted each second, tangled by the wind. Her yellow blouse was stained.

"Now is a good time to drink water. We're almost there." Thane sat on a large slab of broken concrete. "I have a little if you need it."

"I thought we were meeting someone," Nova sat in the rubble where she was standing, while the rest of them moved to large pieces of concrete nearby.

"Sorry. I lied." Thane took a swig from a water skin.

"Big surprise," Nova muttered, only half under her breath.

Thane ignored her disdain. "We've still got a bit of a walk."

Jaxon passed around a water skin from one of the bags Nova had rescued. Reese took a long drink, a trickle escaping to run down her neck, and tossed it back to him. She wished she could pour the rest over her head, but it wouldn't pay to start wasting it now.

"Anyone want food?" Nova dumped out her own bag, sending a slew of readymeals over the ground.

"Where'd you get those?" Thane growled suspiciously.

"Not from your house," Nova retorted, "if that's what you're thinking."

No. Reese was positive the girl had emptied the readymeal dispenser at the C-lodge.

"I wasn't thinking anything." Thane cocked his head, staring at her as if seeing her for the first time. "Your hair is different now."

"What of it?" Nova asked with a little sneer. Apparently, she was a lot more upset about the blindfold than any of them. Reese was glad that no new sketches came to her mind.

"Reminds me of someone." Thane shrugged and looked away.

"I'll have one of those," Eagle said to Nova, and she tossed him a readymeal. They weren't as good cold but safely edible.

Eagle was still pale and his face drawn. They'd have to give him more pain meds soon.

Reese gulped down a readymeal herself, one eye on the empty wasteland around them. When a noise alerted her, she pulled her gun and came swiftly to her feet.

"Easy," Thane said. "There's no one out here. It's just an animal."

How close were they to the South Desolation Zone? That animal might well turn out to be a monster.

"Let's move," Thane said.

He started out quickly, not looking back to see if they followed. Maybe he was even hoping they'd get lost. Nova shoved her food back in her pack, and Reese rose and started after them, checking behind her to see if Eagle was keeping up.

What she saw was Jaxon curled up on the ground beyond Eagle, obviously in the throes of a premonition. Reese hurried back. "Go ahead," she told Eagle. "We'll catch up."

But Jaxon held up his hand as she approached, warning her to stop, probably trying to spare her from his vision. She saw it anyway, though she was still three meters away. Not the sick children, as she expected, but two people wrapped in each other's arms, the telltale flush of passion on their faces.

Her face. And Jaxon's.

She stumbled, catching herself on a bar of rusty iron that jutted from a huge piece of broken concrete. The wind still whipping her hair did nothing to ease the heat crashing over her. Just that fast, the sketch was gone, leaving her hot and breathless and yearning.

Jaxon dragged himself to his feet, concern on his face. His eyes ran over her, the gaze feeling too intimate after what she'd glimpsed. "You okay?" he asked. An odd note in his voice told her he was asking more, that he was wondering if she'd experienced a sketch of what he'd seen. She knew by the lack of surprise in his expression that it wasn't the first time he'd had this vision.

If his visions always came true, where did it leave her? She felt as if she'd already cheated on Alex, or maybe being with Alex was cheating on Jaxon. Whatever it meant, she couldn't deal with it right now. She didn't even know how she felt about it, except angry that he hadn't told her before.

"You're the one who doesn't look okay," she said, leaving the sting in her voice. "You obviously had a premonition. You want to tell me what you saw?"

He took a step toward her, his face open and trusting. For a moment, she thought he might tell her the truth, but he shook his head. "You don't need another sketch bothering you. You're stumbling around as it is. If I tell you, you might see it."

As he spoke, her fingers itched to draw. No, they burned to draw. All the sketches she'd glimpsed today. Sourness scorched her throat. She bent over and vomited onto the rubble.

Jaxon put his arm around her. "Come on. Thane said it's not far. When we get there, you can start drawing."

Reese stifled a snort, not knowing which of them was worse off. They were both hobbling like invalids. Would it pass? Or was this only the beginning of the madness that eventually killed all those with abilities?

CHAPTER 10

D ani sat in a table seat on the sky train, ignoring the man opposite her as she stared out the window. Her hands were cuffed together on the table, her good arm dangling off the edge, while her wounded right arm rested on the flat surface between them, blood dripping through the hasty bandage they'd tied around it. Just a flesh wound, really, and her body would heal in a few days, but for now it ached more than she'd admit even to herself. She'd been clumsy, but it had taken a lot of effort not to break all their necks.

"Talk, fringer whore," growled one of the two Special Forces guards who stood next to the table, their assault rifles at the ready. She didn't respond. He was obviously still angry that she'd thrown him against a building.

It was an insult, really, sending only the three enforcers to escort her to Estlantic, but one of the six Special Forces had died in the shootout, and one would probably succumb soon. That meant only one enforcer from Special Forces remained to rally the local divisions to find her crew, leaving these three pus lickers to watch her. They were really no threat if she'd wanted to escape, at least not on a sky train with so many exits.

"Enforcer Gedet," growled the seated man. "I got this."

Gedet ignored him and plopped himself next to Dani, shoving her over to make room. "What was your goal?" he demanded. "How do you know Sam Kentley? Where did he go?"

Ah, so they haven't caught up to Kentley. That meant the others must have succeeded in their mission. She only hoped they were smart enough to power down their T-links. She'd damaged hers before being captured, but no doubt the pus bags would be able to fix it eventually. As long as the units were linked, there was a risk they could use hers to track them. But Reese and Jaxon were smart. Always had been. She could quit worrying about them and focus on her current goal— freeing her brother and getting him back to Newcali before the Special Forces understood that it wasn't only information about Newcali she was protecting.

Whatever happened, she'd free Tauri, even if she didn't make it out alive. Funny that she could be so attached to a brother she hadn't known existed until much later in her life, but Tauri was everything to her. She loved him above the colonists she'd saved, even the babies she bought from the mothers at Colony 6 who unknowingly sacrificed their children to a life of slavery in exchange for extra rations.

In fact, Tauri's very existence was nothing short of a miracle. Their father, who was supposed to have been seven months dead but was somehow alive, had come back to their tiny house in Colony 6. Dani had awakened in the bed she'd shared with her mother to find them kissing and clinging to one another.

"I'll come back for her next," he'd whispered in the dark room.

"No!" Her mother gave a little sob, clutching his hands as

if to prevent him from leaving. "What if you can't? That's why we agreed she'd go first. It's too big a risk."

Daddy shook his head, his hand caressing the large bulge of her mother's stomach. "Things are different now. It's safer to take the baby out while he's still inside. A few months won't matter for Dani. My mother will take care of her."

"Can't the fringers make room? She's so little."

"There's no room. One slight variation and everyone will be caught."

For a long moment her mother sounded as if she were choking on her tears. Then she straightened her shoulders. "Okay." She noticed Dani watching them and bent to hug her, "Be brave, my little girl. I love you."

Daddy also tried to hug her, his eyes shimmering with moisture in the pale light, but Dani had cringed away from him. He was too strange. He was supposed to be dead.

"I'll come back for you," he promised.

Dani had stared without a response. Then he took her mother away.

Forever.

The next day Dani turned six. She told only one person about that night—her crotchety old gran, who had told her it was a dream. That her mother hadn't run away but had died like her father. For months Dani wondered if the strange growth in her mother's tummy had caused her death. After the first year, it didn't really matter to Dani because if it hadn't been a dream, they had lied and left her. They were lumpers, fringer-lovers, and she didn't need or want them. She didn't need or want anyone, not even her crew, at least not on an emotional level.

Thirteen years had passed, years of danger and fighting and scraping by. Then she'd finally left Colony 6 and was studying for her certificate in manufacturing, when she'd learned her cousin, still in the colony, had attacked an enforcer. It was the beginning of the madness, though they hadn't known it then. Not about the madness or that he'd be shot to death in less than a year.

On her way to plead for his release, the sky train had broken down, and fringers had raided it. She'd bolted with the other passengers and ended up wandering in an empty zone for nearly a day, waiting for rescue.

Fringers caught up with her first. When they'd seen the black of her skin and the unusual white of her spiky hair, so much like Tauri's, they'd taken a blood sample and urged her to go with them to Newcali, promising information about her family. There she'd learned her father had been killed the night he'd come for her mother, and her mother had died in childbirth less than a month later. Maybe it was knowing they hadn't abandoned her that let her love Tauri as much as she did. Knowing about him, her parents had made the only choice they could have. She'd have never wanted him to grow up at Colony 6. Especially with how different he turned out. He would never have survived.

She'd also learned the truth about the CORE and the colonies. Anger and a yearning to right the wrongs grew inside her. So she'd abandoned her life and stayed in Newcali with Tauri. The Newcalian's fight became hers.

"We know who you are, Dani Balak," said the enforcer across from her.

Dani looked at him, glad their slow brains had finally cut across her troubled memories. "You took my blood," she said with a flat little smile, "so I guess that means your boss must have cross-referenced that with the real citizen database because apparently I never existed in the public one, though I distinctly remember attending school in Colony 6."

"Tell me how you know the fringers who took Dr. Kentley," barked Gedet, his twisted face pushing closer to hers.

Dani shifted her gaze to him. Their slow stupidity made her want to scream. "I don't know them at all. I've told you that repeatedly. I came to the doctor for a cure."

Gedet grabbed her upper arm and yanked it toward him, digging his thumb into her wound. Pain ricocheted inside her head and blood gushed from under the bandage, dribbling down her arm and splatting onto the table. The other two enforcers made sounds of protest, but Dani simply took a deep breath, willing her body to be strong, to ignore the pain. She was tempted to bash his face in with his rifle and use his finger-prints to access his gun and shoot the others, but she couldn't afford to do that yet. These enforcers were her ticket to Tauri.

Gedet smirked at her, his too-handsome face contorting with anger. He pulled her arm closer, until her blood-streak skin was near his mouth. Watching her with his dark, hateful eyes, he licked the blood from her arm.

"How much of this do I need to drink before I gain your speed?" he mocked. "One liter? Two?" He gave her arm another long lick, waving his bloodied tongue at her before pulling it slowly into his mouth.

She snorted. "Probably all of it wouldn't be enough for a weak pus licker like you."

His face reddened. "I guess we'll see, won't we?" He jerked out a knife from a side pocket, aiming it at the wound.

There was only so much Dani could take. Dragging in a breath, she snapped the handcuffs and grabbed his knife with her left hand, tossing it with such strength that it embedded into the metal interior of the train. It was a lucky shot, since she was right-handed, but not entirely unexpected.

"That could have been your head," she said, as color leaked from his face. "Now we both know you're not supposed to kill me, and I'm telling you now that if you touch me again, you'll have to kill me"—she smirked—"or try to kill me because I only have so much patience, and I *will* kill you before I let you touch me again."

His color was returning, along with his stupidity. He stood and backed away from her, his hands going to his rifle.

Dumb punk, she thought, keeping an eye on his trigger finger. Still plenty of time to move.

"Stand down!" ordered the seated enforcer. He was slightly higher in rank than the others, though not as high up on the ladder as their leader who had stayed behind in Santoni. "The Controller wants her alive. You don't want him mad at you, do you?" This, said in an urgent voice, somehow managed to penetrate Gedet's sluggish mind.

He removed his finger from the trigger but didn't lower the rifle. Not even after they found new shackles for her, heavy duty ones they thought would keep them safe. As if that would make a difference.

Dani went back to looking out the window. Maybe now they'd give her some peace. Everything was going according to plan.

CHAPTER 11

Their steps came easier as Jaxon and Reese hurried to catch up with the others. Similar to how a body with sore muscles somehow loosens up and moves more easily with walking, Jaxon's mind recovered from the premonition.

He'd finally had the vision of him and Reese again. Was it selfish that he hadn't wanted to leave the vision, that he wouldn't have minded waking up hours later to remember nothing but those moments? No such luck in this place, especially with her coming toward him. But it was a relief knowing it hadn't been his imagination. The vision would eventually come true. He just had to be patient and let her work out her fears or whatever was holding her back.

Of course, the Special Forces' shuttle today was supposed to have blown up and it hadn't. What did that mean? Was it possible a vision might not come true after all?

Like him, Reese was exhausted. Far more than she should be, even with what they'd been through today. Had it only been this morning that they'd gone to see the doctor? Jaxon pushed back the anger the thought brought with it. The doctor might have been able to help Reese. To help him.

In the next moment, Reese stepped away from him. "I'm okay now," she said, and he saw that she was. Tension still gathered on her forehead and her hands clenched, but she was moving faster. Ahead, the others were turning around some debris.

When Jaxon rounded the bend with Reese, the others were standing outside a solid metal wall at least three times as tall as Jaxon. For a stark instant, it reminded him of the gates at the Coop, though the resemblance was superficial. Colony gates were far taller and gleamed silver under the sun while these were black and rusted.

One side of the wall went on for as long as Jaxon could see, until it was obscured by rubble. The other disappeared behind a tall red-bricked building that was more intact than anything else they'd seen, despite its interior being gutted with fire.

Thane banged on the wall, and seconds later, the face of a man with long, stringy black hair popped over. "Hey, Thane," the man called down to them.

"Hey, Namon. Let us in, okay?"

"Only be a minute." The face disappeared.

Jaxon expected a gate to open in the wall, but instead Thane motioned everyone inside the brick building. They dodged around rotting furniture, clumps of ceiling, and what might have been part of an elevator. Behind this last, Jaxon paused, staring at a blackened wall that began moving as they watched. A loud screech made them all cringe as heavy metal scraped against brick. Jaxon could see that the back part of the wall was actually a painted section of the outside metal wall. Once opened, they ducked through the roughly rounded opening.

Jaxon stepped through into green grass, surprise washing

over him. There was still a lot of debris, but much had been cleared, and the grass was nothing short of miraculous in an empty zone.

"Underground spring," Thane supplied at their amazement.

"Hey, I know this place!" Nova mused aloud, her voice filled with wonder.

"You do?" Thane asked.

But Nova was already sprinting through the cleared area. When one of the two men on guard inside started to go after her, Thane shook his head. "I'll take them all inside. Better watch the gate. Special Forces is after them."

The men nodded and gripped their guns more tightly, their eyes digging into Jaxon, Reese, and Eagle.

"One of them has a gray uniform," Reese whispered as they hurried after Nova.

"You recognize him?" Dared Jaxon hope the doctor could be here? The idea wasn't too far-fetched. Safe places to hide in the CORE weren't exactly advertised on the Teev.

"No," Reese said. "Just the uniform."

The house came into view suddenly, appearing in front of them as they passed some kind of holo field like the one masking the back of Silas's safehouse. Nova stood outside a wire fence encircling the house, her fingers clutching at the metal links, her face pushed up against it. Inside the fence two young children, a boy and a girl, played together on the grass

"It was here," she said, as they reached her. "This is where El Cerebro took me after my father died."

Reese's arm slipped around the girl. "You didn't know its location?"

She shook her head. "He was afraid I'd run away. He drugged me and put a tracker in my foot. When I woke up, this was where I was. Same thing when he came to get me. I almost thought it was a dream."

"I can see why they'd want to protect it," Jaxon said. The two children had seen them and now ran into the house.

"How long ago did you leave?" Thane asked.

Nova didn't tear her eyes away from the house but answered his question. "Two years. That's how long I was here too."

Thane's gasp was loud enough for all of them to hear. "I was here sometimes then."

"The laughing boy," Nova whispered. "I remember. Your mother took care of us. Is she still here?"

Thane's expression hardened. "No."

Nova glanced at him then, but apparently decided not to push, which surprised Jaxon. Usually the girl acted heedless of any feelings except her own.

"Come on." Thane removed a loop of wire from a post and opened the narrow gate. "You can rest here. Once things die down, you can leave. The sky station is probably being watched, though, so it's better to find another way out of Santoni."

A thin woman appeared on the porch, beckoning to the children, who ran past her into the house. She looked impossibly old, like a character from a pre-Breakdown Teev show. Obviously, she didn't use any form of Nuface. She wore a flowered dress topped by a stained white apron. Worn brown boots covered her feet. At first Jaxon thought her gray hair was pulled back but realized as they approached that it was simply cut extremely short.

"I'm Debs," she said. "Come on in, and I'll show you where you can rest until you figure out what you're going to do." Her tone, while mild, was clearly not welcoming, and Jaxon didn't blame her. Their very presence put this place at risk. Even the shootout in Santoni had endangered them.

In the tiny entry and the hallway beyond, every centimeter of the short walls was filled with paintings and image receptors, some framed and others unframed, assaulting their eyes and challenging their equilibrium. Even the single wall of the old-fashioned staircase in front of them was lined with the hangings. Half the paintings looked as if they had been created by great masters and others could have been scribbled by children. The image receptors showed copies of paintings or images of people wearing unfamiliar clothes. Jaxon didn't know whether to be impressed by the number of salvaged items or depressed that it meant so many hadn't lived to take care of their own belongings. Only the closed door to their right, so perfectly white it had to be recently painted, was free of clutter.

Debs stood to the side of the stairs as if blocking them from going into the entry any further. She put her hand on what looked like a real wood banister, motioning them upward. "At the top of the stairs, there's a door on your right. If you'll settle in there, I'll bring you some snacks from our garden."

Despite having eaten a readymeal, Jaxon's mouth watered. Fresh food was not generally something found outside a restaurant, and during the past weeks he'd grown accustomed to eating similar foods at Reese's great-aunt's house.

Nova dragged her eyes from the crazy walls and started up the stairs eagerly, clearly lost in memories. Reese and Eagle followed. Jaxon had gone up only two steps when Eagle collapsed in front of him. Jaxon grabbed him as he fell, but it was Reese who somehow managed to stop his head from crashing onto the steps.

"Is he unwell?" Debs glanced nervously behind her.

"He was shot in the back," Reese told her. "He had on a protective vest and the bullets didn't enter, but he doesn't seem to be getting better, even with an injection of nanoparticles. All this walking around isn't helping. He needs somewhere to lie down."

Jaxon looked at the old woman, who still hadn't moved. "Do you have somewhere down here we can put him?"

Debs eyes darted to the closed door behind them but shook her head. Reese grabbed Eagle under the arms. "In there," she said to Jaxon.

"No, you can't go in there." Debs voice had taken on a high pitch. "Upstairs is best."

Ignoring her, Jaxon pushed open the door and grabbed Eagle's feet. Nova and Thane took his arms and together they carried him into a room filled with more clutter—on the walls and in terms of furniture. The soft-looking couch was exactly what they needed.

"Put him on his side," Jaxon said. "In case we need to look at his back."

A man sat at a table with the two children they'd seen earlier. They were eating, but all of them froze as they laid Eagle on the bed. Jaxon didn't like the way the man stared at Reese. As her hands left Eagle, she pulled her gun in a single fluid motion and pointed it at the man, circling to his side but keeping herself angled so she could also keep an eye on the old woman. With her gun pointed at the fringer's chest, she freed his gun from his holster and tucked it into her pocket.

"You took the doctor," she accused. "You were with him. Where is he? Where did you take him?"

Jaxon pulled his own gun and stepped away from the couch, making sure he also covered the man without putting Reese at risk.

"Easy, everyone," Thane said.

"You take it easy," shot Nova. She was brandishing her knife in front of the boy, preventing him from drawing his gun.

"The doctor is safe." The man at the table raised his hands and stood slowly. Jaxon couldn't place the tall man as one of the fringers who'd taken Kentley, but the gray uniform was familiar, and he trusted his partner.

Debs gave a little growl in her throat. "We offer you

sanctuary and this is how you repay us?" Her mouth twisted in disgust. "Kentley is our doctor. *Ours*. We would not survive without him."

A little something inside Jaxon died as he pointed his gun at her. "Take us to him now or I will shoot you and take those two children to the enforcers."

"Do it then," the woman sneered at him.

"No!" Dr. Kentley stepped from the doorway they'd just entered. "I'm right here."

"Sam," Debs chided. "You should have run."

The doctor seemed unperturbed, even down to his wet hair, that appeared freshly washed and combed back from his face. "I don't think they've come to hurt me or anyone." Kentley stared at Jaxon. "Am I right? Come, let's talk. Put away your weapons. We're all on the same side here—or should be."

"First look at our friend," Reese said.

Kentley nodded. "Debs, get my bag."

Jaxon was loath to let the old woman leave, in case she returned with reinforcements, but he wasn't about to abandon his crew. "You come back alone," he told Debs.

She nodded. "Then put that away." Her brown eyes burned accusation.

Jaxon felt scolded as if by his own mother, and the sensation brought a longing he didn't enjoy. A longing for his mother, who had done everything to keep him alive in the Coop and who had paid with her life. Debs didn't wait to see if he complied, but marched from the room, her thin back straight and indignant.

The children took that moment to run to Kentley and bury their faces in his legs. One of them was sniffling, and the doctor bent down to encircle them with his arms. "Shush, now, it's okay."

"Are they going to send us to a colony?" asked the boy. Jaxon had no experience with children and couldn't even begin to guess how old they were, but their heads were at his waist level.

Kentley looked up at Jaxon. "Please let them leave."

Jaxon knew that he shouldn't, that they were the best leverage they had, but he wasn't going to hurt them. He met Reese's gaze and she gave a sharp nod.

"Go play," Dr. Kentley said to the children, rising to his feet. "Go on now." With angry glares at them, the children reluctantly left the room.

"We didn't come to hurt anyone," Jaxon said. "El Cerebro sent us to prevent Special Forces from taking you into custody. He wants to meet with you."

Kentley chuckled. "So your partner over there said earlier. But I'm surprised the leader of the underground in Dallastar even knows I exist. At any rate, if you'll please relax, I can promise you no one will hurt you here."

"How can you promise that?" Nova's lip curled slightly.

Kentley's gaze rested on her a moment before answering. "Because this is my home and has been for a year now. These people are my friends. Who do you think told Silas to bring you here? Though I'd intended to keep out of sight."

"These fringers took you at gunpoint," Reese said. "They threatened to kill you."

"That was just so you'd let us go. I had a patient to see." Kentley pulled a chair from the table and set it close to the couch by Eagle. "But I guess at the end of the day, I should be thanking you." He must have noted the surprise on Jaxon's face because he added, "I knew I was watched and that I didn't have much time before they tried to pick me up. If you hadn't been here and engaged with them, I might have gone back later today. Now keep your guns, if you want, but could you ask this young lady to put away her knife?"

"Okay, fine." Nova's knife disappeared inside her clothes. "But if you try anything, laughing boy," she said to Thane, "I'll gut you."

Thane rolled his eyes. "Sure, you would."

"You don't know the things I've done." Nova stalked away from him toward the door, where she stood like a sentinel.

Debs returned to the room, carrying a large case. She frowned at Jaxon's gun, which he'd lowered but hadn't put away. He met her stare unflinchingly until she retreated from the room. He hadn't told the doctor the whole truth, of course, that the man was going with them back to Amarillo City one way or the other, even if he didn't agree.

Kentley removed a device from his bag and began scanning Eagle. "This will take your friend's vitals and help me know where he's at." He stopped and frowned. "You gave him nanoparticles?"

"Yes." Jaxon moved closer to the couch, still keeping an eye on the fringer man at the table. He'd sat again and resumed eating, but Jaxon wondered if they should have taken away his fork. In Colony 6, they'd used them more than once as a weapon.

"Nanoparticles can fix the body if injected near the damage, but it's mostly hit and miss since we've lost the technology to program them." Kentley put down the device and slid his hand around to Eagle's back. "In this case, they've nearly repaired two broken ribs, but they ignored an internal bleed, which is far more dangerous. No worries, I can fix that." He removed a white hypo and a laser from his bag. "I actually need him on his back, though. Help me turn him."

Once Eagle was on his back, Kentley sedated him and began using the laser. "This is a deep tissue device," he said. "With it, I'm able to pass through the outer layers and repair the bleed. Fortunately, this one isn't bad. If he hadn't been roaming around the tunnels, he might have healed on his own." He flicked off the laser. "There."

"You did that without the aid of a Teev," Jaxon said. "It's because of your ability, isn't it?" He was betting the first scanning device the doctor had used was only for show, though it might have genuinely detected the nanoparticles.

Kentley, still bent over Eagle, stiffened. "How do you know about that?"

"Why else do you think El Cerebro is interested in you?" Nova retorted. "You cure people. It's not like he's looking for just any doctor."

"Is that why you're here?" Kentley asked Jaxon. "To offer me a job? I'm sorry to disappoint you, but I'm not leaving Santoni."

"That's not the only reason we're here," Reese said, approaching the couch. The man at the table stopped chewing and Jaxon shifted toward him.

The doctor looked up at Reese. "Oh? Go ahead and tell me, though it won't make a difference."

"We're from Colony 6 too," she said.

The doctor sat up, his hands resting in his lap. For a long moment, he simply sat there, staring at each of them in turn. "Oh, the good old Coop," he said finally. "That explains the anxiety in all of you. Or you three, at least." He motioned to Jaxon, Reese, and Eagle. "And two of you . . ." He frowned, pausing distastefully. "You don't have long."

"Long before what?" Jaxon barked. Pressure rose in his temples, and he tried to push it back. He didn't need a vision now.

"Before the madness takes over." Kentley sighed. "But I can help. At least temporarily. In fact, it's what I do best."

"What do you mean?" Reese demanded, but Jaxon could

feel the pressure leaking away from his temple. The premonition urge faded. Involuntarily, he stepped closer to Kentley.

"The minute I walked in," Kentley said, "I could feel your friend's bleeding, I could feel the pressure in your heads." He reached out to touch Reese's hand. She tried to pull away, to hide the shaking, but Kentley held on.

"I drain emotion, pain, and everything else," Kentley said. "I can feel where to operate, what's wrong." He took his hand from Reese's, and even from where he stood, Jaxon could see her hands were no longer shaking. "Mostly, it works."

"Mostly?" Nova said. "They said you never lost anyone."

Kentley's laugh was bitter this time. "My ability helps me diagnose people, and I can take their pain, which often gives them enough strength to fight, to live another day, but people still die. Especially if I'm not around at the time they need me." He sounded tired, as if carrying a heavy burden.

Disappointment surged through Jaxon. Until that moment, he hadn't realized how much he'd been counting on Kentley to help him control his ability. "The madness," Jaxon said. "Can you think of any way to stop it?" He hesitated, before adding, "Someone has. Six weeks ago someone giving orders to Special Forces troops tried to take us. They promised treatment, if we'd work for them."

"You should have taken them up on their offer." Kentley's dark eyes were grave. "I've watched three of my best friends succumb. They were the only ones who hadn't been murdered."

"Then you know about the extermination?" Reese said.

Kentley arose, nodding. "I know they've killed everyone who left Colony 6."

"Not just those who left." Reese's voice was tight, and Jaxon could tell she was holding back fury. "Everyone who stayed too. At least everyone with an ability. And now they're paying bonuses for women there to have more children."

The doctor gaped at them. "But why would they do that?"

"Because they need fifty thousand people in each of the six colonies to support everyone on the outside," Reese said. "The colonies grow most of the food and mine most of the raw materials for the CORE. Then we take the best and give them back leftovers and pretend it's charity. Meanwhile, the Elite glut themselves on the taxes we supposedly pay to support the colonies. It's all a huge lie."

Understanding dawned on Kentley's face. "You mean, they really aren't trying to integrate the colonies?" he asked. "They aren't freeing youngsters as they prove they can support themselves?"

Jaxon shook his head. "No. Sometimes they move people around to give the illusion that people leave, but they keep them all in the colonies to replace their parents in the fields or factories as they die. After the murders, Colony 6 only has about forty thousand people left. So that's why they're paying the women bonuses to have more children."

Kentley's shoulder slumped, and he seemed to age before them. "I had no idea, but it explains so much. Why they rarely allow visits, why we never meet anyone who came from a colony, except . . ."

"Except you freaks," Nova said. "Everyone in the underground knows that. It's old news. Colony 6 was the experiment. The *failed* experiment. That's why we gotta do more. Get ready to fight. To free the colonies and everyone."

"Yes!" Thane exclaimed, and Nova smiled at him.

Jaxon studied the doctor's face before adding, "That's why you have to come with us. We're going to need all the help we can get. We"—he motioned to Reese and Eagle—"have abilities, and there are others like us. If you can help find something that will alleviate the symptoms of the madness, we can use our gifts to find out who's responsible and fix what's wrong with the CORE." Without another Breakdown, Jaxon meant. He had to believe they could protect people while freeing them.

"Maybe it's possible." Dr. Kentley rubbed his chin thoughtfully. "But only if I had a sample of the drug they gave us. I've tried using our blood and a million other things, but I haven't been able to pinpoint it."

"You have to try again," Jaxon insisted. "Come with us."

"I can't." Dr. Kentley backed to the door.

Jaxon kept pace with him. "At least talk to El Cerebro. Now that the implant is required, we'll need help taking them back out. Too many are dying."

Kentley stopped, his eyes sweeping over them. "Come with me. I'll show you why I can't leave."

Jaxon glanced back at Reese. She had her gun drawn and pointed at the other man, who had arisen from the table. He held up his hands submissively. "Just going along with you. You have my gun, remember?" He gave her a tight smile. At Reese's nod, he moved to join Jaxon and Kentley at the door.

"Stay with Eagle," Jaxon told Nova. "And we'll need you to look after our supplies." Mostly he meant their blues and Eagle's equipment.

Nova glared at him until Reese gave her a small back up pistol, and then she nodded in agreement. "Fine."

"You stay too, Thane," Dr. Kentley said. "They're already searching for us in the empty zones. You're safer here." Thane glanced at Nova and nodded.

Kentley's voice rose. "Debs, can you come here?"

The old woman appeared outside the door. "I'm bringing a tray in a minute," she told him.

He shook his head. "I'm taking them to the cave. Watch their friend. I've given him something to speed up blood production, but when the sedative wears off, he'll need a lot of water."

A line of irritation formed on her brow "But you haven't eaten. You don't need to go back there now."

"Yes, I do." The doctor pushed past her.

Jaxon glanced again at Eagle. He was still pale, but there was nothing they could do about getting back to Amarillo City before he woke anyway. They might as well see what the doctor thought was more important than freeing the three hundred thousand people in the colonies. Not that it mattered. One way or the other, Dr. Kentley was going with them to see El Cerebro.

CHAPTER 12

Nova was glad she'd stayed behind when the old grand-mother brought them a tray of foods that included fresh vegetables and fruits she didn't recognize. In the underground they mostly ate readymeals or leftovers from restaurants who traded with El Cercbro, so this was a decided treat.

Thane laughed at her. "You act as if you didn't already eat two readymeals."

"You're just as bad."

"It's good food. I always love coming back here." He puffed his chest, making him look older. "But I'm getting a CivID soon. A real one."

"Like that's anything to be proud of," Nova scoffed. "It's nothing but a dog collar."

He shrugged. "You try and earn credits without one. They catch me now, and I'll end up in a colony."

He was right. She looked away from him and concentrated on her food.

Ever since she'd set foot in the house, memories assaulted

her. After her father's death, when her uncle had brought her here, she'd been a legal, non-colony citizen of the CORE. Her father had paid for her freedom from Colony 4 with his trips into the desolation zones to search for new tech, so she wouldn't have to mine oil and make plastic, which would eventually kill her as it had her mother. Nova's freedom for her father's death. The price had been too high.

Back then, she'd been angry even before coming here. Angry because her mother was dead and her father was growing sicker. But after he was gone, the desperation had made her try to attack the enforcer division with nothing but rocks and a knife. Her uncle had forced her to stay here for protection until she was fit to join him in the underground. Every now and then when she did something stupid, he threatened to send her back. She'd always shuddered.

But this house, this place, wasn't all bad; she remembered that now. Beyond the haze of pain, there had been a much younger Thane, who had tried to make her laugh. And other children. She remembered playing in the yard and plotting revenge against the CORE. She remembered Thane's mother, how she'd smelled when she'd put her arms around Nova one night when she'd tried to run away.

"I want to see my old room," she said.

Thane nodded. "Okay. Come on."

She glanced at Eagle, who appeared to be sleeping.

"He's okay," Thane assured her.

She went up the stairs first, letting memory guide her. The house was small, and there was no indoor plumbing since they were in an empty zone, but somehow it was large enough for three bedrooms. She passed up the larger one on the right and went into the tiny room at the end of the hallway. The room was exactly as she remembered, with two sets of mismatched bunkbeds, a metal one with peeling blue paint and one made of scarred wood. There was really no room for anything on the white walls, though someone had drawn on the white ceiling.

She sat on the bottom bunk of the blue bed. "This was where I slept."

"You never talked." Thane sat close to her, so close that their legs were touching.

Her gaze flew to his. He was cute, she had to admit, and she liked him, even after he'd pulled that stupid blindfold stunt. His black hair curled slightly at the ends, and his large nose made him look strong and confident, despite his thinness. But his eyes were his best feature, a warm brown that seemed to understand and forgive her even when she was being rude.

She smiled. "You tried to make us laugh. All of us."

"They're gone now. The others, I mean."

"Dead?" There had been at least six children here then.

He shook his head. "They're still around. Most of them. Out there somewhere. This house isn't big enough for all the fringers who live in the empty zones. It's mostly for children in emergencies."

Nova nodded. "In Amarillo City, I live in the underground. It's kind of like your tunnels but deeper. They used them for trains and they called it the subway—back before the sky trains were made." That was so far before Breakdown that even the oldest people couldn't remember knowing anyone who'd ever used a subway train.

Thane looked like he was going to say something, but he didn't, and Nova guessed that he was protecting someone or something. Probably they had a safe place in the tunnels too. Was that where the doctor was taking Reese and Jaxon?

"Where is the cave?" she asked, watching him carefully.

Thane shrugged. "It's not too far. I've only been there once, though. That man who was here earlier eating, the one your friend recognized? It's where his group lives." He frowned.

"They haven't been here long. They were hoping to join our group, but some of them are sick."

"Sick with what?"

"Radiation poisoning."

With the words, Nova suddenly couldn't find air. "They went into the desolation zones?"

"I guess. Or lived too near."

"My dad died because of radiation."

"I'm sorry." Thane took her hand, his thumb rubbing over her palm. She didn't pull away.

"What about your mom?" She had to know.

His eyes dropped, and his thumb stopped moving. "They caught her last year when she went to help a couple who were expecting an illegal child. They sent her to Colony 4. We haven't seen her since. We've been trying to figure out how to contact her. We don't even know if she's alive."

"I'm sorry. She was nice. I-I remember the way she smelled."

"Like lilacs. It was her favorite fragrance."

He stood and pulled her to her feet, so she had to look up to see his eyes. She still couldn't breathe, but it was because of him now and not their conversation. If she were up to telling the truth, she'd been waiting for this moment since she bested him on his porch.

"I remember other things too," she said. "Like how you tried to kiss me."

He laughed. "I tried to kiss all the girls back then. It made them scream and run away."

"And now?"

He stepped closer. One of his hands entwined in her hair. "I guess I grew up."

Nova had kissed plenty of boys in the underground, but most of those chased her because she was El Cerebro's ward.

She didn't even really want to kiss them. It was a matter of curiosity. But she wanted to kiss Thane.

"You can try now," she said, arching her neck to push her head against his fingers, still tangled in her hair and now gently massaging her scalp.

He grinned. "I don't want to chase you away."

"Well, I am going back to the underground, but that doesn't mean you're chasing me away. You can always come find me there."

Was he going to kiss her or not? Anyway, she wasn't going to wait around. She wasn't a beggar, even though she probably looked like it right now. Kissing him would probably be no different than the smelly, annoying boys back home.

She had taken two steps toward the door when he pulled her back, encircling her into his arms. "You pulled a knife on me."

"You made me wear a blindfold."

His laugh made her insides do funny things. "We're even then," he said.

His lips met hers, and it wasn't at all like the other boys. He was soft and gentle, and he didn't try to take liberties with his hands, liberties that might have made El Cerebro dole out punishments if she told him about the attempts.

Nova put her arms around his neck and kissed him back.

CHAPTER 13

"How far is this cave?" Reese asked. She didn't like being separated from Eagle and Nova, but she had to admit to being curious.

"Not far. Another kilometer maybe." Dr. Kentley glanced her way. "It's not really a cave, though. It's manmade, pre-Breakdown. Apparently, it was a resort at one time. It has a passageway that leads to a cliff overlooking the ocean."

The taller man from the table was leading the way, and Reese felt a little guilty for keeping his gun, but she still didn't trust him. She also had her own gun and the assault rifle Nova had rescued from the C-lodge. Jaxon carried his weapons as well, but in the nyckelira case and in his holster. Kentley had eyed the case in puzzlement a few times but hadn't commented on Jaxon's apparently incongruous burden.

A low growl was all the warning they had before a streak leapt from behind a mound of refuse. The creature landed on the fringer in front of them, knocking him to the ground. The man cried out, bringing his hands up to protect himself. The doglike animal had two misshapen heads, one as large as a bear, the other the size of a poodle. Both heads were covered in a half meter of hair. The big jaws clamped down on both the fringer's arms, while the small one went for his neck. A stench from the creature wafted over them, threatening to gag Reese.

Sprinting forward, she fired her silenced pistol at the same time Jaxon did, hitting it in the larger head. The head jerked back and then went limp, but the body remained unaffected. The eyes of the small head met theirs, its yellow gaze seeming far too bright in the afternoon sun. It growled once, a high, piercing growl that made Reese shudder. In one motion, it turned and leapt, the large head dangling sightlessly, and Reese sent another bullet through the creature's back. It didn't stop.

"Let it go!" Kentley said tensely. "It's too dangerous to be chasing it with Special Forces around." He reached them and bent down to touch the wounded man, who was moaning with pain. "Try to relax, Cooper. You're going to be okay. It's not deep." The fringer calmed almost immediately, but beads of sweat appeared on the doctor's brow. Kentley let go and unshouldered his medical case. "He needs an antibiotic. These creatures are usually poisonous."

"You see a lot of these here?" Jaxon asked.

"Only this close to the South Desolation Zone," the doctor said pressing a blue hypo against Cooper's arm. "Especially the past year. More and more of them are venturing over. I'm not sure if they've lost their way, or if whatever's been sustaining them has run dry. Or maybe their population has become so large that some are being driven off." He gave a mirthless grin as he started to bind the wounds on Cooper's arms. "But I'd take them over the Elite any day. At least you know where you stand with them."

Reese had to agree. For all the time she'd been an enforcer, she'd never seen anything like this in person, but they had erected electronic barriers in Estlantic, which were supposed to keep anything out. Dallastar was less populated, and so far that hadn't been necessary.

Cooper endured the doctor's ministrations without comment, but his eyes radiated hate at Reese when she handed him back his gun. Maybe he would have been able to shoot the creature first, but his unsilenced shot might have also alerted Special Forces to their location.

After another few minutes of walking, Kentley led them into a crumbling building and down a surprisingly intact metal ramp. At the end was a metal door. Kentley banged out a code on it, and the door lurched upward a few painful centimeters at a time, creaking loudly with each jerk.

Two men with guns motioned them inside, and the metal door began its equally painful descent. Inside, the cement walls looked mostly intact and rubble had been cleared away. Cooper, the wounded fringer, stayed behind with the guards as they moved forward.

"How many people live here?" Jaxon asked.

"About forty." Kentley hesitated. "Now."

Reese didn't know if he was hinting that more were coming, or that more had once been here.

"There are many passageways that go to various parts of the resort," he added. "It's more comfortable than most places you'll find in the empty zones."

They turned down one short hallway and paused by a door that opened into a cavernous room whose gloom was lifted by only a few battery-operated lights. Reese recognized the place immediately. The rough walls, the sick children. The air that was still and heavy with suffering.

Beside her, Jaxon was holding his breath, and she almost

expected him to be taken by another vision, but he remained calm. So was she. For that matter, she didn't feel any of the sketches she'd witnessed today pressing her to draw them.

"This is the cave's infirmary," Kentley said. "Of sorts anyway."

There were a dozen children, more than she'd seen from the sketch. No, some of them were adults. They were each lying on folded blankets or scavenged mattresses. Their faces were flushed with running sores. One of the children reached out a thin hand to the doctor and moaned.

Jaxon's gaze met Reese's and held. He was checking to see how she was, but right now only numbness filled every part of her.

"You're not surprised," Dr. Kentley searched their faces. "Why not?"

It wasn't Reese's secret to tell, but Jaxon said slowly, "I have premonitions. I saw this yesterday and then again today. Only it was different. That child didn't make it." Jaxon motioned to a small boy who snuggled under a tattered brown blanket, his head cradled in a man's lap. A man Reese now recognized from the doctor's office this morning, the short man who would do anything to make sure the doctor came with him.

Dr. Kentley shook his head. "He's actually the best of all of them right now. He'll recover, if I continue to work with him. I can stop the degradation and help him heal. He did have convulsions this morning, and it could have been serious if I hadn't come, but it was an unrelated illness that I've since immunized him for. As long as he doesn't have any more radiation exposure, he'll only have a slightly increased chance of cancer as he grows."

Reese could see that Jaxon didn't believe him. Neither did she. "How were they exposed?" she asked.

"Apparently, enforcers in Estlantic are now searching the

empty zones for rebels, and they fled to Dallastar. They found this place and were living here for weeks before we discovered their presence. I told you one of the passageways leads to a cliff overlooking the ocean. Well, at high tide, the water comes inside partway and puddles in a caved-in room. A lot of fish are left stranded and are easy pickings."

Reese gasped. "They didn't test them for radiation?" Only Colony 2 had the safety measures to process seafood. Even eighty years after Breakdown, there were only a few places in the CORE where it was safe to enter the ocean, and those were all in Estlantic.

"Test them with what?" Kentley swallowed hard. "They ate them before understanding how close we are to a desolation zone. It was only after they lost half their group that they started searching for help and stumbled onto one of my contacts."

Silence fell over them as they mourned the unlucky victims.

"You see why I can't leave," Kentley continued more quietly. "No matter how much El Cerebro needs me. There are some here who will die if I abandon them. Children especially. They have no one else. Besides, if it's not them, it's others. They hear about me and they come."

"I understand the dilemma." Jaxon watched the short fringer stroke his son's face. "But don't you think it's more important to save all the colonies?"

The doctor sighed. "The age-old question about what's more important—do we save the individual or the group?"

"In this case if we manage to save the group, there won't be any more individuals to worry about," Jaxon said. "At least not like this. They would all be in a hospital."

Kentley motioned to the boy. "By the time change came it would be too late for him. Now, if you'll excuse me, I'll just check on my patients and then we'll return to the house. We still need to figure out a way to get you back to wherever you're headed."

Jaxon's mouth opened to speak as the doctor moved away, but Reese put her hand on Jaxon's arm. "He's right. He has to stay. We have to let him help these children."

She could see he wanted to protest, but she also knew he couldn't condemn the people here to death any more than she could.

Jaxon and Reese watched while the doctor visited his patients. After the first few, his shoulders started to slump and his face paled. He began to shuffle instead of walk between the makeshift beds.

"You can see him taking their pain," she mused.

"But it's all wrong," Jaxon said, his eyes roaming the room. "That boy was dead, and yet he's not. And we're not likely to come back to see them again. Why isn't it like I saw?"

Reese searched his face and saw concern under his relief at the boy's survival. "Maybe if we hadn't arrived when we did, Special Forces would have taken Kentley and the child would have died. It's also possible we interrupted you during the premonition, and you might have gone on to see an alternate version like you did with our last encounter with Special Forces."

"Or maybe we were wrong about how it works."

Reese wanted to reassure him, but at the same time the upset she'd felt at the sketch he'd sent her, the one of them together, sealed her lips. Why had he kept it from her? She knew he was attracted to her. Saca, she was attracted to him, but he was her best friend, and they had to work together every day, and she didn't want anything to confuse that. Because what happened when the passion died, as it always did? Better to put the friendship first. He meant too much to risk.

Then why was she so angry? Was it that he'd had the premonition, or the fact that he hadn't told her?

"We're not wrong about anything," she forced herself to say. "It's all a part of the craziness we're feeling, that's all."

His gaze skidded away as the doctor reappeared. "Looks like everyone's okay," Kentley said. "We can go now."

Jaxon shifted the nyckelira case to his other side. "You said we're near the ocean, right? That one of the passageways leads there. Is the way safe to see?"

Reese knew he was asking not for himself but because of her. Once he'd asked her about the ocean view in her tiny office, and she'd told him about the best vacation she'd ever had at a C-lodge on a beach in Haven. Just sitting on the beach and hearing the waves battering at the shore had given her peace. The images were a reminder now of what they were fighting for, every bit as much as the water transfer station at Colony 6.

"Sure," the doctor said with a little smile. "They don't trap the fish anymore, and the ocean itself leaves little residue after this long. I wouldn't mind seeing it myself. Your friend is likely to need more time to heal anyway." He motioned for them to follow him.

Reese looked back at the dim room once more as they left. Most of the patients were sleeping now, and even the short man was lying with his son on the floor, his eyes shut. She wanted to remember it this way, instead of how it had been in the sketch.

Kentley led them through one long hallway and then another, some parts blocked with partial cave-ins but for the most part largely intact. "This must have been one of the finer buildings pre-Breakdown," he said. "It's actually a very good place to live, despite the problem with the water. It may be that Thane and Silas's group will join them here, once the threat of radiation subsides."

"Are you saying the patients can poison others?" Reese asked.

"No and yes. No because as long as safety measures are taken, nothing will pass to others." He stopped talking momentarily as they deviated around a slab of cement that cut through the high ceiling, revealing pinpoints of sky. "But because the exposure was internal, there is a possibility of contamination as their bodies shed the radiation. I'm giving them everything I can to help them recover. We wash them regularly, and we're careful with bodily wastes. But we are right to be concerned. Our children are particularly susceptible. But I think those who haven't already died will slowly recover and survive."

"How much further?" Jaxon asked. The smell of the ocean was closer now.

"Almost there," Kentley said. "I don't know if you've noticed, but we've been angling downward. At this point it levels out." His steps were faster than they had been when leaving the children, as if each pace gave him back his strength.

Reese hadn't really noticed the slope, but the hallway was wet now. Old paint peeled away from the cement walls and shell deposits clung to odd places. Turning a corner, they came upon it suddenly—a large room with an opening nine meters high through which she could see ocean and sky.

"It used to be covered in some kind of safety glass, which apparently didn't survive Breakdown," Kentley said. "I imagine it was a favorite pastime of whoever stayed here to come down when the tide was high and water covered the glass."

"Good thing it's low now." Jaxon peered out the opening.

Kentley laughed. "The passageway we came down, as well as several others, aren't passable during high tide."

Reese stepped forward, leaning out of the hole to see the ocean below. The beach was closer than she expected, only five or six meters down, and a thin strip of soft-looking sand lined the base of the cliff. She could almost taste the salt as the breeze blew back her hair. She was tempted to jump down and wet her feet, even knowing the danger of contamination this close to the South Desolation Zone. Instead, she watched the waves rolling in, and the steady rhythm brought the peace she remembered.

Jaxon sat down at the edge, dangling his feet over. He looked more rested than he had all day. "Look," he said. "Seagulls." Sure enough, two of the rare birds were on the shore scavenging. Another was dead on the sand. Reese wondered if it was because of the contaminated fish, or if the bird was a twisted version like the monster dog they'd seen.

"Doctor," she said, leaning against a relatively dry part of the wall. "My ability hasn't manifested since I've been with you."

He laughed. "Don't worry. It's still there. You're likely able to control it, though. In my experience, gifts manifest more often and are more difficult to control as the madness encroaches. But I've been draining that pressure for you—and it should help for a time."

Reese didn't really care to try to control anything right then. "What about you and the madness?"

He shrugged. "I don't feel it affecting me. Well, as long as I don't have too many patients at once. My ability seems inherently able to fix myself as well."

"How long can you help people like us?"

"It depends on the person." His gaze was knowing. "It's not a permanent fix, though, not by a long shot."

Reese sighed. "It couldn't be that easy, I guess."

After watching the water for a few minutes more, Kentley said, "If you don't mind, what is your ability?"

"I'll show you." Reese stepped closer to him and concentrated, but nothing came from Kentley's mind. For a moment panic swelled inside her. Maybe the doctor had lied. Maybe her ability was gone forever.

No, that was ridiculous. She took a deep breath to steady her thoughts.

"You don't have to show me if it's too stressful," Kentley said, recoiling from her slightly. "I was just curious."

She gave a self-deprecating snort. "I usually can't stop it. But this should give you an idea." She pulled her notebook from her bag and flipped to the page she'd drawn last night of the sick children. "I see images from people's minds. I call them sketches, mostly because after I see them I have to sketch them or I feel unsettled, and if I leave it too long or see too many, I lose it."

She didn't add that his presence had seemed to erase all need to record the sketches she'd seen since leaving the C-lodge that morning.

He studied the sketch, a deep furrow in his forehead. He had to notice the dead boy, but when he spoke, it wasn't about the child. "You're lucky you have the drawing outlet," he said. "It's the ones who can't ever get a release that the madness takes first."

People like Jaxon, she thought, glancing in his direction.

But what about Dani, Eagle, and the twins? Dani was in constant motion, Eagle was regularly translating his 3D through the Teev in the underground, and Lyssa and Lyra claimed their spirits physically traveled during their episodes. By contrast, Jaxon was held motionless by his visions.

Jaxon climbed to his feet, hefting the nyckelira case. "We'd better get back." To Kentley, he added, "We'll talk to El Cerebro and let him know what's going on here, but he's not one to take no lightly."

"You have orders to take me if I don't come willingly, don't you?"

"Yes. But instead, we'll report your answer."

"If he sends you back, I still won't go with you."

"I know."

As the men talked, Reese watched the two seagulls, now winging away in the incredibly blue sky. She waited for the birds to disappear before following the men.

They'd passed the wet corridors and Reese now felt the incline as they traversed the passageway. They had reached the slab of concrete and the partially caved-in roof when they heard the sounds. *Pop, pop, pop!* So far away that it sounded something from a child's game.

"What's that?" Kentley stopped walking and tilted his head.

"Gunfire!" Jaxon skirted the cement slab, bringing around the nyckelira case, opening it as he jogged forward.

Kentley stared. "You have an assault rifle in there?"

Jaxon gave him a flat grin. "I'm no musician, that's for sure."

Reese drew her pistol, shoved it at the doctor, and pulled out her assault rifle.

"Wait, what? Why are you giving me this?" Kentley demanded.

Reese turned to see him standing in the hallway, a confused expression on his face. "To defend yourself. We have no idea what's going on."

"I-I can't shoot anyone. I took an oath."

"Then you might have a choice to make. Hopefully it won't come to that." She turned and ran to catch up with Jaxon. Thoughts tumbled through her mind. Had Special Forces found these fringers or had some monster attacked?

Another burst of shots broke the silence, louder now as they neared the end of the hallway. Several isolated shots followed. Reese's lungs burned from her sprint. "Careful," she cautioned Jaxon. "We don't know what we're walking into."

He nodded and continued forward. As they reached the bend, they heard shuffling, and Jaxon threw himself against the wall. Reese did the same, bringing up her gun, ready to pick off any he didn't take.

"Hold!" Jaxon grunted as a man stumbled around the bend.

Reese eased her finger from the trigger as she identified Cooper, the tall fringer who had led them to the cave. He staggered toward them, his arm bandages drenched with blood. Why was he still bleeding?

He gasped as he saw them, taking a few more steps toward Reese, his face angling past her toward Kentley, who was still some distance down the hall.

"Help!" he called. "Help them. Please." He turned and fell into Reese, and she caught him, realizing the blood on his arms wasn't from his earlier wounds but welling from his stomach and chest.

She saw the enforcers in his mind. They were in the chamber where the sick children lay. In the image, a sketch now frozen inside her, she saw one man staring mockingly down into a pleading face . . . and firing.

"They killed them all," Cooper rasped. "They're dead, all dead. Your friends too. I'm sorry."

His body went completely limp, threatening to take Reese down with him to the floor, but Jaxon was already pulling him away. He lay the man on his back in the corridor, his unseeing eyes staring upward.

Kentley reached them. "What happened?" He placed his hand on Cooper's chest, closing his eyes as if mentally feeling for a heartbeat.

"Enforcers," Reese said, "They're inside." She struggled to maintain composure, though the sketch burned at her. "He said they're shooting everyone."

"Can you help him?" Jaxon asked Kentley.

The doctor shook his head. "He's gone." He put his hands over the man's eyes, pulling the lids shut.

"Is there any other way out?" Jaxon asked.

Kentley shook his head. "Not that we could get through.

Just the sea. But there is barely a strip of sand, and the tide's coming up. It's too dangerous. We might be able to hide."

Jaxon shook his head. "We'd better get out now while they're spread out and searching. Otherwise we'll get trapped." He looked at Reese. "You okay?"

She nodded. And she was. The horror still resonated inside her, and she felt the urge to draw, but the panic was gone. By contrast, the doctor was shaking. Reese put an arm through his and dragged him to his feet.

"Lead the way," she told Jaxon.

Jaxon hurried to the next bend, where he signaled that two enforcers in full battle gear, blues plus helmets, were coming their way. Jaxon and Reese retraced their steps and hid in another hallway until the men passed. They'd gone only a few meters when they found another bloodied victim—a woman this time, lying on her side in a fetal position.

Kentley didn't even check her pulse. "Gone," he whispered.

A shot whizzed past them, barely missing Reese, but Jaxon was already firing. He hit the enforcer in the chest, and the force of the shot in his body armor slammed him into the wall. Jaxon pounced on him, punching the bit of exposed face again and again until he lay still. Another enforcer skidded around a corner, and Reese blasted him with three shots. He fell and didn't get up, though his suit would probably save his life.

They were moving again, but Kentley was a dead weight. His shaking was worse now, and he began sobbing softly to himself. "We have to get him out of here," she said. "He's taking in too much emotion."

Jaxon leaned over Kentley and said, "Doctor, you need to focus. We're trying to get you out of here. Are we going the right way?"

Kentley's eyes fixated on him, as if trying to process the words. Finally he nodded. "Always to the right from here.

We're almost to the infirmary. After that, it's only a short hall before the exit."

They ran softly up the passageway for a good stretch. Then Jaxon skidded to a stop, holding up a fist. His eyes were glazed and unfocused, as if seeing something only he could see. One, two, three heartbeats passed until Reese wanted to scream with the inaction. Abruptly, Jaxon fired as an enforcer rounded the bend. He followed with a jab of his rifle into the man's face that sent him crashing to the floor. They hurried on.

Jaxon picked off two more enforcers in the same way as Reese struggled to pull the doctor along. She understood that somehow with the doctor's presence, Jaxon had gained a temporary control over his premonitions, perhaps dampening them until they were only useful glimpses that didn't incapacitate him.

The path back seemed to take far longer than Reese expected, but they finally stood outside the infirmary in the hallway leading to the entrance. "We have to save them," Kentley said, his words coming in short gasps.

With a grimace, Jaxon pushed open the infirmary door, and they stepped inside. Reese dropped the doctor's arm as he stumbled to the first bed, but one look had told Reese there were no survivors. Even the short fringer, the man who had stroked his son's face so lovingly, lay draped over his son as if trying to protect him. Fury built in Reese, and she pointed her gun at the door, almost willing the Special Forces leader to enter. She knew he'd made this call because local enforcers would have arrested and sent them to the colonies.

Jaxon grabbed the doctor, who had fallen to his knees clutching his head and moaning, and hauled him to his feet. "Let's go," he growled.

Kentley let himself be pushed toward the door. The short hallway leading to the entrance was still empty. As they reached the end of it, Reese noticed the doctor had stopped trembling and carried the pistol in his hand as if finally serious about using it.

Jaxon closed his eyes briefly, then raised two fingers. Reese nodded.

They rounded the bend together. Two enforcers stood guard before the metal door that was pulled halfway upward. One leaned over the bodies of two dead fringers, rifling through their pockets. Neither got off a shot before Reese and Jaxon peppered them with enough bullets to cut them down.

Kentley also fired, and Reese turned to see an enforcer staggering under the hit in the hallway behind them. She let off a burst from her assault rifle as he tried to fire back. He stumbled and fell. Shouts and the sound of running feet reached them as she and Jaxon grabbed Kentley and rushed to the metal door, ducking under it. The iTeevs of the men they shot would be registering their conditions, whether dead or unconscious, and reinforcements and detection drones would be on the way.

They ran as fast as they could drag Kentley through the rubble of the empty zone, and the farther away from the cave, the more he kept up. "Go right," he said as they reached a particularly large mass of twisted metal. "There's an opening under this that goes for several kilometers. Used to be a sky train rail. It'll confuse the drones."

They dived into the small hole, wiggling under the metal. Pounding feet ran by and Reese was sure she heard the buzz of one of the larger drones.

"This way," Kentley said.

The direction was pointless as forward was the only option. For some time, they had to crawl, dust clogging their throats and rocks digging into their hands and knees, but the way soon opened up and they were able to crouch over and run, making better time.

The trail came out suddenly in open space, where Kentley lifted a hand, asking them to stop. His face was flushed with physical effort, but he seemed to be stable emotionally now. "I need to warn Debs and the others at the house, in case someone at the cave told the enforcers about them." He began texting on his iTeev.

Reese's stomach clenched. "Cooper said our friends were dead," she remembered. "That he was sorry." She hadn't let herself dwell on that until now. How much had he told enforcers before they'd shot him?

Jaxon surveyed the rubble-strewn area, his rifle ready. "Are you sure your message won't be detected?"

"Drones will be able to pick up the emissions if they're nearby, but the message is encrypted. We have a relay that's piggybacked on the Teev. It doesn't allow voice calls, but we get texts through. After I'm finished, I'll turn it off."

Whatever Kentley was doing, it was taking too long. Reese felt exposed and anxious. She watched the sky for drones, though if enforcers used the smaller ones, any sound warning would come too late.

Color bled from the doctor's face. He sat down heavily, missing a boulder and sliding into the dirt. "No one is answering. They always answer. I think we're too late."

CHAPTER 14

Laughter pierced Eagle's awareness. *Clud!* he thought. His head was pounding, and his chest felt as if a huge rock compressed his lungs. Had he passed out in the empty zone when something fell on him?

No, he'd fallen on the stairs, but they'd carried him somewhere. He'd heard them talking.

The room gradually came into focus with the help of his special glasses, the ones he'd created to allow him to see as his vision decreased. He could "see" people in the room now, even with his eyes shut. The glasses translated everything they recorded and sent the information through the connection in his temples. Opening his eyes did help some, but he was so close to blind that it wasn't all that important, except his brain seemed to like his eyes open when the glasses were on.

With the numerous paintings and image receptors staring back at him as they had done in the hallway, he felt dizzy. Colors assaulted him, colors he knew were different from what others saw with their naked eyes. Some things simply glowed. His brain calculated how many of the images there were, how far apart, and the sizes of the frames. Every centimeter was diagrammed. He could even tell the exact weight if he correctly guessed the composition. But he had to signal the glasses with a few eye movements to block some of the infrared on the spectrum until his brain was fully functional and his senses could catch up.

"He's awake!" Nova moved toward him and knelt beside the couch where he lay. "How are you feeling?"

"Head hurts, and it feels like someone's been using me as a punching bag, but besides that, I'm fine."

"That good, huh? Well, you're supposed to drink lots of water." She reached for something out of view and came back with a plastic skin.

He took a gulp while lying down, only because he couldn't imagine moving. Water sloshed out of his mouth and dribbled down his face to the couch. He closed his eyes. He could still see the room in his mind and calculate each section.

"Is he going to die?" asked a child's voice, a little girl.

"No, silly," Nova said. "Go back and deal those cards. It's your turn." To Eagle, she added. "The doctor fixed your internal bleeding and gave you something to help you make more blood. I think that's where the water comes in. The more you drink, the better."

Eagle could feel Nova starting to move, but he put his hand on her shoulder without opening his eyes. "Wait. Help me sit up."

"Are you sure?"

Eagle nodded and then wished he hadn't. "Yes." He slowly opened his eyes and looked around the room. The assault was less now, as the habit of filtering out light and sound waves that didn't matter kicked in. Nova pulled him up none-too-gently, and he stifled a groan. He had to remind himself that she was only fourteen.

Now seated, his brain perfectly flipped the schematic it had drawn, so the original dizziness didn't recur. His brain also began dimming the brightness of the infrared, so the glasses didn't have to. No one understood how he could see so much with the dark glasses, and he'd given up trying to explain that they were simply a way to bypass his eyes to give his brain the information it would have ordinarily received. The glass lenses themselves didn't "fix" his eyes, as they did for people as they aged.

"I'm going back to play the game, okay?" Nova said. "Let me know if you need me."

Eagle traced her steps back to the table. Twelve steps for Nova, though it had been fifteen for the little girl, and five point four eight meters for both of them. Thane was there with a young boy, and they were playing some kind of game with cards that looked similar to cash credits. He calculated the size of the cards, noted their color as a dark purple that the children would translate as pure black, then took another deep gulp of the water. The pounding in his head was easing, and he did feel stronger than when they'd arrived. The internal bleeding must not have been too severe, or he would have collapsed sooner.

With his fingers, he tested his back ribs. He could feel bruising, but not the cutting pain he'd experienced before. He drank again.

The old woman, Debs, appeared in the doorway. Eagle recognized her more for her body measurements than for her face, as light from the sun and the holo emitters outside angled through the window, partially masking her features. By habit, he calculated the angle of light and how it would look a minute later.

"So, you're up," she said, stepping forward out of the direct light. "Would you like something to eat?"

Nausea choked Eagle's throat. "Thank you, but not now."

"You really should eat," Nova said from the table. "Her food is amazing."

Did the woman's wrinkled face soften? Eagle could see that it did. She liked Nova, at least, though the feelings didn't extend to him.

"I'll bring you something," Debs said, "and you can eat it when you do feel like it. You look like you could use a cup of brew too."

Eagle nodded agreement, and when she brought the tray, with cut apples, raspberries, broccoli twigs, pungent cheese, and soft bread, he suddenly was hungry. The brew was bitter, but he'd expected that, and downed it in two long gulps despite the heat. As he ate, Nova filled him in on finding the doctor and where he'd taken Jaxon and Reese.

"How long have they been gone?" he asked.

Nova frowned. "At least an hour. You think that's too long?"

"I don't know."

When Debs came in to collect the tray, nodding in satisfaction at his short work of it, he asked, "How long does it usually take to visit the place where my friends went?"

"The doctor is always gone several hours, but that's when he's treating patients. They should be back any minute." She set the nearly empty water skin on the tray. "I'll get you more to drink."

"Thank you."

She had barely returned with the skin when the front door opened and one of the men who had been guarding the fence hurtled into the house, passing the doorway in his haste before seeing them and backpedaling. He leapt more than walked into the room.

"Enforcers!" he said. "They're cutting down the gate. With something strong. We have only a few minutes. Maybe a bit more until they pass the holo emitters and find the house."

Debs gasped. "Where's Namon?"

"He's letting out the beast. That might give us more time."

Beast? Eagle thought the way he said it was ominous.

"I'm going to hold them off with Namon until you're out," the fringer added.

"No, come with us," Debs pleaded.

For an answer, he shook his head and rushed from the room. Debs stared after him for a few seconds, her face one of pure agony. Then it was gone. She clapped her hands. "Children! Grab the packs. Run to the back gate and wait for me there. This is not a drill." Her gaze fell on Eagle. "You're welcome to come, but you'll have to keep up and carry your own things."

Nova was already grabbing one of the bags. Eagle pulled his rifle from the other one, slinging the strap over his shoulder, and started to pick up the bag. Nova thrust hers at Thane and grabbed the straps of the second bag from Eagle.

"I got it." She sounded determined enough that he let her do it.

The children led the way down the hall, and Eagle turned to see Debs pouring something from a large green container. He went to help her and the stench of accelerant filled his nostrils.

"Just go!" The woman shouted at him. "Keep your gun ready. The beast will be attracted by their noise, but it might attack the kids."

Attack the kids? What kind of beast was it?

He hurried after the children, down the hall, through a tiny kitchen, and out the back of the house. From there they cut right, running along a path near a garden that was verdant with greens even in mid-October. Beyond that was a squat greenhouse bordered by apple trees.

"Where's Debs?" the little boy shouted when they reached the gate to the inner wire fence that surrounded the house and yard. Thane was already opening it.

"There!" Nova shouted.

Debs ran toward them, fire blossoming in the windows of the house behind them. The old woman didn't so much as look at the garden or the greenhouse but ran with her eyes fixed on the children. An oversized pack bounced against her back, until Eagle wondered if it might knock her over.

Eagle heard an explosion beyond the front of the house, and then shouts. The enforcers were through the metal outer gate, or would be in a few seconds.

"Go, go, go!" Debs shouted as she ran toward them. "You know the way."

Thane ran across the open space, curving further right. Eagle wondered if he was heading toward the hole they'd entered because if so, they would probably be seen by the enforcers.

All thoughts fled as an inhuman roar sliced through mortal shouts. The sound made Eagle's skin crawl and his blood pound in his ears. *What in Breakdown is that?*

Thane darted around a bush and began pushing on what looked like a patch in the outer metal wall. Nova surged forward to help. "It won't open!" her voice was panicked.

Debs caught up with them and threw herself at the door scraping and pulling. "It's fused shut. I can't open it."

By Eagle's calculations, they were thirty meters from the other opening but only a few meters from where he'd heard the explosions. The shouts they heard were coming closer.

Eagle tried his hand at moving the top piece of metal, but he had no success either.

"We'll have to go through the front." Debs voice was defeated.

"No," he said, reaching for his bag and pulling it from Nova's shoulder. "All of you, step back behind the bush. Now!"

It took him three seconds longer than he'd hoped to find the least powerful of his plastic explosives but less time to set it. Given the size and the composition, he needed exactly two centimeters to loosen the door. Any more than that might twist the metal, making it impossible to open. He slapped in a fuse and stepped back, blowing it.

The loud *boom!* was muffled by another ferocious, other-worldly scream coming from the front of the compound.

Eagle jumped forward and pushed back the metal patch, revealing an opening as tall as his waist. "Hurry!" he urged.

The four children scrambled through, and Debs threw herself after them, her pack catching briefly on the door.

A heart-wrenching scream, this time human, made Eagle pause. He turned his head in time to see an enormous *thing* bearing down on a comparatively tiny enforcer. It was some-thing from a nightmare—a hairy thing with a twisted bearlike face and claws that were as long as Eagle's fingers. His brain told him it had the mass of an elephant and automatically calculated the result of its impact on the human. The enforcer's assault rifle barked out an angry-sounding *rat-tat-tat*. The bullets seemed to have no effect as the creature slammed into the man, sending him flying backwards with the impact. Its maw opened, crunching down, and blood spurted over the ground.

Sickened, Eagle turned away and pushed through the hole, pulling the metal cover back into place. The enforcers would find it soon enough, but hopefully not before they got away. Maybe the two guards would be able to get out as well, though he wasn't hopeful after seeing the beast. Even if they got free of the enforcers, who could defeat that?

Thane and Nova hurried heedlessly through the rubble of the empty zone, and Eagle had to force himself to sprint. "Stop!" he called as loudly as he dared. "Stop!"

Glancing behind her, Nova saw his face and pulled Thane to a standstill.

Behind them, Debs also stopped, whirling around to challenge him. "We have to hurry!" Her voice came with effort and her face was so flushed it would be comical in another setting. He suspected the old woman wouldn't be able to take much more.

"No," he said. "They'll have drones out. If they get close enough, they'll detect our heat signatures. And Santoni is so small, I'm betting they've pulled in reinforcements from other towns, which means more drones. Our only chance is to hide until I figure out how to get us safely to the tunnels."

Nova paled and scanned the sky, as if expecting to see one of the drones poised above them.

Eagle could see the full electromagnet spectrum, but that was only useful if he had direct sight of a person or object, which would be too late for a drone warning. Otherwise the lights bending and distorting around objects simply confused the issue. A piece of metal warmed by the sun might seem to emit the same light as an enforcer. Or an enforcer using his suit's cooling mechanism might emit less light than a pile of rubble.

He wished he could send up one of his own drones, but without activating the fringer T-link addition on his special glasses, he couldn't do that. Activating it was out of the question until it was reprogrammed so that Dani's unit couldn't track his. But maybe there was another way . . .

"Nova, give me your iTeev." As an illegal rip-off, it already had protocols in place to keep from being noticed by the main Teev feed, and a little on-the-spot adjustment might make it compatible with his drone. Too bad he'd have to do it manually instead of through the neural connection to his special glasses, which her iTeev didn't have. The iTeev's emissions would still be detected by a drone, but with their own drone up, they could power her device down if one got too close.

Eagle dug in his bag. "I might be able to send up our own little spy."

"Their drones will sense another drone," Nova said.

"Not this one." From a small container, he dumped out a tiny object twice the size of a mosquito. "It doesn't radiate more heat or electrical emissions than an average real-life bug, so the drones should overlook it." He hoped. He tapped on Nova's iTeev screen, working around the protocols to connect the bug. "It can't send back images, only short number texts, but it'll pick up electrical radiation within a thirty-meter radius. Well, it has to be fairly strong emissions, but all the enforcers have iTeevs, so it'll register them, as well as the spy drones."

"This is taking too long," Debs complained. "They'll be on us soon."

Eagle didn't look her way, though the light she was emitting increased with her anxiety. "It might be the only chance we have."

"That's not much," she said bitterly.

"No," he agreed, "but it's more than we had." He finished the connection and the bug arose from his hand and flew off. "Good, it's working. When we receive numbers from it, I'll be able to plot a course around them." Already his mind showed him the way to the tunnels Thane had taken them through, like a 3D map only he could see. They might have to deviate to avoid drones or enforcers, but they would be able to make it—and within thirty minutes.

"Nice," Thane said. "Too bad you can't equip it with a mini gun or explosives."

Eagle smiled at the teen's eagerness. "It's tiny, so weight's an issue."

Nova reached for the iTeev. "I'll tell you when the numbers come in."

When, not if. He was glad she understood their danger. "I'll lead," he said. "Thane and Nova. Take up the rear. Have your guns ready."

As the teens moved back, the little girl slumped to the ground and began crying. "I want the doctor," she sobbed. "I hurt my foot."

Eagle leaned over and picked her up with one arm. His ribs ached, but she really wasn't very heavy. He let his rifle dangle on his shoulder, replacing it with a pistol instead. "Let's go."

He took the most direct course, which didn't include revisiting the place where Thane had them stop to drink water. The farther they moved away from the house, the more hope he had.

But what about Reese and Jaxon? He had no way of warning them without the T-links. Should he risk contacting? If they didn't have their T-links on, he would be exposing his group for nothing.

No T-links, he decided. *Not yet.* If the doctor was with Reese and Jaxon, he'd probably take them to the tunnels anyway, or to the hidden lair Eagle suspected was located in the tunnels. Of course, if the doctor wasn't still with Reese and Jaxon, that might be a problem. Anger at Dani flared inside him. She'd always been one to strike out on her own, even back in the Coop. Her impulsiveness had brought down as much trouble on them as children as it had saved them.

Nova ran up to him. "Numbers," she said, holding her folded iTeev screen up for him to see. His enhanced glasses easily picked out the numbers and translated them to his brain. "Its height says it has to be a drone. Let's turn by that green slab and angle along our same direction for a while. That should keep us away from its path."

Nova wrinkled her nose. "Green slab? They're all gray or blackish."

"I mean that slab there." He pointed ten meters to his left and started forward.

While people generally understood his inborn ability to judge distance, velocity, depth, volume, and weight with a glance, seeing electromagnetic emissions was harder to explain, so he usually didn't.

By the time they reached the slab, his body ached from the effort of walking and carrying the child, but he'd endured worse his last few years in the Coop. Life outside the colony had made him weak.

"More numbers," Nova said, still at his side.

Three, in fact. Two near the ground that must be enforcers and another in the air that would be a drone.

"No deviating around both of those," he said. "We need a place to hide."

She looked around carefully before pointing to a skeletal building. Eagle didn't like the huge gaps in the concrete, but maybe inside they'd find something thick enough to mask their body heat from the drone.

Seconds later they were hunched together inside the building under a slab of concrete that leaned against one of the remaining sections of the wall. Eagle calculated the rate of approach and then powered down Nova's iTeev until the drone flew by and was far enough away so it couldn't detect the emissions. After turning it back on, he verified that the other two numbers were changing regularly, showing that the enforcers, or at least their iTeevs, were still approaching at a constant speed.

"They'll pass far enough from the building that they won't

detect us," he said, "But wait here just in case. I'll check it out." To Debs, he added, "Keep the kids quiet."

She nodded. The old woman was nicer to him now that he'd helped them avoid the drones, but he didn't trust her exactly. Non-enforcers often let panic drive them in stressful situations, and he didn't want to lose control now.

He left the building and headed toward a large pile of concrete he'd noted as they entered. He crawled up it, slowly, avoiding loose rubble that might give him away. Once near the top, he rested, closing his eyes briefly and fighting the desire to sleep. A piece of metal jutted uncomfortably into his stomach, and that helped.

Voices came to him faintly, and he opened his eyes. In that instant, his brain put together pieces of strew rubble, reforming it, and showed him a 3D image of what the area might have looked like pre-Breakdown. Before the bombs, before the killing, before the CORE. Half of it was from estimation of the rubble, the other half from his own inventiveness. This city would have been one of the greats. How many people had died here?

For a moment he felt doubt. The CORE Elite's highest goal was to create a world in which another Breakdown could never happen. Fighting against them . . . it was either insane or the bravest thing he'd ever done.

The enforcers came into view. Regular ones, not Special Forces, a man and a woman. But they weren't alone. Namon, the guard Eagle and his crew had first seen peer over the metal fence was in front of them, his hands cuffed behind his back. His face was bloodied and beaten, and his clothes full of dirt. As Eagle watched, he stumbled to his knees.

He said something Eagle couldn't make out, but the male enforcer gave him a drink from a skin of water. Then the woman jabbed her rifle into him. "Go on," she ordered. "Or you'll end up like your friend."

Calculating their direction, Eagle surmised they were heading to the tunnels in a path roughly parallel to the one Eagle had calculated. At least for the time being. Namon was either planning to sell out his fringer buddies, or he was trying to find the courage to die. Eagle didn't care to guess which.

He waited until they started walking again to slip down from his perch. He hurried as fast as he dared back to the ruined building. "Bad news," he said. "The two enforcers have your friend Namon."

Debs perked up. "Is he okay?"

Eagle shrugged. "For now."

"What can we do?" Urgency made her voice sharp.

In light of her expression when she'd made the choice to leave him behind, Eagle wasn't surprised. "We have to stop them, one way or another. He's leading them to the tunnels."

Thane frowned. "How do you know that?"

"Because their direction is parallel to ours and I was taking us back to the tunnels."

Thane gaped at him. "I thought you were just avoiding the drones. You didn't say anything about the tunnels." He paused before rushing on, "You were blindfolded, so how do you know where the tunnels even are?"

Nova sighed in exasperation. "He's from Colony 6, remember? Like the doctor. Eagle's brain is weird, that's all."

Fear rose in Thane's eyes, which Eagle thought might be for the best. "So that's why you didn't fight the blindfolds," Thane muttered.

"No, we didn't fight because we wanted you to help us." Nova put a hand on his arm and the boy settled. Eagle would have teased them about it in another setting, but now he grabbed his bag and pulled out his enforcer uniform.

"What did you mean, when you said we have to stop them one way or the other?" Debs asked.

"Just that. We can't let Namon take them to the tunnels." He pulled out Reese's uniform as well from the bag Thane had been carrying. It wouldn't fit Nova, but Thane could make it work. Jaxon's would dwarf the boy. He tossed the uniform to Thane. "Put this on."

Thane looked down at the uniform, taking a moment to realize what it was. "You guys stole enforcer uniforms?" His voice held both envy and awe.

Eagle gave Nova a warning stare. "Something like that," he said, digging inside the bag again for battle helmets.

Putting on his own uniform was more painful than Eagle expected, and by the time he'd finished, Thane was ready. The top looked odd where no breasts filled it out, but a carefully situated rifle strap and the strap of an emptied bag made it work.

"Nova," he said, "give me your iTeev. And you make sure everyone stays put." He finished his preparations by filling his pockets with his favorite explosives.

Debs jumped up to grab his hand. "Please, bring my son back to me."

Her son, he thought with a mental groan. That would make what he'd have to do worse if things went sideways.

"I'll try," he said. He glanced at Nova, whose somber face showed understanding. He hated that she had to understand such things at all.

"Come on," he told Thane. "Keep up."

CHAPTER 15

Eagle jogged through the rubble, skirting around obstacles. Thane followed willingly, a happy expression on his face. Eagle hoped the boy could still smile after it was over.

"Where are we going?" Thane asked.

"Around to confront them from the other side. Shouldn't be too hard. They can't make Namon move fast after beating him so much, and they apparently don't have a shuttle."

"The shuttles are useless in this area," Thane said. "Too much rubble they'd have to move. They use them in other areas of the empty zones, though. They visit those areas mostly for target practice."

"You've watched them."

"Yeah. Some."

Eagle's chest hurt, his back was on fire, and he pretty much wanted to die. *Later,* he promised himself.

"That should be enough," he said after ten minutes. "But we're not far ahead, and I still need to do a few things. Come on." He cut into the path he expected the enforcers to come along in three point four minutes.

"Wait here," he told Thane. He jogged down the path where the enforcers would approach and planted a charge inside a tangled mass of metal and concrete on the right side. Farther down, across the narrow passageway, he planted another one. Finally, he planted two more on his way back to Thane.

"Stay here with your back to the path like you're walking. When they show up, they'll see the uniforms and think we're friendly. We'll let them catch up to us. By the time they see our faces and think to check for CivIDs, it'll be too late."

"What if they shoot us in the back?"

Eagle winced internally. "It'll hurt, but you'll live."

Turning, Eagle sprinted ahead to the nearest ruined building. The structure was already so damaged that it wouldn't take much to collapse the rest, but the calculations couldn't be off by much or it would fail. If he targeted the weakest areas, it could definitely work. He ran a mental 3D simulation three times to be sure.

Next, he hurried to a pile of rubble with an overhanging slab and did the same thing. This was his backup. Not as good a location as the building.

He was almost back to Thane when the enforcers came into view. They paused and waved. He waved back. He'd chosen this spot specifically near a bend in the path through the debris so the enforcers would be able to see their uniforms without iTeev magnification. Otherwise, they might check his CivID and find it and his face masked by his skin tag.

"It's time," he said to Thane. "Keep quiet, and when things start exploding, stay in the middle of the path away from my charges, even if I run elsewhere. Got it?"

Thane nodded and rotated slightly to glance out of the corner of his eyes at the oncoming enforcer pair. "Are you going to tell me when to shoot?"

"No shooting, but if you have to, make sure you do it in their face or neck. Otherwise their uniforms and helmets will protect them."

Thane nodded firmly, but the fear was back in his eyes. *I shouldn't have brought him,* Eagle thought. But searching the empty zone alone wasn't exactly protocol, and Thane's presence gave him legitimacy. Besides, he needed Namon's cooperation, and he might not remember Eagle from their brief meeting in his civilian clothes.

The enforcers were upon them now, the woman occasionally prodding their prisoner to encourage him to move faster. Recognition flared briefly in Namon's eyes when he saw Thane, but he lowered his gaze almost instantly. Was it only Eagle's imagination that he looked like his mother? Certainly their light emissions were nothing alike. Namon's emissions were brighter, those of a man terrified. Probably not a man about to make the ultimate sacrifice, which meant he was taking his captors to the tunnels.

"Hey, you guys find anything?" asked the male enforcer.

"Nothing, but it looks like you guys have," Eagle said.

The woman nodded. "You one of the guys from Riverton?"

Had they really made it that easy? But he couldn't agree in case they noticed the Armarillo Enforcer Division patch on his shoulder. "Sort of," he said. "My team was nearby conducting some training when the call came. We're glad to help out." Eagle made a show of studying Namon. "We were just debating if we should head back to the shuttles. Is that where you're taking this fringer?"

"Not yet," the woman said. "He knows something, and he's taking us there. We keep having to do a little convincing, but he'll spill it in the end. We showed him what would happen to him if he didn't."

"This punk let a monster loose," the man added. "One of those things changed by the radiation from the desolation zone. It killed two of our guys. Ripped their heads clean off." He kicked out at the fringer's leg. "Whore wrangling, fringer clud has no feelings for his own kind. Then again, we're not his kind, are we? What do you bet, he's also been changed by the radiation? Probably has twelve toes or an extra stomach. He's certainly not human."

The woman laughed. "Maybe he eats rocks. We could shove a few down his throat and see how they go down." She swept up a small piece of splintered concrete, pelting Namon in the head with it. Blood welled from a new cut the rock made on his cheek.

Were the enforcers he worked with like this? Eagle didn't think they were. But then, most of his work memories were from back east where life was so regimented that enforcers there dealt primarily with jukeheads or disgruntled kids studying for their certificates.

"Well, I'm thinking we'd better just get wherever he's taking you," Eagle said. "Mind if we tag along? You might need backup, I don't think there's anything else out here."

"Sure, but we get the credit for catching him."

"Of course."

The woman's eyes drifted to Thane. "They make 'em younger and younger."

"Yeah," Eagle said. "Training sucks."

The woman jabbed her rifle into Namon's upper arm. "Get going. Every time you stop, you're going to swallow a rock. Just in case stopping means you're hungry."

"Wait." Eagle held up a hand and lifted his eyes to the path beyond them. "Did you hear something?"

They turned to stare, shaking their heads. Eagle set off the first explosion with the detonator in his pocket.

"That's something big," the male enforcer said, his face crunching with concern.

"Lucky shot," the woman retorted with a sneer. "Fringers are probably randomly launching some of their stolen weapons in the hope they won't be caught with them. I bet they haven't seen us."

Eagle set off the second charge while they were still staring down the path, followed closely by the third. "We'd better take cover," he said, pointing at the ruined building. "That's our best bet. We checked it out earlier, and it's solid. Has an escape route out the back too. Let's go!"

He started running, but slowly to make sure they kept up. He situated himself between them and took Namon's arm as the woman pulled him forward. It would be easier to let the enforcers go into the building with Namon, but Eagle couldn't forget his mother's pleas. He had to try to save the man. He pulled back on Namon's arm, slowing him considerably.

When they were near the building, he set off the fourth distraction charge. This one was larger and close enough to spatter debris over them. As it did, Eagle pushed out his rifle and tripped Namon, who fell. Eagle threw himself on top of the man. "Stay down," he gritted near Namon's ear.

The woman enforcer had let go of Namon as he fell, but as Eagle faked a struggle to his feet, she pointed her rifle at him. "Get up fringer, or I'll put a bullet through you."

Eagle made a show of checking his pulse. "He's alive but unconscious. I'll carry him. Get to the building!" This was the weak point of his plan. If the woman didn't follow her partner, who was already ducking inside the building, he'd have to shoot her and set off the charge before her companion could return fire.

Without waiting for a reply, he bent to lift Namon, his body protesting at the effort. Eagle knew he wouldn't be able to carry him for more than a few steps, if at all. The woman hesitated, then moved to help him. Cursing under his breath, Eagle dumped Namon's full weight on her, bringing up his rifle to slam into her face. She went down without a fight, crumpling under Namon's weight. The fringer rolled away and dived behind a twisted freezer as bullets sprayed from the ruined building.

Eagle jumped away, tucking and rolling as he hit the ground. He reached inside his pocket to set off the building's charge. *Boom!* It came down just as planned, and the shooting abruptly ceased.

"You okay?" Eagle asked Namon, who nodded. As miraculous as it seemed, they were both uninjured.

They staggered to their feet. Eagle freed Namon from his cuffs and replaced them on the woman. "We should kill her," Namon growled as Eagle removed her iTeev, careful not to leave fingerprints, and smashed it with a rock.

"I know, but we're not going to." With his helmet and glasses on, it was unlikely she could identify him. Eagle jerked his head to the path. "Come on. We've got to get back to your mother and the kids."

Namon blinked at him, his shoulders straightening. "They're safe?"

"For now. Let's go find Thane."

They found Thane near where they'd left him, but to Eagle's horror, he was sprawled on the ground. Blood gushed from the side of his neck, seeping into the dry earth beneath him.

"No!" He hurried to the boy.

Eagle clapped a hand over the bloody mess, trying to stem the flow. Red gore continued dripping between his fingers. Desperately, he searched for something to tie around the wound. But Namon was already taking off his shirt, folding it inside out, so they could press the cleaner portion against Thane's neck.

Thane's eyes fluttered. "I-I stayed put," he said, his body jerking.

"You did great." Eagle was furious at himself that he hadn't acted fast enough to stop the male enforcer from firing. Furious that he'd traded Namon's life for Thane's.

Eagle's emergency medical training didn't give him enough experience to know if the wound would be fatal, even if they could get the bleeding stopped. They had to try. "Let's get him to cover. I have a med kit. I'll go get it."

They carried Thane awkwardly to the rubble pile where Eagle had set the final unused charge. The slab of cement atop the refuse was angled enough that it might possibly keep them safe from passing drones.

Eagle ripped off his sweat-soaked helmet, tossing it to the ground. "Don't take your hand off the wound," he told Namon. "Constant pressure. No matter what."

Without waiting for a response, Eagle turned and ran. He continued until his sides ached and he felt like falling down and dying. Then he pushed himself harder. He wasted three precious minutes hiding when a drone's path led it close enough to detect him. Then he was off again.

He arrived at the place where he'd left the others, taking no care for stealth. Nova lowered the gun in her hand when she identified him. "Where's Thane?" she asked, digging into him with anxious eyes.

"He's been hurt. Hurry. We need the med kit."

"And my son?" asked Debs hopefully.

"He's with Thane." Did his bitterness show in the words?

Eagle turned from the gladness in her face and went through their equipment, discarding everything except the medical bag, the weapons, and Jaxon's enforcer uniform, which might leave clues about their identity. He could replace his tech, eventually, but right now speed was more important. Without the second bag that was still with Thane, they couldn't carry it all anyway.

He shoved the bag at Nova and picked up the little girl. "Let's go."

The journey back to Thane seemed to take forever, but at least they didn't run into any drones. When the rubble pile was in view, Eagle and Nova sprinted ahead, leaving Debs to catch up with the two children. Nova threw herself to the ground as Eagle grabbed the medical supplies from the bag.

"Thane, Thane!" Nova said urgently. "Please wake up."

His eyes opened slowly, and he smiled, his eyes unfocused. "It doesn't hurt anymore."

Eagle didn't think that was a good thing. He took out a container of skin sealant. If the wound wasn't too bad, it might slow the blood flow enough to save his life. "We need to turn him on his side and then take away the cloth," he told Namon. "Nova, you turn his head. Namon will rotate his body. On the count of three. One, two, three."

They turned Thane, and Eagle dumped half the container of skin sealant over the wound, discouraged at the amount of blood already soaking the dirt beneath him. This wasn't going to work. He sprinkled more over the wound. The blood flow slowed. By the time the bleeding stopped, he'd used all the powder.

They rolled him once more onto his back, and his eyes opened again. "I'm glad I got to kiss you," he said to Nova.

Tears ran down her face. "You're not going to die, you idiot."

He grinned. "I'm still glad. Anyway, I'm not afraid. I've already lived seventeen years longer than the CORE wanted, and I didn't have to die in a colony like my mom."

"You don't know that she's dead." Nova clutched at his hands, as if her touch could stop the inevitable.

"Yes, I do."

Had he hidden the truth from Nova, or was he just guessing? Eagle had no way of knowing.

Thane let out a sigh and closed his eyes. He didn't take another breath.

Eagle grabbed a red hypo stim and slammed it into Thane's chest. Nothing. He put his hands on his chest and started pumping. "Get the oxygen on him," he barked.

Nova fumbled, but Debs took the folded mask from her and put it over Thane's mouth. Eagle kept pumping. At last Debs put her hand on Eagle's arm. "He's gone."

Nova stared down at Thane's face for a long moment. She was still holding one of his hands, but she dropped it and stepped away, her tears drying on her face. "Leave him," she said harshly. "Other enforcers will be here soon. The drones will detect the heat from the explosions and the shooting, if they haven't already."

Eagle shook his head. "We're taking him with us. It's less than ten minutes to the tunnels."

"He's dead." Her voice was cold. "It's a waste of energy. We could still get caught."

"Yes, but we'll do it anyway. For his father."

Not only for Silas, but also for Eagle. Because at that moment, everything they'd been fighting for came into focus. He had to stop real monsters from hurting innocent people like Thane. He would never doubt their cause again.

Using twisted metal and Jaxon's enforcer uniform, he made a simple stretcher to carry Thane's body. He and Namon picked it up, while Nova, her face without expression, picked up the little girl with the hurt ankle.

Mere moments later, they passed the stark line that marked the border of the woods and the rubble. *They had been so close,* Eagle thought. For all the good it had done the boy.

They were nearly at the tunnels when he heard movement in the trees ahead of them. He motioned for everyone to stop as he set down his end of the stretcher.

"What?" Nova mouthed as they crouched behind the brush. The little girl whimpered, burying her face in Nova's neck. Eagle knew exactly how she felt.

He shrugged and whispered, "Stay here while I check it out."

CHAPTER 16

Jaxon stared down at the burnt-out house. Nothing could have survived there. He could almost smell the soot, though that would be impossible at this distance. He handed Dr. Kentley back his iTeev, glad the magnification feature didn't require being connected to the Teev feed.

"That's actually a good sign," Kentley said as they climbed down the remains of what had once been a sky train station. "Debs is supposed to do that when they leave. They didn't leave me a message, but that means they got out." He powered down the unit again to keep it from being detected by any passing drones. Body heat was easier to hide in the wreckage than an iTeev signal, even one not connected to the feed.

"No telling how far they got," Reese said.

A furrow creased Kentley's brow. "They'd go to the tunnels." For a moment, he seemed despondent, and Reese touched his arm.

"Are the two children yours?" she asked gently. Her eyes

were troubled, and Jaxon guessed she'd received a sketch from the doctor.

Kentley shook his head and then nodded. "Not biological, but they are mine. One was the result of a hidden pregnancy. The woman's implant didn't work, and she wanted a child so much, she didn't abort. The other was the child of a friend."

He didn't need to tell them the friend was dead. "So they're mine now," he said. "Though the boy's mother does visit him periodically. The fringers told me about the house, and so I took them there, and stayed myself to help. There have been other women there besides Debs, but she's the only one now."

"You know the way to the tunnels?" Jaxon asked.

"Yes. But they'll have drones out. We'll have to stay close to the sky train line, or what's left of it. We can use its cover most of the way, and by then we'll probably be far enough that they won't detect us. We should hurry."

They followed Kentley, who moved like a man in a dream— or a nightmare, rather. His face was haunted, his movements robotic. Jaxon figured he was in shock.

A flash of a premonition made Jaxon stumble. It was the nyckelira case again, but this time with Dani opening the secret compartment and drawing out weapons. This was followed by another vision of two enforcers waiting for them in a place very like the one they were walking in now. He pushed at the images in his mind, trying to see more.

The next thing he knew, Reese was gently slapping his face. Rocks poked painfully into his back. He opened his eyes to find Reese and the doctor poised over him.

"What did you see?" Reese asked.

The vision of Dani was irrelevant at the moment, but the other could be important. "Two enforcers near the end of this line. I-I think."

Reese glanced at the doctor. "We'll have to choose another path. His visions always come true."

"They didn't this time," Jaxon said. "I didn't see everyone dying. Just the boy, and not like this." The helplessness he'd often felt with his gift had become an impossible burden. Before, he'd always trusted that there was nothing he could do to change his visions, but today something had changed.

"The children were still there," Reese insisted. "And so are those enforcers." The way she said it told him she'd seen the image from his mind.

He pushed himself to a seated position. "Maybe. I can't tell if we're going to be safe."

"You were out fifteen minutes," she said. "You should have been able to see more alternates, if there were any. The enforcers will be there. So we have to choose another way."

She had more confidence in his ability than he did at the moment.

His eyes lifted to the doctor, who shook his head. "I don't know, but all that tension I felt earlier in you is back. I'm sorry. Some of that is my fault. I don't always have a choice about when or who I take pain or emotion from, and when it stops . . . I must be tired." He paused and looked down at the ground as he added, "You need to understand that eventually nothing I do will help the madness. Until I find a cure. But without a sample, that's not happening soon. I'm sorry."

"What about my vision of those sick children?" Jaxon asked. "Normally my premonitions come true down to the last detail. At least it always has before today. Any idea, medically speaking, why that would change?"

Kentley raised his gaze and heaved a sigh. "Maybe every-thing changes with the choices we make. Or maybe there are always alternatives, but most choices lead to the one you see. Or maybe your ability is growing." He hesitated a moment before adding, "It's also possible it's a symptom of your madness."

Great. Nothing like giving a man hope.

"I'm not sure if I should say this," Kentley went on, "but it might be important to you or anyone else looking for a cure. It's about the effect the hallucinogen juke has on people with abilities."

"Juke?" Jaxon couldn't imagine what effect the illegal recreational drug could possibly have on their abilities. Certainly nothing good.

"Yes. You know juke's everywhere, even in the colonies." Kentley gave a snort of disgust. "Maybe especially in the colonies where they can least afford it—anything to find relief from what they endure. When it all began—the madness, I mean— those who used the drug soon discovered that it intensified or increased the occurrence of their abilities."

"Are you telling me that if I took a hit of juke I could cause myself to see a sketch?" Reese asked, "even when nothing was coming to me?"

The doctor nodded. "But ultimately, it speeds up the development of the ability, which also speeds up onset of the madness. Jukeheads were the first to go mad, and then because the madness has no cure, more and more turned to juke for relief."

"Which made them more crazy," Jaxon said.

Kentley nodded. "Afraid so. I tried making an antidote from the juke, thinking it had to be related, but it was missing something. I still believe they're related. Maybe derivatives of the same original concoction."

Jaxon wondered how many people from Colony 6 had been killed by Special Forces before the Elite realized their science project was the cause of the craziness.

Reese offered him a hand up. "Let's go. We can't stay here. We'll continue on the sky train line for a while and then veer off and make a run for it."

"I'm going with you," Kentley said.

Jaxon blinked at him. "Of course you are. We'll get you safely to the tunnels."

"I mean to Amarillo City."

Jaxon didn't hide his surprise. "What about your patients? I thought you had others."

Kentley nodded and was quiet a moment before adding, "Back there, in the middle of all that shooting and death, I just wanted out. I didn't care about looking for survivors or trying to save anyone." A sob shook his throat. "I hate myself for that. I hate that I didn't even think about my two wards, that I thought only about my own life until we escaped. With El Cerebro in the Underground, it's safe, right?"

"As safe as anywhere these days." Jaxon steadied himself on a twisted metal beam. Something was battering at his mind, the pressure of a vision, but he had to stay on his feet.

"Ultimately, everything I did for those people means nothing," Kentley went on. "Same thing for all the others I've helped. They still have no CivIDs, no rights, no freedom. I have to help you stop this. For them—and for my kids."

Jaxon should have been pleased that the doctor had given into their argument of the many versus the one, but he wasn't pleased. He was angry that it was necessary. He couldn't bear looking at Reese because he knew she'd feel the same.

Kentley stared down at his useless iTeev. "I would like to try to find Debs and the children first, see if they're alive, but after I'll go with you to the underground."

"First let's get out of this place." Reese started forward and the men filed along behind her.

They followed the ruined sky train rails nearly to the end

and then veered left. The sun beat down on them more now that they were out in the open. Jaxon's shakiness had eased, but he felt on edge. Dani would soon be in New York at HED, and Eagle and Nova were still somewhere out there. Time wasn't in their favor.

"Look, the trees!" Reese said, redirecting his attention to the line of scraggly trees that bordered the empty zone. "We're almost there."

Before they could move forward, several explosions reached their ears, one after the other, then a pause and another blast. Definitely in the empty zone, and fairly close. Kentley cringed momentarily before sprinting for the trees. Jaxon and Reese ran after him. The distance was longer than Jaxon expected, and he felt exposed, as if at any moment a drone would find them. When they finally did reach the sparse shade of the trees, he felt immediately safer, though he knew there was no safety until they'd entered the tunnels.

"This way." The doctor waved them to a path on the right before hurrying away. Maybe he was anxious to see if his children had made it inside and were waiting, but Jaxon suspected he was driven mostly by fear. Jaxon couldn't blame him.

"Should we check out the explosion?" Reese asked.

"Let's look in the tunnels first."

She nodded and they continued onward. When they reached the top of the entrance, the doctor was already coming back up the sloping ground, his eyes reddened. "They're not inside." He glanced fearfully around them. "What do we do now?"

Jaxon's brain felt steeped in ice. He should be able to consider their next move, but all at once he was riveted to the spot. Almost as if his body was trying to show him a premonition but was simply too tired to follow through. But somehow he knew he couldn't leave this place, just as he'd known in the cave when enforcers were coming around each bend. Only then, the glimpses he'd seen had been clear and certain. Now everything was hazy. He felt weak and sick.

Maybe it was the madness.

"We should probably wait inside," Reese began.

"No," Jaxon said. "I feel . . . we have to stay here."

"We can't." Kentley shook his head vigorously. "They're either inside already, deeper in the tunnels. Or they're gone." He turned to go, but Reese clamped a hand on his shoulder.

"We can wait for a few minutes," she said.

More than those few minutes slid by as Jaxon began to doubt himself. He had orders to save the doctor. He could do that now, if he could make himself move. His feet refused to obey.

"Take him to the tunnels," he told Reese finally. "You can't wait any longer."

"If you think I'm leaving you, you're . . ." She trailed off, her gaze going to a point beyond Jaxon.

Her surprise freed his limbs. He turned and there was Eagle, emerging from the trees, striding like a man with a purpose, a strong man who wouldn't yield. Blood ran down one cheek, and the rest of his face and hair were caked with dirt and sweat. He carried one end of a stretcher. With him was a wild-haired Nova, the two children, Debs, and another man Jaxon vaguely recognized as a guard at the house. All of them looked stunned and beaten, especially the guard, who struggled to carry the other end of the stretcher. Jaxon suspected he only moved forward because Eagle pulled him.

Kentley let out a coarse cry, dropped his bag, and leapt at Nova, taking the little girl from her. The little boy ran to meet him, and Kentley fell to his knees as he encircled the children, crushing them to his chest. His sobs came roughly.

While Reese took up a guard position, Jaxon went to Eagle. "Glad to see you. We were worried when we saw the house had been burnt out."

"We almost didn't make it." His eyes were hidden as usual by his black glasses, but his voice hinted at unspeakable horrors like the ones that haunted Jaxon after his time in the cave.

Jaxon's gaze fell to the stretcher where Thane sprawled unmoving, too pale to be simply sleeping. "No," Jaxon said. A weight descended on him that threatened to crush his chest. "Is he . . .?"

Without waiting for Eagle's response, Jaxon whirled and grabbed Kentley by the back of his shirt, hauling him to his feet, despite the protests of the children. "Take a look at Thane." He shoved the doctor toward the stretcher.

"It's too late," Eagle said, as he and the fringer guard gently lowered Thane to the ground. "We gave him a stim and oxygen, but he wouldn't revive."

Jaxon glanced at Nova, whose face tightened as she looked away. That told him everything.

"We'd better get inside the tunnels," Reese said. "We're too exposed out here."

Ignoring her, Kentley knelt next to Thane, the children clutching at his waist, and put his hand on Thane's chest. "How long's he been gone?"

"Fourteen minutes and thirty-two seconds," Eagle said in a dead-sounding monotone.

"Then it might not be too late." With one hand on Thane, the doctor motioned for his bag. "I need the red hypo. Then the green. Hurry."

Jaxon dived for the bag, riffling through the contents. He shoved a hypo at the doctor, who stabbed it into Thane's heart.

"What are you doing?" Nova demanded.

"I'm getting his heart beating. Sometimes they'll wake."

"There'll be too much damage," Nova said. "He'll be a vegetable like after medical enhancement. Or worse."

Thane's body jerked, and he started to breathe. Someone gasped—or maybe they all did.

"I don't have time to explain," the doctor said, "but tissue death occurs after the circulation is restored, not before, and I sometimes can fix it because I see where to put the medication. If you gave him stim, that adds time, even if it doesn't seem to work."

He was touching Thane's head now, the other hand doing something to the green hypo. An impossibly thin needle popped out of the end.

He pressed it against the right side of Thane's skull, and the hypo began whirring, digging itself into the bone. When it stopped, Kentley pressed in the medication.

Everyone stood in fascination as Kentley drilled ten more micro holes in Thane's head, injecting medication and stopping them with a silicone plug. "To prevent infection," he said.

When he finished, they all stared down at Thane. He was breathing and his heart beat out a steady rhythm, but he didn't open his eyes.

"You were too late," Nova said bitterly. Jaxon understood that losing hope was worse than never having it.

"Maybe." The doctor leaned back. "He may just be in a temporary coma." He hesitated before adding, "Whatever his condition . . . if he doesn't awake, the fringers here need his organs. They don't have the luxury of hospitals or mechanical implants."

Nova launched herself at Kentley. "You half-witted pus licker!" she shouted. "You, saucebag, warthog-faced fringer!"

Jaxon grabbed her an instant before her hooked fingers reached the doctor. He held her tightly, and she struggled against him, her arms flailing. "Calm down, Nova," he whispered in her ear. "You have to calm down."

"I don't have to do anything except hurt this stinking

lumper!" She pushed at Jaxon, trying to get away. "He made Thane into a . . . thing! That's worse than death. Thane wouldn't have wanted it." She struggled furiously against Jaxon's arms, but he held on.

He became aware of Reese urging the others on to the tunnels without them. "Jaxon and I'll catch up to you with Nova in a bit," she promised.

Kentley scooped up both his children and led the way. Eagle and Namon followed with Thane on the stretcher, and Debs cast a pitying glance at Nova as she hurried after them. Jaxon held the girl's rigid figure until she went limp and started sobbing. He spat out curly hair that had lodged in his mouth.

Reese moved closer then, her hand going to Nova's arm. "I'm sorry. I really am. It's a terrible thing that happened, but we really need you right now. We have to get into the tunnels and contact your uncle. We can still help Dani. But they have a big jump on us, and she'll be in New York by morning. We can't stop now. We need her and her friends in Newcali to fix the CORE."

Nova went utterly still, so still Jaxon couldn't even feel her breathing. Then she pulled herself away from him without looking at either of them and hurried down to the tunnel entrance.

Reese surveyed the area with a sigh. Her hands were shaking, and Jaxon knew she'd received a sketch from Nova. That meant whatever effect the doctor had on her was also wearing off.

"Even with what happened to the boy, we were lucky," she said.

"I know." But losing a child meant it wasn't a win of any kind. One more nightmare to add to the others plaguing them.

They met the others inside the tunnel, where they debated what to do. Debs and Namon refused to take them to their main hideout, and after what had happened, Jaxon didn't blame them.

"Just take us to another entrance," Jaxon said. "One far enough away from here that it won't be suspect if we suddenly appear."

Debs and Namon agreed, but before they arrived at their destination, two fringers appeared and relieved Eagle and Namon of their burden. Jaxon had no idea how they'd known where to find them, but he didn't ask.

"Just get him there and keep him warm," Kentley told them. "Tell Ennah what I did. She'll know what to do for him. I'll come and visit when I can."

Namon hugged his mother. Then with a hard stare at the doctor, he disappeared with the fringers.

Debs continued on, her shoulders slightly hunched now. When they reached their destination, everyone stood by the exit while Jaxon emerged far enough to get a signal to contact Brogan on Nova's iTeev.

A response in the form of coordinates came back quickly. "Can you get us here? I told him we're in the tunnels, so I think it's another entrance." Jaxon showed Eagle the screen.

Eagle nodded. "We might have to take a few odd turns, or backtrack at dead ends, but we can find it."

"Okay then," Debs said. "Good luck."

"What?" Dr. Kentley's head swung toward her, the front part of his hair hanging into his eyes. "You have to come with us. It's not safe here."

"Come with us, Debs," added the little boy. "We need you. Who will take care of us?"

The girl simply stared at her with wide, pleading eyes.

Tears rolled down Debs weathered cheeks, but in the end, she shook her head. "My place is with my son. I know he's grown, but Namon still needs me." With a kiss to each child, she hurried away and didn't look back.

Jaxon watched her fade into the darkness. She'd probably raised these kids every bit as much as the doctor had, but losing her home and leaving her son was apparently more than she was willing to endure even for the love of these two young ones. His hatred of the CORE grew.

"We'll be okay," Kentley whispered through the children's quiet sobs.

Jaxon was going to make sure it was one promise he kept.

CHAPTER 17

Reese felt more like herself after a sonic cleansing and changing into a fresh enforcer uniform. She'd drawn all the sketches she'd seen over the day, even those she didn't feel compelled to put on paper, presumably because of Kentley's influence. She drew the sketches mostly to record anything that might turn out to be important but also because she was still feeling a bit jumpy. She theorized that the doctor's ability might only temporarily lessen her urge to draw the sketches instead of removing it completely.

She took her seat in the C-lodge's main room with Jaxon, Eagle, and the twins, Lyssa and Lyra. Evan Hammer, Brogan, and Kentley talked quietly near a bedroom door, where Kentley's children were sleeping. Nova had commandeered one of the other rooms, and Reese hoped she was also asleep. She hadn't spoken a word since Thane's strange revival.

After Nova's communication about Dani, Brogan had started immediately for Santoni with the twins and Hammer. As Captain Brogan, he'd offered official assistance to the local enforcer division, which allowed him to comb the streets near the woods in the hopes of providing his team an escape from the city. Brogan himself had met them at the coordinates he'd sent and brought them by shuttle to this C-lodge in nearby Riverton where the others waited. Kentley and the children were traveling under new false CivIDs, but the rest of them were now using their own identities. Reese hoped that meant they were out of immediate danger. Kentley still didn't know that Brogan was El Cerebro, but he understood the captain was on their side.

Lyssa handed Reese a hot readymeal, and Eagle extended a bag of pretzels one of the twins had brought for him. He was still pale and moved slowly but was obviously recovering from his ordeal in the empty zone, a fact he loudly credited to his favorite snack. Reese was glad someone could joke because it was the only thing easing the tense, unhappy atmosphere.

Brogan said something to Kentley, who nodded and disappeared into the room with his children. Then he and Hammer joined the rest on the couches.

"You've done a good job in very hard circumstances," Brogan began. "I know it wasn't easy, but somehow you managed to complete your mission and get out safely. Or most of you, anyway." He paused a moment. "Thank you for taking care of Nova."

"She helped us too," Reese said for all of them. "She brought the supplies, and without her iTeev, we would have had to risk turning on Dani's T-links again to contact you."

"I'm glad you didn't. They were tracking the connection within an hour of the confrontation with Special Forces—after they repaired the damage Dani did to her unit. But we can wipe the connection and reboot with another code, so we'll be able to use them again, if we need to."

"To go after Dani, you mean," Jaxon said.

Brogan held up a hand. "We'll get to that in a minute. First, you might be interested to know that Dr. Kentley has disappeared from the database."

"Maybe they thought they killed him in the Empty Zone," Reese suggested.

"Or maybe they realize we've got him." Brogan sat back in his chair, crossing his legs and steepling his fingers over his broad chest. "They would take samples from everyone they killed." He paused and added, "You should also know that Special Forces came to get the men you arrested at the fountain."

Jaxon snorted. "That's good for us. We don't have time to deal with crazies like that, even if he was right in everything he was saying."

"True." Brogan uncrossed his legs and leaned forward abruptly. "But it concerns me that they were so quick in taking our prisoners. That means they have Special Forces in or near Amarillo City. They were at our division before I could question any of the prisoners."

"What do you think it means?" Eagle asked slowly.

Brogan's frown made him look menacing. "I'm not sure, but I'm hoping it doesn't mean they don't trust us. Or that they're going to become more active in Dallastar. I'm only telling you so that you're aware our division is being monitored."

"We also know Special Forces has been clearing people out of the empty zones in Estlantic," Jaxon said. "Maybe they're working their way west."

"If it comes to it, we'll leave the underground and fight!" A yearning for vengeance rankled in the young voice. They turned to see Nova standing at the edge of the room.

Brogan shook his head and rose to his feet. "I know we've made progress, but we're not ready for that yet. We don't have enough weapons, and we certainly don't have enough people. We need to find out if anyone among the Elite will back us."

"We don't need those pus bags," Nova said. "Newcali will help. I know they will."

Brogan walked over to her, putting his arm around her. "We'll talk later, I promise. Can you go lie down?" His tone was firm, and everyone knew the girl had no choice, despite the gentle phrasing. She turned without another word and walked away.

Nova had been angry before, but now there was an added fatality to her actions. Reese missed her stomping and her protests. She worried about this quieter, angrier little girl.

"I thought we were going to try to resolve this without evoking a war," Jaxon said, when Brogan returned to his seat. "We don't want to hurt innocent people."

"That would be the preferred method," Brogan agreed, "but we may need to prepare for more. There may be no way except another Breakdown."

Silence met his comment. Reese felt they were on a sky train, heading for a break in the line with no way to bail out. The CORE had been created to prevent another Breakdown, and Brogan's words went against everything they'd ever been taught.

"But—" Jaxon began.

Brogan overrode the protest with a near growl. "I will *never* accept that some people are disposable. People like those children who died in the empty zone today, or the three hundred thousand in the colonies. If any of you are not willing to go the distance, you need to let me know now."

He waited. They all waited.

But Reese was all in. Even if she had a true choice, even if she didn't know Brogan would kill them in order to maintain the secrecy of the underground, she wouldn't leave.

Neither would the others.

"What's the plan for Dani?" she asked. "They already have

most of the day on us. There's no way we could beat them to HED, even if her fringers lent us one of their hovers."

Hammer gave them a wry grin from his seat next to Lyra. This evening the large man's long black hair was loose instead of in its customary ponytail, reminding Reese of an ancient movie she'd seen on the history feed. "Believe me, we thought of asking for a hover, but it would be useless anyway. We've lost a lot of pre-Breakdown tech, but Estlantic has heavy drone patrol along most of their inhabited borders. There are only a few places we'd be able to approach through the empty zones, and none of them are near your final destination."

"That means you'll have to go by sky train," Brogan said. "Hammer has given you all a cover story for why you will be in New York. Reese, Jaxon, and Eagle will be attending a memorial of a Special Forces team supervisor they all worked with or knew during the past ten years. It will be held late tomorrow afternoon at HED."

"How did you manage that?" Eagle asked. "You didn't kill someone, did you?" His tone was only half joking.

Hammer looked amused. "This enforcer was killed three days ago, chasing fringers from the empty zones."

"They fought back?" Reese asked. Because from what she'd seen of the enforcers today, they didn't give the rebels any chance to fight back.

"No, a building collapsed on him," Hammer said. "But Jaxon is the only one who ever worked with him, back before the man transferred to Special Forces. We found the invite in Jaxon's enforcer messages this morning after Dani was taken, so that's where I got the idea. I know, I know," he held up a hand, "you hate anyone reading your mail, but that's what you signed on for. Besides, your enforcer files are never really private, you know that. With the hacking codes Dani provided, we adjusted a few work dates to make him overlap divisions with Eagle and had the system send an invite. Then we adjusted online posts about his dating Reese six years ago and had her request a belated invite from the family."

Brogan nodded. "So you're all expected, or at least invited. In addition, Lyssa will see the dispatch manager at HED about a possible job opening. Cover story is that she's not thrilled with life in Dallastar and is seeking other options. This is probably the most important of our plans because she can request a tour. The manager may be a little confused about the scheduling, but we put her on his calendar tomorrow at noon."

"So we're assuming Dani will be held at HED?" Reese asked.

"We're reasonably certain," Hammer said. "We did have positive identification that her brother was seen there, days after he was captured, though we didn't know where they're keeping him. But while you were gone, Lyssa set up some commands on the HED's TAD-Alert, and we think we've identified a potential location within HED."

Lyssa picked up the story. "I know we think of our TAD-Alert as being separate from the TADs in the other divisions, but they're all connected ultimately to each other and HED, who controls them all. The commands I put in yesterday resemble the mirroring program Hammer used when we were tracing the Teev clean spots in our search for the missing scientists."

Which had led them to Dani and the Newcali fringers. Reese leaned forward eagerly. "So instead of searching for something that's there, you recorded the locations of where it was not."

Lyssa gave a self-satisfied grin. "Exactly. I told it we needed to search for humans who didn't have implanted CivIDs. The cameras have always recorded people who weren't carrying cards, reporting that back to the TADs, but now that implantation is mandatory here, whoever programmed the TADs added all kinds of updates and alerts." She gave another smirk before adding, "They just didn't expect me to use those at HED. The TAD came back with a list of everywhere it had checked. And of course there were places it didn't check, even though I told it to check everywhere."

"Which means if it didn't check certain places, it had primary orders not to check or give out information on those locations," Jaxon said. "But that could be dozens of places. I visited HED when I was thinking about joining Special Forces. It's a maze."

"Guess again," Lyssa said. "I got back only two places it didn't report on, one on the fourth floor and one on the fifth, which are the top two stories at HED. Cross-referencing that with the office assignments, we know that one of those belong to the Controller himself. Not even his Special Forces captain's office was off-limits to that search, though I'd tried other searches that it did block."

Hammer reached to help himself to some of Eagle's pretzels. "This could change, of course. The information was correct as of this morning, but I'll double check before you do anything. Keep in mind if they discover our search, it'll be over before it starts."

"Look, I don't mean to put a damper on this discovery," Eagle said. "But they've had plenty of time to implant Dani's brother, haven't they? Would they risk not implanting him in case someone did attempt a rescue?"

Brogan frowned. "There is that, but since the CORE was established, there has never been a Fringer attack in New York. Ever. They won't be expecting any rescue attempt." He paused and added thoughtfully, "While we're on the subject of Dani's brother, we don't know if he has any kind of ability. Dani's been closed-mouthed on that. But he does have information on Newcali, and while Dani says he'd die before disclosing anything, we don't know that's true."

"He might not do it to save himself," Jaxon added, "but what about saving Dani? We already know she's willing to risk her life to save him."

Silence fell over the room as they all digested this idea.

"So what's the plan?" Jaxon asked finally. "The prisoners aren't going to be in the Controller's personal office, so obviously they'd be in the second location, if they're still at HED, but getting in and out of there, even knowing where Dani might be, is next to impossible."

The hope that had been building in Reese plummeted. He was right. HED would be near impregnable to any but enforcers, and they didn't have the manpower to go in with guns blazing. Not without a lot more planning.

Brogan exchanged a glance with Hammer and then sighed. "Exactly. The intel is good because we know the location of something they're hiding onsite, and it's probably where Dani will be, but we don't know much more than that. There are too many variables. I think for now, you need to do reconnaissance and see if anything stands out." He nodded at Jaxon. "Maybe once you're closer, you'll have a premonition, or Reese"—his gaze shifted to her—"will see an important sketch. Or Lyssa might learn something on her tour of HED."

"And if we find a way?" Reese asked.

A smile tugged at one corner of Brogan's mouth. "If the opportunity presents itself, get in, get Dani and her brother, and run like Breakdown."

Reese felt a little surge of anger that Dani had allowed herself to be caught, risking even more than was at risk before. Did love make them all crazy? Apparently, because they were risking exposure going to HED, especially without an end plan.

"I have connections in the New York underground," Brogan continued. "They can lend a hand with transportation if we come up with a plan. Hammer will make sure the T-links can't be traced by Dani's unit in case you need them. While he's working on that, you can load up on new CivID cards, ammo, and other supplies we brought, then Hammer will take you all to the sky train."

Hammer took that as his cue to add, "There's an express sleeper train coming in within the hour, and it'll be faster than any shuttle. I need maybe thirty minutes for the T-links. Can you be ready by then?"

Reese nodded with the others as Brogan said, "Don't worry. This time Nova will not be following you."

Eagle arose, taller than Brogan and far leaner. "Captain," he said, his voice low. "That kid we told you about? Just wanted you to know that Nova seemed close to him. She's been different since it happened."

"I'll talk to her," Brogan said.

Reese, Jaxon, and Eagle followed Hammer into the C-lodge's third bedroom where bags of supplies littered the floor and bed. Reese had already checked her guns and ammunition, but she was happy to add another uniform and civilian clothes to her bag. And a full med kit.

Jaxon also found clothes to pack, but Eagle stood in the middle of the room, as if seeing nothing. "I let him die," he said into the silence. There was no trace of humor now.

Reese shook her head. "You couldn't have known. And you saved Namon and the others. You did your job."

Eagle picked up a box of rounds and didn't reply.

Jaxon moved toward him, his mouth open to speak, but he'd taken only two steps when he stopped, clutching his head.

"Jaxon?" Reese rushed to him. "What is it?" No response.

Eagle dropped his bag. "Is it a premonition?"

"Has to be." She steadied Jaxon so he wouldn't fall. "Jaxon, you need to snap out of it. Jaxon?"

"Maybe he'll see something about Dani," Eagle said.

She supposed he might. "Help me get him onto the bed. Saca, it keeps getting worse and worse."

Eagle cleared a few bags and together they wrested Jaxon to the bed. "Well, he didn't fall to the ground," Eagle said. "That's good, right?"

"No, but he's checking out of reality altogether. He doesn't seem to hear me. I'm—" She broke off as a sketch appeared in her mind, the image waving instantly to life. "Wait. I see a sketch of Dani with your nyckelira case. She's wearing some kind of white body suit. The case is sitting on a desk, and she's opened the secret compartment and has removed that big temper laser you took from the men at the train station in Amarillo City." In the still image, Dani's face was turned, as if looking at someone who was with her.

Reese caught Eagle's stare. "Did Dani know about the hidden compartment in the case?" she asked. "She wasn't there this morning when you gave it to Jaxon."

"I showed it to her last week. She helped me with the security sequence. I ended up changing the original code, but she was a lot of help." Eagle looked thoughtful, and a hint of eagerness entered his voice. "If we could get the case to her, Dani could break herself out. She's fast enough and strong enough. I'd change the code back to the one we were experimenting with so she'd be able to get inside. We'd only need to be nearby, ready to run interference and hide her once they mount a search."

For the first time since Dani's capture, Reese thought they might all have a chance to walk out of HED alive. "We'd have to find out where that room in Jaxon's vision is. I'll draw it for us."

"What about him?" Eagle motioned to Jaxon, whose hands had fallen from his head and who now looked peaceful as if he were simply sleeping.

"You start loading the stuff. I'll wake him up."

"Good idea." Hefting her bag and his own, Eagle started for the open door.

"And Eagle?" she said.

He paused. "Yeah?"

"Don't tell the others about Jaxon, okay? Not yet."

"But you said he's getting worse."

"I know. But he can handle it." She hoped. Jaxon hadn't checked out anytime they'd really needed him. Yet.

"So am I," Eagle added. "Getting worse, that is. It's taking more time for me to filter and organize everything I see. Especially close to the desolation zones where there are so many more stray emissions."

"Why didn't you say anything?"

His smile reminded her of the boy with the thick-glasses back in the Coop—engaging, knowing, yet somehow innocent. "I'm telling you now. I've been taking off my glasses at night because at least that way I can't see the colors or the dimensions of things, which helps. But we're going to need a cure soon."

"We need a sample of whatever they gave us," she said. "Maybe we can find one at HED."

Eagle shrugged, his right shoulder lifting slightly before the left as it always had. "That's not likely. We don't even know who's behind this yet. Or if it's all of them. We have no idea where a sample might be. Or even what the drug is called."

Reese looked down at her hands as something niggled at her memory. Something about her great-aunt. She'd had this same feeling before, once when they had visited Colony 6, but there had been other times, usually at her aunt's. It was as if something lingered just out of reach. Something important. What did it mean?

Then all at once she knew.

"By the CORE," she said, sinking to the bed, feeling her heart starting to pound erratically. "What kind of sample?"

"Water would be the best, naturally, since that was the delivery system, but maybe we could test other things. Clothes, furniture. Even if the drug was only put into our water, people would have excreted it." He sighed. "But finding a strong enough concentration after ten years isn't likely."

"Maybe not so unlikely." She stood again and paced to the door. "I took a bag when I left the Coop. My extra pair of clothes, my drawing pads, my dad's empty sauce skins that I kept under my bed filled with water. When I ran from the Coop, I took it all with me. Whatever's left is still in my aunt's attic."

"You think there might be water?" Excitement spilled from his voice, and for the millionth time, Reese wished she could see his eyes.

She shook her head. "That I can't say. I found a lake and at one point I took the sky train, and it had plenty of water, but I don't know what I arrived with. I do remember that my aunt put all my clothes in the bag and put it away. She didn't think any of it was proper for me to wear. I'm assuming even if she kept the skins, she might have dumped out the water."

Eagle's shoulder slumped just a little. "There could be some residue on the clothes."

"She could have washed them." Reese sighed, discouragement overtaking her again. "I'm sorry. I shouldn't have started thinking out loud. It's probably nothing we can use."

"It's still worth a try. You're the only one who has anything from that time." He sounded sad now. He'd become an orphan like the rest of their crew shortly after he'd left Colony

6, and he rarely mentioned his family. She didn't know if they'd been killed or had died from exposure in one of the colony's manufacturing plants, but she understood that he regretted leaving them.

"Maybe you can tell Brogan while I take care of Jaxon," she said. She didn't like the intimacy of anyone going through her childhood treasures, whatever they were, but if there was any chance to help Jaxon and the others, she had to let Brogan try.

"Will do." With a nod, he left the room, shutting the door behind him.

Reese turned back to Jaxon. "Wake up," she said.

He didn't move. In the empty zone, he'd passed out for fifteen minutes, and they really didn't have that much time now. He looked peaceful though, almost happy. She wished she could let him stay that way.

"Jaxon!" She tried slapping his face gently. When that didn't work, she shook his shoulders.

She'd barely let him go when an image leapt into her mind. The two of them were in bed together, their mouths locked in such a passionate kiss that she felt the heat and movement, though the sketch was motionless in her mind, vivid and clear, as if it had happened only minutes ago. Her pulse raced and all the sensual thoughts she'd ever had about Jaxon threatened to break through the barriers she'd created.

She slapped him harder. "Wake up!"

His hand shot out and grabbed her. Then he was pulling her toward him. "Reese," he murmured. His eyes were open, but was he seeing her?

He tugged at her, and she fell over him, feeling his strong arms wrap around her body. His lips came closer, stopping just short of touching hers. Tension sizzled between them until she felt that if she didn't kiss him, the ache that had appeared inside her would grow and grow until it ate her completely.

He'd seen them together in a vision, which meant it was going to happen. Why should she fight it when deep down she knew this was what she wanted? She'd loved him as a boy and loved him more as a man. Loved him so much that losing him would be the end of her.

Her body was afire with want and need. They didn't have time for this, and yet what better time when they were headed into uncertainty? They'd both been through a lot today, and a few minutes wouldn't hurt.

"I love you, Reese," Jaxon whispered against her lips. He rolled, pulling her with him until he was on top of her. He kissed her nose, her cheeks, and tasted her neck with his tongue. Reese arched against him. Her hand ran down his back along the tight fit of his uniform.

Finally, he brought his mouth to hers in a slow, sensual kiss that made her close her eyes. This was exactly how she'd felt at their first kiss over six weeks ago, and she'd imagined repeating it ever since. Her hands went up around his neck, pulling him closer.

Satisfaction spread through her as their kiss deepened. His lips moved against hers as if he knew exactly what made her want him more. Every centimeter of her skin was alive with his closeness. The moment seemed to last forever. It was just the two of them alone, as it always should have been.

All too soon voices in the next room reached them, and she pulled away as duty kicked in. She released him and pushed at his chest. "We have to get to the sky train," she murmured. "We'll talk about this later."

He froze on top of her, and she opened her eyes to see something akin to horror on his face. "What did you say?" he asked.

"I said we have to go. The others are waiting."

He rolled off her, jumping to his feet by the bed, staring down at her uncertainly. "This isn't a premonition," he said.

Understanding dawned on Reese. He'd come out of his reverie, only to find her there, and he'd thought it was another vision. He wasn't really kissing her, but a dream woman.

"No," she snapped, standing and pushing past him. "It's not."

He touched her shoulder. "But you . . . you didn't want . . ."

"You said it was adrenaline the last time you kissed me." She turned to face him. "You said it was because I'm beautiful."

"You looked so afraid. I didn't want to scare you off."

"Well, that didn't mean there wasn't a chance." A chance that at some point she could believe that loving him wouldn't mean losing him.

He smiled without mirth. "You've been with Alex. That's a pretty strong message."

She stepped toward him, jabbing an aggressive finger at his chest with each point she made. "We're friends. We work together. We eat together. We do pretty much everything together. You should have told me about the premonitions." The ones about them, she meant, but she could tell he understood.

His head shook back and forth. "You're seeing Alex."

"That makes no difference. Not if you saw the future. If we're going to be together, why would I waste time being with Alex?"

Hurt spread over his face. "If I told you about it, it would take away your choices. I don't want you to be with me because I saw it. I want you to be with me because you feel the same way about me as I do about you."

With those words that delicious tension was back, enticing her body toward him. She resisted only because she was still mad at him.

"I figured if you wanted anything more between us," he added, "you wouldn't be wasting time with Alex."

Was he that dense? She *loved* him. That had never been the

problem. The problem was they had barely been reunited, and she'd pretty much screwed up any relationship she'd ever had, or her ability messed it up, and she needed his friendship more than she needed a lover. But if she'd had any idea that she could have both, and have it work long term, she might have made a different choice.

"And now it doesn't really matter," Jaxon continued. "Because it's only one timeline. Like Kentley said, all roads may not lead where we think. And who's to say how much of my vision is only because I want it so bad?"

His voice broke on the last few words, ripping her heart into shreds. "Kentley doesn't know what we know. You can't listen to him. One alternate scene with the children in the cave doesn't mean you mistrust all your premonitions."

Jaxon's blue eyes seemed to grow even more intense, their stare searing her. "This morning during the gunfire, I told Eagle to target the Special Forces shuttle. Then I had a premonition. I saw Dani in front of the shuttle and when it exploded, she was ripped apart. I told Eagle not to fire."

"That's a good thing. You saved her."

"But it means that vision of us isn't certain, no matter what I thought. Telling you would have only forced you to make the choice to be with me."

"No," she said. "*Not* telling me took away that choice altogether. We're never going to be normal, Jaxon. You should know that by now."

His chin jutted out stubbornly, but was that hope in his eyes? Or rejection? Reese knew him so well, but for once she couldn't be sure. She wanted to throw off the anger that had settled on her and step into his arms, but stubbornness immobilized her feet.

A knock came on the door, and a second later Eagle stuck his head inside. "We're heading out," he said. "Even on the night train, we won't make it to New York before ten, and Lyssa has her meeting two hours later."

Reese exchanged a glance with Jaxon, and this time she understood his expression. They were soldiers first and whatever was between them would have to wait.

"Later then," she said.

He nodded and followed her out to the waiting shuttle.

CHAPTER 18

Dani was wide awake as Special Forces marched her through the deserted corridors of the Headquarters Enforcer Division. Exhaustion leaked from them, and she had to stifle a feeling of superiority. It wouldn't do to under-estimate anyone here.

Would they put her near Tauri? Back in Dallastar it seemed reasonable they would take her to the same place, but now she worried. How many cells did they have for people like them? Both of them were fringers, both of them were missing from the public database, both of them had an ability. Except the enforcers shouldn't know about Tauri's gift yet. If they did, he might be dead already.

Someone likely knew about their relationship, even if they hadn't shared it with the enforcers who'd brought her here. She anticipated that it would be used against them. But she trusted in her ability and Tauri's related one. However less sustainable, it was deadly—if she could get him to use it.

Not for the first time, she pondered that she should have

been gifted with his ability. She'd gladly suffer the consequences if it meant she could use it in the upcoming fight. Tauri didn't feel the same. Still atoning for actions he hadn't been responsible for, he wanted to pretend his ability didn't exist.

They weren't heading to the underground level where the prison cells for "regular" people were located, cells she knew were full of jukeheads or saucebags that would likely face reconditioning, or students who needed to be put back in their place before they grew up to become a real problem. Only occasionally would a more serious violator be captured. Like a man trying to create an alternate to the Teev, or a pregnant woman whose birth control implant didn't work. The former would face permanent employment for the CORE, and the latter, if she was lucky, might be permitted to give birth for one of the Elites. The babies from accidental pregnancies were never permitted to remain with the birth parents. Not ever. Only those with a birth order could have and raise a child. Besides, too many of the children born by accident had genetic problems that would require termination. At least that was what everyone was told.

They went up four levels, which surprised Dani. Maybe they realized she'd have slightly more difficulty escaping from the upper floors. But if it meant she'd be reunited with Tauri, she didn't care. Her hands itched to break free of the shackles—and this place. It felt oppressive. She forced herself to take a deep, steadying breath. The panic faded into confidence and strength. It would work out. Besides, her crew would be coming for her, Jaxon and the others. But they were only her backup, and she didn't plan to need them.

The guards left the elevator and marched her down a wide hallway to a set of double doors. Enforcer Gedet pushed a call button and the door emitted a soft whir as it opened. Inside, the enforcers indicated that she should approach a wide desk where two more enforcers sat in front of a huge holo screen. Her eyes riveted on it. In the main image, doors lined a long white corridor, a least a dozen of them, illuminated by dim lights at regular intervals. The holo looked as real as if she could walk down it herself. Below the main image were two smaller feeds of individual prisoners.

Only two, she thought, not sure if she should be relieved or appalled that of so many who had disappeared only these few were saved. Or maybe only these two had refused to cooperate. The lights in the rooms were dark, and she couldn't tell by the faint outline of the people in the narrow beds if one of them was Tauri.

"Arm," said one of the enforcers at the desk, a large woman of indeterminate age. Her skin was darker than most, but still three shades lighter than Dani's. When Gedet grabbed her arms and extended them over the desk, the woman rolled her eyes. "Remove the cuffs."

"Not until she goes into her cell."

She stared at him flatly. "I can't put this on with the cuff, and she can't change and shower either."

"What, you scared I'm going to hurt you?" Dani sent a mocking smile at the man.

"Shut up," Gedet snarled at her. But reluctantly, he unlocked the shackles. All three male enforcers took a step back and pointed their assault rifles at Dani.

The woman put a thick strip of what looked like pliable metal under Dani's left wrist, curling it up and fastening the ends, one on top of the other. Dani flexed her muscles to make sure it didn't go on too tight. "That's your ID," the enforcer told Dani. "Since you don't have an implant." She smiled. "Yet."

Dani didn't react. Would her skin tag mask that ID as well if she reactivated it? She'd have to experiment later. So far these idiots hadn't found it on her neck. If it didn't mask the wristband ID, she'd have to try to break it, and there was a limit to her strength. At least the band was on her left arm and not her right, which would be the stronger of the two after her wound healed.

A signal chimed and the male enforcer behind the desk brought up a holo screen in front of him and pressed something. The door to the hallway opened and a man with a medical bag strode into the room.

"Couldn't you bring her to my office?"

"Apparently not," said the woman enforcer.

Dani stood quietly as the doctor looked at her wound. "This looks like it's already healing," the doctor said after cleaning it. "Nothing more I can do but give you an injection of antibiotic and a patch of RealSkin."

"No injection," Dani said. Who knew what would really be in it? "Use a topical and the RealSkin."

The doctor regarded her for a moment, amusement on his face. "I don't typically inject anything dangerous into my patients."

"I think you do anything the Controller tells you to," Dani retorted.

The doctor looked suddenly uncomfortable. He hurried with the RealSkin, topping it with a bandage that was more to hide the wound from sight than to protect it.

"Come with me," the woman said when the doctor finished. She waved at Dani's escorts. "You too, if she's that dangerous."

The female enforcer walked to a place in the wall where seams indicated a sliding door. As she approached, the door opened to reveal a small bathroom. With her handprint, the enforcer unlocked a cabinet and removed a white bodysuit that would cover most of Dani's body but left nothing to the imagination. No one was hiding any weapons wearing that.

Dani had taken two steps toward the door when Gedet's

rough hand shoved her forward. She stumbled and fell to her knees on the floor's hard, glossy surface.

"Undress and get into the sonic cleanser," the woman said. "If you are carrying any weapons hidden in interesting orifices, you need to dump them in the disposal unit there." She pointed to a hole in the wall. "The doorway will scan you for electrical emissions on your way out. It's the most advanced of its kind and will find anything with even the faintest signal, activated or not." She sneered at Dani. "Don't make me fish for anything. Tap on the door when you're finished."

Dani nodded, surprised when the woman left the room and shut the door on the eager faces of the male enforcers.

Stripping quickly, Dani removed and discarded a knife strapped to her inner thigh that the other enforcers had missed. She hesitated over the skin tag. It was mostly plastic, but there was more than a chance it would set off the scanner, and she couldn't risk them becoming aware of the tech that allowed fringers to walk among them, or risk her escorts taking out their frustration on her because of disobedience. No matter how they treated her, she couldn't kill any of them until she found Tauri.

With regret, she pretended to rub her neck—for the benefit of any possible cameras—to peel it off, and then used the toilet, subtly sending the tag into the sewer.

She stepped into the cleansing unit, a curl of disgust on her lips. The cleanser resembled the real-water shower she had in her apartment in Newcali, and while it removed all the bacteria and dirt, she never really felt as clean as water made her feel.

She stepped out and pulled off the doctor's bandage. She wouldn't need it now and had only left it on to protect the RealSkin patch in the shower. She pulled on the bodysuit. It was comfortable, at least, and not see-through or as tight as she'd expected. It still hugged her curves and screamed that she was a prisoner. She lifted her hand to examine the metal wristband, which was snug without being uncomfortable. The edges were rounded and smooth, the color gold. It had sealed without any break that she could see, and the surface was hard now, as if it had been welded into place on her wrist.

She tapped on the door and it slid open. The men still had their weapons out, and the woman held the stiff shackles. She motioned Dani to come out of the room, her eyes on something above the door. "Come out slowly."

Dani did as requested and the woman nodded. "Good. I see you know how to follow rules."

So the weapon and maybe the skin tag had registered on her way in. Dani held out her arms and the enforcer put the shackles back on. They were little more than two thirty-centi-meter pieces of thin metal with curved indents for her wrists, and a locking mechanism that ratcheted down to imprison her securely. The left arm with the metal bracelet felt slightly more snug but not too noticeable.

She expected to be taken to the corridor of cells, but the door the enforcers marched her through opened to a circular room in what could have been the sitting room of an expensive house. Unease rippled through Dani. Everything was decorated in tones of white, from the walls and carpets to the two facing couches on the right side of the room. The lights overhead were too bright, making everything seem whiter. The only thing not white was the elaborately carved, golden-brown wood desk, set so far to the left near the wall that it almost seemed to be in another room. The plush chair behind it was also off-white.

Besides two Special Forces who stood inside the door with assault rifles, the only occupant of the room was a man resting on one of the luxurious couches. He had medium brown hair, burning blue eyes, and a strong face that could belong to a forty-something Teev star. His smooth cheeks had to be a result of Nuface therapy, but his face didn't have the plastic appearance that was normal for so many of the older population who'd had the therapy for too long.

He unfolded his tall frame and arose, inclining his head as he came toward her. "Hello, Dani Balak."

He looked familiar, but it took a few seconds for Dani to recognize him. This was the Controller himself, the Elite CORE leader who was second only to the Director, and debatably more powerful. In concept, the Administrator, who oversaw transportation, food, water, electricity, and city managers, and the Regulator, who was over population control and birth orders, were equal in power to the Controller, all three reporting to the Director, but every enforcer in the CORE Territories ultimately answered to the Controller, which meant he was the one with the true power. He'd given the command to carry out all the deaths at Colony 6, and for that she hated him.

Fighting down both her panic and fury, she dipped her head calmly. "I see you have me at a disadvantage," she said. "Who are you?"

He smiled indulgently, as if not quite believing she didn't recognize him but willing to let her pretend. "I'm Warrick Ramsey. In case that doesn't ring a bell, I am the CORE Controller."

She cocked her head, studying him. He wore shimmering black pants and a deep V-neck shirt with long sleeves and cuffs. The blue eyes and the high widow's peak on his short hair reminded her of Bensell Summers, the pus bag who'd tried to capture Jaxon and the others six weeks ago. But was it a true resemblance, or simply the air of an Elite, which registered on her senses like a stench?

"I thought you'd look older," she said. "You've been Controller since before I was born thirty years ago." That meant his hair couldn't be his own color, unless they'd found a way to regenerate that too. "I'd say it was nice to meet you, but that would be lying."

His smile didn't change. He transferred his gaze to Gedet and the other enforcers who had accompanied her to Estlantic. "You may go."

Gedet looked ready to protest, but he glanced at the Controllers' two guards and nodded, stepping back with the others. The door slid shut and hid them from sight.

"Please, have a seat," Ramsey said.

Dani sat on the nearest couch, noting as he passed her to sit on the opposite one that he had a cowlick on the back of his head. He'd come from his bed to meet her, and apparently either used a sonic shower or came without cleansing altogether. That showed he wasn't as calm as he appeared.

"You have your office adjoining a prison cell?" she said. "That surprises me."

"This is simply an observation room." With a few hand motions, the walls at the far end of the room shimmered and the holo screens embedded there now showed three different rooms.

Dani sat up straighter to see inside, noting immediately that the rooms weren't for observation as Ramsey had indicated but for experimentation. Or testing. One of the rooms beyond the glass had metal walls, while the other two were concrete. Heavy vault-like doors stood open at the end of each room. One of them was scorched black.

"Let's cut right to it," Ramsey said, "as I'm sure you're tired from your long journey."

She gave him a bland smile, leaning back into the couch that cradled her body like the softest of beds. "Actually, I feel quite rested, thank you."

He nodded. "Ah, yes. You're from Colony 6."

"We called it the Coop," she offered without expression.

"As in a dirty, stinking coop for chickens, which, by the way, some of our residents sometimes kept inside their tiny houses to supplement those horrid, subpar readymeals."

He leaned forward. "And yet those readymeals kept you alive. You had food, lodging, an education. The colony was an investment in your future. In all our futures. You were supposed to become a contributor to the whole. But you took advantage of the generosity of the people because since leaving the core, you haven't given back. Don't you feel you owe us?"

She regarded him, bitterness welling up past her caution. "I do owe you. I owe you for imprisoning my family in the guise of helping them. I owe you for my parents' deaths. I owe you for experimenting on us. I owe you for killing ten thousand of my people." Her nostrils flared and her muscles clenched, sending a pleasant buzz of readiness throughout her body.

"We took care of you." His voice was forceful.

"No, my grandmother paid for me by working in your factory. As my father and mother did before you killed them. They paid for me with their blood and their lives." Strength flowed through her, and without thought, she yanked her arms in opposite directions and the shackles popped apart, falling to the carpet.

The Special Forces started forward, their guns pointing at her, but Ramsey raised a hand, signaling them to stop. They froze but didn't lower their rifles.

"Look," Dani grated, "I am not one of your pus licking, mindless punks that you can control with pretty words and empty promises. Or with threats."

He sat back slowly, crossing his legs. "I'm sorry you feel this way," he said mildly. "We have had to react to violence in Colony 6, but I assure you the rest of your accusations are unfounded. The Commonwealth Objective for Reform and Efficiency saved our people after Breakdown, and you now have the choice to willingly participate in building up our great nation or return to a colony to live out your life."

Dani knew better, but she'd play along to prove the lie. "Then send me to a colony. I'm willing to work."

Anger flared in his eyes. "You will first have to undergo psychological reconditioning," he said. "That may take some time."

The rest of her life, she bet, or until the madness caused by her ability took over. The only signs of that so far was that she could no longer sleep the entire four hours that had once been her normal, and her thoughts often raced too fast for her to concentrate. Usually a vigorous, three-hour run would put her to rights, but for how long that would work, she had no idea.

They sat watching each other, and Dani suspected he was trying hard to remain calm. At last he took a deep breath and began talking, his voice soothing and reasonable. "In the first two decades after Breakdown, there was chaos, as you well know. Bodies heaped all over the earth, even in the sections that hadn't been hit by the nuclear bombs. People fought and killed each other for every scrap of food. After the first decade, my father and people like him stood up and took charge. They began setting the building blocks of the CORE and started construction of the colonies to save lives, to teach the less fortunate to provide for themselves."

"And to use them to support everyone else."

He sighed and uncrossed his legs, leaning forward, elbows on his knees, pinning her with his intense eyes. "It didn't start out that way. That wasn't the intention."

"You're not denying it, though."

"No." He looked down at his hands. "That came much later. But the colonies were successful, and they saved lives. My father and the other Elite brought everyone safety."

Safety? Did he really believe that delusion?

"They imprisoned three hundred thousand people and controlled everyone else," she said. "They experimented on us—*you* experimented on everyone in Colony 6. I found the canisters at the water transfer station, dripping your drugs every day into our water. You tested them on children. On pregnant women!"

He stood abruptly and started pacing. "The viribus was to make you stronger."

Viribus. Finally a name to put to the horror. "Why?"

"They wanted to create a human that was stronger, and who would be able to withstand another Breakdown. We were but a tiny fraction of what we'd been, and as a society we couldn't afford to lose any more. My father had been testing people with a history of unusual abilities before Breakdown, and when they built the colonies, he convinced them to send anyone who tested strongly to Colony 6. That way the people would intermarry, and with the drugs enhancing the abilities . . . it was the best way."

"Until they went crazy."

"That was a serious setback." He returned to the couch and sat down. "But we've found a cure to the madness. Well, not really a cure because it is an ongoing treatment, but you can live a normal life here. We can help you."

"If I work for you, you mean. Why not give it to everyone who needs it? Why not put the treatment in the water at Colony 6 so no one else goes mad? There may still be people there with abilities that you haven't yet murdered."

He frowned, a genuinely sad expression on his face that was somehow familiar. "We can't. Not unless they're working for us. We have a fragile existence here, and without control, more lives will be lost." He gestured to the shackles on the floor. "With strength like that, I'm betting enforcers aren't much of a challenge for you. Imagine ten thousand more just like you. No. We've learned the hard way that genetic change like this can't be done on a population level. The good of the whole must always be considered more important than the individual."

A thousand responses pressed at Dani, begging for her attention. She held her breath for a moment, willing them to ease as she scanned the room with deliberation. "I guess that's where we'll have to disagree. As long as people are still living in a colony in a tiny box working sixty hours a week so you can live and work in a place like this, I'd say the needs of the individual are much more important than the wants of a few Elite."

His eyes hardened. "Tell me where your people are. Where did they take the doctor? We won't hurt any of them."

"I don't know."

"You're lying."

She couldn't help answering, "So are you."

He came to his feet again. "You want honesty? Okay, here it is. You now work for me. If I don't find you useful, I will kill you. Think about that."

Dani didn't feel any triumph at getting to the truth she'd known all along.

He strode toward the door where his guards waited and placed his hand over the reader. The door slid open. "You should also think about who else your decision will affect."

Dani stared beyond him. Standing outside the door with the woman enforcer was Tauri, looking as if he'd been pulled from bed and had been standing too long waiting. Should she pretend not to know him or had Tauri already told him he had a sister?

"This is your brother," Ramsey said, cutting short her deliberation. "Tauri Balak."

She lifted her chin coolly "I don't have a brother."

"DNA says otherwise. He may or may not have been born

in Colony 6, but he is genetically your full sibling. We suspect he knows more than what he's saying about where he comes from and about the death and disappearance of some of our Special Forces in the empty zone north of Amarillo City where he was picked up. You would do good to encourage him to talk. You have ten minutes before you are shown to your cell. We'll talk later." With that, he and his two guards left the room.

Tauri walked toward her, looking good, though as thin as ever, a fact accentuated by the white bodysuit. His skin was black like hers, and his hair the same white, though they'd shaved his once-long hair close to his head. He wasn't shackled, so they apparently didn't consider him a danger.

He started to talk, but she signaled him to stay quiet with a shake of her head.

"Have a seat." She motioned for Tauri to sit, hoping the couches and their positions would partially block the cameras she knew must be in the room.

She sat next to him and offered her hand, low enough that it skimmed the couch between them. "Nice to meet you Tauri, but I don't have a brother." Keeping her hands low, she said in Handspeak, *Take you home.*

You shouldn't be here, he answered. Aloud he said, "Nice to meet you. I don't know anything about being your brother. Maybe their test isn't accurate." His voice held only a trace of inflection that remained from his non-hearing days.

Of course I'm here, she signed.

I'm sorry.

Not your fault.

"They are probably lying," she said. "Anyway, where are you from?"

"The empty zone near Colony 5." That was near where he'd been caught, so he hadn't told them details about Newcali—yet. She relaxed slightly.

They know Handspeak? she asked.

No. They scanned my hearing implant. Luckily, they have no use for it.

Dani understood why. Each couple had to undergo rigorous genetic testing to be allowed a birth order. Deafness still occurred, and no one could prevent all accidents, but now any affected children born outside the colonies were automatically fitted with an implant. When she and the others lived in the Coop, Dani had known one non-hearing child who'd simply disappeared and never returned. As a child she hadn't questioned the absence, but as an adult, she suspected the worst. Children with anything that might be viewed as a disability for future work had often disappeared from the colony. Eagle had been lucky his gift prevented him from becoming one of the missing. Smuggling these children from the colonies to Newcali before the CORE acted against them—as well as any other child she could pay for—had become a priority.

"I've never been near Colony 5," she lied. Because six weeks ago, that was where they'd killed Bensell Summers, that pus bag the Controller had reminded her of, as well as his Special Forces.

Wait—a thought occurred to her. Were those the same Special Forces the Controller thought Tauri had been mixed up with? But Tauri had gone missing before the encounter.

Plan? Tauri asked. *Break out?*

She nodded. *Be ready. May need your gift.*

His lips turned pale. *No. Please.*

Dani had pity on him. *Maybe not.*

She drew away, holding her hands together in her lap, already knowing anyone watching would be suspicious at their hand motions, however subtle they'd tried to make them. Maybe they'd consider it some fringer ritual.

"How long have you been here?" Dani asked, though she already knew the answer.

"Two months."

"Doing what?"

"Lots of tests. Not sure why. There is a room they take me to with cement walls. They make me stay there, sometimes giving me food, or starving me. Sometimes they talk to me and ask me to do things."

"Like what?"

"Break things, climb the wall, push something away from me, levitate, predict an image from a set of cards or a holo screen. It goes on. I've lost track. But I'm not much good at any of it, which is a nice way to say I've failed at everything. Sometimes they put different gasses into the room." He made a face of disgust. "Haven't killed me—yet."

Ramsey was testing him for known abilities, no doubt. In case Tauri had been born in Colony 6.

"They said yesterday they were finished," he added. "Next week I'm to be implanted with a CivID and start reconditioning. Then I'll go to a colony. But I'm not really sure that's true. They've said it before."

Dani tried to hide her anger—and also the relief she felt for getting here in time. "If you're holding anything back you should tell them everything." She added a sharp *no* in Handspeak, though Tauri would already know she was speaking for the cameras.

"I already did. I'm an orphan, raised by people who found me." He shrugged. "They were nice."

Nearly the truth, and Dani found herself smiling. When she'd first met Tauri, he'd been thirteen and used only Handspeak or a T-link to communicate. A data discovery in the North Desolation Zone and his implant two years later had changed everything, but she was glad now that he and others like him in Newcali still practiced their first language.

The door opened to reveal the same woman enforcer who'd taken Dani to the sonic cleanser, along with the other man from behind the desk. Neither commented on the lack of Dani's shackles but ushered them from the room. Dani saw the two enforcer guards that had been with the Controller now standing on either side of another doorway, and it was to this that the woman enforcer motioned them. She placed her hand on a reader next to one of the guards and then leaned over for it to scan her eye. The door opened to the corridor depicted on the holo screen. Brighter lights came on down the corridor as they entered, and the air that rushed out at them was slightly different than the scrubbed air of the outer office, but not by much, which was a comfort to Dani. At least she wouldn't have to breathe in stench.

The enforcer pushed the first cell door inward and Tauri shuffled inside, glancing back at Dani, his brown eyes warm and trusting. A rush of love spread through her. *I love you,* she signed, keeping her hand low.

The door shut with a metal clang, leaving only his face staring from the small square window in the top part of the cell door. The enforcer put her hand on a pad and locked it.

The enforcer opened the next door and stepped back to let Dani enter. Without warning, exhaustion descended on Dani, a sensation she rarely experienced. When had she last slept? She didn't know, but she needed to rest now so she could concentrate on a way to escape—with Tauri. Sleep would reduce her oxygen intake to almost nothing, and she'd finally be able to turn off the racing thoughts.

She waited until the brighter lights in the hall winked out before she lay on the bed and tried to sleep.

CHAPTER 19

"What happened between you and Jaxon anyway?" Lyra asked Reese as they sat in a C-lodge in New York, waiting for Lyssa to finish her appointment at HED.

"Nothing is going on." Reese shifted uncomfortably at the question, which told Lyra something certainly was happening between her and Jaxon. Lyra knew it because of the way she herself acted around Kansas. Loving someone didn't make life easier if you couldn't fix what was broken.

Why can't I be satisfied with Tamsin? Lyra thought. She had raised her niece every bit as much as Lyssa and Kansas had, and she'd sacrifice her life for Tamsin. Yet still the primordial urge to have her own child haunted her sleep and all her waking hours. As if having Tamsin only whet her appetite for her own baby.

She pushed the thoughts aside and dragged her mind back to the mission. So far, little of interest had occurred at Lyssa's meeting except amusement at watching her twin pretend innocence at the surprise of the dispatch manager, who couldn't remember making the appointment. Lyssa had glossed over the confusion easily, flirting with the man and making him laugh. Being confident with men was one of Lyssa's talents. She'd always been the outgoing twin, the one to speak her mind and stand up for what was right.

And also the one who screwed up. Lyra had saved her sister and Tamsin, and she didn't regret doing so. Never would she regret it. Tamsin was the center of her life.

And yet . . .

"What are they doing now?" Reese asked.

"They're still in the conference room, but she's finally asked for a tour. She's just waiting now for him to finish a Teev call." Lyra was amazed at how easy it was to keep an eye on Lyssa and also chat with Reese at the same time. Her traveling ability was increasing. Three nights ago, she'd found herself hovering incorporeally near Kansas in his bedroom after one of their seemingly constant disagreements. The crew had always theorized that as the twins grew they'd be able to project their conscious thoughts elsewhere besides to where the other one was, but until that night, it hadn't happened. In fact, Lyra didn't know if it actually had happened. Possibly it was a dream, or maybe she could go anywhere in their apartment because Lyssa was close. If it occurred again, especially if Lyssa was at Ty's, she'd have to tell the others.

The separate bedrooms had been meant to keep Tamsin from realizing that Lyra—whom Tamsin called Aunt Lyssa—was the twin officially married to Kansas and to increase her opportunity to be alone with him. When they'd lived in Estlantic, they'd even had a secret door adjoining their rooms. But they didn't have that here, and it hadn't seemed to matter; lately Kansas spent more time in his bed than in hers. On most nights, a little bit more of Lyra died, even though she knew she was in large part to blame.

If only Kansas could understand how important a baby was to her. And the past six weeks of hiding that she was part of the underground was only adding to the strain between them.

Reese jumped up and paced the room, going to the window where she rubbed her fingers over the decorative trim. After a few moments, she said quietly, "They always deviate around the enforcers. I never noticed that when I lived here."

"That's because you were the enforcer." Lyra moved to stand with her. Down below, people moved with purpose, tension in every step.

This C-lodge was eight stories and took up half a block, and its amenities made the one in Santoni feel like a colony hovel by comparison. Because of the strict laws controlling building height, it was one of the tallest buildings in New York and in all of Estlantic, taller even than HED.

New York had endured a beating in the Breakdown bombings, fortunately not nuclear, and rubble from much taller pre-Breakdown buildings had taken decades to clear. But the surrounding areas had been far worse off, so half the CORE's non-colony residents ended up here, somewhere near a million people.

"I always knew something wasn't right," Reese said. "Once a father attacked me on the sky train. They'd sent his son in for medical enhancement. I didn't have anything to do with his arrest, so I think the father was just taking it out on the first available enforcer. I tried to explain that enhancement involved only removing a tiny portion of the brain, the part that made him violent."

Reese sank abruptly on the plush velvet bench next to the window. "How could I have said that? I knew what happens to people who are enhanced. They are never the same."

Lyra put her hand on Reese's shoulder in sympathy. At the same time, she was also walking next to Lyssa in the halls of

HED. "We all wanted to believe, and you have to remember that you weren't the reason for his son's problems."

"No, but my actions sent others to enhancement."

"Well, some deserved it, like that executive at Kordell Corp." His partners hadn't taken the enhancement well, and because of Reese's involvement in the drug bust, they'd nearly killed her. Which was why they'd all agreed Reese should remain here in the room with Lyra instead of going with Jaxon and Eagle to catch up with enforcer buddies at the local sauce bar in the hopes of identifying the desk in Jaxon's vision. In case the KC still carried a vendetta against her, there was no use flaunting Reese's presence until the memorial, by which time they hoped to have a plan in place to free Dani.

"I'm worried Jaxon's going to do something rash," Reese said suddenly.

Lyra sank down next to her. "He say something to make you think that?"

"No, but he spent all night on the train trying to have another vision of the desk. He wanted to see more of the room." Reese stared down at her hands. "But something else kept coming instead."

"What did he see?"

Reese's eyes dragged up to her, almost startled. "Nothing important."

Lyra could see that whatever Jaxon had seen, it was important to Reese, though probably not to the operation at hand. Lyra was about to probe when an exclamation from Lyssa pulled her back to her traveling duties.

Lyra sat back against the wall and closed her eyes, grabbing onto the scene around her twin with greater concentration. "Just a minute," she said. "I need to concentrate on Lyssa."

"Nice desk," Lyssa said, faking excitement when in reality disappointment pushed at her. The desk appeared to be real wood, but it was small and lacked the elaborate carvings of the one in Reese's sketch. Too bad because getting the nyckelira case here wouldn't have been difficult. She lifted her gaze to meet Lyra's, who had become visible in the small room. Lyra frowned, sharing her frustration.

"I got that desk in New Jersey," said Connor Simmons, the HED dispatch manager, whipping out his arm in a flourish and sending it through Lyra's incorporeal image. "Pre-Breakdown, of course."

"Of course." Lyssa gave him a demure smile.

"Full of himself, isn't he?" Lyra said, rolling her eyes at the man. "Too bad he can't hear me or I'd make him think the desk was haunted."

Lyssa managed to hold back a laugh of agreement. Simmons was a little too good looking for her tastes, and in her heels she towered over him, not something she was accustomed to. He wore a marriage band around his finger, the kind that couldn't be removed until the marriage was broken. While not yet mandated by the CORE, it was all the rage, and Lyssa guessed it would be mandated soon. Breaking a union wasn't against the law, unless you had a child under eighteen, but you had to file and receive permission. Affairs by those in valid unions were punishable by huge fines and even psychological reconditioning. None of this seemed to prevent Simmons from touching her waist whenever possible.

On her iTeev, Lyssa brought up a copy of the drawing Reese had made of the desk—after removing Dani from the image.

"This is one owned by a friend of mine," she said. "You ever see anything like it?"

He studied the sketch. "No, but those are nice carvings." He glanced at his own desk, a slight frown on his face. "Well, this is where you can reach me if we need to talk. I guess we should continue our tour now."

"Poor baby's jealous." Lyra made a show of shooing Simmons as he led Lyssa from the room. At least someone was having a good time.

From his office, Simmons took her back down the corridor past their dispatch room, which was triple the size of theirs in Amarillo City, and up to the cafeteria and the exercise room. "All Special Forces employees are encouraged to reach optimum physical conditioning. Supporting personnel don't train for combat with them in the mornings, of course, but we do need to stay healthy as well."

He rattled on. About shifts, employees, recent advances of the TAD-Alert. Not until he started talking about prisoners did she finally perk up.

"Mostly disgruntled youth and juke users, huh?" she said. "That's like us in Amarillo City, but what about fringers? I know enforcers have been sweeping the empty zones here, and we always send our fringer prisoners to you." She shivered, as if the idea frightened her, and moved closer to him.

His grin widened. "That's because we're equipped to handle them here. And you're right. We have been working overtime on clearing the empty zones."

"I guess you keep the fringers onsite with the other prisoners."

"No. Well, they're here but in a special suite upstairs. It has cells and experiment rooms."

"Experiment rooms?" Lyssa pretended surprise. "Why would they need those?"

His gaze slid away from hers, his smile vanishing. "I meant interrogation rooms." So, he knew or suspected about the abilities at Colony 6, but apparently it wasn't common knowledge. He took a deep breath. "Anyway, most of them aren't here long."

"What do they do with them after interrogation and processing?"

Simmons shrugged. "The colonies, I believe. That's what they exist for."

"I wonder what will happen once the colonies are integrated with the rest of the CORE?" she mused. "That's a goal that probably isn't far off." She watched him carefully for his response. If he believed this, he probably didn't know anything about the real situation in the colonies.

"I'm sure they'll figure something out. Maybe combine them. We still have to help those in need." He winked at her, causing a shudder of unease to ripple up her spine. "It'll be nice not to send half our earnings to support their dead weight."

His words made her momentarily dizzy. She could almost see the factories, the places of horror where her parents and grandparents had put in sixty hours a week and died while still in their fifties.

"You okay?" Simmons asked, his hand snaking around her waist. "You zoned out there for a moment."

Zoned out? That was something she only did when visiting Lyra.

"You did look strange for a moment," Lyra said worriedly, her ghostly body gliding closer to her. "You sure you're all right?"

"I'm fine," Lyssa said to both of them. "This is all just a bit overwhelming. I mean, I've lived in Estlantic before, but mostly in Virginia and Haven, but you know how small those cities are."

"That's because they were completely destroyed during Breakdown," Simmons said importantly. "But you'll get used to it here."

"I'm sure I will."

"Ask him if you can see where they keep the fringers," Lyra prompted, bringing Lyssa back to the work at hand.

Shaking herself, Lyssa said, "Can I see where they keep the fringers? I mean, I know if I worked here, I'd have no reason to see where they're detained, but I confess to being curious." She set a hand on his arm and smiled.

He placed his hand over hers, exerting more pressure than was strictly necessary. His hand felt moist and unpleasant. "I think that can be arranged. This way."

Lyssa was pleased when they got off at the fourth floor, one of the only places besides the Controller's office the TAD hadn't been able to check for missing CivIDs.

"Dani has to be here," Lyra murmured. Lyssa thought so too.

When they arrived at a set of double doors, Simmons didn't put his hand on the panel to open the door or press the call button. Instead, he called someone on his iTeev. "Hey, I'm outside the door, and I'd like to show a future employee the reception room, if you're not busy. No, look on your screen. We're already here." A pause. "Of course not. I know the cells are off-limits. Yes. Thank you. I owe you one."

So Simmons didn't have access to the "reception" room, much less the prison cells or experimentation rooms, which destroyed the plan forming in Lyssa's head. But at least the location device she carried would compare the location to the information the TAD had given them.

The door opened, and an unsmiling male enforcer motioned them inside. "Make it quick," he said, backing up a few steps to let them in.

Simmons nodded at the man and swaggered into the room. "This," he said to Lyssa, "is where they bring fringers." He gestured to the holo screen over the desk where another man stood watching them. "Those show the cells. Small rooms really. We're not barbarians."

"We don't have different holding cells for fringers and CORE residents in Amarillo City," Lyssa said. There were four doors in the room but only one had two guards standing in front of it, so that must lead to the cells.

"That's because you send fringers here," Simmons said.

"Well, it's not like they're dangerous, right?" Lyssa strained to see the holo screen. She needed to get closer, but the enforcer who'd opened the door was blocking her path, and he didn't look as if he'd allow them to step further into the room.

"I'll go look," Lyra said. She passed through Simmons and the enforcers, moving her feet without really touching the ground.

"Oh, fringers are plenty dangerous," Simmons said. "They—" He broke off at a stare from the enforcer, then began again a bit hesitantly. "Some of them have been living too close to the desolation zones. They've been affected by radiation."

After hearing about the beasts her crew had seen yesterday, Lyssa guessed this could be an accepted explanation. Simmons might have suspicions about what went on up here, but she guessed he had no idea that the abilities coming out of Colony 6 were induced by CORE experiments.

"What's with the extra muscle?" Simmons asked, thumbing at the two Special Forces with the assault rifles.

"New fringer arrived in the night," the enforcer told him. "Apparently, she's special." His voice stressed the "special" as if Simmons should know what that meant. "The Controller has taken particular interest in her. She's the one responsible for killing two of our own in Dallastar yesterday."

Simmons paled and his jauntiness lessened slightly. "Yeah. Well, uh, good they caught her."

"It's Dani all right," Lyra called from the desk area. "And one of the other two looks just like her—black skin, white hair. If you'll try to come in closer, I'll see if I can get through the door to her. Not that she'll be able to hear me . . ."

Simmons was turning to go, and Lyra knew she had to act fast. "So," she said, stepping around the enforcer and moving at an angle toward the guarded door. "We see animals affected by radiation in Dallastar. It mutates their genes into horrific creatures. Is it the same with people? How has the radiation affected this fringer? What kind of stuff are you guys dealing with here?"

No one spoke for long seconds, and then the enforcer said, with a quick look at his partner behind the desk, "That's not for us to say."

Lyssa took two more steps before turning and saying, "Good thing all of you are here. I don't know what these fringers think they're doing. They can't win against the CORE." She snorted in disgust, daring a glance over her shoulder to see what Lyra was doing.

Lyra was partially inside the closed door, but her face was contorted "Sorry," she said, emerging. "I can't seem to leave you."

Was that an odd inflection in her sister's voice? It was hard to tell when the sound was only in your head, but Lyssa didn't have time to worry about that now.

"You won't need to deal with fringers when you come to work here," Simmons said, his voice sure again. "The TAD will help you route it to the right team."

"Of course it will." Lyssa faked a smile.

"We need to get back to work," the enforcer said, one hand

coming to rest casually on his stunner. "We haven't fed the prisoners yet."

Simmons inclined his head. "Thank you for your time."

Lyssa had no choice except to follow him from the room.

"It would have been nice to tell Dani to look for the nyck-elira case," Lyra mumbled beside her.

But Lyssa was sure Dani would know what to do if she found the case. Where they should leave it was the issue. The desk had to be close. But where?

CHAPTER 20

Jaxon looked up from his glass of chotks and grimaced at Eagle across the tiny table they shared. "This is a bust. Half these guys are Special Forces and the other half want to be. They don't know or care about wood desks."

They'd come to the Coaster, a restaurant near HED, to intercept as many enforcers as possible, and while they'd both seen half a dozen people they had known from their previous years working in Estlantic and also chatted up complete strangers, no one had identified the desk in Reese's drawing. Their cover story of finding a gift for their captain was wearing thin.

These enforcers also had no idea what was going on in the colonies. A few alluded to strange abilities among the radiation-crazed fringers, but even the Special Forces who mentioned going on missions to Dallastar, and who might have been a part of the Colony 6 extermination, didn't seem to understand the full ramifications. Whoever had ordered the murders wasn't giving enforcers the full truth.

"We've still got a few hours before the memorial," Eagle

said, grinning as if enjoying himself. "And we can explore HED while we're there."

Exhaustion rocked Jaxon. "Everyone here seems to have their own agenda." He thumbed at Ekan Donnel, who he'd been with back in the academy and who was with Special Forces now. "He actually asked me if I knew anyone at HED I could put in a good word with so he could become a team leader faster."

"That's not unusual. Sometimes a promotion is just a matter of standing out." Eagle swept a hand over the talkative crowd. "With all the competition, you have to get ahead somehow."

"Yeah, I guess. Hey, I need to stretch my legs. Let's take a break." Jaxon lurched to his feet. "Lyssa should be finished at HED by now too. I want to see if she learned anything."

They emerged into the bright light outside the restaurant and a chill wind blew through Jaxon. He wished he were wearing his enforcer blues so he could turn on the warming feature. He fastened the magnetized opening in his jacket instead, nearly bumping into a small group of women, who glanced over at him but didn't smile. Had New York always been this unfriendly? Or was it because they were coming from a known enforcer hangout?

Eagle walked in a distracted manner that told Jaxon he was checking messages through the link in his special glasses. "Lyssa's back at the C-lodge," Eagle said after a minute. "No desk, but she verified that Dani is being held at the coordinates we suspected."

"That's something at least."

The walking made him feel better, but he was still anxious. Ever since he and Reese had talked last night, the only vision he'd seen was of them together, and it was driving him insane. He understood that the reoccurrence stemmed from his anxiety about the future, but at the moment the premonition was blocking everything else.

Pinning all their hopes on finding a certain desk from a vision that might not be real seemed impossible. But having Dani break herself out was the best solution, the only solution that might not get some or all of them killed. Whatever happened, if they didn't act soon, Dani was as good as dead. Her brother too.

Unless he tried something different.

He waited a block before saying, "Look, there might be another way. Before you found us outside the tunnels in the empty zone, Kentley was telling us that juke enhances abilities."

"It does? That's interesting. I wonder if—" Eagle slowed his step. "Wait, are you suggesting we buy drugs?"

"If it saves Dani. And us. One time shouldn't have an effect on me long-term." At least not physically. He wasn't sure about the madness, but even that wasn't as important as Dani's life. The madness was close—he could feel it—so just once really couldn't make it worse. Maybe.

"They did make us take it once in training," Eagle said. "Just to make sure we understood what we were up against. But that was under doctor supervision, and they don't do it now with new recruits. Only the smeg, and that's a lot less destructive. Do you think that would work? At least it's not illegal."

Smeg was a mildly addictive drug that heated the entire body, imitating sexual stimulation, and there was no way Jaxon needed that now with his visions of Reese. "I think he would have said."

"It's a lousy idea."

"What about Dani?"

Eagle's jaw clenched. "I won't risk one friend for another."

"Fine." Jaxon would have to ditch Eagle and do it on his own. "Let's go back to the restaurant. Maybe we'll find someone who knows something about that stupid desk." It wouldn't be hard to slip away when Eagle was talking to someone else.

They turned around, retracing their steps a half block before Eagle sighed and came to an abrupt stop. "Okay, let's do it. I know you well enough to know that you're going to do it with or without me, and I'd rather someone be there to watch you."

Jaxon grinned at him. "This has to remain between the two of us." He instinctively looked in the direction of the nearby C-lodge where Reese was supposed to be waiting.

"That depends on how well the counter agent we get works," Eagle said dryly. "I think the others will notice if you can't wake up for the memorial this afternoon."

"Good point. We'll get it."

Buying juke turned out to be more difficult than either expected, but Jaxon hadn't spent a third of his life arresting jukeheads for nothing. They finally tracked down a dealer near a marketplace at the edge of town where illegal exchanges often occurred right under the noses of enforcers. Using the untraceable cash credits Brogan had given them, they bought two black hypos—the juke and the counter agent that dealers now sold in an attempt to prevent the overdose deaths of their best customers.

"You won't need the counter for only one dose," the man who looked like a school teacher told them, but it was with a smile that expected them to be back for more. "Just a lot of sleep. Best sleep you'll ever have."

"Now what?" Eagle asked as they left the marketplace.

"We need a shuttle."

"Maybe we should get an ambulance."

"Very funny."

The shuttle arrived within two minutes. Jaxon climbed in and lay back in the seat. "Okay, I'm ready."

"You sure about this?" Eagle asked.

For an answer, Jaxon pushed the small hypo against his neck and released the juke. They waited a few seconds.

"Anything?" Eagle's face was impassive, but his voice oozed tension. "You'll have about thirty minutes of high before you crash. Then I'll give you the counter agent to wake you up. Better sooner than later."

Jaxon shook his head. "I don't feel anything. Maybe I'm immune like with the temper laser."

"This is totally different. No one is immune."

"Well, I don't—" Jaxon cut off. Something shifted inside his brain. Eagle's face split in two and then rejoined. Jaxon felt like laughing. Power and confidence surged through him. He could do anything he wanted, figure out anything, including breaking into any room in HED to plant the nyckelira case. In fact, he could rescue Dani himself and win Reese in the bargain. He had nothing to fear from Alex. He and Reese were a team. They'd always been a team. Together they could find out who was behind the continuing imprisonment of the colonies. They might even discover who his father was.

"Uh, Jaxon, that's a terrifying smile," Eagle said. "Are you okay? Are you having a vision yet?"

Jaxon stifled irritation at the intrusion of his plans. But of course he could have a vision. He was different, and he liked being different. His visions always came true.

A fleeting thought crossed his brain about the two times his premonitions hadn't come exactly true yesterday, but that made no real difference. Not with how good and strong he felt now. Power pulsed through his brain.

"Jaxon," Eagle's voice wouldn't let him go. "Concentrate on the nyckelira. Where is the desk? I know you're probably feeling all kinds of high right now, but that's going to end soon, and you'll pass out. Come on. Concentrate. Where is the desk?"

Right, Jaxon thought. *I have a job to do. Should be easy for me. I can do anything.* He shut his eyes concentrating on the memory he had of Dani and the case.

Nothing.

He pushed harder. Sleep nibbled at the edges of his mind. *Already?* he thought.

When something finally did happen, the vision came so quickly and with so much reality that for a moment his surprise penetrated his juke rush.

An enforcer carries the nyckelira over his shoulder. A crowd of uniformed enforcers stream past the man, filing into a large auditorium where they sit in anticipation. The man takes a deep breath and surges forward to the stage where a leader Jaxon knows only too well from his appearances on the Teev is talking to a bereaved couple, perhaps telling them how sorry he is for the loss of their son. The Controller himself.

The enforcer waits for the conversation to end, but when it does, the Controller strides off the stage in the opposite direction, a guard on either side, though he has to be safer than anywhere else in the CORE, surrounded as he is by at least a thousand enforcers.

The enforcer with the nyckelira case follows, far too slow to catch up with the Controller's longer strides. Then someone stands up from a seat and steps into the aisle. It's Reese. The Controller stops.

The enforcer reaches the Controller and touches his elbow. He turns to gaze down at the shorter man.

"Sir," the enforcer says, pulling the case from his shoulder. "I'm Special Forces Ekan Donnel. I work with the hepta team. This is a one-of-a kind case I found in the marketplace. It looks like a musical instrument case but actually holds an assault rifle. If you'll forgive my presumption and this interruption, I thought you might want to add it to your collection."

The Controller's face changes from bored indifference to interest. "Show me," he says.

They move out of the auditorium where Donnel opens the case and holds it as the Controller runs his hand over the interior velvet. He motions one of his guards to put in his assault rifle.

"Nice," the guard murmurs in appreciation.

"Thank you," the Controller says. "What did you say your name was?"

Ha! Jaxon thought. I did it! He was soaring at the top of his game. So easy this premonition thing. He could see anything he wanted. Maybe even who was behind the horrors at the colonies and who among the Elite might be willing to help them. *Show it all to me,* he demanded. Of himself, of the juke, of anyone who might be listening.

"Show you what?" Eagle's voice came from far away. "Jaxon? Jaxon? Can you hear me?"

Jaxon tried to speak, but all at once the euphoria drained from him. Then he was falling as though from a huge summit. Falling, falling, falling. He struggled to open his eyes, but weight held them down. Was he actually dropping? At this rate of descent, he didn't have much hope of survival.

Images rushed at him as he fell, a rapid flow that made him weak and nauseated. People and places he'd never seen. Would these visions all come true? No, he was nothing. His ability was useless. Nothing he'd ever done in his life meant anything. Reese would never be his. He welcomed the crash and impending oblivion.

A sharp needle poked his neck. "I've given you the counter drug," Eagle said, still sounding as if he were in another room. "But what did you see? You were mumbling for nearly a half hour."

Slowly reality returned to Jaxon. He wasn't dead after all,

and he was mostly glad. "It's Donnel," he forced out. "He has to give the case to the Controller."

"The Controller? Are you sure? Because getting close to him is impossible."

"Tonight he'll be there." But even as Jaxon voiced the words, doubt trickled in. What was he thinking, betting Dani's life on a drug-induced hallucination?

Now the other visions were crowding in, coming more rapidly: Ty's funeral, Reese in his arms, Dani with the nyckelira case, Lyssa—or was it Lyra?—with an extended belly. The voice of a man claiming to be his father.

All of it jumbled until he felt ready to scream. No, he *was* screaming.

Then everything went blissfully dark.

CHAPTER 21

At the C-lodge, Reese paused in her research of pre-Breakdown furniture to answer a phone call from her aunt. She was getting nowhere anyway and needed a break.

"Hey," she said, activating the holo feature. "What's up?"

Her aunt's eyes wandered over her uniform. "I know you're on a mission, and I tried not to call, but I finally decided to anyway. It might be important."

Worry shot through Reese. "What happened?"

"Your captain came to the house this morning. Very early when I was still half asleep."

Reese wilted with relief. "I texted you last night. I told you he'd be there for the bag," she said it quickly so Theena wouldn't clarify that it was her bag from Colony 6. Since Hammer had tinkered with her background, she'd asked Theena not to mention the colony, alluding to a connection with her gift, which was a secret Theena had already protected for years, but the request was new enough that her aunt might slip.

Theena nodded. "Right. I gave it to him like you said, but

then I got to worrying about what else might be in the bag. What if he . . .? You know."

Reese did know. Theena was worried Brogan might learn about her ability. "It's okay," she said. "There's nothing in there that he can't see. But speaking of the bag, did you notice if I had any water still in the skins?"

"I'm sorry. I should have looked to see exactly what was inside, but I was a little flustered and still half asleep. I almost shut the door on him, you know, before I remembered your text."

Reese smiled at the idea of the frail Theena trying to prevent Captain Brogan from entering her house. "You did great."

"If you don't mind my asking, why did he come for it? Couldn't you wait until you got back from wherever you are? You didn't say in your text."

Reese searched her brain for a reason that would sound valid. She'd known last night that Theena would demand more, but she'd been too tired to come up with any excuse. "It's just a little thing I'm working on," she said. "I'll explain when I get back." It wouldn't be easy explaining why her captain drove all the way out to Big Horn for a bag of childhood treasures. "Right now, though, I'm in the middle of something. In fact, I have to go."

"Of course. Well, I'm glad to know you're safe. A text just isn't the same thing."

Was that the real reason her aunt had called? To make sure she was all right?

"I should have called you this morning," Reese said. "I'll come see you as soon as I get home, even if it's only for a few hours. I love you."

"Love you too, dear."

Reese hung up to find Lyssa and Lyra watching her. "Did the skins have any water?" Lyssa asked.

"She didn't look."

The twin's faces showed identical expressions of disappointment. "She's sweet to check up on you," Lyra said.

"I'm lucky to have her." Reese meant it, and not only because Theena had literally saved her life as a child.

A commotion at the door to the suite prevented conversation. The door cracked and then a foot shoved through the narrow opening, and finally Eagle pushed open the door, and staggered in, supporting what appeared to be a hung-over Jaxon.

Reese ran to help. "You're cutting things close. We have to leave in an hour for the memorial. Why haven't you been answering our texts?"

Eagle dragged Jaxon forward a step. "We've been working."

Jaxon stumbled, nearly falling into Reese's arms. A kaleidoscope of sketches burst from him, each too brief for details but definitely images she'd have to draw. She pushed him at Eagle and retreated, feeling dizzy and nauseated.

"What's wrong with him?" she demanded when the flow didn't cease. "It's like he's having dozens of premonitions at once." She grabbed her drawing pad and backed all the way to the spacious adjoining kitchen, glad when the image assault subsided at that distance.

"I'm not sure. He was okay a minute ago when we started up on the elevator."

"Must have had too much sauce." Lyssa popped up from her chair near the window to help Eagle get Jaxon to the couch. "I hope you had some luck because besides verifying that Dani's at HED and still alive, we are no further than we were before."

"Give me a brew?" Eagle asked Reese as he propped Jaxon in a seated position on the couch. "For him, I mean."

She nodded and went to the dispenser. Lyra hurried over and took the steaming mug from her. "I'll take it to him."

"Thanks." Reese's jitters were back with all the additional images, and if Jaxon didn't find a way to control this sudden influx of visions, she'd have to stay well away from him.

"We didn't find out where the desk is," Eagle said, "But Jaxon did have a premonition of *who* we need to get the case to."

Lyssa snapped her fingers. "Yes, of course, that makes sense. We're not ever getting inside the holding cells where they have Dani, but someone who works there can. We should have been researching people who have access, not the desk itself."

Lyra sat next to Jaxon and held the mug to his mouth. "Drink this," she said. Jaxon muttered something Reese couldn't hear, but he took the mug from Lyra, which was a good sign.

Reese opened her drawing pad and began sketching the most pressing image of a man's distorted face. Quickly, it came to life under her fingers, simple lines that didn't have much substance. As if Jaxon saw it through a cup of water. There would be no identifying this man.

"Unfortunately, we may have a problem." Eagle slumped into a chair near the couch. "It's none other than the Controller who ends up with the nyckelira case. One of the guys Jaxon knows will give it to him. Tonight, we think. At the memorial. At least he will if we can make it happen. We have no idea when the Controller will put it on the desk where Dani will find it, but presumably before he takes it home, which means soon. Probably before he leaves for the day."

Lyssa nodded. "One of the guards did say the Controller had taken a special interest in Dani. Probably because of her ability. And he'd have access to wherever she's at. But convincing anyone to give the case to the Controller is definitely a problem."

Reese's hand stilled as she stared down at her drawing of a

man holding something out in his hands. It was blurry, but he could be offering the other man the nyckelira case.

"Why would Jaxon's friend give the Controller the case?" Lyssa put on her iTeevs and began swiping screens that no one else could see. "Ah, okay, here it is. Apparently, the Controller collects musical instruments, some of which aren't in use anymore, so he's had them recreated from old Teev footage. He also has two children and four grandchildren, all of whom play different instruments."

Eagle tilted his head. "The guy Jaxon knows is already with Special Forces, but he's looking to move up. We'll have to approach him about the case, and do it fast. He's probably home getting ready."

"Donnel was already wearing his uniform at the Coaster." Jaxon lifted up the square of his iTeev and began unfolding the screen. His hand shook. "I'll text him."

"Give it to me," Lyra reached for the iTeev.

Jaxon held it away from her. "I can do it."

Lyra frowned. "If Donnel gives the case to the Controller, and Dani uses the weapons inside the secret compartment to escape, won't he question Donnel? That'd be a death sentence for him."

Jaxon lowered his iTeev. "Not if we leave a note inside telling Dani to lock up the secret compartment after she removes the weapons."

"They have cameras everywhere," Lyssa countered. "And if that's her means of escape, they'll eventually ask Donnel where he got it."

Everyone fell silent as they pondered the question. "Maybe not," Eagle said after a few minutes. "I could put a jammer in the case that activates once it's open, and that would disrupt the camera, and the note would do the rest."

Reese left her drawing pad and approached the couch slowly.

No images battered at her yet, so maybe Jaxon was becoming sober again. "What about security? The invite said no weapons at the memorial, and that makes sense with so many outside people, especially if the Controller will be present."

"It'll get through the scanners," Eagle said confidently. "They'll want to open it up, but I've lined the hidden compartments with special metals, and with the design it will look innocuous under a scan. It'll get through. I'll remove the fingerprint requirement on the weapons, in case she gives one to her brother."

"So we just give it to Donnel?" Reese asked.

"Yes. Or convince him he wants it." Jaxon turned to look at her, his eyes clear now, but he lowered his gaze almost instantly. "And it has to be tonight. I also saw enforcers streaming out to the street after an alarm was raised."

"Great," Lyssa muttered. "Just great. We have to try to break her out on the one night half the enforcers in the CORE will be present."

"At least most of them won't be armed," Reese said.

Lyssa shook her head. "Maybe not inside the building, but how many will have weapons waiting for them nearby on the outside, or will be given them once she breaks out?"

"I think it's perfect, actually." Eagle's shoulders lifted in his uneven shrug. "On another night, more would have their weapons ready."

"But you guys have to know there's no guarantee, right?" Jaxon insisted. "I don't know that Dani will get the case. None of us do."

Reese felt his doubt, and to be honest, she was feeling it too. That distorted medley of visions had shaken her. Shoving aside the misgivings, she moved around the couch and sat on Jaxon's other side. "She'll get the case." Still no sketches burst out at her, not even when their legs touched and heat rushed through her at his nearness, at the memory of the sketch she'd seen from him last night.

He smiled at her, but the unsteadiness of his grin told her he wasn't well. His hands, spread now on the front of his thighs, were still shaking, and his breath was shallow, coming faster than normal.

"You text your friend," Reese said. "I'll contact Brogan on the T-link. We'll need transportation Special Forces can't lock down. Once we make sure Donnel delivers the case, we'll go outside and be ready to pick Dani and Tauri up once they're out."

"I'd like to remain inside for as long as possible," Eagle said. "I may be able to set off a few distractions to help Dani."

Reese had been expecting that. "Good idea." She stood, pulling her borrowed T-link over her eyes. She needed to brief the captain on a secure channel, and with Jaxon out of commission, that fell to her. "Just remember, they'll have cameras everywhere."

"Which I know how to temporarily disrupt, if necessary." Eagle flashed her his usual confident grin, which had been lacking since their experience in Santoni.

"What about us?" Lyssa asked.

"HED has two entrances," Lyra said. "You and I can watch them and let Reese and Jaxon know which way Dani comes out."

Lyssa smiled. "I'll take the back. There's a roof nearby that I'm confident I can get to. I'll be able to watch the whole back-side of the building."

"There's a snack shop directly in front," Lyra added. "I'll shop for something to take home, and linger over a drink if I need to."

"Someone will need to stash our weapons and battle gear inside our escape vehicle." Eagle picked up a helmet someone had left on the table. "Just in case it doesn't go smoothly."

"Does anything ever go smoothly?" Lyssa shot back.

The crew continued to discuss the plan, but Reese's attention was drawn by Brogan's voice coming through the T-link. "We think we've found a way," she told him on audio only, walking away from the others.

Quickly, she outlined the plan to put the nyckelira case where Dani would be able to access it and escape on her own. "Eagle will stay inside to lend what aid he can, and the twins will let us know where to pick her up, but we're going to need transportation."

"I've already contacted the underground there to let them know we'll need support," he said. "Apparently there has been a change of leadership recently, but my contact assured me our agreements would remain unchanged. He's let me know I can have a shuttle wherever you want it. I'll also send you the address of our safehouse in Morry. I think that will be the best location for your retreat."

"Not a shuttle," she said. "At least not at first. If Special Forces closes down the public shuttles, we'll be blocked, even if the one you give us is off the grid. What we need is a pair of scramblers." The two-wheel motorized cycles were always the best way to get around the shuttle traffic in New York, especially on a Saturday night.

Brogan chuckled. "I'm sure the underground there has managed to lift a few from enforcers."

"We'll also need a shuttle waiting for us outside the city, and a way to avoid cameras until we're closer to the safehouse and won't be noticed. Special Forces will be looking for a shuttle nearby that doesn't obey their commands."

"The shuttle they'll give you will know the cameras to avoid. I'll send you the scrambler coordinates when it's done."

"Send them to all of us," Reese told him. "And any codes we'll need to activate them or open their storage compartments.

We'll need to stash our weapons and battle helmets on them as soon as possible."

"Will do." Brogan paused and added, "How confident are you about this plan?"

Reese looked over to where the others were getting ready to leave. "I don't know, but it's all we've got, short of storming the place, and you know where that would leave us."

"With a whole lot of collateral damage."

"Right."

"Okay. Good luck."

They would need it. She cut the connection and returned to the others.

"Do we have transportation?" Jaxon asked, sounding more like his old self.

She grinned. "How do you feel about riding a scrambler again?"

Jaxon chuckled. "Nice!"

"Clud," Eagle said with an exaggerated sigh, "You guys have all the fun. I almost regret volunteering to stay behind."

Jaxon, Reese, and Eagle stopped off at the Coaster barely in time to catch Jaxon's friend Ekan Donnel, who was leaving despite the texts he'd exchanged with Jaxon. "Thanks for waiting," Jaxon said, waving him back to his seat and setting the nyckelira on the table with a flourish. "Look what I found at the marketplace."

Donnel eyed the case with doubt. "Is that the instrument that's currently making the rounds in the streets?"

"Nope." Jaxon sat, his legs still wobbly from his encounter with the juke. "Well, it could hold a nyckelira, but it's designed for something much more useful." He opened the case to show the velvet interior, then motioned to an enforcer at the next table. "Come here a minute, would you? Let me see your rifle."

The enforcer stood and joined them, followed by a few of his Special Forces buddies. He handed Jaxon the rifle, obviously expecting him to ooh and aah over the gleaming surface. Instead, Jaxon set it deftly inside the nyckelira case. "See? Fits a couple of magazines as well."

Eagle chuckled. "Sweet, isn't it? The designer must be a genius. What a great present for our captain."

"Yeah, too bad he doesn't actually play the nyckelira," Reese put in. "Does he have any kids who do?"

"No." Jaxon pretended to study the rifle inside the case. "But it works so well to disguise a weapon that he'll like it anyway. Or maybe he'll use it to grease the wheels for a promotion for himself. It's all the same to me, as long as I'm the recipient of his good graces." He laughed, watching Donnel from the corner of one eye. Would he have to bring up the Controller?

"Hey, our captain might like one of these too," said the enforcer whose rifle they'd put inside the case. "But he'd probably pass it on to the Controller."

Donnel's hand landed possessively on the edge of the case. He leaned close to Jaxon. "I'll buy it from you." Urgency laced his voice.

"You can go get another one." Jaxon tried not to smile. "I'll show you where."

"Has to be tonight." Donnel leaned closer and whispered so Jaxon alone could hear. "The Controller collects instruments. I hear he'll be in attendance tonight. This is my chance to move up. Maybe even be chosen for his personal guard."

Jaxon felt a twinge of remorse. If he gave Donnel the case, he'd probably end up in more danger, even if the case's part in their plan was never discovered.

"Please, man. I'll pay extra." Donnel dragged a hand through his thick head of black hair, his eyes digging into Jaxon. "You can get another one tomorrow for your captain."

Jaxon stared at the shorter man for a good ten seconds before nodding finally. "Sure. Whatever you need. I got time. But it'll cost you five hundred credits."

"That puts me out," said the other enforcer, who removed his rifle from the case and left the table with a friendly wave.

"Done," Donnel said.

The price was high for an average case, but far less than it was actually worth. With a few taps of Donnel's iTeev the funds were transferred, and the man slung it over his wiry shoulder, muttering something about wrapping the gift.

Jaxon waited until Donnel was gone and they were all out on the street before saying, "That went well."

Reese nodded. "Let's walk over to HED. We can chat outside until Donnel shows up. I want to make sure he gets through security."

They strode toward HED behind a group of other enforcers from the restaurant. Reese had her T-link over her eyes and swiped to read her messages. "Our scramblers are in place," she reported. "Lyssa just dropped off the weapons, using a fake CivID, of course, and Lyra is heading to the shop. They'll have both exits covered within three minutes."

Eagle snorted. "Dani might not use a typical exit. They know that, right?"

"Of course, but she's got her brother with her," Reese said. "Hopefully. So that will make her choices more limited."

If Dani didn't have access to her brother, would she leave HED, even if she found the weapons in the nyckelira case? Jaxon doubted it. *Trust in the vision,* he told himself. Doing so wasn't easy. It had been so vivid, but the use of juke changed everything.

Reese bumped him with her arm, as if knowing he needed a jolt. "This is going to work," she said. "But you should review Brogan's recommended escape route. Depending on pursuit, we may have to deviate."

As a plan, it was simple, but everything hinged on the nyckelira case, which made it the worst plan in history. "She might not get the case until tomorrow," Jaxon said.

Reese shrugged. "Then we'll wait."

But they all knew each minute that ticked by was one more opportunity for Dani or her brother to break. Or for something else to go wrong.

Jaxon's attention was distracted as a sleek blue car drove past, the windows tinted as dark as those on any shuttle. He paused to watch the surface of the vehicle change from glittering navy to star-studded black as it drove past, but he couldn't tell if it was actually changing color or if the effect came from the way light hit the surface. Whoever was driving had a healthy bank account, and Jaxon bet it wasn't someone coming to the memorial.

Unless it was the Controller himself. Jaxon watched the car until it was out of sight.

Next to him, Reese had also stopped and was studying the increasing number of enforcers who were jumping out of shuttles or walking down the sidewalk, angling toward the building ahead of them. "Donnel should be here," she said. "Do you see him?"

Jaxon shook his head. "He'll be here, but maybe you should go inside and find a seat while we wait for him. We need to make sure you're in the right position to help him catch up to the Controller."

Reese's mouth lifted at the corners, obviously finding his reminder amusing. "There's still time."

Jaxon experienced a sudden urge to pull her to his chest,

to kiss her until she looked at him through half-shuttered eyes like in his premonitions. An ache started in his gut, deep and wide, and his shakiness returned. Would those premonitions ever come true? What he wouldn't give that moment for another hit of juke. He craved the feeling of invincibility and unending confidence. To know he was right and that he could do anything. Maybe if he used it again, he'd know for sure when Dani would escape. There was at least one more hit in the hypo they'd purchased.

No, that was not going to happen. The danger of addiction quadrupled or more with each use of juke. He understood that. Yes, it had given him visions, but at what cost? He'd already seen Dani escaping among a crowd of enforcers. That was enough to pinpoint it to tonight or some other large event.

If the visions were real.

"Hey, don't look now," Eagle leaned over to whisper to them. "But there's this weird car with changing blues and blacks that's been around the block three times now. It's stopped in front of that group of scramblers. See? Someone inside is talking to a man on the sidewalk, the one dressed in that fancy gray outfit. Ordinarily, I wouldn't have thought anything of it, but three times around is weird, and they've been looking this way for the past minute. Not at us necessarily, but in this direction. Maybe at the enforcers going inside."

Reese gave a slight gasp. "I know that man, the one on the walk. He had longer hair then, but he's from KC. He was there the night they attacked me." Reaching for a gun she wasn't carrying, she started forward, but Jaxon grabbed her and hauled her instead to the double glass doors leading into HED.

"Saca, Reese!" he said. "What are you going to do, confront him?"

She stopped struggling. "Maybe." She gave a tight smile

to the Special Forces guarding the door as he gestured them toward one of the two scanners.

Jaxon lifted one hand in a waiting gesture as they stepped to the side to allow other enforcers to enter and move through the security. A few civilians also came inside, but not the man dressed in gray.

"He can't hurt me in front of all these enforcers, can he?" Reese stepped in front of the door, ignoring the jostling of an enforcer trying to get past her. "And I've got a bone to pick with him."

Jaxon pulled her back to the side. "Who knows what they can do," he whispered fiercely in her ear. "Besides, we need to focus on Dani."

Reese's jaw worked, but she nodded. "Okay. Look, there's Donnel. He's finally here. We can go on through. This thing isn't going to pick up our skin tags, will it?"

"No," Eagle said. "It won't register anything more than the heating units in our suits or our iTeevs, which are permitted inside. Or T-links in our case, and they look enough alike to pass. Just keep them powered down until we're through so the scanner won't pick up any unusual emissions. It's not like they're expecting trouble."

Jaxon followed Reese through a scanner, feeling more than a little exposed without even a stunner. He glanced over his shoulder to see that Donnel had made it to the other scanner, where two Special Forces were removing festive wrap from the nyckelira case. His heart beat heavily as they opened the lid and ran their hand-held scanners over the entire surface.

"Relax," Eagle said from behind him. "They won't even be able to sense the additional compartment, not with the density of the material. It'll come across as molded plastic. I tested it on ours back home."

Still Jaxon worried until the enforcers returned the nyckelira case to a disgruntled looking Donnel, who crumpled the ruined wrapping paper and tossed it into a garbage bin.

"Let's go," Jaxon said.

"You guys go ahead." Eagle reached into a pocket. "I've got to join some perfectly innocent substances I brought. In case we need a distraction."

Jaxon nodded. "We'll let you know when it's done."

They followed the crowd until they reached a huge auditorium. Jaxon remembered now that he'd been here several times before in training, but the sense of déjà vu came from the vision, not those more distant memories. The walls were alight with holo feeds from other enforcer districts, showing the faces of people who for whatever reason hadn't been able to make the trip to New York to honor the lost team supervisor.

Reese led the way down the aisle until they reached a pair of empty seats. It looked about right, so Jaxon slid into a chair. Anxiously, he stared across the heads of the people. The parents of the dead enforcer were on the stage with an official Jaxon assumed was HED's captain. Where was the Controller?

Then he saw him in full dress blues, stepping onto the stage and bending over the mother, then shaking the father's hand. Both arose, awe at the honor of meeting the Controller himself shining through even their grief.

A figure moved hastily toward the stage, down the far aisle, just like in Jaxon's vision. It was Donnel, the nyckelira case awkwardly slung over his shoulder. That's when Jaxon noticed a pair of musicians on the far end of the stage motioning to him. Thankfully, Donnel ignored them.

When the Controller left the parents, striding across the stage and into the near aisle with broad steps, Donnel hurried after him, scrambling in an awkward way that made everyone stare. But he was forgotten the minute he stepped off the stage.

Jaxon glanced over at Reese. Her fists were shut tight, and

he knew she was probably receiving sketches from the people around her. Her face looked okay, though, strong and determined. She didn't glance his way, but one hand opened and gently touched his thigh. He was so aware of her that even through the thick enforcer uniform, her touch penetrated. He felt calmer having her close.

They waited as the Controller approached.

Now, Jaxon thought. But she didn't stand.

Finally, as the Controller was about to pass, Reese stood up in his path. The man moved to step around her.

Jaxon's gaze shifted momentarily to Donnel, who was still too far away. *It's not going to work,* he thought.

That was when his gaze met the Controller's. Something flickered in the man's blue eyes and he stopped. Familiarity washed over Jaxon. He'd seen those eyes before, and the high widow peak in the hair. The patrician nose and confident expression. Was it only from his appearance on the Teev? Or from his vision? But why wouldn't the eyes leave Jaxon's?

Then the man turned away as Donnel tugged on his sleeve. The Controller's guards tensed but they allowed the man to speak, and in the next moment the four moved up the aisle together. Jaxon watched them go, knowing he shouldn't. The Controller didn't look back.

He'd imagined it then.

Reese sank to her seat next to him. "I think we have a problem."

"The guy in gray?" Jaxon immediately began scanning the crowd.

"No." She leaned so close he could smell her scent, musky and compelling. "The Controller. He knows you, Jaxon. He didn't stop because of me. He stopped because of you."

Jaxon remembered the visions he'd had under the influence of juke. In the whirlwind of premonitions, someone had been talking about being his father, the man he'd never known. A man he could never have known with the influx of men visiting his mother in the Coop. For years he'd believed his father would come back, to rescue him and his mother. He'd given up that hope twenty years ago when his mother was murdered.

But Captain Brogan hadn't been able to mask Jaxon's origin from Colony 6 as he had the others in the crew, and Bensell Summers, before Jaxon had shot him, had hinted at Jaxon's parentage. He'd insinuated that he'd been at Jaxon's house in Colony 6 on someone else's command.

"You think he's the one Summers reported to?" Reese asked. "The reason Summers was at your house that day?" The week before his mother died, she meant.

Jaxon felt another wave of nausea. "I think he knows something about me."

Reese gave him a penetrating look. "Let's get out of here. We've done what we came to do. The rest is up to Dani."

CHAPTER 22

D ani had slept four hours, at least, since talking to the Controller, and spent the rest of the day pacing or exercising. Two large steps brought her across the cell, but taking six smaller steps and bringing her knees to her chest gave her more movement. Push-ups on the floor or off the wall kept her focus away from how small the room really was. Pulling on the bed was even better, her neck straining with effort—until the bolts jerked free and she ended up with bruises on her legs where the bed crashed into her.

Bruises that were almost gone, like the gunshot wound which she barely noticed anymore.

She was going to die in here. Or go stir crazy until she beat her own head into the wall to stop the fidgeting. Maybe she'd tear down the door of the cell and all the walls. Then they'd probably lock her up in one of the observation rooms the Controller had shown her—the ones with concrete or metal walls and heavy vault doors. Better that she keep her cool and wait for an opportunity to escape with Tauri.

They'd brought her a single lukewarm readymeal for breakfast and another for lunch. The boxes were supposed to contain all the nutrition a person needed. For her it would have been ample, if not for the drive that forced her to stay moving. Once she could have sat perfectly still all day—she had done it just for discipline. She'd slow her breath until it was almost nonexistent, reserving all her strength. But that was before her gift started to malfunction.

Yes, she was going to die, or starve in this little box. She took a deep breath, which filled her with more energy—and hunger.

Still she couldn't stop moving.

When the two enforcers opened her cell door, she experienced a sense of inevitability. She'd have to act sooner rather than later. While she was still able.

"Where are you taking me?" she asked as they fastened new shackles over her wrists.

The male enforcer, one she hadn't seen before, grunted out a reply, "The Controller wants to see you."

She thought about taking them both out and going for Tauri right now, but she didn't know who else was watching the monitors. Better to see what Ramsey wanted, maybe take him hostage. She craned her neck as she passed Tauri's room, but she couldn't see him inside.

The guards led her from the cell block out into the reception, where two more enforcers manned the desk like before. One was heating a readymeal in the wall microwave, presumably to take to the other prisoners, and her stomach growled. Just her luck that the Controller wanted to see her now instead of after dinner. The holo screens behind the desks showed only empty rooms. Where was Tauri? Could he be with the Controller now?

She could take them all with little effort, but getting out of this room and the building itself was another thing altogether.

How many people would she have to kill? She'd do it, though, if she had to.

The guards opened the door to the white room where she had met the Controller before and pushed her inside. Warrick Ramsey arose from one of the pale couches and dipped his head in greeting. He had lost the shimmering pants of earlier and now wore an enforcer uniform, but the black outfit sported a high collar that jutted nearly to the ends of his earlobes. Dress uniform, she knew, but why was he wearing it? Was it something she could work into an escape?

She almost didn't care as her gaze slid past him to a gilt, three-tier food trolley that had been rolled next to the couch. It was filled with a kettle, fancy mugs, and numerous baked goods she couldn't name. Her stomach growled.

Ramsey saw her gaze and motioned to the guards to remove her shackles. After complying, they retreated near the door, where they stood with their rifles ready.

"Help yourself," Ramsey invited. "I thought we'd get acquainted a little." He moved two objects that were round like Newcali bread drops to a plate before lifting the kettle to pour liquid that looked and smelled like expensive brew.

She didn't wait for a second invitation but strode to the trolley, taking up the plate he'd made for himself. Just in case the others weren't safe.

He stared at her a minute before a smile broke his face. He handed her the mug of brew. "Please, take this. I'll pour more for myself."

Dani accepted the mug and sat close as she could to the trolley, plate on her lap, and began eating. She'd downed both of the drops before he'd seated himself opposite her. She gulped the hot brew—the best she'd ever tasted—before stretching her hand out for another bread drop and two flat cookies that might have been sprinkled with sugar and cinnamon.

"We had these made especially for the memorial this afternoon," the Controller said, watching her.

"Memorial?" Dani tried to make herself chew more slowly. The cookies were amazing, the delicious flavor tantalized her taste buds, urging her to eat more.

Ramsey sighed. "Yes. One of my Special Forces supervisors was killed in the empty zone south of Colony 2. The memorial is nearly over now."

"I'm sorry to hear that." She wasn't really, but it seemed the thing to say. She was eating his food, after all, and it wasn't an odious readymeal.

"Thank you." He paused a moment to savor his drink. "The guards tell me you've been . . . restless today."

She shrugged and took another bite, swallowing before saying into the silence, "I'm not used to being kept prisoner."

"You don't have to be a prisoner," Ramsey said. "I can help you."

Dani was already feeling good. More steady now. Maybe all she'd needed was decent food, even if it was sweeter than she was accustomed to.

"It's your ability, you know," Ramsey said conversationally.

She stopped chewing. "What?"

"Why you can't sit still. I've seen others gifted with strength like yours, and it gets worse as the madness increases. They usually fatally injure themselves or others if they don't accept the therapy we can give them."

"I'm fine," Dani said.

He studied her. "For now." Ramsey arose and moved to sit next to her, looking toward the back of the room. With a few motions directed at the Teev sensors embedded in the wall, the holos covering two of the experiment rooms shimmered and disappeared.

Stiffening, Dani stared inside them, her mind instantly

processing what she was seeing. The cookie in her mouth turned to ash. She jumped to her feet, unable to control the gasp that escaped her lips.

In each of the rooms, a man sat imprisoned in an interrogation chair. One of them was Tauri. Despite the blood on his face and his haggard expression, he was still breathing, his eyes open and angry. The other man, one she didn't know, was unmarked by blood, but he was slumped, his head twisted and hanging to the side at an unnatural angle.

"Your brother's okay," Ramsey said, still sitting and casually sipping his drink. "However, I'm afraid the other man is gone." He made a motion to open the audio feed. "Go ahead and take him down to medical," he ordered some unseen underlings. "They'll want an autopsy."

The heavy door at the back of the room opened and two guards entered with a body board. They opened the arm and leg locks on the chair, released the waist strap, and spread the limp man on the board before carrying him out.

"What did you do to him?" Dani's throat felt so dry she could barely speak past the horror. What was wrong with her? She'd seen Special Forces do far worse than this to her people. And she'd never let it affect her this way.

It's because I'm afraid for Tauri, she thought.

Ramsey shrugged. "He wouldn't join us, so we didn't give him the antidote. As for what we did, we were simply testing him. He had the ability to push things away from him, but his madness made him reckless. My theory is that he essentially pushed his own body apart. Broke his neck, it looks like. Maybe more. The autopsy will determine if I'm correct."

"You whore wrangling pus bag," she ground out.

He stood and met her accusing eyes without expression. "He made his choice. Just like you will make yours. We both know I can never let you go. You're far too dangerous." His mouth turned up in a mirthless smile. "On the other hand, your brother doesn't seem to test positive for an ability."

Dani knew Tauri's ability wouldn't have manifested as long as no one was in the room with him, and if someone had been in the room . . . well, Tauri had somehow managed enough control to fool them so far.

At Dani's silence Ramsey added, "Maybe your mother left the colony before the drugs took effect on him, or maybe he's just lucky. We could possibly let him leave."

Should she pretend not to care? But Dani was certain it was already too late for that. Her reaction to seeing her brother strapped to the chair had been too obvious. "If he's not gifted, you should have already let him go."

"I'm certain he's not telling us everything he knows about the people responsible for my brother's death," Ramsey added.

"Brother?" She was confused. The Controller had mentioned deaths in the empty zone near Colony 5, and she had mentally connected that with the men she'd helped Jaxon and the others fight six weeks earlier. But all the enforcers they'd killed that day had seemed too young to be a sibling to the Controller. Only their Elite leader, that pus bag Bensell Summers, might have run in the same circles as Ramsey. Which meant that slight resemblance she'd noted on her first meeting with Ramsey wasn't because of their Elite status after all.

"His name was Bensell Summers," Ramsey said, verifying her guess. His mouth tightened. "He was my only brother. Same mother, different father. He was on an errand for me at the time of his death. Losing him not only set back my plans but affected me on a personal level."

Dani dragged her mug to her mouth and downed the rest of her drink. Mostly to hide the swirl of emotions. The Controller didn't seem affected on a personal level. He seemed dispassionate and in control. She wondered if his brother had hated and envied him.

None of this could change the fact that Jaxon had killed Summers to prevent him from dragging them all back here for detainment. Summers was the man Jaxon believed had ordered the death of his mother. If Ramsey had any idea Dani had been there when his brother died, no doubt he'd torture her until he learned the truth, until she betrayed Jaxon.

"Bensell was killed near where your brother was picked up," Ramsey continued, his gaze not leaving hers. "Admittedly, he died after we found Tauri, but I believe he knows more than he's told us about activity there and that he could direct us to those who were involved. But I'd be willing to consider releasing him back to Colony 6 anyway."

"You mean if I agree to work for you." She had no doubt today's fatal demonstration had been meant for her.

"Yes. Having a brother yourself, you might begin to imagine the sacrifice it would be for me."

She did know, and she also understood that he would never let Tauri go. If she capitulated, Tauri would be dragged back whenever she refused to obey. The Controller would own her heart, body, and soul until she killed herself or he killed Tauri. The hopelessness of her situation shook her.

Allowing enforcers to bring her to HED had been a terrible idea. Had it been the madness that made her act so rashly? She'd waited twenty years to reunite with her Colony 6 crew, waited and built and planned. She'd spent several years planning and enacting an operation that had allowed her soldiers to deviate part of the Dallastar water supply so they had clean water in the empty zones where Newcali had bases. It had taken six months to organize a single raid that had given them enough drugs to sedate dozens of people fighting madness brought on by their abilities. Waiting had always been a detested but necessary part of her fight. But Tauri had been missing only two months, and she'd gotten herself captured at nearly the first opportunity.

She had to escape this place, and it had to be soon. Before she betrayed her brother and her people. Even if that meant she and Tauri died. Because getting out of the building would be next to impossible without a weapon, especially if Tauri wouldn't use his ability. Even if she took out the guards by the door and the other two outside, she wouldn't be able to use their guns, which would be linked to their fingerprints.

She'd half expected the buzzing in her head to return as her mind flew through the options, but she was thinking more clearly than she had in weeks. And the clear thinking told her the only viable option was taking the Controller hostage and forcing him to provide a weapon for her. Without a weapon she could use from a distance, all the strength in the world wouldn't be enough, not when she had Tauri to worry about. But dragging a hostage would slow her down and make her a target to whatever tech the Special Forces had available. It would only take a few well-placed bullets to put her down. Or a simple gas could make both her and Tauri lose consciousness. She needed something to sway the tide in their direction.

"More brew?" Ramsey asked.

When she nodded absently, he reached for her mug and rose in a fluid movement. It was as he poured the brew that she spied the nyckelira case on the desk beyond him against the far wall. Her heartbeat increased, but she took a steady breath, willing it to slow. There were thousands of nyckeliras spreading throughout the CORE, and a corresponding number of cases. It didn't mean anything.

But she knew it did. Exactly as she'd known Jaxon and the

others would be forced to come for her. That meant there was hope. A calm settled over her.

"You play the nyckelira?" she asked.

Ramsey followed her gaze to the case. "No. But my grand-children do. This is actually more of a collector's item." He handed her the full mug, and she sipped it carefully. It wasn't hot enough to burn her tongue, but almost.

She waited for more, but she guessed it would be too much to expect him to explain the real function of the case. "May I see it?"

He gave a flourishing wave. "Be my guest." He walked with her to the desk and opened the case. The dark velvet interior was exactly as Eagle had shown her, and she knew that in the hidden compartment, something special waited for her, something that meant her way out. All she needed now was Tauri.

"It's beautiful." She ran her fingers along the velvet before moving away.

"I think so. It was a gift."

"You have nice friends."

He smiled. "You could too, if you worked for me."

More likely he'd expect gifts from her. Like killing his enemies. Or betraying her friends. She waited until she was back at the food cart before saying, "Can I talk to my brother again?"

"I'll arrange it in the morning."

"Please, could I see him now? I need to be sure he's all right before I decide what I'm going to do." Would he believe she was actually considering his offer? If not, it was over before it started.

Ramsey searched her face, his expression calculating. "Okay. I'll have him brought here. But you should finish your drink."

Suspicion crept through her mind. "You drugged it, didn't you?" Panic threatened the calm she'd experienced since spying the case. If this drug put her out or dulled her ability, she might not make it out, even with whatever treasure the nyckelira case held for her.

"I gave you an antidote to the madness is all. As I said at our last meeting, it's not permanent. You've taken enough to give you a hint of what you could be if you worked for the people of the CORE. You can think again, can't you? The jitters are gone. The buzzing in your head."

There was truth in what he was saying. Her mind was clear, and her body felt stronger than ever. How many people had he tortured in order to know her so well? "You drank it too."

He nodded placidly. "The treatment has no effect on people without abilities. And it tastes great as an additive to brew."

Dani returned to the couch, debating whether she should drink the rest. For all she knew, it would hasten the madness. But she needed a clear head now. She downed the cup in one long drink.

Ramsey laughed, and again she felt the odd sensation that he reminded her of someone else. But not his brother this time. "Good choice," he said. "It only lasts a few days, probably fewer with you, but as long as you cooperate, you'll have access to more. You'll sleep better tonight, I assure you."

She tried to eat more food, but her stomach rebelled. She kept seeing the lolling head of the man in the experiment room. Ramsey had restored the holos when he'd given the order to bring Tauri, but her brain remembered only too well.

She didn't have long to wait. Three minutes after Ramsey gave the order, Tauri arrived. He wore a fresh white bodysuit and someone had plastered a bandage on his cheek. The guards brought him into the room instead of pushing him, and Dani realized her brother must have been brought to the edge of his endurance today. How much longer before he told them everything?

His hand waved a discreet greeting to Dani before his gaze settled on the Controller, hatred burning in his eyes. Guilt rushed through her as she realized she might be able to use this to her advantage. If Tauri would fight with her, no one could stop them.

Leave soon, she said in Handspeak to Tauri, keeping her hands near her stomach and her body angled away from the Controller. "Hello," she said aloud. "We saved you some food."

Who knew when he'd eaten last or how long this latest "experiment" had gone on. She'd taken only a few steps in his direction, but one of the guards pointed his rifle at her. Dani lifted her hands and backed away. The Controller watched them all, his gaze calculating. He wasn't armed that she could see, though he probably had a hidden weapon, which meant she'd have to disable the guards first.

The guards left Tauri near the food trolley but didn't immediately return to the door. She knew why as Tauri wavered slightly, looking ready to collapse.

"Can you remove his handcuffs?" She tried to pour Tauri some of the brew into her empty mug to help him regain his energy, but only a few drops drizzled from the kettle.

Ramsey smirked at her, showing that he'd known exactly how much had been inside and hadn't wanted her to receive more than necessary. He motioned to the guards, and one began to unlock Tauri's cuffs.

We leave now, she signed to Tauri. *Maybe need your ability.*

He gave her the single abrupt sign for *no* above the plate of bread drops. His expression looked worse than it had seconds ago. It didn't stop him from grabbing a drop and stuffing it into his mouth.

Not your fault, she told him. *You followed orders.*

My fault, he signed. *Always.*

Her heart ached for him, for what she might make him do.

Three years had passed since the terrible night when he'd accidentally suffocated an entire team of enforcers—as well as his best friend, who had been their unwitting captive. He hadn't used his ability since, and they had to pull him off anything but the most routine of missions. With each passing month, he feared the madness would take him, and he'd kill everyone he loved. She still didn't know how to help him, because he might be right.

"Please fill a plate and have a seat," Ramsey told Tauri, who had grabbed a handful of cookies. Dani suspected Tauri's eagerness was amusing to the Controller. She hated him more for that.

Maybe need you, she tried again with Tauri.

Again the sign for *no*.

The guards were staring at her, their weapons still ready, their faces puzzled at her hand motions. Even if Ramsey couldn't tell something was passing between them, no doubt the guards and the cameras would fill in the details later. With mistrusting stares, the guards began retreating to their place by the door, seemingly satisfied that Tauri would be able to keep his feet on his own. Dani also eased away from the trolley so Tauri would be farther from the line of fire.

The time had come to act.

With a single step, she bounced onto the couch and kicked off, hurtling toward the guards. She struck hard as she landed, taking down the female with a single kick. The man took two punches, but he was falling before his partner hit the floor. Neither had a chance to fire.

In the next breath, Dani was back over the couch and lunging at the Controller. Her arm wrapped around his throat, squeezing. He smelled of brew and something spicy. He didn't struggle.

This is almost too easy, she thought. As long as the guards outside didn't come into the room, they'd have all the time they needed to question him about escape routes before knocking him out. If enforcers did come in, she'd threaten to kill their precious Controller. Either way, she figured they had at least a few minutes.

Tauri had stopped eating and was staring at her, relief etched on his face. "I guess I didn't need your help," she said.

He laughed. "Good."

A sharp pain in her left wrist drew her attention. She looked down to see that the gold band around her wrist was tightening. "Saca," she muttered.

"It will keep growing smaller," Ramsey rasped through the pressure she was putting on his throat.

"What do you mean?" The pain was growing by the second, changing from a sharp pressure to a burning. She flexed the muscles in her wrist, pushing back at the band.

Ramsey tried to speak, but she was clenching him too tightly now. She eased up and he said, "Do you really think I'd be anywhere near you without a backup? I saw the feed from the enforcers in Santoni and on the sky train. I saw what you're capable of. The pressure band you're wearing is pre-Breakdown tech we uncovered in the North Desolation Zone. Right now that band is tightening, and thinning on the edges. It's cutting through your skin, and in a few minutes your muscles and tendons will be gone. Then all that will be left is bone until even that snaps in two."

Blood began leaking from the edges of the band. As the agony increased, Dani fell to her knees, dragging the Controller with her. Blood splattered on the white carpet. She ripped at the band with her right hand, only to slice her fingers.

By the CORE, she thought, the instinctive saying coming to her lips like a prayer. Pain painted black splotches across her vision.

"I can stop it," the Controller said. "Just let me go."

"How?"

He snorted. "Let me go, and I'll show you. The pain will only get worse. And next time I'll put it around your neck."

The pain was too great. More than the bullets she'd taken, more than the bite of a beast from a desolation zone, more than running out of breath deep under the water. More than the fever that had almost taken her life.

"Tauri," Dani gasped, her voice rising slightly with the torture. Tauri stared at her, his once-handsome face changed with terror.

"Still conscious?" Ramsey asked, mocking now. "You have serious endurance."

She couldn't let him go. No matter what. He'd own her and Tauri and they'd betray Newcali and everyone who was fighting for freedom. She had to hold on until the hand was off, until the pain stopped. She'd kill him then. And she and Tauri would still escape. Somehow.

"It's okay," she told Tauri. Sweat ran down her face, blocking what little she could see beyond the blackness.

She gripped the Controller's neck tighter and screamed.

CHAPTER 23

Eagle had set two charges, one in the bathroom and one he'd dropped casually behind a decorative pot near the entrance to the auditorium. Neither was strong enough to hurt anyone with the blast, but the resulting smoke would confuse things.

"Let me know if you see any activity out there," he told the twins through his T-link. "I have a couple of surprises I can set off."

"Reese and Jaxon are already in place," Lyra told him. "They've activated their skin tags so their IDs can't be traced and are less than thirty seconds from either of the entrances."

"Good. I'll stay here in case I can do more. I'll let you know if I see Dani."

Not wanting to attend the memorial, Eagle struck up a conversation with a knot of other enforcers chatting outside the auditorium doors. They had all known the deceased, but not well, and had used the invitation more for the opportunity to come to the CORE's capital city than to mourn his passing.

"How'd you know him?" One of the women asked.

Eagle laughed. "Well, that's kind of a long story."

"We've still got at least twenty minutes until this thing ends," said a man. "And we already tried to raid the refreshment tables over there, but they gave us the evil eye, so we're just passing time. Spill it."

Eagle fed them a slightly off-colored story about dating the same woman, who turned out to be using both of them to spread rumors about her ex, who also worked as an enforcer. "Since I was in weapons and not out in the field," Eagle finished, "She thought she'd ruin his reputation at both ends."

His audience laughed, and one of the women tried to peer past his special glasses, but he ignored her curiosity. They looked different from iTeevs, but not so much that they couldn't be a fancy upgrade. Even if she suspected they were to aid his sight, she wouldn't be able to tell they had fringer T-link capabilities.

The doors behind them opened and a group of Special Forces emerged, hurrying past them as if on a mission. "What's with them?" someone in his group muttered.

Another team of Special Forces spilled from the memorial. "Is it over?" Eagle asked.

One of them shook his head. "Nothing you need to worry about." But he lurched into a run.

Eagle backed away from the others in his group, who had begun to speculate on what their Special Forces brothers were actually doing. "Something's happening in here," he told his crew through the T-link. "I'm going to see if I can find out what. It's probably best if we all tap in to the comlink now, if you aren't already. Leaving mine open so you can hear what's happening."

"Be careful," Lyssa said in his ear.

Eagle followed the Special Forces until they disappeared into an elevator. He bet anything they would be going to the fourth floor.

"What are you doing here!" barked someone behind him.

Eagle turned to see a half dozen more Special Forces. One of them had a captain's patch and was pointing his iTeev in Eagle's direction, no doubt scanning his CivID and perusing his records. Not just any captain, but Captain Walsh of HED. Unlike most captains, he didn't answer to a chief, but directly to the Controller himself. Thirty minutes ago when Eagle had poked his head into the auditorium, he'd been up on the stage with the grieving parents of the deceased enforcer.

With Captain Walsh was a man Eagle recognized. Since the crew had begun looking for people from Colony 6, he'd grown accustomed to comparing every face he saw to those Brogan showed him or the faces from his childhood memories. This enforcer was from the latter. He was definitely someone Eagle had known in the Coop, though he couldn't remember his name. He was maybe a few years older. His face was different after twenty years, wider, and his hair far shorter, but the underlying squarish facial structure was the same. More interesting was that he radiated brighter on the electromagnetic spectrum than everyone else around him.

"Sorry Captain Walsh," Eagle said, with a proper salute. "I'm just here for the memorial."

"Then why aren't you inside?"

"Bathroom break, sir. Must have taken a wrong turn. Haven't been to HED in a long time."

"How is Amarillo City?"

"Warm, sir."

The captain's mouth twitched slightly. "Carry on."

Eagle nodded and walked away, glancing backward at the man from Colony 6. He hadn't shared Eagle's recognition, for which he was grateful, seeing as the last time enforcers had known he was from Colony 6 they'd tried to capture him.

With a few eye movements, Eagle saved the 3D images of

the enforcer to a T-link file—minus the spectrum glow—to share with the others later.

If the captain had been called from the memorial, something was definitely happening. He hoped Dani was all right.

Pain was all she knew, sharp and lasting. Concentrated. Her stomach convulsed with nausea. She must hold on a little longer. Then it would be over. She'd get her revenge. But only if she clung to consciousness.

The air around Dani seemed to pulse. She recognized the sensation and blinked to clear her eyes. She could barely see a portion of her brother as he stood by the food trolley, his face intense. Furious.

The air around her thinned.

The Controller began to gasp, clawing at her arm, though she hadn't tightened her hold. "Not only will I take your hand for this," he growled with a sneer. "But I'll personally kill your brother."

In the next instant, there was no air. Nothing to breathe. So she stopped breathing. Though it was costing her to stay conscious through the pain, she had plenty of reserve. Or would have as long as Tauri maintained enough control so he didn't suck the oxygen from her pores.

She released the Controller. He tried to drag in a breath, then his eyes widened as he realized no oxygen seeped into his lungs. Did he think she was stealing his air, or would he realize it was Tauri?

She tried to speak, but no sound reached her ears. The pain in her wrist had lessened now, and she wasn't sure that was a good sign.

She waved her right arm to get Tauri's attention. *Ask him . . . turn off,* she signed.

Tauri moved toward them, his eyes too bright. He kicked out at Ramsey. "Tell me how to stop the band. Or you will suffocate."

Ramsey's body was heaving, searching for air. He'd die in a bit, and that would also mean the end of her hand.

"Now!" Tauri thundered, sounding more like the brother she'd known and lost.

Still convulsing as his body struggled for air, Ramsey reached into his pocket for his iTeev. He tapped in a code.

Instantly, the pressure on her wrist ceased. The band loosened and dropped to the carpet, taking flesh with it. Blood still gushed from the cut circle of her wrist. Dani came to her feet, searching for something to stem the flow.

She stepped on the Controller, who had passed out. Maybe he was already dead.

Stop! she signed to Tauri. *Stop!*

He didn't look at her or appear to hear her. His face was a mask of pain and anger as he stared at the Controller. Dani crossed the few steps between them, ramming her shoulder into him and shaking her blood-drenched arm in his face.

In the space of a single heartbeat, the air seeped back around her. She reached for the elaborate cloth napkins on the trolley, folding one around her wrist. She tossed Tauri another one. "Tie it up. Hurry. Before I bleed to death." That wasn't likely now that the band was no longer cutting into her, but even her rapid healing couldn't fix this. They needed to get out.

Tauri took a deep, shaky breath, as if waking from a nightmare. He tied the napkin around her arm, followed by another one for good measure.

She sprinted across the room to the nyckelira case. A few special taps brought the secret compartment open. A miniature nine mil fell to the table, along with the oversized temper Eagle had taken from the men at the gathering in Amarillo city. Two fake CivID cards and a small disk completed the package.

Nice, she thought, reading the accompanying note: *Take jammer disk with you and relock the case. We're outside waiting. E.*

She shoved the tiny gun inside the top of her bodysuit, slipped the jammer into her wrist bandage, and grabbed the temper.

Tauri stood up from the Controller. *Dead,* he signed.

Good. That only saved her from having to do the job herself. Shutting the case, she went to check the guards, and they also had no pulse. The female was much too small for the uniform to be of any use to her, so Dani put down the temper laser and began removing the uniform of the male enforcer. Her wrist was throbbing now, but Tauri helped her change, and the tightness of the long-sleeved uniform helped some.

"We'll get you a uniform out there." She thumbed toward the door.

He nodded, staring down at the guards' faces, for a moment looking as lost as he had three years ago.

She glared at him, mouthing the words and signing at the same time. *You saved me. You protected information. You did good.*

The haunted look receded a bit. She thought about giving him the pistol, but any hesitation could still mean failure, and she wasn't sure he was all there. She pushed the temper laser at him instead, then pointed at one of the enforcer's hands and motioned toward the door. He tucked the temper under his arm and leaned over, heaving the woman up and carrying her to the handprint reader.

Dani tested her wounded arm. Not good, but the fingers still moved. Maybe it was strong enough for a hit or two, but she'd better not depend on it.

How many enforcers outside, I don't know, she signed. *Stay back. I'll distract them. You use temper laser.*

He nodded with determination, as he had on so many other operations before the accident. Maybe he'd be okay.

When Tauri opened the door with the fallen guard's hand, Dani jumped out, diving into a forward roll. A dozen Special Forces, all dressed in battle gear, began shooting. So much for hoping she hadn't alerted anyone. They might not have known what happened after she opened the nyckelira case, but they'd obviously seen her attack the guards and the Controller and had been preparing to enter the room.

She let off two bullets from the nine mil as she came to her feet, hitting one man in his helmet and another in the chest. They fell back at the blasts. She ducked behind a third man as bullets peppered her former location. Placing her good hand on the enforcer's, she held him with her bad arm and forced him to fire his assault rifle on his companions, who dived out of the way, or were hit, their uniforms protecting them from immediate death but doing little for the force of impact. Bullets ricocheted around the room.

In a few seconds, it was over. From the corner of her eye, she saw Tauri aiming the temper in slow, repeating sweeps. "Put down your weapons," she yelled.

All the enforcers except one lost interest in the battle, dropping their weapons. Dani sprinted toward the holdout—who was probably immune like Jaxon—yanked his rifle from him, and slammed it into his face. One-handed, the move didn't put him out, but she followed it with a kick to his head. He'd stay down now.

"Are there any more prisoners up here?" she barked at one of the enforcers who had previously been behind the desk.

He shook his head. "Not anymore."

Dani's gut wrenched, remembering the lolling head of the

prisoner in the observation room. "Get around the desk now and bring up the feeds to all the cameras. Put them on the main screen."

The man obeyed, but casually, as if the temper laser had sapped his energy. She wanted him to hurry. How long before reinforcements arrived?

Little squares finally began marching across the holo screen. "What about the cameras in here?" she asked to be sure.

He frowned. "I can't get them to work."

"Good. Show me the exits." She was stunned to see what looked like hundreds of enforcers in the front lobby. "Why are so many enforcers here?" she asked. Were they all here to stop her? But no one was running or had their weapons out.

"For the memorial," the man answered.

She studied the feed a few more seconds. "You," she said to the other man who'd been manning the desk earlier. "Help Tauri escort the enforcers to a cell. Remove their iTeevs and helmets first. Carry anyone who can't make it on their own. Then go into the cell yourself when you're finished."

The enforcer obeyed her orders. To be sure everyone remained compliant, Tauri kept hitting them periodically with the temper, except for the man behind the desk. She wondered if repeated use of the powerful temper might be causing permanent damage, but they really had no choice. This was the enemy, even if these men themselves were unwitting pawns.

Two dead, Tauri signed to her when he'd finished. Dani acknowledged the count. This close, it was to be expected despite the battle gear.

She made the enforcer behind the desk remove his uniform and give it to Tauri. Now in his underwear, the enforcer stared at her with anger, a sure sign his faculties were returning, which was what she needed.

"Now I want you to call in an alarm," Dani told him. "Tell whoever you're supposed to report to that the fringers are heading out the back entrance. To send all forces there." She held the gun against his temple. "Please sound convincing. And know that all of your friend's lives are at risk. I will shoot every one of them if you try anything."

The enforcer glared at her and pulled up a new holo screen over the desk. "No," Dani said. "Tell me what to push. Give me your authorization code." She couldn't have him setting off a different kind of alarm.

He hesitated, and she jerked the pistol downward, firing. He screamed and doubled over in agony as blood spattered down his leg. "Now," she said. "Or I can put a bullet in the other leg."

To Tauri, she added, "Get one of the others. We'll make an example of him."

Tauri nodded and was almost to the door when the enforcer capitulated. "Five, nine, zero, four, alpha, delta, ten," he said. "You put it in here."

Dani could feel her brother's sense of relief as she followed the enforcer's direction and gestured for him to speak.

"The prisoners are escaping," he yelled. "They're heading to the rear entrance. All forces move to stop them!"

"What happened?" barked a return voice. "Why are the cameras disabled? We detected weapons fire."

The enforcer hesitated, and Dani jabbed him with the gun. There weren't any bullets left, but he couldn't know that. "Prisoners somehow obtained weapons," he said with a gasp. "Must have control of the camera. I can't get it to work."

"Is everyone okay? We're getting no images from the helmet cameras either."

Say you're fine, Dani mouthed.

"We're fine. No casualties. Please get them!"

"But we don't have images of them leaving the fringer unit," came the voice.

Dani closed the connection. She had to hope that whoever the enforcer was talking to would be more interested in making sure she wasn't escaping out the back than in what the hallway cameras told him. The sooner she disrupted the cameras outside this room—any camera—the better.

"Thank you," she said to the enforcer. Then she punched him hard with her right fist. "You'll thank me later," she told him as he crumbled. "They can't blame you this way."

She looked to see Tauri watching her. "We should have killed them all," he said.

She nodded. "I know, but it's really not their fault, and I know how you feel about it." She hadn't wanted to risk him withdrawing into himself, not after killing the three in the observation room.

Thank you, he signed.

They pulled on two of the discarded helmets to hide the white of their hair that would stand out even more than their black skin. "Turn off the cameras on the helmets," she said to Tauri. The cameras wouldn't broadcast as long as she held the jammer, but those watching the cameras would soon understand that they had only to follow the disrupted feeds to find her. She'd have to ditch the jammer at the first opportunity, and once she did, she didn't want the helmet cameras active.

She activated both the CivID cards Eagle had placed inside the case and gave one to her brother. She would have preferred skin tags, but these would be more useful inside HED if he'd given them IDs of actual enforcers. She'd have to trust that he knew what he was doing.

Let's go, she signed. *More enforcers outside.*

If more enforcers weren't already outside in the hallway, they'd run into more soon enough. Whoever was in charge would send a team to secure the cells and make sure the Controller was alive.

She smiled in satisfaction. At least that bit had gone absolutely right. Controller Warrick Ramsey would never again hurt more of her people.

Together she and Tauri dragged the unconscious enforcer to the door and used his handprint to exit. Only three enforcers were sprinting down the hallway toward their location. They waved in greeting, and Dani responded, motioning for them to hurry. When they were close enough, she took two by surprise with her good hand and a foot before Tauri finished using the temper laser on the other.

"Stand down," Dani told him. "We're friends."

"I'm supposed to protect the Controller," the enforcer said, sounding as if he really wasn't sure.

"Right, but now you have a different mission." Dani marched the enforcer to the elevator and gave him the jammer disk. "Go to the back entrance. Give this to the Special Forces there. You want to do this. You'll get everything you want if you do. But hurry."

The man nodded. "I should use the back elevator."

Dani hadn't known there was more than one set, but it made sense given the size of HED. "The Controller will be so pleased," she added, motioning for Tauri to give him another dose of the temper laser.

"Thank you." Holding the jammer tightly in his hand, the enforcer hurried off.

Depending on his force of will, he might shake off the effects of the temper before he got to his destination, but hopefully by then they'd be far away.

Eagle had barely made it down the hallway near the auditorium when the doors opened and people began to stream past. The memorial was over then, and still nothing new on Dani.

"Get out of the way! Get out of the way!" someone yelled.

Eagle threw himself against the wall as Captain Walsh thundered past, his entourage of Special Forces having quadrupled since Eagle had talked with him minutes earlier. Others coming from the auditorium weren't as quick, and the enforcers surrounding the captain pushed them roughly aside.

"Ouch," someone shouted. "By the CORE. What's going on? Did you feel that flash of heat?"

Eagle craned to see the speaker in the growing crowd of enforcers. He had seen the flash but not its origin. Neither of his distractions would have resulted in anything resembling a heat flash, so someone else was responsible.

"You're lucky you got out of the way," a voice said behind him.

Eagle turned to see Donnel at his shoulder. "Why's that?"

"That guy with the captain? Name's Queran. I've worked with him before. He's . . . he's . . ." Donnel shuddered. "The radiation must have changed him. He can fry a person's insides without even touching them. Whatever you do, stay on his good side."

Eagle didn't feel satisfaction at knowing he'd been right about the enforcer coming from Colony 6. "What's going on, do you know?"

Donnel nodded. "Some. A notice just went out to every Special Forces here. At least one prisoner has escaped from the fringer holding cell. I'm supposed to help clear the crowd and make sure only valid enforcers leave."

"They have a description?"

"A woman with black skin and white hair. Hard to hide." Donnel punched his arm playfully. "You don't fit the description. Better get out while you can." He winked at Eagle and turned into the crowd.

"You get that?" Eagle whispered.

Reese's voice came over the comlink. "Yes," she said. "All units confirm. Dani is on the move."

Each member of the crew began to check in. The last response was lost to Eagle as an emergency siren blasted throughout HED.

Dani and Tauri slipped inside the doors to the stairs as the elevator chimed, warning them of new arrivals. They ducked into the stairwell and ran down four flights, seeing no one until they emerged on the main floor. There, Tauri stumbled over a tall man in a blue lab uniform.

He stared at the temper laser in Tauri's hand. "Why do you have one of my ultratemp prototypes? Who gave you permission? And what did you do to the barrel?"

This made Dani blink in surprise. The temper was a HED prototype? So her flippant guess back in Amarillo City hadn't been far off. But did that mean the men they'd picked up at the Amarillo City train station had been connected with this man? Or that the weapons had been stolen?

Tauri was already using the temper, but casually to fool any cameras.

"The Controller gave it to us," she said, which in a way was the truth. "We're searching for the prisoners."

"Oh, of course. So that's what's going on."

"You should go back to your lab," Dani suggested.

"I think I'll go back to my lab," the scientist wandered off.

Tauri kept the temper pointed unobtrusively downward

at his side as they hurried through the hallway. The crowd of enforcers she'd glimpsed in the camera feed hadn't thinned at all, and in a few moments, Dani saw why—there was a line to get out. She stepped in line with Tauri, scanning the crowd. They were the only enforcers wearing battle helmets here, except for those checking people through the exits. That might be a problem.

She made the signs for "fight" and "go out," keeping her movements to a minimum. Tauri had to understand that she'd need his ability again.

He tucked the temper under his arm. *Can't. Many people.*

You strong, she signed back and looked away from the expression in his eyes. Maybe his breakthrough hadn't really been a breakthrough at all. Maybe he was only being strong to get her out.

Tauri touched her shoulder to make her look at him again. *He watches.* He jerked his head at a man who wasn't in the outgoing line, a man who was searching the crowd despite the covering of dark glasses over his eyes. It was Eagle. His movement didn't change when he passed them, but his eyes met hers briefly across the room.

Dani felt a distinct sense of relief. Eagle would back her up, even if it meant he'd blow his cover and have to go into hiding.

Dani didn't dare make the sign for friend because the cameras were still broadcasting down here, but she turned her back slightly on Eagle. Tauri would understand that sign. It meant she wasn't afraid of him.

There were two security counters, but only one was active. Precious seconds ticked by as they slowly approached the counter. When it was finally their turn, the enforcer frowned at the screen. "Why are you wearing Special Forces uniforms? That doesn't match up with your CivIDs. And you'll have to remove your helmets if—" he broke off as he looked more closely at them, his eyes widening at the color of their skin.

"We're new," Dani said. "The IDs aren't updated." But she knew their cover was blown.

Tauri shifted, aiming the temper, but already the enforcer and those around him were reaching for their weapons. Their movements were slow to Dani, and she'd have plenty of time to take them all out, or at least those between her and the door. But she couldn't take on all the other enforcers in the line.

She whipped her head to Tauri, who seemed frozen like the others. Fear radiated in his eyes, fear that he'd kill everyone here. He was right to be afraid, and where it hadn't mattered to her minutes before, it mattered to her now that Eagle would also die.

And Tauri would have more horror to live with. Dani clenched her muscles to act. She'd at least take out as many as she could. Maybe if she moved fast enough, Tauri could somehow get free.

A shout came from behind them. "Help!" someone yelled. Smoke billowed through the lobby, though Dani hadn't heard any explosion. Murmurs spread through the crowd as everyone turned in that direction.

"It's the prisoners!" The voice came from far behind them, sounding a lot like Eagle. "This way—everyone head them off." The enforcers in line behind Dani jumped to obey.

She snatched the temper from her brother and squeezed the trigger at the Special Forces behind the scanner, sweeping over those in front of the door as well. "You'd better go help," she told them. "I'll take over here."

Without waiting for a response, she grabbed Tauri with her bad hand and pushed him hard in the direction of the door. A shot slammed into the glass, and Dani turned to see one of the Special Forces stepping from behind the counter. Less than one percent of people were immune to the temper laser, and she'd run into two of them today. It was probably one of the qualities most sought by HED.

She dropped the temper and sprang for the man, knocking his gun to the floor and slamming her fist into his face. She whirled, grabbing Tauri and pulling him out the door. Bullets sprayed the glass behind them. She risked a backward glance and saw a group of angry-looking Special Forces emerging from the building, pushing people out of the way.

Was it her imagination, or was heat waving toward her?

She held on more tightly to Tauri and ran into the street. The sun had set, but barely so, and it was still light enough that it would be difficult to hide.

"Run!" she screamed.

CHAPTER 24

"Dani just came out the front," Lyra's voice said in Jaxon's ear.

Jaxon engaged his scrambler engine and followed Reese out of the alley where they'd been waiting. The scramblers ran on pre-Breakdown tech that used fuel cells for power. They were fast, maneuverable, and ran for a month without refueling. Riding them always made Jaxon feel powerful.

"Special Forces are in pursuit." Lyra paused and added. "On foot for now, but I'm sure that won't be for long. Oh, no. Looks like Dani's heading for an alley that doesn't have an exit. Hurry!"

He and Reese pushed the scramblers to the max. They ripped past a group of Special Forces, who cheered, probably thinking they were on their side. They looked the part with the helmets, but that would only last until the real Special Forces noticed the black bands obscuring their division patch or checked the camera feed to scan for their now-masked CivIDs.

"I see the alley," Reese said. "Wish they knew we were coming."

"Dani will be expecting us." Jaxon rounded the corner a little too fast. For a thrilling and terrifying moment, he thought he was going to lose control. His years in Amarillo City without the daily use of a scrambler had taken their toll. Or possibly his instability was the lingering effect of the juke.

He recovered as Reese screeched to a stop in front of Dani, who looked ready to pounce. "Get on!" Reese shouted, patting the seat behind her.

Dani nodded once and pushed her brother toward Reese. Tauri straddled the scrambler and they took off.

The next second, Dani was climbing on behind Jaxon. "Hold on tight!" he yelled.

But before he could get the scrambler moving, a vision flashed over him. Nothing concrete, except a man in gray staring down the barrel of Reese's gun, her lowering it and following him. Numberless other images crowded in after that glimpse, threatening to steal his sanity.

A sharp dig in his side became noticeable, and Jaxon struggled to focus. Dani had her left arm around him, but it was dripping blood. "Drive!" she ordered. "Or do you need me to do it?"

"Jaxon! Where are you?" Reese said urgently through his comlink.

"They've got scramblers in play," Lyra added. "And all the shuttles in the area have pulled to the side of the road. They must have used the emergency override. Brogan said something about your scramblers having extra power, but that only makes a difference if they don't trap you."

Gritting his teeth, Jaxon fingered the power controls, and Dani crashed against his back as they leapt into motion. He skidded into the main street, barely missing a shuttle. Special

Forces on scramblers had reached the alley, and he took them by surprise as he roared passed. Shots sounded around them. Dani felt for the gun she must have known he kept in his suit, the one with the disabled fingerprint reader. She returned fire.

Jaxon spied Reese ahead and pushed his scrambler harder. He concentrated only on her back. He could feel the weight of the cameras lining the streets throughout the city. Until they made it out of town, they couldn't stop or they'd be cornered. His heart thundered, his breathing was fast and shallow. He kept his eyes ahead.

She glanced back at him. "Once we leave the city, it's over the bridge and into the trees," she said in his comlink. "Ten more minutes. The shuttle from the local Undergrounders will be there."

"Okay." Ten minutes. He could push back the tide of visions until then.

"Are you okay?" she asked. "Because you're weaving a lot."

"To avoid bullets," he lied.

He didn't dare glance behind him, but Dani had actually stopped firing, which meant she'd taken out those close enough to reach. As if to taunt him, a drone whirred by, only feet above them. It couldn't shoot, but that meant there was no way to shake their pursuit, even if they left the cameras behind. Reese stayed on the main road and he followed, zigzagging between the few cars on the street that had no automatic controls or Teev overrides.

"At least they cleared the way for us," Reese said, her voice mocking.

"Kind of them," he agreed.

An eternity seemed to pass until he spied the bridge. That marked the last of the regular cameras, which meant they'd have to do something about the drones before they made it to the rendezvous with the shuttle.

"Uh-oh," Reese said. "Looks like TAD found someone to head us off."

A silver enforcer shuttle had appeared at the far end of the bridge, obviously having been out of the city on some other business. But the solitary vehicle couldn't block the entire bridge. Already the enforcers were running to the open space next to the shuttle, kneeling down and bringing up their assault rifles.

Jaxon grinned. "Let's show them how we sixers do this."

"Sixers?" Reese asked.

"Us," he supplied. "People with abilities from Colony 6."

She laughed and ducked behind the bulletproof plexiglass rising in front of the handlebars. Jaxon also hunched and felt Dani press her helmet against his back. They careened toward the enforcers. A battery of shots crashed against the plexiglass. It splintered but held, the bullets suspended in spiderwebs of damaged glass. Both he and Reese plunged on ahead, their scramblers dangerously close at this velocity.

More shots hit the glass, and a shard flew up and banged against his helmet. At the last second, the enforcers dived to the side and the scramblers sped on through.

Jaxon couldn't tell if the sigh of relief was his or Reese's.

"You guys okay?" Lyra asked. "That was an awful lot of shooting."

"We're fine." Reese sounded tough and determined, and Jaxon was sure he was the only one to hear worry in her voice.

"Good. I've got Eagle with me," Lyra added. "We're heading back to the C-lodge."

"I'm already at the C-lodge," Lyssa said. "I'm following the pursuit on the enforcer feed. They aren't saying much, though. Just that a fringer was spotted in town. Nothing about an escape from HED. Watch for police shuttles on the outskirts of the city. They've called in everyone."

"We're out of camera range," Reese said, "but we still have a drone on our tail. No, make that two."

"Pull over," Jaxon said. "We have to take care of them now." They skidded to a stop and he, Reese, and Dani started firing at the drones. Jaxon's hand shook but he emptied his clip, satisfaction spilling through him as one of the drones burst into flame. The second followed in a brilliant fireball.

"Let's move," he grunted.

The landscape around him sped by as they pushed the scramblers to the max speed. He could see a sparse forest ahead now. At the thought of the forest, his vision abruptly clouded, showing him another momentary flash of the man in gray. Just as fast, it was gone.

"Reese," he said, "Be careful."

"You see something?" She glanced backward at the sky, presumably for drones.

"Maybe. But not up there."

Her resulting "Oh" was loaded with . . . something, and he was glad he couldn't see her expression.

Less than a minute later, they turned off the main road onto a narrow trail leading into the trees. Slowing their speed considerably, they bounced along. It was darker here, but not dangerously so. At this point, darkness was their friend.

They'd been inside the tree line for only two minutes when a figure stepped out in front of them. Jaxon slammed on his brakes and swerved to avoid hitting the man. Dani cursed as their scrambler crashed into a tree.

By the time Jaxon and Dani were on their feet, undamaged but rattled, Reese was already confronting the man, her gun drawn and pointed at his heart. "Why are you following us?" Her voice was harsh. "Come to finish what you started seven months ago?"

The man blinked slowly. His eyes were dark and his hair even darker, cropped short like an enforcer's. He was still wearing the fancy gray pants and high collared shirt that opened in a deep V, topped now by a long black jacket. Jaxon glimpsed a handgun in a holster under his arm. A gun he hadn't drawn. He had the kind of handsome face that made women swoon and men want to punch him out. Smooth and confident, not the kind to dirty his hands but capable of finding someone who would.

"I'm Xavier," the man said. "And I'm not sure what you mean."

Reese pulled off her helmet. "What about now?"

The man started noticeably with recognition. "I heard you were in town, and I did see you outside HED, but until this moment, I didn't know I would be meeting you. I assure you, I'm here only to collect the scramblers and to provide a shuttle that will allow you to get wherever El Cerebro is sending you. But we need to hurry. After the attack on HED, the Controller will be out for blood."

"He's dead," Dani said. "He's not going to be out for anything."

Xavier's attention shifted to her. "That's good news indeed."

Dead? Jaxon felt Dani's words like a jab to his stomach. Had he only imagined the recognition in the Controller's eyes? He didn't know if he should be relieved that the monster would never again interfere with his life, or if he should scream out at the unfairness of it all. So many years he'd hoped to find answers, and now whatever knowledge this man held for him was lost.

He pulled off his helmet and tossed it on the ground next to his fallen scrambler. Dani looked over at him in concern, but he shook his head to ward off comment. His head pounded and dizziness threatened his vision, but he'd be fine.

"You will not make it far on the scramblers," Xavier was

saying to Reese. "Special Forces is already searching the area for you, and I estimate they'll reach our position in ten minutes. There will be drones, I'm sure."

Reese didn't waver. "El Cerebro contacted New York's underground, not KC," she spat.

Xavier smiled, one side of his mouth rising higher than the other. "A lot has changed in seven months. For both of us, apparently." His gaze at Reese was pointed. "As CORE Elite continued to tighten their choke-hold over Estlantic, Kordell Corp has expanded its interests. As have you, or so it would appear."

"We are *not* on the same side," Reese retorted. "When I investigated your company, I was doing my job. Your company was running juke. *Is* running juke. You destroy lives."

Xavier was unperturbed. "Yet tonight we're working together. We now have about seven minutes until enforcers reach this area. Are you going to shoot me or follow me to your shuttle?"

"Reese." Jaxon moved slowly to her side. "We have to get out of here."

Her face turned toward him. "This was what you saw? Us meeting him?"

He nodded. "And you have to let him go." His gaze swung first to one side of the trees and then the other. It was growing steadily darker, but he could still see crouching shadows out there. He added quietly, "He's not alone. With Dani we could probably take them out, even if she's one-handed, but maybe not. We got what we came for. Now's not the time for a confrontation with Kordell Corp."

Reese's chest heaved, and he could tell she wanted to reject his words. But she gave a sharp nod and jerked her face back to Xavier, lowering her gun but not putting it away. "Lead on."

Xavier turned his back and led them through the woods,

checking only once to see if they were following. Dani left her brother and slipped between Reese and Jaxon. "Six more in the trees. Want me to dispatch them?"

Jaxon shook his head. "We need to get you and Tauri somewhere safe." He gestured to her arm. "In case you hadn't noticed, you're bleeding."

She nodded and didn't contest his suggestion, which told Jaxon more than anything that she was worried about her arm and perhaps her brother, who seemed too quiet to be okay.

"He'll be fine," Dani said, seeing Jaxon's glance behind them. "He saved me in there. I couldn't have escaped without him. Or without you guys." There was a hitch in her voice, but Jaxon couldn't tell if it was because she hadn't expected them to come for her or if she was simply grateful.

It was probably the closest thing they'd get to an apology for her rashness, but Jaxon didn't care. His crew was safe. They might be half insane, but they were safe.

For now.

Two minutes later, they reached a clearing near a wide dirt road leading off through the trees. Parked on the road was a shuttle. "Follow this road until it leaves the trees," Xavier said. "I recommend taking the back roads. The shuttle has programming to avoid roads with cameras, but they've killed all the shuttle traffic in and around the city, so you'll be noticed even without cameras. The shuttle will begin broadcasting a nonconsequential ID in twenty minutes. If you're stopped, you'll have to fight, and I won't be able to help you." He sounded almost happy at that. "When you're finished using it, just leave it. We'll pick it up when everything dies down."

"And the scramblers?" Reese asked. "How will you hide those?"

One brow arched. "If I didn't know better, I'd say you're worried about me."

Reese rolled her eyes and started to get inside the shuttle. Xavier's hand reached out to touch her arm but stopped as she flinched away from him, her face stiff. Jaxon moved to step between them, his hand going to his gun. Not that Reese couldn't defend herself, but because whatever sketch she must have received from him, it hadn't been anything pleasant.

Xavier's gaze met his briefly and then slid past him to Reese. "It isn't over between us," he said. To Jaxon, he added, "Tell El Cerebro he now owes KC a favor." He turned and strode away as Reese glared at him.

"I know," Jaxon told her. "I . . ." Whatever he'd been going to say was lost as a premonition settled over him.

The Controller stares at him, much as he had in the auditorium at HED. "There's something I need to tell you," he says.

"Stay away from me," Jaxon retorts. "I have nothing to say to you."

Pain shoots through him. He opens his mouth to scream.

"Jaxon!" Reese's voice sounded far away. He tried to assure her it was just a vision—and obviously not a real one since the Controller was dead—but before anything escaped his lips, the medley of images pressed against his mind.

He saw Reese in a bed sleeping with a bare shoulder peeking above the covers, Eagle without his special glasses as his face twisted in pain, Lyssa—or was it Lyra?—holding an infant, Lyssa's boyfriend with a broken neck, Lyra—or was it Lyssa?—quivering at the wrong end of a loaded pistol, himself as he stared down at Brogan's still face, enforcers and Fringers firing at each other, Reese with tears skidding down her face as she beat out a rhythm on a prone man's chest. His chest.

Then everything went black.

CHAPTER 25

Reese's anger and upset at her confrontation with Xavier was overshadowed by the sketch about the Controller from Jaxon's mind. Before she could process what she'd seen, the kaleidoscope of sketches he'd emitted at the C-lodge in New York were back, rushing at her with a rapidity that made her nauseated.

"Help me get him in the car," she said to the others. Dani and Tauri grabbed Jaxon and helped settle him in the back seat.

Reese climbed in next to him, and the others took the front. She leaned forward to give orders to the shuttle. "Go to Morry. Take the back roads at maximum possible speed. But avoid any cameras for as long as possible." The shuttle bumped into life. Hopefully, they wouldn't be picked up by drones.

"Reese?" Lyssa said in her ear. "What's wrong? What happened to Jaxon?"

"I'm not sure." Reese ran shaking fingers over his uniform, checking for any possible cause but knowing the rush of images had to stem from his ability.

"Um, I might know what's wrong," Eagle said, his voice hesitant and subdued in Reese's comlink. "It could be the juke."

"What are you talking about?" Reese worked her arm under Jaxon's neck and checked his pulse. It was slow now, and the rapid images had disappeared since he'd lost consciousness. Except in her own mind, where the sketches demanded to be put on paper.

"Apparently, Dr. Kentley told him juke intensified abilities."

"I know that." Fury shot through Reese. "I was there. Did Jaxon also tell you it speeds up onset of the madness?"

"He didn't mention that." Eagle sounded miserable. "I knew it was a bad idea. But he was determined to figure out how to get the nyckelira case to Dani. I gave him the counter agent when he passed out. He should be okay."

"Okay?" Reese mocked. "You can't be serious. Juke can be addictive with a single dose. That's why they don't let enforcers test it in training anymore." In one of Jaxon's pockets, she found a black hypo marked with a white J and tossed it to the floor in disgust.

"I know, but he's strong. And he was going to do it anyway, with or without me."

Reese's fury died a quick death. "I know how stubborn he can be, but you saw how bad he was already. You should have stopped him."

No, *she* should have stopped him instead of hiding at the C-lodge from Kordell Corp. What if Jaxon never fully recovered? What if this rush of images became his constant world until the insanity killed him?

"Please make the report to the captain. We'll call when we get to the safehouse." She cut the connection, too upset at Eagle and Jaxon to remain connected over the T-link.

She scooted closer to Jaxon, stroking his cheek and

murmuring in his ear. "I'm sorry," she said. "I'm not angry with you anymore. Please wake up."

No response. In fact, his pulse was even fainter.

She called Brogan on her T-link. "Something's wrong with Jaxon," she said. "He won't wake up. Is Kentley with you? Maybe he knows something I can do. Tell him Jaxon took juke to find out where to leave the nyckelira case. He also took the counter agent. I don't have any medical supplies, except the standard kit in my suit. So if he can't help, I'm taking him to a hospital." She could do that alone and send Dani and Tauri on to the safehouse.

"Kentley and I will intercept you," Brogan said. "But I'm sending new coordinates. We'll have to risk you traveling farther west. In the meantime, Kentley says to give him a hypo with a stim."

Reese scrounged in her kit for the medicine. "Okay, I've done that. He doesn't seem to be reacting."

"Let us know if there's any change."

"Okay. But hurry!"

After staring at Jaxon for ten minutes, checking his pulse every few, Reese fished for the tiny drawing pad in the pocket of her uniform and began drawing. As the images formed under her pencil, her shaking stopped.

Feeling a gaze on her, she looked up to meet Dani's eyes. There was something different about her, but Reese couldn't pinpoint what.

"I didn't know that's how you got the case to me." Dani's voice was low and husky in the dim light.

"It wasn't your fault," Reese said without conviction. Because if Dani hadn't taken off as she had, Jaxon might be okay.

"They would have killed Tauri," Dani glanced at her brother, whose face tightened. "And me."

"I had no choice," Tauri said, making no sense to Reese.

"Yes, you did." Dani's voice grew hard. "You could have let them cut off my hand. You made the right choice. If you'd used your ability sooner, they wouldn't have been able to take you at all."

"Maybe." Tauri's jaw clenched as he gestured at Jaxon. "But what happens when the madness takes me like that? No one I know will be safe." His voice grew as hard as Dani's. "You should have left me there."

"They would have used you."

"I wouldn't have given in."

"Then you would be dead. You saw what that man was capable of."

Tauri's voice was soft. "Yes."

Reese didn't know anything of what had happened to them at HED, or what Tauri's ability was, and now wasn't the time to ask, but whatever happened had shaken them both. Jaxon would be happy his sacrifice had saved them from certain death. For Reese the idea of losing Jaxon was more than she could bear.

Dani was silent for a moment. "If juke increases the ability, maybe it's related. Maybe it's part of the treatment. The Controller said it had to be administered often. That sounds like a drug, not a cure."

"Kentley tried using a derivative for a cure," Reese told her. "It didn't work."

Dani nodded. "Well, if the doctor is as good as everyone in Santoni seems to think, he'll be able to do something for Jaxon, at least temporarily. And then we'll figure out a more permanent solution. We won't give up."

Dani was right. They rescued her and her brother at great odds, and she wouldn't expect less for Jaxon. Reese dared to hope.

But a short time later as their shuttle made a descent on a dark, winding road that had Reese longing for the sky train, Jaxon stopped breathing. Reese pushed him down on the seat and began pounding on his chest.

"Breathe!" she yelled at him.

Nothing.

"We need another stim!" she shouted.

Dani stopped the shuttle, and they pulled Jaxon out onto the road. Reese kept pumping his chest as Dani administered the medicine.

Still nothing.

She felt Dani's hand on her shoulder, willing her to stop, but she didn't. She couldn't. Not until there was some reaction.

Then she remembered the juke. The drug in its first stages was a stimulant. She dived for the open shuttle door and fumbled for the hypo. A few precious seconds later she stabbed it into his neck and then continued her compressions.

Less than five seconds later, Jaxon took a shuddering breath. His eyes opened. "Reese?"

"I'm here." She leaned over to put her cheek next to his. What was she going to do when he crashed again as he inevitably would?

She pulled away and saw that his eyes were shut, but he was smiling.

"Let's get him back into the shuttle," she said. "And check your suits for stims. I want to have them ready just in case."

"I can walk," Jaxon protested. She and Dani ignored him.

Back in the shuttle, as they sped into the night, Jaxon put his arms around her, and only then did she realize she was shaking. "It's okay," he murmured in her ear. "It's okay. I feel great."

Of course he did. That was the juke talking.

Jaxon pulled her tighter and kissed her neck, her ear, the

tears on her cheeks, moving in a trail until he found her lips, pushing them open with his own.

Reese kissed him back, the fear making her anxious and greedy.

"Woah," Jaxon drew back as the visions began to come again.

Visions of them. Reese clung to him, seeing rapid sketches in his mind, one after another, vivid and bright, filled with emotion. Until she didn't know what was real, his touch or the sketches. His hands knew all the right places to caress, the hard lines of his body fit along hers perfectly.

She never wanted the sketches to end. This was how it was always supposed to be, the two of them together. She understood that now.

But it did end. All too soon.

The sketches of them together ceased abruptly. Innumerable images came next, reaching her in distorted, horrific sketches. With a cry, Reese doubled over and heaved, but nothing came up. Again and again she heaved. Her hands shook and her head felt ready to explode.

"Sorry," Jaxon muttered. She wiped her mouth and clung to him anyway.

Just when she couldn't take anymore, Jaxon passed out and the images ceased. With a shaking hand, she checked for a pulse. Still strong but fading fast. She'd get the stims ready. Should she give them to him now? What if they did nothing for him like the last time?

"We're almost there," Dani said.

How long had it been since they'd spoken to Brogan? Reese had no concept of passing time. She knew only that she might fly apart at any moment.

"But there's no way this is the halfway point," Dani muttered as if reading her mind. "It's only been a few hours. Give me your T-link. I want to check the coordinates. Okay, it's right. But unless they . . ."

Whatever else she said was lost as the multitude of sketches claimed Reese's attention. She fought to stay alert. For Jaxon. But her mind wouldn't obey. She began sketching in the air, not coherent enough to reach for her drawing pad.

Then hands were pulling at her, and she was vaguely aware of Kentley's hands rubbing her arms. The terrible compulsion to sketch leaked away, in a mere trickle at first and then in a flood. She sighed with relief.

"Get them inside," she heard Brogan say.

Dani's arm went around Reese as she half dragged her out of the shuttle. All around them houses rose in every direction, but no lights penetrated the darkness except those in the house in front of them. Reese watched Brogan carry Jaxon inside, his thick arms and shoulders barely straining at the effort. Reese felt a sense of safety that somehow Brogan always emitted, and the fear inside her seeped away like the sketches in her mind.

Brogan set Jaxon on a couch, and Kentley knelt beside him, running his hands over his body. "You're just in time."

"I gave him more juke," Reese admitted. "He stopped breathing. It was the only thing we could do."

Kentley twisted his head to stare up at her. "Right. That would work. But only because you got him here quickly. I'll take care of that in a minute, but first . . ." He injected a hypo into Jaxon's neck. "This should reverse the madness."

Reese gaped at him, the suddenness of the declaration taking her by surprise. "You found a cure?"

Brogan stepped away from the couch, turning to her. "We found water in several of the old sauce skins you left at your aunt's house. The doctor did an analysis and was able to separate the drug they gave all of you from the water and other additives."

"Viribus," Dani said. When Brogan looked at her in confusion, she added, "That's what the Controller called what they gave us."

Brogan snorted. "Finally, a name for it. So after plugging this viribus into the formulas he'd already developed, Kentley thinks it's a cure. But it's never been tested."

"It will work," Kentley said. "I know it. I *feel* it."

Reese looked down on Jaxon, who was still out but breathing more steadily now. Was that because of Kentley's presence or the cure?

"It's going to take me longer to get the juke from his system," Kentley said. "I can't guarantee he won't crave it, but I can limit the effects."

"Then the cure isn't connected to juke?" Reese had to be sure. The last thing they needed was to cure Jaxon of the madness and hook him permanently on the drug.

Kentley's narrow face grimaced. "On the contrary. It is connected, as I suspected all along. Juke is positively a byproduct of the, uh, viribus. Historically they both appeared about sixty years ago after the colonies were created. But the viribus isn't a hallucinogen or anything like it."

"How long will your cure last?" Dani asked.

Reese stared at her and then looked back at Kentley. "It's not permanent?" She'd assumed it was.

Kentley glanced at Brogan, whose heavy-lidded eye shut momentarily. "You can tell them."

"Using the viribus inside the water at your aunt's," Kentley began, "I was able to create a treatment which is basically an infusion of the drug, which I think will last at least some weeks. Possibly months. And there was enough for a few more doses."

"Only a few?" Reese asked. "You can't synthesize it?"

"Not effectively. Not without a larger sample of the original drug, undiluted would be best. The yield would just be too low.

And without a pure sample, I also can't begin to make a permanent cure to the madness. There are too many factors." He hesitated before adding, "The drug didn't so much as change us as it did enhance latent abilities that ran in our families. By finding which part of the drug causes the madness, I believe I can counter that permanently. But I need more viribus to run the tests."

"That fits with what the Controller told me." Dani said. "They purposely sent those with any kind of ability to Colony 6. They wanted to make stronger humans who could withstand another Breakdown." Dani paced the length of the room, her wounded hand held across her stomach. She stopped and faced them, her black face somber. "But I don't think there's a cure. They gave me something in a mug of brew, and it stopped my jitters completely. I felt strong and clear. In control. Like I did years ago. The Controller said it would only last a short time. I'd get more only if I agreed to help him. If I didn't . . ." She swallowed hard. "He showed us a man whose ability made him self-destruct."

Kentley made a sound of disgust. "There's a cure. But we'll never get it from the Elite."

Dani nodded. "They're afraid of us." She glanced toward Tauri and away again. "They *should* be afraid."

Kentley arose and motioned Dani to a table that stood in the corner of the room. "Come, let me look at your arm."

Reese finally collapsed to a chair and gazed at their surroundings. The house was very old, with minimal furniture. Just the couch, the table, and a few chairs. Nothing on the gray walls, and only bare, uneven wood strips on the floor. The dust was so thick that it must have been months since anyone had come here.

Brogan sat down in a chair next to her. "You'll have to return to New York," he said. "Maybe look up a few old friends. We have to leave a clear trail of you two going home from your visit."

Reese nodded. "But not in the KC shuttle. We need to send it somewhere fast. In fact, we shouldn't stay here long. I don't trust them."

"Sorry about the KC involvement." Brogan's dark eyes were brooding and his strong shoulders slightly hunched. "I didn't realize they were involved until it was too late. I would be lying if I didn't say I was worried. The KC might be undermining the CORE, but their goals are very different from ours."

"I'm glad you see that."

"But don't worry about this place," Brogan added. "It's too near the East Desolation Zone to be inhabited long term. That's why it's deserted despite how untouched the city is. It's also hidden from most of the CORE surveillance because of the nearby mountains. It was the only place close enough to you that we were confident we could take a Newcalian hover to without being detected."

"A hover?" Now Reese understood what Dani had already figured out in the shuttle. "I'm glad you managed that for Jaxon's sake, but I don't want to know what you promised the fringers to get one of their precious hovers."

"Actually, they offered it free of charge to El Cerebro shortly after you left for New York on the sky train, and I took them up on it, just in case we needed a backup. They were worried about the information Tauri and Dani might spill once they had each other to worry about."

Meaning it was easier to sacrifice your own life than someone you loved. Reese understood that today more than she ever had before.

"I did have to give them some insurance that I'd return it," Brogan added, sounding troubled.

Reese stared. What could El Cerebro possibly have that

they'd trust him to return a hover? There was only one thing—or one person—she knew he'd sacrifice anything for. "Nova?" she said with a little gasp.

He nodded. "It's just a visit, and she volunteered. She needed to get away."

"I'm sorry."

"They want their hover. She'll be okay." His smile looked forced. "I'm actually betting she comes back with some good intel."

"No doubt."

Jaxon stirred on the couch, and Reese rose to her feet quickly, casting an apologetic look at the captain, but Brogan was already moving off to join the doctor, who was using a laser on Dani's wrist.

"Why do I feel like someone's been banging on me?" Jaxon asked.

Reese gripped his hand. "Because maybe someone has, but you're going to be all right. Dr. Kentley found a treatment."

"That's good."

His tone told her he understood what she wasn't saying, that a treatment wasn't a cure. Still, it was a lot better than the nothing they'd had before.

A week later, Jaxon took a bottle of chotks to the couch where Reese was sketching in the light that came through the glass doors leading to her balcony. Though her need to record her sketches had diminished in the short time Kentley had been working with them in the underground, they'd interviewed a number of people today as they tracked the oversized temper laser and the preacher who had brought them to Amarillo City.

Ever since Dani had asserted that HED was responsible for the weapon's creation, Brogan wanted to determine whether the preacher and his men had stolen the weapon or if the Controller had sent them to the city on a mission.

The news feed was alive on Reese's holo screen, still showing information about Dani's escape from HED, which someone had finally made public, though no mention was made of Tauri or the Controller's demise. An image of Dani in her white prison uniform, her face snarling and her white hair sticking out at every angle, had been plastered all over the Teev feed. Brogan had immediately sent Dani back to Newcali with the fringer hover, and Hammer had altered the division's records to show a transfer. Her official image was already not the correct one, so anyone looking at the records would see a smiling woman with light brown skin and long brown hair—nothing like the madwoman fringer escapee. As Brogan's personal assistant, she hadn't interacted much with the rest of his employees, but they could never be too careful.

"Anything?" Jaxon asked, indicating Reese's drawing pad.

She shook her head. "Nothing of value. Just images of family. But I'm finished now." She put her notebook aside and accepted a glass of chotks, moving closer to him as he sat on the couch. He put his arm around her, running the tips of his fingers down her bare arm, hardly believing she was here with him like this.

Reese had ended her relationship with Alex after returning from New York, but Alex didn't give up easily. There had been a scene with him last night in this very room, one that embarrassed all of them. He'd pleaded with Reese to give the two of them another chance, and it was obvious Reese felt terrible as she tried to explain—and she was shaking with sketches by the time it was over. In the end, the medical examiner had no choice but to walk away.

Even irritation at his former friend didn't stem Jaxon's pity. He remembered too well what it was like to have only half of what he wanted most. But he knew Alex would be okay. He was charming and popular with all the women at the district, and Jaxon suspected it wouldn't be long before he found consolation.

Jaxon set down his glass and kissed Reese deeply, tasting the drink's light fruitiness on her tongue. Her mouth was soft and warm, and she gazed at him through half-lidded eyes that invited more. He took her glass from her unresisting hand and set it on her sofa table. He couldn't get enough of her, would never have enough of her.

He didn't know what the change between them would do for their working relationship, but he was too exultant to think about it now. From the moment they'd become best friends in the Coop, he and Reese had always been heading to this spot. For tonight, nothing else mattered.

He shifted his position, still kissing her as she worked an arm out from his grasp to shut down the Teev. The Teev and its connection to the TAD that was always alert and watching. But instead of sweeping downward, her hand remained hovering in the air, her body growing stiff under him. Air pulled from his mouth as she drew in a quick breath.

Breaking away, he turned to see Controller Warrick Ramsey staring out at them from the holo screen, looking every bit as strong and healthy as he had last week in person at the memorial. Jaxon flicked his fingers to turn up the volume.

"I'm happy to announce that Special Forces has recaptured the escaped fringer, Dani Balak," Ramsey was saying, "and also all those responsible for helping her. While I am deeply saddened over the lives of the Special Forces that were lost, and my sincerest condolences go out to their families, I want everyone to know their sacrifice wasn't in vain. The fringer has given us information that will save many lives. We will never allow another Breakdown to destroy our great nation."

Jaxon couldn't take his eyes from the man, his face larger than life as it hovered over them. He had wondered about the visions he'd seen of the Controller under the influence of the juke. He'd almost hoped they'd stemmed from his imagination. But here was Ramsey staring out at them, healthy and vibrant, his lies about Dani rolling as easily off his tongue as any truth.

"We knew he had to be alive," Reese whispered. "I saw the sketch of him in your mind. Looks like he wants people to believe he caught Dani, for all the good it does him."

"It destroys hope, that's what it does." With an impatient movement, Jaxon killed the screen. One day soon there would be a confrontation, and Jaxon would learn what the man was hiding. But not now.

Now there was only Reese. He reached for her again, and she came willingly into his arms. For a long time they forgot everything except each other.

GLOSSARY OF TERMS

Birth order – permission to have a child. You must first submit a birth application to be awarded one of these. The application process takes three months with a six-month waiting period between rejected applications. This means couples can apply every nine months until they have two children.

Blues, or enforcer blues – the black, bulletproof uniforms worn by enforcers with built-in iTeev connectors and heating/cooling units.

Breakdown – total economic collapse and nuclear warfare that occurred in what was formerly known as America in 2198. Sometimes used as a curse.

Breathers – gas masks.

Brew – a stimulating drink made from the guardana plant grown in Colony 2. There are two versions, a rich, tasty brew that comes from the leaves and a bitter drink derived from the stems that has the same kick.

C-lodges (capitalized) – Commonwealth lodges owned by the CORE.

Cash credits – plastic card encoded with different credit (money) amounts.

Chotks – an expensive, light-colored alcoholic drink that is slightly sweet.

CivID – identification that must be carried by all CORE citizens. CivIDs constantly emit a signal that can be easily picked up by surveillance cameras. There are blockers sold on the black market to mask this signal. A CivID allows access to the sky trains.

Clean spots – used to obscure online Teev activities. Use is directly against CORE law.

Cleaners – boxy, Teev-driven, automated cleaning machines that are roughly sixty square centimeters in circumference and one hundred and twenty centimeters tall. Used to vacuum and clean the floors in many large buildings. Often people who have been medically enhanced will follow these cleaners to help them navigate any difficult objects, but the job is basically nonessential. Because of this, the term "walk with the cleaners" is both a reference to a mental condition and as a comment on a person's low intelligence.

Clipper – derogative nickname for an enforcer.

Clud – a mild curse.

Colonies – settlements created to support the poor, needy, and displaced after Breakdown. There are six colonies, three in Estlantic and three in Dallastar, and each is assigned to a primary industry, except Colony 6. In Estlantic: Colony 1, farming and forestry; Colony 2, farming and fishing; Colony 3, mining and metals. In Dallastar: Colony 4, oils and plastics; Colony 5 (also known as the Sty), cattle and livestock; Colony 6 (see below).

Commontongue (capitalized) – language of the CORE.

Coop, or Colony 6 – as in chicken coop. They create raw textiles, metals, or plastics from materials created by the other colonies. Located southwest of Amarillo City in Dallastar Territory.

CORE Elite – wealthy people who lead the government of the CORE. These include the Director (overall ruler), Controller (over all enforcers), Administrator (finances and city affairs), Regulator (controls population and gives out birth orders) and all their highest advisors and underlings.

CORE Identification Unit, or CIU – an enforcer unit that specializes on discovering the identities of criminals. Serves all of Estlantic.

CORE, or Commonwealth Objective for Reform and Efficiency – name of the country and government of Estlantic and Dallastar territories, short for. Often used as an exclamation in sentences like, "Thank CORE."

Credits – money, method of exchange, normally transferred via iTeev or Teev feed.

Crew – gangs in the Coop.

Dallastar – smaller territory of the CORE, located in the mid-south of the continent and borders Fringer territory.

Data square – a tiny, thin, square, flash drive.

Desolation zones – areas affected by nuclear fallout during Breakdown.

Ditch digger – a person who does dirty work for someone powerful

Empty zones – rubble-filled areas destroyed during Breakdown and not yet inhabited or reclaimed.

Enforce weapons – weapons used by enforcers, pre-Breakdown tech that uses fingerprint identity to enable the weapons.

Enforcer – Police officer. Usually called enforcers. Besides their normal job hours, they must log three to six hours of physical efficiency training per week, depending on their location.

Enforcer divisions – like police precincts. There are ten in Estlantic and five in Dallastar, with subdivisions. Some important divisions are Amarillo Enforcer Division (AED), New York Enforcer Division (NYD), Headquarters Enforcer Division (HED).

Enhancement, or enhancing – a medical procedure where lasers are used on aggressive centers of the brain. Worse than a lobotomy.

Estlantic – largest territory of the CORE, located on the east coast of the continent.

Freedom Fountain, or the Fountain – a fountain erected in the plaza outside CORE buildings in Amarillo City to celebrate the CORE's victory against fringers during the fight for Amarillo City. Famous in all of the CORE, and almost revered in Dallastar.

Fringers – people who separated from those who created the CORE after Breakdown. Viewed as crazy and dangerous rebels suffering from nuclear radiation, fringers still fight to undermine the CORE. There are different bands of fringers living in various empty zones. A large band of fringers, population unknown, inhabit Newcali on the west coast. People in the CORE often use fringer as a derogatory term, such as "half-witted fringer."

Gathering limit – public and private gatherings are limited to twenty citizens, unless a permit is acquired from the city manager.

Handspeak (capitalized) – sign language

Holos – holographs; pre-Breakdown technology used by Teevs and iTeevs.

Hover, or hover car, or hovercraft – a small personal flying ship, a technology believed to have been lost after Breakdown.

Hypo – a small cylinder used to inject medications. A hypo can hold several doses and can be used on different people without fear of cross-contamination. Certain colors of hypos are often used to hold a specific medicine, so they can be found and used quickly. Common ones are blue for a painkiller, red for a stimulant, and white for a sedative.

Image receptors – a nearly indestructible, reusable screen the thickness of a paper. Receptors are pre-Breakdown tech that are now only available within the enforcer divisions or by CORE Elite. Images can be loaded into the receptors.

iTeev – a portable Teev (see Teev description below) that can be held in the hand or used over the eyes like glasses to communicate or view holo feeds anywhere, even outdoors, without the use of holo emitters. Normally activated and used by direct touch on the foldable screen, through hand signals, or verbal commands. Limited eye movement controls are also supported but rarely used by the general population. Has a mini earbud connected with a thin wire that can pull out of a compartment for more private communication when used over the eyes.

Juke – a recreational hallucinogen, an addictive drug that was originally discovered as a byproduct of viribus, the experimental drug used in Colony 6. Outlawed in all of the CORE. Provides thirty or more minutes of rush or high followed by exhaustion or unconsciousness unless a counter agent is used. Juke enhances the development of abilities found in Colony 6, and also speeds up onset of the madness. Often sold in a black hypo marked with a white J.

Jukehead – a juke addict. Sometimes also called a "cotton-headed juke addict" or a "warthog-faced jukehead," which are mild curses.

Level – nursery or school grade that corresponds exactly with a child's age. When a child graduates, they "level out."

Lumper – a person who ventures into the empty zones or edges of the desolation zones and is stupid enough to get taken by fringers (or presumed taken). This has evolved into Terms like "I lumping hate you" or "I don't give a lump."

Magglue – glue for metals, contains magnetic nanites.

Marriage band – a wedding band that can't be removed until the marriage is broken. Not mandated by the CORE but growing popular among the residents. Breaking a union isn't against the law, unless you have a child under eighteen, but couples must receive permission. Affairs by those in valid unions are punishable by huge fines and even psychological reconditioning when minors are involved.

Nanobots – used to be common for fixing ailments pre-Breakdown. More rare now. A similar tech is used in Nuface therapy.

Nanoparticles – the less effective little brother of nanobots. Nanoparticles can fix internal wounds if injected near the damage, but it's mostly hit and miss since the CORE has lost the technology to program them.

Newcali – A territory that is home to a large group of fringers who live outside CORE control. Located on the west coast of the continent. Little is known about the territory's size or population, but the people are powerful enough to have resisted CORE attempts of takeover. They allow free study and invention. After leaving Colony 6, Dani Balak became associated with them and now considers them her people.

Newcali bread drops – small rolls that are very soft and lightly sweetened, cross between a doughnut and a roll.

Nuface therapy – nanite treatments to preserve youth.

Nyckelira – a sixteen-string fiddle-like instrument with dozens of keys intersecting the strings. Strings are played with a short bow and the keys are played with the fingers. A modified version of current day Swedish nyckelharpa. A current rage among the youth of the CORE, bought at local furniture shops, though no one seems to know exactly who is manufacturing them.

Pressure pad – pre-Breakdown tech now utilized only by

Newcalians. A thin, clear pad with sensors connected wirelessly to a transmitter that signals whenever it senses pressure, such as the weight of a person stepping on it.

Punk – person who didn't finish school, works on the underbelly of society.

Punk bucket – any job that sucks, related to the buckets of waste a punk had to carry away from the work settlements when the colonies were being built.

Pus bag – derogative term for a CORE Elite (leader).

Pus licker – derogative term for a person who does the bidding of a Core Elite.

Readymeal – a flat carton of mixed processed foods and synthesized food substitutes, similar to current-day microwaveable meals. Usually heated in a microwave or inside a readymade dispenser. Often tasteless compared with fresh food but inexpensive and convenient. Primary sustenance for daily use throughout the CORE. Each carton contains immunizations and vitamins and comes with a plastic fork. Substandard readymeals are distributed in the colonies.

RealSkin – used as bandages over repaired wounds.

Reconditioning – psychological therapy for people who have disobeyed minor CORE laws.

Saca – a mild curse.

Sauce – a stiff alcoholic drink made of equal parts coarse alcohol and synthetic fillers. The drink of the poor. The taste is tart and the sour smell tends to linger on the breath.

Sauced or sauce-crazed – drunk.

Scramblers – enforcer motorcycles equipped with pre-Breakdown tech that uses fuel cells for power. Scramblers are fast, maneuverable, and can be used for a month without refueling. Mostly used in Estlantic (New York in particular).

Shuttle, or automated shuttle – a roughly tetrahedron-shaped blue car that is a Teev-driven taxi. All CORE residents outside the colonies have a limited monthly allotment of time they are permitted to use the public shuttle without cost. There are also automatic ambulance shuttles people can call for assistance. The doors on all shuttles slide back into built-in door pockets and the windows are normally darkened for privacy. Shuttle use pre-Breakdown fuel cells for power. Unlike the public shuttles that are a calming sky blue color, enforcer shuttles are silver with black and red stripes. They are also larger and faster, and their metal tops can fold back inside the rear compartment for use as a convertible. Instead of only being driven automatically by Teev, enforcer shuttles have optional manual controls.

Sixers – newly coined word for those with abilities that are from Colony 6.

Skin – a collapsible membrane with a flip top that can hold water, sauce, juice or other liquids.

Skin sealant – a powdered substance used in emergency as a temporary fix to slow or stop bleeding.

Skin tag – a circular patch of indeterminate color that immediately takes on the skin color of the user. Once activated, a tag will distort the wearer's face on any electronic recording. Activated with one long press of a finger. A two-fingered long press will distort both appearance and override any active CivIDs, including implanted ones. Three short taps with one finger turns it off. Wearer experiences a tingle as it is activated. Skin tags last up to two months and are nearly imperceptible to the naked eye.

Sky train – free, pre-Breakdown public transport that runs throughout the CORE. Runs on solar energy.

Smeg – a mildly addictive drug like marijuana that heats the entire body, giving the user a sexual reaction that emulates the flush of sex. Not outlawed in the CORE, but use is not viewed favorably.

Smegger – a person who often uses or is addicted to smeg.

Sonic cleansing – the no-water cleaning system used by most of the CORE.

Stunner, or stun – a weapon similar to a taser.

T-link – fringer version of the Teev. Also has holo capabilities and a portable wearable version that is nearly indistinguishable from an iTeev, except for the wireless earbud.

Cleaner – a boxy cleaning machine with gently rounded edges. Roughly a square meter wide and several meters tall.

Teev (capitalized) – television, Internet, and phone hardware/software combo. You can view, search, call, or read on the Teev. Teevs provide holographic feed indoors through holograph emitters embedded in the walls and are found in every household. Hand motions are used to activate or deactivate. Guests can normally access a certain feed on any Teev, but to access all the abilities, a password can be required.

Teev Aided Dispatch Alert System, or TAD-Alert – an enforcer system that tracks callers, prioritizes calls, and suggests names of enforcers to respond to any emergency. It can link to most home or work Teevs to have immediate eyes on any situation where enforcers might be called.

Teev feed – the connection between all Teevs and iTeevs, owned and controlled exclusively by the CORE.

Temper laser – mood altering laser that will calm most people. Effects last about fifteen minutes. However, 1% of people in the CORE are immune.

Ultratemp – larger, more powerful temper laser.

Underground, or the underground (not capitalized) – black market organization that skirts CORE law.

Undergrounders (not capitalized) – people who live underground in old metro tunnels. They usually work for the underground leader and trade on the black market.

Viribus (not capitalized) – the experimental drug placed secretly in the water at Colony 6 over a period of fifty-two years, about twenty-two to seventy-four years after Breakdown. Viribus enhances inborn psychic and physical abilities. The hope was to create stronger, more resilient humans, but if a person with abilities is exposed and left untreated, the universal side effect is madness and violence.

Voice modulator – a device worn at the throat to disguise your voice.

Whore wrangler – someone who visits a prostitute, which is illegal in the CORE.

X-Fang – a popular band in the CORE.

Teyla Branton grew up avidly reading science fiction and fantasy and watching Star Trek reruns with her large family. They lived on a little farm where she loved to visit the solitary cow and collect (and juggle) the eggs, usually making it back to the house with most of them intact. On that same farm she once owned thirty-three gerbils and eighteen cats, not a good mix, as it turns out. Teyla always had her nose in a book and daydreamed about someday creating her own worlds.

Teyla is now married, mostly grown up, and has seven kids, so life at her house can be very interesting (and loud), but writing keeps her sane. She thrives on the energy and daily amusement offered by her children, the semi-ordered chaos giving her a constant source of writing material. Teyla grabs any bit of free time from her hectic life to write. She's been known to wear pajamas all day when working on a deadline, and is often distracted enough to burn dinner. (Okay, pretty much 90% of the time.)

She loves writing fiction and traveling, and she hopes to write and travel a lot more. She also loves shooting guns, martial arts, and belly dancing. She has worked in the publishing business for over twenty years. Teyla also writes romance and suspense under the name Rachel Branton. For more information or to join her mailing list and get a free ebook, please visit http://www.TeylaBranton.com.